D1577458

TRUST

Also by Chris Hammer

Scrublands

Silver

CHRIS HAMMER

TRUST

WILDFIRE

First published in 2020 by ALLEN & UNWIN

First published in Great Britain in 2020 by
WILDFIRE
an imprint of HEADLINE PUBLISHING GROUP

1

Cataloguing in Publication Data is available from the British Library

Hardback ISBN 978 1 4722 7290 4
Trade Paperback ISBN 978 1 4722 7291 1

Map by Aleksander J. Potočnik

Typeset in 13/18 pt Granjon LT Std by Bookhouse, Sydney

Printed and bound in Great Britain by Clays Ltd, Elcograf S.p.A.

MIX
Paper from
responsible sources
FSC® C104740

Headline's policy is to use papers that are natural, renewable and recyclable
products and made from wood grown in well-managed forests and other
controlled sources. The logging and manufacturing processes are expected
to conform to the environmental regulations of the country of origin.

FOR ELENA AND CAMERON

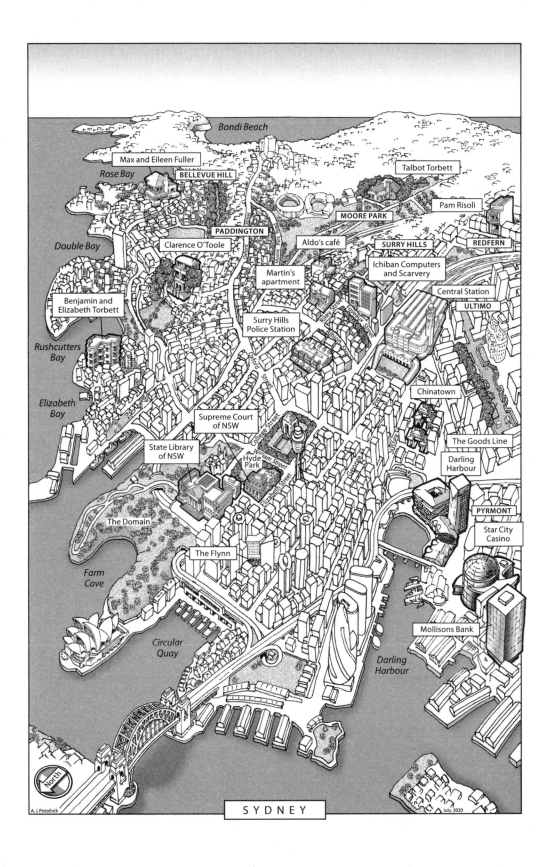

prologue

THE REALISATION SWELLS WITHIN HIM, LIKE A BIRTHING. IT'S HAPPENING RIGHT now, today, in this moment of time, in this sliver of history. After months of gestation—after all the connections and the cultivations, all the plotting and the intrigues, all the threats and the black-mail—it's this simple. He's going to get away with it. The files are downloading, faster than he could ever have imagined, transcribing the guilt, the corruption, the criminality, all neatly packaged, all digitised, all pre-digested, pouring from the computer through a supposedly disabled USB port onto the bright blue thumb drive, encryption broken, the truth laid bare, the drive itself hidden by nothing more than his bravado and a takeaway coffee cup. He stands and looks around, his mind electric but his exterior calm, the consummate actor. The consummate spy. He smiles—but, then, he is always smiling.

The trading floor is a hive of activity, brokers swarming, abuzz with corporate fervour and personal ambition, banks of monitors alive with bonds and equities and derivatives and exchange rates, all fluid, all flickering, all demanding their attention. Simply by standing still, he's rendered himself invisible. No one is looking at him, no one cares about his monitor, they're all focused on their own ephemera: numbers and charts and transactions; losses, margins and gains. He feels he is the only point of stillness, the cyclone swirling about him, that he alone possesses the perspective to know what is truly happening across these epochal seconds. It completes his victory; carried out in plain sight, the audacity of it, his own subterfuge disguised by the bank's own much larger deception. It will make the retelling all the better; this will be the making of him, the stuff of legends. He catches a reflection of himself, only slightly distorted, in the surface of a golden wall panel. He's pleased with what he sees: hair bouffant, face tanned, eyes bright and teeth even. He likes his face; everyone likes his face. It's a likeable face. More importantly, it's a trustworthy face.

The transfer is almost done. He lifts the coffee. It tastes excellent. Through the windows of the office tower, he can see the perfect Sydney day, blue and white, the sun pouring benevolence across the skyline, harbour alight, as if the city itself approves the righteousness of his actions.

He looks back to the computer, startled to see it's finished. Already. He blinks, savouring the moment, this tipping point, this culmination. If nothing else, he'll miss the bank's state-of-the-art tech, so much faster and efficient than the antiquated systems at his real workplace. He sits. Quickly, he imposes his own encryption on the thumb drive, then runs a purpose-built program to cover his tracks. It takes mere minutes. Then he ejects the drive, pockets it and logs off. Done.

'Early lunch?' he asks, pausing at the cubicle of Raff, the shift supervisor—the one person he knows won't accept his invitation.

'Sorry. Bit under the pump,' says Raff, not lifting his eyes from his screens. 'Maybe later in the week.'

'No worries,' says Tarquin, grinning at his colleague's predictability. 'I'll be an hour or so. You want anything?'

'No. Brought my lunch in.'

'Okay, see you, then.'

And Tarquin Molloy walks away, his gait confident, as always; his eyes shining, as always; his smile every bit as generous and unflappable as on his first day here. But inside, his stomach is churning and his mind is bubbling with what he has achieved.

He enters the lift, hits the button for the lobby, for glory, taking one last look across the trading floor as the doors begin to close, the curtains falling on the final scene. He commits it to memory, for the recounting. Then, at the last, an arm reaches in, forcing the doors open. Tarquin Molloy beams at the newcomer, a tall man, thin and dressed in a vintage suit of coarse brown wool. The doors ease shut.

'Morning,' says the gentleman, inviting engagement.

'It certainly is,' he replies. And to Tarquin, he *does* look like a gentleman. The suit is three-piece, of heavy cloth, as if it's been transported from somewhere in the mid-twentieth century, immaculately maintained despite its age. There is a patterned kerchief in the suit's breast pocket and a Legacy badge on its lapel. The man's face is long, as is his hair, oiled so it stays in place behind his ears. The hair oil, or something, has a pleasant aroma in the confined space. The smell, like the suit and the man's demeanour, is old-fashioned. His complexion is touched with sepia. A smoker, thinks Tarquin. Old for a trading floor.

'California Poppy,' says the man.

'Sorry?'

'The hair oil. California Poppy.'

'It smells very nice.'

'Thank you,' says the man genially. One of his teeth has a gold cap. 'Hard to come by nowadays.'

The lift shudders to a halt, but the doors don't open. They're stuck between floors.

'That's strange,' says Tarquin.

'You don't know the half of it,' says the man in the brown suit. He unbuttons his coat and withdraws a revolver. A six-gun, a prop from a Western, a massive thing, matt black and menacing, its handle inlaid with pearl shell. Tarquin's stomach plummets and his mind begins to reel. The muzzle is pointed at his chest.

SUNDAY

chapter one

THE BOY IS LAUGHING WITH THE JOY OF IT, THE SENSATION OF IT, SLAPPING AT the sea water with his hands, sending it spraying about him. Martin laughs too; Liam's pleasure is contagious. They're side by side, the man and the infant, sitting in a briny puddle formed when Martin scooped out sand to build a castle, now demolished. The excavation won't last much longer either, its sides slowly collapsing as another wave rolls up the beach, the tide on its way back in. *Splat, splat, splat*, go Liam's pudgy hands. *Splat, splat, splat*, go Martin's as he emulates his stepson, inciting more delight. Oh, how he loves the boy's laugh, that distinctive chortle that has always been his and his alone, pre-dating words.

Martin can hear his phone ringing in the beach bag further up the sand, below the steps to the house, but he doesn't move, doesn't consider answering it. Nothing is urgent here, not anymore. The days of subjugation, to the dictates of phone calls and editors, to deadlines and scoops, to egos and rivalries, are past. For sixteen months they've lived here at Port Silver—Martin, Mandalay and Liam—repairing their house on the cliffs above the beach, repairing their lives. Constructing a new and more robust reality, quarantined from the past.

'Marn. Look. Marn!'

'What?'

'Whale! Marn, whale!' The boy is on his feet, pointing excitedly out beyond the bar where the river meets the ocean. Martin hears it before he sees it, the exhalation of breath, the fizzing spray of a mist, the whale's blow. And now, as if to greet them, one white fin rises from the water, waving as it catches the early afternoon sun.

'Humpback. It's a humpback,' says Martin, smiling broadly, but Liam is too busy waving back to attempt the word.

The phone rings again. And again he ignores it. This mid-winter day is too perfect to lose: the sky clear, the day warm, the sea gentle. Even on the far north coast of New South Wales, winter southerlies can bite, bringing rain and cold. Days like this, the first after a week of cloud and squalls, are not to be interrupted. But when the phone rings for a third time, insistent, he knows he must answer it. Nobody rings three times unless it's urgent.

'Right back,' he says to Liam as he stands. He moves up the beach, no more than twenty metres. He walks backwards, not taking his eyes from the boy. Liam is well past two, twenty-seven months, a real toddler, walking and talking. Even so, Martin is taking no chances, not with the boy close to the water. Still looking at Liam, he picks up his phone and answers the call. 'Martin Scarsden.'

'Martin. Long time.'

'Max?' Martin takes a quick glance at the screen, shading it from the sun, confirming it's his former editor, his old mentor, Max Fuller.

'Where are you? Port Silver?'

'Yes, on the beach.'

'Lucky you. How's work?'

'Yeah, good. The book's doing well, the one about the killings up here last year.'

'Good. So you're at a loose end?'

'Lot to be said for that, Max.'

'I've got wind of a big story. A cracker. I could do with your help.'

Martin hesitates before responding; he still feels residual guilt for his part in Max being stripped of the *Herald*'s editorship. Liam has plopped back onto his bare arse and is splashing about in the puddle. Since when would Max need his help? 'You don't mean just a feature, do you? You wouldn't need me for that.'

'It's early days, but this could be huge. An investigative series. A book as well.'

'What is it?'

'Not on the phone. You in Sydney anytime soon?'

'I wasn't planning to be.'

'Well, see if you can make it down. Don't wait too long.'

Liam is standing again, taking a few unsteady steps towards the sea, apparently intent on paddling.

'Okay. But don't take it for granted I'll come on board.'

'You will when you see what I've got. We're not talking about a few pissy murders here, son. We're talking grand conspiracy. I promise you, you'll want in.'

9

'Okay. I'll talk to Mandy, see what I can do. Sorry I didn't pick up first time.'

There's a pause. 'What do you mean?'

'Wasn't that you ringing just a moment ago?'

'Not me.'

'Okay. I'll be in touch.' Martin ends the call and checks his phone. Sure enough, the two previous calls were from Mandy: his partner, Liam's mum. Unusual for her to call; she usually texts. Liam is heading towards him now, holding up a seashell.

'Mumma,' says the lad.

'She'll love it.' It's something Mandy and Liam do together, collect shells on the beach below their house.

Martin looks back at his phone; she's left a voice message. He opens it, holds the phone to his ear. But it's not words, it's a scream: one long shriek, full of desperation and danger, ten seconds long. It cuts through the tranquillity of the day like a blade. It doesn't finish; instead it ends abruptly, as if cut off.

'Fuck,' says Martin.

'Fuck,' says Liam, the irrepressible mimic.

Martin is already moving. He lifts the infant and starts running towards the stairs behind the beach, leaving everything else behind, taking only his son and his phone, nothing else matters.

Almost instantly the boy is crying, shocked by the rough handling, but Martin doesn't care, not now. He reaches the steps carved into the sandstone, leading up to their clifftop house, starts bounding up, the boy squirming and wailing. Up they go. Ten metres, twenty. Martin is breathing hard, slowed by Liam's weight. The steps finish at a zigzagging path. He scrambles along to the start of another flight, wooden stairs this time, suspended from a near vertical rockface. He doesn't hesitate; up they go, the boy becoming sullen and silent.

The stairs end. They're close now. Another couple of switchbacks through the rainforest, the rise not as steep, and the house appears through the foliage. He stops again. He can see nothing wrong, nothing unusual; he can hear nothing other than the noise of his own panting and the now distant sound of the surf . . . No, wait. There. Just visible around the corner of their home: a white car. *Shit.* Someone is in the house. He pauses, torn. Mandy's scream is still reverberating around his skull, but he can't take Liam in there, into possible danger. *Shit.* Then he knows what to do.

'Drive, Liam.'

He jogs up to the house, hoping no one is watching, still holding his stepson firmly. Ducking down below the windows, he moves along the building's side. He pauses at the corner, peering around it to where the unfamiliar car is parked. An SUV. New. Queensland number plates. A rental? He steps quickly past it to Mandy's Subaru, sitting unlocked in the shade of some trees. He places Liam in the booster seat and fastens the belt.

'Drive!' enthuses Liam.

'Soon. I'll be back soon. You wait here, okay?'

'Mumma?'

'Yes. I'll get Mumma.'

Liam looks uncertain, but there is no time to reassure him. Leaving the car door open—even in winter, a locked car can grow dangerously hot—Martin scuttles to the house, sheltering below the kitchen window. He looks back: the open door is out of sight on the far side of the car; Liam is silent and almost impossible to see. Martin turns his full attention to the house. He can hear

11

nothing unusual; just the wind, the surf and birdsong. How can the birds be so insensitive? Didn't they hear her scream?

He eases the kitchen door open and slides inside. There is no sound, a stillness has settled. The door to the dining room is open. Again, nothing. No: there is, there is. On the table: her phone. The one she screamed into. She must be here; she wouldn't leave her phone.

He moves through the room, looks around the open doorway into the living room . . . And sees a man in a suit face down on the floor. Adrenaline hits him, and his already surging heartbeat accelerates. He tries to listen for the sound of an intruder, but the blood in his ears is too loud; that and the memory of Mandy's scream. He takes a breath and edges forward, knowing he's exposing himself, knowing he may be walking into danger. But she's in jeopardy; standing still is not an option.

Nothing happens. There is no one else. He moves to the body, squats, feels for a pulse. It's there, in the neck, strong and consistent. The man is alive. Martin can hear him breathing: a little ragged, but steady enough. There is blood seeping from the back of his skull, out through his hair. There is no other sign of injury. Someone has king hit him from behind, laid him flat. Did Mandy do this, knock the man unconscious? Where *is* Mandy? Martin needs to get upstairs, explore the rest of the house, try to find her. But first he rolls the man onto his side, into the recovery position. He's a dead weight, showing no sign of waking. Only when Martin has him in position does he look at his face—and is shocked to recognise him. It's Claus Vandenbruk, the ill-tempered policeman Martin encountered a year and a half ago in far western New South Wales. What the hell is Vandenbruk doing here? Back then, Vandenbruk was on secondment to the Australian Criminal Intelligence Commission, the ACIC; he'd played a major role in bringing down an organised crime syndicate. What is he doing here? The questions flood Martin's mind, but he dismisses them: right now he needs to get help, and he needs to find Mandy.

He dials triple zero, asks for the police, explains quickly, voice low, what he's found, requests that police and ambulance both attend, warning that there is the potential for danger, that the police should enter first. The dispatcher starts to ask questions, but Martin can't afford to wait any longer. He interrupts to tell them of the boy in the car—if anything happens to him, at least they'll find Liam. Then he hangs up and starts moving towards the stairs.

chapter two

SHE OPENS HER EYES, BUT CANNOT SEE; TRIES TO SPEAK, BUT CANNOT TALK.
She closes her eyes again, almost slips back into sleep. It must be dark. No. It's not that. There is motion, a sense of movement. She feels the vibration, can hear the sound. A car. She's in a car. Or a van or a truck. But the weight of fatigue is too great. Her eyes close and she drifts away.

A loud sound, a vibration. She comes awake, and still she cannot see. But now she can feel the cloth that brushes her eyelashes when she blinks. She's blindfolded. She rolls her eyes around. Yes: there, to her lower left, the slightest seepage of light. She tries to open her mouth to speak, but it's taped shut. A fog comes rolling across her mind and it's all she can do to stay awake, to stave off the temptation to fall under once again. But it is coming in too strong, a dark tide. She feels herself taken.

*

Awareness comes seeping back in; again, she opens her eyes to darkness. But the mist is lifting from her mind. She's sitting upright, in a car. She can feel the cushioning beneath and behind, the shape of the seat. There are industrial smells: oils and grease and solvents. She tries to move her hands but they're tied together. She attempts to lift them to her eyes, to remove the blindfold, but it's no good: their movement is restricted. *Breathe*, she tells herself, *breathe. And don't betray your weakness.* She realises she's not fully gagged; there is nothing in her mouth, it's just been taped shut. She can't speak, but she could easily make a noise. She decides against trying. Instead, she sits back in the seat, feigns unconsciousness, while trying to work through what has happened to her, what might happen next.

The man. She remembers him now. The man in the suit, as unfamiliar and unlikely in her coastal home as a priest or a politician, out of place with his fidgety nervousness and abrupt manner. What had he said? That he knew her, that they had met before? In Riversend, her home town in western New South Wales. Had he said that, or did she dream it? There were no men in suits in Riversend. Only at funerals were there men in suits. And then she remembers: at the end, after the killings, the policemen and the reporters, all wearing suits, setting themselves apart, setting themselves above. That was it: a policeman. He'd said he was a policeman, had shown her identification. She remembers that now. A policeman.

God, she feels tired. Remembering is like lifting weights.

She closes her useless eyes, trying to concentrate, to push her mind through the treacle. Her memory of the detective is hazy, but she feels it wasn't so long ago that she was talking to him. In her lounge room. In their house on the cliff. Claus. He said his name was Claus. Why is it so hard to remember? Has she been hit? Has she been drugged? She pushes against the headrest, slowly flexing her neck muscles, but there is no pain. Not hit then; drugged. She congratulates herself for working that out, then realises that it doesn't help. She flexes her arms one way, then the other, testing the restraints: her wrists are bound painfully together, so too her ankles, with another cord threaded through the seatbelt, preventing her from lifting her hands above her midriff. She tries moving in her seat: but the belt holds her firm. To her left, there is nothing, but to her right she encounters resistance. The side of the vehicle. She leans as far as she can, presses her bare arm against the hardness. It's warm. The sun, she thinks. The sun warming the side of the vehicle. If it's the afternoon, then they're driving south. But she can feel no sunlight on her face. So not a window, then. She must be in a van, or a truck. Makes sense. They could hardly have her sitting up, bound, blindfolded and gagged next to a window. She tries to follow the pattern of movement; there is no accelerating and decelerating, no rounding of corners. The engine and road noise have a constant pitch. They must be on the freeway, heading south. South towards Sydney.

South towards the past.

She breathes deeply, trying to quell the rising sense of panic. A detective came to her home, drugged her and kidnapped her. She tries to make sense of it, to imagine alternatives, but only one conclusion is possible: it's the past, come to claim her. After all these years, just as she was beginning to believe she had achieved escape velocity, fled its orbital pull once and for all. The past; she's sure of it.

MONDAY

chapter three

THE SUN RISES FROM THE DISTANT SEA, RAYS SPEARING ABOVE PORT SILVER TO catch the upper ramparts of the escarpment, before gradually bathing the twin towns of Longton, up on the plateau, and Port Silver, down on the coast, setting the landscape in soft relief with its golden light bestowing solar benevolence on a second day of mid-winter perfection. But Martin Scarsden is unaware of the dawn. He sits inside Longton Base Hospital, bathed in the hard fluorescent light of a waiting room. Hospitals and casinos: where time runs its own race, disdainful of external chronologies.

He hasn't slept, hasn't thought of sleeping. Mandy has gone. Vanished. There was no sign of blood at their home on the cliffs, no sign of a struggle. Just her phone left on the dining-room table and an unconscious policeman on the floor. The ambulance had come, so too the local police. The paramedics had acted decisively, stabilising the obstinately unresponsive Claus Vandenbruk before whisking him away, here, to this hospital. By comparison, the police had dithered, unsure of their protocols. They'd taken Martin's statement and, as if to reassure themselves he wasn't a fantasist, they'd plodded about upstairs in an ill-disciplined search, despite his pleas not to contaminate the crime scene.

'What crime scene?' the young constable had asked.

Martin waited at home until almost midnight, feeding and bathing Liam, putting the boy to bed, all the time listening, alert to any sign, imagining her voice, hoping that Mandy might return. A flimsy theory of hope constructed itself in his mind, built on the soft foundation of too few facts and too much yearning: she had knocked out Vandenbruk, flattening him with a candle-stick or frying pan or laptop, before fleeing into the bush to hide. You'd want to hide, he reasoned, if you'd belted a cop. They only own one car now, the Subaru, so she hadn't left, not by herself. And so he listened, even as he tried to present an air of confidence and normalcy to Liam. But the child, sensing Martin's anxiety, became quarrelsome. He cried for his mother, something he rarely did.

When the boy finally fell asleep, hours past his normal bedtime, Martin left the house. Standing at the edge of the bush, he called Mandy's name. But the more he thought about it, the less likely it seemed she could be hiding in the forest: why would she ring him twice, scream into her phone, then leave it lying on the dining-room table? And would she be screaming, ringing him in extremis, running into the forest, if the policeman was already unconscious on the floor? No. There must have been someone else in the house. Or someones.

He crouched on the damp ground by the house with a torch, seeking tyre tracks, but the ground had been thoroughly trampled, all evidence obliterated by the feet and vehicles of paramedics and police. He should have thought to look earlier, before the emergency services had arrived.

Eventually, he returned inside, but the house was not large enough to contain his anxieties, his mind not quiet enough to contain his speculations. At midnight, he packed a bag for Liam and another for himself, then carried the sleeping child to the car.

Now he lingers in the hospital because he doesn't know where else to wait. Liam is safe and secure with Martin's uncle Vern and his family. Martin has left Mandy's phone at home: if she returns, she will call, explain what happened. But if she doesn't, then the only person who might know where she has gone is Claus Vandenbruk, the comatose policeman.

Maybe he nods off, maybe he just closes his eyes, but the voice rouses him. 'Martin?'

He's instantly alert, but unprepared nevertheless: it's Morris Montifore, homicide detective. 'You?' *Homicide.*

Montifore must see the panic in his eyes. 'Are you all right?'

'Mandy. Where is she? Is she okay?'

'As far as I know.' The policeman offers an approximation of a smile.

'Have you found her?'

The smile vanishes. 'Not yet.'

'So who's dead?'

Montifore sits down. There's a weariness to the man that follows him, a weight that seldom lifts. 'Not Mandy.'

'Vandenbruk?'

'No. He's still unconscious. Stable, though. He'll be choppered to Sydney as soon as possible, have all the scans. They reckon he should be okay, but they don't want to take any chances.'

Martin stares at the detective. 'What's happening? What is Vandenbruk doing here? What are *you* doing here?'

Montifore matches the intensity of his gaze before looking away, choosing his words. 'You ever watch the news up here? Read the papers?'

'Not as much as I used to.'

'You seen any of those stories about dodgy Sydney apartment blocks?'

'Some.' Even in Port Silver, they've been hard to miss. Entire residential blocks evacuated because of structural flaws, unsound foundations and fire-trap cladding.

Montifore is looking at Martin again. 'There's a big one out at Parramatta, called Sublimity—whatever the fuck that's meant to mean. Only five years old. Huge crack, going from the sub-basement up to the second or third floor. Creeps up a few more centimetres every day. All the residents have been kicked out.'

'And?'

'The structural engineers are on to it. They've been X-raying the foundations. They've got these huge machines, ground-penetrating radar or some such. The whole thing is as suss as all fuck. Not enough steel, too much sand, fuck-all cement.'

'Let me guess: they found something.'

'A cavity.'

'A cavity?'

'And a body. A very well-preserved body.'

'Whose?'

'A man known as Tarquin Molloy.'

'What do you mean "known as"?'

'An alias. You don't need to know his real name.' Montifore is examining Martin's face, looking for a reaction. 'Have you ever heard his name before?'

'No. Never. Who was he?'

'An undercover cop.'

'What makes you think I would have heard of him?'

'At the time of his death, he was engaged to be married. To Mandalay Blonde.'

chapter four

SHE WAKES, DISORIENTED ONCE MORE. SHE LIES STILL, TRYING TO GATHER HER consciousness around her, to assert her faculties, to take control. They've drugged her again, she realises. She struggles against the fog, straining to make sense of her predicament. She's lying on her side, on a bed or maybe a mattress, constrained. The blindfold is still in place, and the gag. The smells are still there, same as in the van, but stronger now, more pungent. Petrol, solvents, above a sense of dampness and mould. Her tongue feels thick and pasty; her thirst immediate and pressing. She feels the chafing on her wrists: they are bound together by something thin and cutting, so too her ankles. Plastic ties, with more threaded through her belt, preventing her from lifting her hands to her face. Her arms and legs are stiff, her back hurts. She badly needs to piss.

Emotions wash through: helplessness and frustration; anger and determination. And beyond them, a sense of dread, a malevolence threatening to come for her. She pushes back, concentrates, listens. White noise, the muffled sound of traffic. The distant whine of a plane. A city, then. Sydney? She pinches at her bedding: nothing more than a slab of foam rubber. She can feel the air on her cheek: still, cool, damp. She's somewhere without light, a basement or an internal room. She shivers, an involuntary response. Who has brought her here? And why?

The dread threatens to deprive her of rationality, inviting her to panic. It's the past, coming after her, propelled by karma. For an instant, she thinks of Liam. Of Martin. The future. She prays that they're safe, that Martin has Liam, is holding him close, will care for her son.

There's a lift in volume, the city momentarily louder, accompanied by a shift in the air, a zephyr of movement. A door opening and closing again.

'Good morning.' A woman's voice.

Mandy freezes.

'We'll remove the gag. Stay still.' Her captor's tone sounds malicious in its neutrality.

Mandy nods. A hand takes her chin, holds it firm. A man's hand? He pulls the tape away, his actions abrupt. The pain is sharp, as if skin has been lifted along with the tape.

'You're welcome to scream,' says the woman. 'No one can hear you.' Her voice is coming from beyond the end of the bed. So there are at least two of them: a woman and a man. The woman is talking; she's the one in charge.

'I need to pee,' says Mandy, keeping her voice calm.

'I'm not surprised. Cooperate and you can.'

Jesus. That voice. 'Zelda?'

Silence.

'It's you, isn't it? Zelda.'

More silence. Then hands, the man's hands, lifting Mandy's head, removing the blindfold.

A light hangs directly above her: a single bulb, incandescent, a relic from another era. Mandy blinks. But there's no mistaking who is sitting on a chair at the end of the mattress. 'Jesus. It *is* you.'

Zelda Forshaw. Smiling, but with a furrow of concern bisecting her forehead. She looks older, harder; her foundation is thicker, and the cupid's bow of her mouth has developed a sneer.

'I thought you were in prison,' says Mandy.

'Yeah, I was. Thanks to you. You bitch.'

'I didn't testify.'

'You didn't have to.'

Mandy looks about her. She's on the floor, on the foam mattress. A man is standing over her, dressed in jeans, cheap running shoes, a faded Nike sweatshirt. And a ski mask. He's shifting his weight uneasily from leg to leg, as if he doesn't really want to be here, as if unsure of his role. They're in some sort of disused storeroom, its walls streaked with mould and lined with metal storage racks. Their shelves are rusting and empty, save for some old oil cans and plastic buckets.

'What's going on, Zelda? Why this?'

'What do you think?'

'The policeman. In a suit. He was in my house. What happened?'

'He'll be fine.'

'What do you mean, he'll be fine?'

'Nothing to concern you. I just wanted to get in first—before he arrested you.'

'Arrested me? For what?'

'It's me, Mandy—you don't have to pretend.'

'Arrest me for *what*?' Mandy repeats.

'For Tarquin.'

'Tarquin?' Of course, Tarquin. It was always going to be about Tarquin. 'Tarquin Molloy? Why would they arrest me?' She can't help it; panic is rising. Something is happening and she doesn't know what it is. Five years pass without incident, then all of a sudden, on the same day, a policeman arrives and she is kidnapped. 'I have no idea where Tarquin is, where he went, but I'll tell you everything I can. Just let me take a piss.'

But Zelda Forshaw is impervious to the appeal, her smile flickering. 'Tell me where the money is, and you can piss to your heart's content. Niagara fucking Falls. In fact, tell me where Mollisons' money is and I'll let you go.'

'I never knew anything about any money. You know that.'

Zelda stands. She towers over Mandy. 'Don't play the dumb blonde with me, bitch. I want the money I went to prison for.'

'It was Tarquin. That's what the bank said; that's what the court found. Tarquin took it.'

'No he fucking didn't.' The anger in Zelda's voice is rising.

'How can you know that?'

'The same way you do.'

'What do you mean?'

'He's dead. Shot through the head.'

Mandy's breath sticks in her throat, a jagged thing, unable to be moved. 'Dead? He's dead?'

'Not just dead. Murdered.'

'But when? Where?'

'Enough bullshit. I went to prison for that fucking money. I want my share.'

Mandy doesn't know how to respond; another denial is not going to get her anywhere. She looks around, but there is nothing to see: the uneasy-looking enforcer, the stained walls, the empty shelves.

'Last chance. Tell me. Or we walk out and leave you here.'

'I don't have the money.'

'Bullshit. I checked you out. First thing I did when I heard he was dead. You're fucking rolling in it.'

Mandy shakes her head. 'No. It's an inheritance. From my grandfather. All of it. You can ask my lawyer. I'll give you her name. She can send a copy of the will.'

'I told you.' It's the man, the enforcer, voice tentative.

'Shut up,' Zelda spits back, before returning her attention to Mandy. 'Sorry. I'm not accepting any more bullshit from lawyers. Tarquin was a lawyer, and look what a lying bastard he was.'

'My partner. He's a journalist. Martin Scarsden. Works for the *Sydney Morning Herald*. He wrote a book about it. It's all there, in the epilogue.'

'Yes, Martin Scarsden,' Zelda scoffs. 'Your latest lover. Who shares your wealth, your palace up there on the cliffs. No bushfires for you, no viruses, no recessions.' She shakes her head. 'I don't think so.'

Mandy looks at the enforcer with his masked face, still rocking from foot to foot.

'Truth serum,' says the man, suddenly enthusiastic. 'We can try truth serum.'

'Quiet, mate. Quiet. We'll be done soon.' Now Zelda's voice is surprisingly soft.

Mandy looks at the man. There is something not quite right there, something askew, his voice childish, not threatening. Maybe she can appeal to him, convince him of her innocence, of her ignorance. Maybe she can simply buy her freedom. 'How much money is it?'

'Tarquin told me ten million,' says Zelda. 'What did he tell you?'

'I told you: he never said anything to me. Not about money.'

Zelda's eyes are boring into hers. 'What did he tell you, then?'

Mandy blinks, doesn't know what to say, opts for truth. 'That he loved me.' And to her surprise she feels a rising emotion. It must be the lingering effect of the drugs.

'You think you were the only one?' says Zelda contemptuously.

'We were engaged. We were getting married. He didn't have to offer me money.'

'But you knew what he was planning?'

'No. He told me nothing. Made sure I wasn't around to interfere. He sent me to the Gold Coast. A romantic weekend away—that's what he said.' Again, the rising of residual emotion, this time of distress, of betrayal. 'But he never showed. By the time I got back to Sydney, he was gone. Then Mollisons called in the cops.'

There is a change in Zelda's face; the hardness is joined by an intensity, a concentration. 'So what did you think happened?' Her voice is lower, engaged, no longer dismissive.

'Same as everyone else, once I heard the rumours. I thought he'd scarpered, taken the bank's money, played me for a fool.' A sob escapes from somewhere, catching Mandy unawares. Surely she is beyond this, beyond Tarquin Molloy. 'I heard he'd embezzled it and fled overseas.' Now she can no longer meet her jailer's gaze.

'I was interrogated by the security people. Clarity Sparkes and Harry Sweetwater. They cleared me.'

'They sacked you,' says Zelda. 'They must have suspected you of something.'

'They sacked my whole team. And . . .' Her voice trails off.

'And what?'

Mandy looks back at Zelda Forshaw. 'And they charged you. Convicted you. I figured it must be true, that you were in it together, you and Tarquin—that you stole the money.' She swallows. 'And I knew about the two of you.'

'What do you mean?'

'I knew that he was screwing you.'

'Is that what you told the cops?'

'I didn't have to.'

'So what did you do?'

'Cried. I cried a lot. We were engaged, I loved him. But he used me and then pissed off with the money. What do you think I should have done?'

For a moment, there is no reaction. For a moment, it seems as if their mutual gaze might connect the two women. But then it breaks, and Zelda laughs, a brittle and uncertain sound. 'Yeah, right.'

Mandy just stares. There is nothing left to say.

'Zel, can we go?' asks the man, sounding almost plaintive.

The impasse holds. And then, from somewhere beyond the storeroom, comes the sound of breaking glass. Once, twice, thrice. Shattering glass, cascading.

'Shit.' Zelda Forshaw turns to the man. 'Check it out. Fast.'

Mandy is holding her breath. By the look of her, her captor is doing the same. Now Zelda brings a single finger to her lips, signalling for her to remain silent. Mandy considers yelling. Should she risk it? Zelda removes her finger, appears about to whisper something, when they hear it: a single gunshot. It crackles through the air, electric, like bottled lightning. Close by. The next room.

'Shit,' whispers Zelda. And she's off, past Mandy and away.

Mandy cranes her neck, straining against her bonds: there must be a second door at the back of the storeroom. She squirms, the ties cutting into her wrists, but there is no getting away. Seconds pass. She can hear the sound of feet grinding across the top of broken glass.

The door opens, the door through which the ski-masked minion passed, and a tall man enters, his face long and sallow, his thin body slightly stooped. He's wearing a three-piece suit, navy with pinstripes. And he's holding a large handgun, some sort of antique. From her position on the floor, she can see he's wearing polished riding boots. He looks like Doc Holliday without the spurs and the handlebar moustache.

Mandy doesn't move, can't move. Only her bladder screams its insistence.

'Well, hello,' says the man. 'What have we here?'

He stalks past her, gun before him. His hair is long and greasy. No, not greasy: oiled. For a minute or more he's gone, out the same door as Zelda. And then he's back, moving easily, unhurried.

He gets the chair from the end of the mattress, the one Zelda had been sitting on, moves it closer to Mandy, so he's next to her. He places his gun in a holster beneath his coat and sits. He extends his hand, large and bony-fingered, yellow-stained, and rests it on her shoulder. Mandy can smell nicotine. 'It's okay, love. You're safe now.' He looks about forty, but something about him seems much older; not his age so much as his appearance, his demeanour borrowed from a past century.

'Who are you?' she asks.

'Police.'

'Police?'

'Yes. You're safe now.'

'Can you release me?'

'Of course.' The man reaches out, lifts her bound wrists. He turns to the door. 'Sergeant!' he calls. 'In here. Now!'

A man appears, short and powerful, with a shaven head, dressed in a black t-shirt, grimy jeans and industrial boots. There is a spider-web tattoo crawling up his neck, vivid blues and reds. His eyes are like pebbles: small and hard and perceptive.

'Cable ties. A prisoner,' explains the policeman, gesturing towards Mandy. 'The constable. Get him to cut her free.'

The man nods and disappears back the way he came.

'Who's that?' asks Mandy.

'Forget him. He's undercover. Understand? You never saw him.'

Mandy nods her comprehension.

'Now. I'm assuming that was Zelda Forshaw who was holding you here.'

'Yes. It was her.'

The man looks around the room, as if considering something. 'We've been looking for her. You're Mandalay Blonde, correct?' His hair glistens in the fluorescent light. There is a sweet smell.

Mandy feels suddenly emboldened. 'You say you're a policeman.'

The man smiles, one tooth glinting with gold. 'Detective Inspector Henry Livingstone, at your service.' He reaches into the inside of his coat pocket, withdraws a wallet. He flicks it open, revealing a police badge. 'Internal investigations.' He holds it out for her fleeting examination, then returns it to his coat. 'Now, while we wait for the constable and his wire-cutters, why don't you tell me what happened here.'

And so Mandy explains. Her abduction, being drugged, waking to find herself a captive of Zelda Forshaw.

Inspector Livingstone listens intently, not speaking until Mandy has finished. 'And this policeman who came to see you at your home—what was his name?'

'It was Claus something. He said he'd met me before.'

'I see.' Livingstone frowns, as if considering the gravity of the situation. 'I remember hearing all about you. You were the innocent; the fool.' He smiles apologetically. 'Tell me about the money. Why does Zelda Forshaw think you know where the money is?'

'I have no idea. I don't know anything about the money. I told them, back then, the police and the bank. I never knew about it. That was Tarquin. And her: Zelda.'

'It's okay,' Livingstone says, reassuring. 'I believe you.'

'Is it true?' Mandy asks. 'Is he really dead?'

'Who's that, love?'

'Tarquin Molloy. She said he's dead.'

The man nods, eyes sad, face gaunt. 'Oh yes. I'm sorry to say it is. I have it on the best authority.' He reaches out his hand, places it gently on her bound hands. In the distance, Mandy can hear a siren.

The bald undercover agent puts his head back through the door. 'Boss. Backup is almost here.'

'Right. Thanks.' He turns to Mandy. 'I'd better go and speak with them. And I'll see what's keeping that constable.' He's almost to the door when he turns and says quietly, 'A word to the wise. Don't get mixed up in this thing. It's going to get ugly.' And he leaves.

It's only later, after her bladder has surrendered but well before the police find her lying there, soaked and shivering, hands and feet still bound, that she realises Livingstone isn't coming back. And that the man can't possibly be a police officer.

chapter five

MARTIN DRIVES SOUTH TOWARDS SYDNEY, THE FREEWAY LONG AND SINUOUS, lined with state forest, far enough inland to be unimpeded by development, rising and falling with the gentle folding of the land. Exits come and go, promising beachside resorts to the east and heritage towns to the west, while signs assure him there are strategically spaced rest areas and service centres along the kilometres to come.

He guides the car automatically, eyes on the road but thoughts elsewhere, already stalking city streets. Somewhere down there, amid the office towers and the endless suburbs, the concrete and the bitumen, among the unmindful millions, there will be answers. Answers and Mandy—but how does he find them? He's sure now that she's no longer in Port Silver. She would have contacted him. And someone would have seen her; the town is too small, she is too well known, if not personally then by reputation. No, she's gone; taken. He thinks again of her phone, left on the dining-room table, the screaming voice message. Her wallet in the bedroom, her clothes still there, their luggage. No, she's been abducted; there can be no other explanation. So he's brought her phone with him, and her wallet, hoping he can reunite them with their owner.

He tries to discipline his thoughts, to control them, just as he keeps the car in its lane; he mustn't permit his imagination to swerve onto the fearful verge. He tries instead to concentrate on the future, the coming days, what needs to be done. He needs a plan. But the road is mesmeric, the forest unchanging. His mind wanders across the white lines, veering onto the soft shoulder of speculation.

Has he ever known her? Really, known her? They've been together for a year and a half now, sharing their thoughts, sharing their bed, sharing every intimacy. Building a life together. They've been refurbishing the old house on the cliffs, Hartigan's. They've been raising her son Liam together, *their* son, the jewel in their existence. And slowly, amid the warmth of the coast, the warmth of this unexpected family, Martin has felt himself unfurling, growing, transforming. Because of her. Because of this stranger.

For she has never mentioned, not once, not even hinted at this other life, this other man, this Tarquin Molloy. Even as Martin gradually peeled back the layers of his own repressed past, the trauma of his youth, his lost family, she remained silent. Gradually he'd begun to heal, felt himself becoming a better man, more compassionate, more empathetic, spurred on by her love for him and his love for her and Liam. They'd hidden away in their redoubt, their fortress on the clifftops, removed from the traumas of the world. And in all that time together, she had never confided.

Yet she had been engaged to be married; not something easily forgotten, not something to paper over. He acknowledges what it means: that he doesn't know her after all. For if he didn't know about that, how can he know what else she has redacted from her past? How can he trust those things she has told him? Can he trust himself to feel the same about her?

The cruise control rushes him up behind a semi-trailer. He changes lanes, taps the accelerator, moves past the truck, changes back.

An idea occurs to him, an unexplored line of inquiry. He speaks to his phone, mounted on the dash, and calls Winifred Barbicombe, Mandy's Melbourne-based lawyer, her fiercest defender.

'Martin? Is that you?'

'Yes.'

'Where are you?'

'Driving to Sydney.'

'How can I help?'

'Mandalay's disappeared. I think she's been abducted. The police are looking for her.'

Looming on the road ahead is a wallaby, mowed down mid-lane. Martin veers, hitting the horn, sending ravens scrambling aloft. He passes the matted red mass without decelerating and returns to his lane.

'Tell me what's happened,' instructs the lawyer.

Martin runs through the sequence of events: the screaming voicemail message, Claus Vandenbruk unconscious on the floor, bleeding from the head, Mandy gone. The Subaru parked, none of Mandy's clothes or belongings touched, her phone on the dining-room table, her wallet and passport upstairs.

Winifred listens without comment, waiting for him to finish, before prompting him. 'So why are you going to Sydney?'

'She was engaged, Winifred. To an undercover policeman. Tarquin Molloy.'

There is no response, nothing for long seconds. Then: 'When was this?'

'You didn't know?'

'No.'

'How could you not?' Martin can't help it; he can't keep the accusatory note from his voice.

'She's my client. I work for her. I don't spy on her.'

'Not even in those years before she turned thirty, before she came into her inheritance?'

'No. I was explicitly instructed not to contact her. What about you? Were you aware of her engagement?'

That puts Martin back in his box. 'No. No, I wasn't.'

'Right. So tell me what you've learnt.'

Martin recounts the scant information Morris Montifore shared with him: the body in the foundations, the undercover policeman, the engagement five years earlier.

'That's incredible,' says the solicitor. 'I didn't know. You didn't know. She didn't tell anyone.'

'Apparently not.'

'Why not? Why didn't she tell anyone?'

'If we knew that, we'd be halfway there.'

'But, Martin, her name was everywhere. The events at Riversend, then again at Port Silver. She was big news, nationwide. Don't you think it's uncanny that no journalist discovered she'd been engaged to a missing policeman, thought it worthy of reporting?'

Martin can't help but agree. 'I guess Molloy's disappearance wasn't ever reported. I'd never heard of it.'

'Surely the murder of an undercover cop would have been newsworthy. Did you check?'

'I googled it. Nothing.'

'It must have been suppressed. But why?'

'So as not to compromise an ongoing investigation?' Martin leaves his guess hanging.

'Investigating what?'

'Montifore wouldn't tell me. But he did say that no one knew Molloy was dead, not even the cops. He was listed as missing right up until his body was found.'

'And there's no doubt that it's him they found?'

'Apparently not.'

More silence before the lawyer resumes, her voice thoughtful. 'And Montifore told you all of this?'

'That's right. He's got the job of finding who killed Tarquin Molloy.'

'I think Montifore may know more than he's saying.'

'How do you mean?'

'Down in Riversend, he was happy to hang Mandy out for you vultures of the press, but in Port Silver he was far more circumspect.'

'Maybe he just didn't want to stuff up the second time around.'

'Maybe.' She sounds unconvinced.

'Did the police ever raise her past with you? With Mandy?'

'Not with me. And not with her. Not directly anyway.'

'What does that mean?'

'There was one occasion when Montifore was interviewing her and he threw in a couple of unconnected names—people who lived in Sydney, not Port Silver.'

'Do you have a transcript?'

'No. But I took notes. I'll have the names. I remember checking them out.'

'Can you send them to me?'

'Of course.'

They talk some more, strategise, before Martin rings off. The road continues, the traffic sparse, the day calm. Then, abruptly, the eucalypt forest changes from khaki to more emphatic tones: black trunks wrapped in bright green foliage, recovering from the bushfires of summer. But the ground is still white with ash, the undergrowth slow to regenerate. Maybe it's waiting for spring, maybe it's waiting for rain. Maybe the fire had burnt too fiercely.

Martin goes over what he knows yet again. The body of Mandy's fiancé was found in Sydney, murdered, concreted into the foundations of a high-rise. And within days she's disappeared, most likely abducted. The police had come for her: Claus Vandenbruk, investigator with the Australian Criminal Intelligence Commission, no doubt motivated by the discovery of Tarquin Molloy's remains. Morris Montifore didn't say as much, but clearly the homicide detective believes the discovery of Molloy, the assault on Vandenbruk and Mandy's disappearance are connected. Now Vandenbruk has been medivacked to Sydney's Royal Prince Alfred, and Montifore is back in the state capital. Soon, Martin will be too.

He changes lanes, powers past a motor home—ADVENTURE BEFORE DEMENTIA painted across the back in old-fashioned cursive. The grey nomads, like the forest, slowly returning. He looks at the speedo, is surprised to see he's crept up to twenty-five kilometres per hour beyond the limit, overriding the cruise control in his urgency. He winds the speed back, engages the speed limiter for the third or fourth time.

His phone rings, the sound coming through the speaker system. He answers it.

'Martin. It's Max Fuller. Thought I would have heard back by now.'

God. Max and his story. 'Sorry. Something important has come up.'

'So you won't be heading to Sydney any time soon?'

Martin smiles despite himself. 'I'm on my way.'

'Good man. I knew you couldn't resist. You won't regret it. It's a ball-tearer.'

'Max, I can't help you. Mandy has disappeared. I think she's been kidnapped.'

There is a momentary silence then: 'Shit. You sure?'

'The police think so.'

'So why are you coming to Sydney?'

'Because I think she might have been taken there.'

'Right.'

'Sorry, Max, but she's my priority. I wouldn't be able to concentrate on anything else.'

'Absolutely. Understood. I'm sure we can press on without you. But let me know if there is anything I can do to help.'

'Actually there is. Have you ever heard of a man called Tarquin Molloy?'

There's no response. For a moment Martin thinks he's lost the connection. 'Max?'

'I'm still here.'

'Molloy was an undercover police officer.'

'Martin, this is important. Come and see me. As soon as you can.'

'What is it?'

'No, mate. Not on an open line. Come first thing tomorrow.'

'I'll be there.'

Somewhere north of Newcastle, the seasons change. A wall of grey cloud comes roiling up the coast, pushed by the cold thrust of a southerly, overwhelming the pretence of summer, the temperature dropping by ten degrees in ten minutes. The sun retreats and the rain starts spattering, insistent on the windshield. Martin closes the windows, the wipers engage, he turns on the demister. By the time he reaches Sydney, the rain is sheeting down and night has fallen. Red tail-lights bounce in reflected patterns from oily streets, the traffic slowed to a hydrophobic crawl. He inches onto the Gore Hill Freeway to find the flow of cars no less viscous, the endless river of red beacons shining on black. There must be an accident somewhere; it takes him another hour to get across the bridge, navigate the southern reaches of the city and arrive at his apartment in Surry Hills. Even then, his journey is not yet complete: there is nowhere to park. It was difficult enough back when he still owned his old Toyota, its residents' parking sticker worth more than the car itself. He finds himself feeling lost in his old neighbourhood, circling the block twice, then a wider circle twice more, winding further and further from his place before giving up and heading down the hill towards Central Station, finding paid parking in an underground lot. The overnight fee isn't so bad, but he can't leave the car here for long.

He's still wearing his north coast attire: t-shirt, shorts and sandals, ineffectual the moment he steps from the car's heating. He extracts a sweatshirt from his suitcase, then another. He has no umbrella and no raincoat. The downpour pauses long enough for him to get a block from the car park before it starts in again, rifling in from the south, soaking him through, rendering the sweatshirts cold, soggy and heavy. He trudges with his head lowered, his case rattling along behind him, a small river washing down the hill as he ascends Foveaux Street. Intermittent awnings offer shelter, not that they make any difference now; there is no part of him that isn't wet.

The street is both familiar and unfamiliar, the footpath widened from when he first bought his apartment here fifteen years ago, the boutiques and cafes and noodle bars seemingly ever-changing, new entries emerging from the bankruptcies of corona, the remaining pubs evolving further and further from their workers' origins. He passes a homeless couple in brand-new sleeping bags, tucked into the doorway of a design business, a craftily constructed dam made of polystyrene boxes diverting water out and around them. He pauses under an awning, giving his arm a rest from pulling his case. ICHIBAN COMPUTERS AND SCARVERY says a sign, but there are no displays of either electronics or fashion accessories; the windows are painted black and caged in tempered steel grilles, more like a crack den than a shop. Maybe it's a front for stolen goods; it has that sort of look. A skateboarder captures his attention, pelting down the hill in the middle of the road, bare-chested and his arms extended, as if flying, carried by the torrent and propelled by life. Martin watches him go, reckless in the night, down towards the lights of Central. By the time Martin reaches his place, he's given up trying to control his shivering.

The apartment block looks unwelcoming, a two-storey brown brick remnant of the 1940s, two apartments on the top floor, two on the bottom, none of them with lights in their windows. The gate opens with resistance, screeching on its hinges. There are steps up to twin entrances sheltering under a pair of expansive porticos. Someone has been sleeping in the left-hand entryway, their swag pushed to one side, surrounded by the halo of homelessness: a mattress of flattened cardboard, plastic bags, empty bottles, the smell of piss and poverty. He threads his way through it, treading carefully, unlocks the door, pushes through.

There is a slurry of junk mail scattered inside on the floor. His downstairs neighbour must also be away. He sorts through it, but there is nothing of importance, not even a bill, just lotteries for dream houses on the Gold Coast, an invitation to join a Zumba class and various takeaway menus for everything from pizza to Portuguese chicken. He climbs the stairs, unlocks the door to his apartment.

Inside, it's dank, dark and cold. There's that pungent inner-city smell, a mix of mould and cockroaches, with the added tincture of leaking gas. It's a smell he'd found intoxicating as a uni student, fresh from the north coast, but no longer. It's been two months since he was last here—a fleeting visit, back when autumn was perpetuating an Indian summer, when the climate was at its most agreeable and he could open the windows. Now he extracts a small blow heater, gets it going, blowing enough dust to make him sneeze but not enough to warm him: the cold and damp are in the walls, in the bones of the place, and will not easily be exorcised. He finds a second heater in a cupboard, an oil-filled column variety, sets it going in the single bedroom.

Sydney in winter: the most miserable of seasons. As a correspondent, he'd reported from truly frigid places: Moscow, Mongolia, Northern Quebec, but he's never in his life been as cold as in a Sydney winter. In the northern hemisphere, the denizens respect the seasons, embrace their variability. The same in Canberra and Melbourne, where houses have central heating and double glazing, but not here, not in these remnants of the twentieth century. Here, there is a collective agreement that if winter is ignored it will disappear soon enough.

He shivers, desperate for a shower, before remembering the boiler will need to be powered up. No hot water, not until morning. He really needs to install reverse-cycle air-conditioning: the place is small enough and it gets stinking in summer. He wonders why he's never thought of it before. He heaves his suitcase up onto the old leather couch, strips off his wet clothes and pulls on jeans, a t-shirt, a long-sleeved shirt, socks and boots, an old woollen jumper and a puffer jacket. He feels slightly ridiculous. And no warmer.

He sits on the couch, swathed in a blanket. He phones Max, wondering why his old boss needed to see him so urgently; he must know something about Molloy. But the call rings out. He gives it away and Facetimes Vern and Liam instead. The boy's face comes streaming through the ether onto his screen, bright and full of cheer, bringing warmth into the frigid flat. They talk, Liam initially excited and cheerful before, for no apparent reason, he starts to cry. Vern takes the phone back, says the boy will be fine, that he's just tired. Martin feels guilty for upsetting his stepson's equilibrium, for reminding him of his absence, of Mandy's. He tells Vern there is no news of Mandy: he'll make some calls tonight, start searching tomorrow. The life flows back out of the apartment as he says his goodbyes and cuts the connection.

He tries Max again. Still no answer. What is he up to? What does he know about Tarquin Molloy? Martin closes his eyes, starts to drift, growing warm at last, his mind returning to those early days at the *Herald*, to the night of his humiliation, the night he started to become a real journalist. Throughout that first year as a cadet he'd been intimidated by Max, the chief of staff; been so eager to please him, or at least appease him. He'd been so full of himself, with his honours degree in history, wanting to tell great stories, like Livy, A.J.P. Taylor and Manning Clark. Max had been scathing. 'Cadets don't tell stories; cadets report facts.' And, 'It's a news story, Scarsden, not the rise and fall of the Roman fucking Empire.' That particular quip had stuck; for a time his fellow cadets nicknamed him Gibbon.

So Martin had buckled under, tried to stick to the facts, keeping his writing as simple as possible, even while D'Arcy Defoe won praise for his eloquence. That hurt. One time, D'Arcy was sent to cover a council meeting but had found it so boring, he'd filed a sketch, a satirical piece. Max praised his initiative and the piece was published online.

When Martin was revolved through the same round, he'd encountered the same problem: council proceedings were mundane, not significant enough to warrant space in a paper distributed statewide. So he'd tried a different tack, tried digging, tried to substantiate rumours of corruption, of illegal rezoning to benefit property developers. Even now he cringes at the memory. A councillor had gone out of business, was unable to pay his debts. Martin had replaced a sentence with a word, labelled the man a 'bankrupt'. It wasn't accurate, the man threatened to sue, and was only persuaded out of it by a fellow councillor keen to curry favour with the *Herald*. Max's silence was more scathing than any words could ever be.

Three weeks later, promotions were announced, cadets graduating into rounds. D'Arcy got the plum: state parliament. Not Martin. Max gruffly told him he'd make the cut next time, maybe in three months, maybe in six. Martin considered quitting.

That night at the pub, upstairs in the roof garden, while everyone else was celebrating around him, or pretending to, Max found Martin nursing a beer and tending his ego. The chief of staff sat with him, put his imposing persona to one side, and spoke with sincerity.

'Listen, Martin. Local government is a backwater. Everyone knows it. Reporting the facts isn't enough; the stories will almost never be important enough for a paper like ours. The only two in your whole intake who realised that were you and D'Arcy. Everyone else just obeyed the rules, followed the formula and had their efforts spiked. You would have been promoted as well, if you hadn't fucked up. But trust me, that fuck-up will serve you in just as good a stead as D'Arcy getting his story published. Always check your facts; double-check them. Never rely on one source when you can use two.'

After that, Max bought him a beer and they sat talking into the night, like equals, his colleagues looking on with jealousy until a couple joined them, and then more. By the end of the night, the table was packed, full of drunken camaraderie. That was the night Martin had found his new family, after the trauma of his Port Silver childhood and the cut-price fellowship of university.

He opens his eyes, looks around him at the apartment's walls, decorated with trophies of his career as a correspondent: a poster of Lenin purchased from a market in the outskirts of Moscow, a woven palm hat from the Pacific, a carving of Christ from deep in the Amazon. A declaration of rebellion from the Arab Spring, a bullet-holed road sign from Africa, a Hamas flag from the Gaza Strip. He'd once been proud of them, impressed by his own achievements, curating an exhibition in his own honour, but now they seem try-hard and sad. Who else decorates the walls of their living room with work-related memorabilia? Dentists with X-rays of recalcitrant mandibles, accountants with challenging spreadsheets, politicians with high-denomination brown paper bags? He shakes his head. The museum of Martin had been useful enough back in the day, projecting his man-of-the-world persona, impressing his intermittent lovers. He looks around him and wonders how he ever managed to live here, in this small world, his personal diorama. He decides he needs to redecorate, clear most of it out, although the hand-woven rug shipped back from Afghanistan, spreading warmth across the floorboards, can stay.

He tries Max again. Again, the call rings out. Jesus, where is he? What's so important that he doesn't answer?

Martin stands, starts pacing. Driven by some old habit, he absent-mindedly opens the refrigerator. There is nothing edible: jars of condiments, a bottle of beer left over from autumn, a crisper with a slowly decaying vegetable. He needs to scrub it out, soak up the smells with bicarbonate of soda. He closes the fridge door; it's a mission for another day. He feels the compulsion to get out, to find something to eat. He's thinking takeaway, maybe a curry and the heat it might lend him.

Outside, it's stopped raining, a small mercy. In the portico, he nudges the detritus aside with his boot, reaches the power box, opens it and flicks on the hot-water circuit.

'Oi! What do you want?'

A grizzled man is coming up through the gate, stooped, with a grey beard, water dripping from a large green poncho fashioned from garbage bags.

Martin sighs. 'I live here. Upstairs.'

'Oh, right,' says the man, aggression leaving his voice. 'You Scarsden?'

'That's me.'

'Mrs Jones said I could shelter here.'

Martin nods. His downstairs neighbour, a real Samaritan. Lost her husband in the pandemic. Martin wonders where she might be, if she's all right.

'You've got mail.'

'Right. Anything important?'

'Doesn't look like it.'

'I'll get it later, then.' And Martin walks past the man, down the three exterior steps, through the gate and onto the street. He's making his way up to Crown Street when a slow drizzle starts. He shelters under an awning, deciding he doesn't want to get soaked a second time. His phone rings. The screen says Morris Montifore.

'Morris? Any news?'

'We've got her. She's safe.'

And the city lights glow with joy, and the rain dances from the pavement.

chapter six

MANDY IS FEELING BETTER BY THE MINUTE, HER ORDEAL BEGINNING TO RECEDE.
Morris Montifore is treating her with respect and hard-faced tender-
ness, hovering, more like a concerned parent than a veteran detective,
making sure she can shower, insisting she gets clean clothes and,
best of all, lending her his own mobile phone. She rings Martin,
who doesn't answer, and Winifred, who does. She rings Vern and
Liam, the sound of her son's voice a digital balm, enough to set the
world to rights. He's safe, she's free, normalcy beckons. A doctor
declares her unharmed, taking blood and urine samples, hoping
to establish the substance used to drug her.

And then, instead of an interview room or an office, the
detective takes her to eat: Chinese on Sussex Street, a small place,
upstairs, warm and quiet and out of the rain on this Monday night.
He orders stir-fried noodles and honeyed prawns; she gets a long
soup and steamed vegetables. Only when she has made her way

through most of her meal does he begin gently to question her, starting with her abduction.

She tells him she remembers only fragments of what happened. She recalls a policeman called Claus knocking at the front door, recalls leading him into the lounge room, but little else. A hazy memory of being in a van, waking briefly to find herself bound and blindfolded, then regaining consciousness in the storeroom. And she remembers Zelda Forshaw.

'Tell me about her,' Montifore prompts.

'She said Tarquin Molloy is dead.'

The policeman inclines his head, as if in sympathy. 'That's correct; he is. They found his body on Friday. That's why I'm involved. I want to find out who killed him.'

'He died here? In Australia? I thought he was long gone. Living the high life somewhere overseas.'

'That's what everyone thought. Until his body was found.'

Mandy looks down at her bowl, the vegetables floating in the thin brown liquid. 'Zelda said he was shot.'

'That's right.'

'How did she know that?'

'I told her. She was the first person I interviewed, Saturday afternoon, as soon as I got the case.'

'Of course. His accomplice.' Mandy looks up at the detective. 'Why was he still here? If he had all that money, why stay? Does it mean he didn't steal it after all?'

Montifore says nothing for a moment, watching her, as if considering what to say next. 'The theft was real; Zelda Forshaw went to prison as an accessory. Convicted in a court of law. You must remember that. But it looks like he may have died before he could get away. Before he could spend it.'

Mandy blinks, assimilating the implication of the detective's statement. 'So it's not recent? He died back then?'

Montifore squints, as if trying to improve his focus. 'His body was sealed into the foundations of an apartment block in western Sydney. We've been through the building records. Most likely he was cemented in within days of you last seeing him.'

Mandy's eyes drift away. A waitress is hovering by the bar, flirting with the barman. 'I see. Poor Tarquin.' The waitress does a little wiggle, as if miming, or imitating someone, and the bartender laughs as if he doesn't have a care in the world. 'I always imagined him off on the Riviera, awash with bimbos.'

Montifore gives her a few seconds before continuing. 'So Zelda Forshaw thinks you know where the money is.'

'So she said. You don't think that, do you?'

'No, I don't. We got a warrant. I've been through your accounts. You're wealthy now, but we can see where it's all come from, and how recently. Every cent is legitimate.'

Mandy squirms. She knows the policeman is doing his job, realises the audit of her affairs is in her own interest, but she feels uneasy, as if he's been sifting through her underwear drawer. 'So what happened to the money Tarquin stole?'

'We don't know,' says Montifore. He pokes at a honeyed prawn with his chopsticks, chasing it round the plate, before picking it up and popping it into his mouth, chewing without apparent enjoyment. 'What was Zelda Forshaw to Tarquin Molloy?' It's a brutal question; not even Montifore's gentle manner can disguise that.

Mandy looks him in the eye. 'She was his lover. And maybe his dupe. Like me.'

'So you knew her back then?'

'Not that well. We both worked for the bank, for Mollisons. But she was in a different department and more senior. I was just a clerk, a dogsbody. She was an accountant. But yes, I knew her.'

'Right. Did you interact with her at work?'

'No, not at work. A bit socially. Parties, after-work drinks. We were both young. I was mid-twenties, she was about the same, maybe a year or two older. She was always flirting, thrusting those tits of hers about the place.' Mandy hears the bitchiness in her voice, hates it, but even five years later Zelda Forshaw still gets under her skin.

'Sounds like you didn't get on so well.'

'No. Even after Tarquin and I were engaged, she was still trying to get into his pants.'

'Succeeding?'

Mandy again examines the remnants of her meal, the heat going out from her. 'Yes. Probably.'

Montifore studies her face before changing tack. 'Tell me what happened in the storeroom. What did she say? And why did she abandon you?'

Mandy smiles grimly, glad to be back in the present day, distanced from the past. 'She was questioning me, threatening me. It was all about the money. Then there was the sound of breaking glass. She sent her flunky off to find out what it was.'

'Her flunky?'

'A man. He was wearing a mask. Full face. I have no idea who he was.'

'Go on.'

'Is he okay?'

'The flunky?'

'Yes. She sent him to find out what the noise was. Then there was a gunshot. Is he alive?'

Montifore blinks, as if he's been momentarily wrong-footed by her question. 'I'd say so. There was broken glass everywhere, a few specks of blood, but not much. So no evidence he was shot.' He considers another prawn, decides against it. 'What happened next?'

She tells him of Zelda escaping through the back door, of the appearance of the gaunt man in the tailored suit. 'He claimed he was a policeman, but he didn't release me.'

'You believed him?'

'Yes. He had a badge.'

Montifore reaches into his pocket, extracts his wallet, flips it open, revealing his own glistening identity. 'Like this?'

'Similar.' She frowns. 'Maybe with more bling.'

'Of course. More bling.' The detective repeats her words, scowling. 'Describe him for me, please.'

So she does: the height, the slight stoop, the immaculate suit and the polished shoes. The horse face, the sallow complexion, the long hair, the nicotine-stained fingers, a gold tooth, the sweet smell of his hair oil.

'California Poppy,' whispers Morris Montifore, as if talking to himself.

'Pardon?'

'His hair oil. California Poppy. Very popular once upon a time, sixty or seventy years ago. Almost impossible to find now.'

'He said his name was Henry Livingstone.'

Montifore looks stunned, as if not quite able to believe it. 'Yes, that's him. His real name. Why would he tell you his real name?'

'I don't know.'

'Was he alone?'

'No. There was another man. Short, a ball of muscles, like a powerlifter or something.'

'Bald? With tattoos?'

'That's him. A spider web on his neck. Livingstone claimed he was an undercover cop.'

That elicits a derisory grunt from the policeman. 'Joshua Spitt,' he says. 'Livingstone's little mate. Fresh out of Silverwater.'

Mandy can see the concern on the detective's face. 'What is it?'

'Spitt and Livingstone. Hard men. Killers. They didn't harm you?'

'No.'

'I guess there's a first time for everything.' He's about to say something else, but seems to think better of it. 'I'll need to speak with you some more. Tomorrow. More formally. And after I do, you and Martin should leave Sydney. As soon as possible.'

'Martin? Where is he?'

The policeman smiles, gesturing towards something behind her.

Mandy turns. Martin Scarsden is standing at the top of the stairs, breathing hard, his face flushed. He sees them and starts towards her, a smile breaking across his face, and her spirits lift her to her feet.

—

In an apartment slowly warming, after the joy and the relief and the love-making, Martin can't sleep, the normal post-coital stupor absent. He rolls over, and in the half-light of the city, leaking in through the blinds and onto their bed, he can see that Mandy is also awake, lying still, staring at the ceiling, eyes wide open. She's told him all about her ordeal: held captive by Zelda Forshaw, tied to the shabby mattress, the appearance of the two fake policemen, Morris Montifore identifying them as the underworld thugs Spitt and Livingstone. And yet so much remains unsaid. He hesitates, bites his lip, a gesture learnt from her, but realises neither of them can escape into unconsciousness.

'Tell me about him,' he says quietly. 'Tell me about Tarquin Molloy.'

She sighs, but says nothing, not for a very long time. When she does speak, her eyes remain fixed on the ceiling, her voice remote. 'I loved him. It was the first time I ever properly loved anyone. We were engaged to be married—a fairy tale come true. But he cheated on me. He lied to me. And then he abandoned me.'

'You don't know that. He was killed. Murdered.'

'Only after he had deceived me.'

'What do you mean?'

'He stole millions. He was planning it the whole time. He used me.'

'Maybe he was trying to protect you?'

'No. He used me, kept me in the dark. He never loved me.' There is a hard edge to her voice.

Martin is unsure what to say. 'You knew he was a cop?'

'What?'

'Montifore didn't tell you?'

There is no response, but he senses her contained distress. Through the window comes the sound of sirens, cutting above the background orchestra of traffic. Martin feels a surge of compassion.

He thinks of her life—childhood poverty and scandal in small-town Australia. And her three lovers: the murdered undercover cop Tarquin Molloy, the homicidal priest Byron Swift and the damaged journalist Martin Scarsden. Lucky her.

Finally she speaks. 'All that means is that he played the cops for fools, like he did me and everyone else.'

He rolls over towards her, reaches out to comfort her, but she shrugs his hand away. 'Don't.'

He rolls back, joins her in staring at the ceiling. There are cobwebs and stains. He should clean, get someone in to repaint. He considers staying silent, to hope for sleep. Instead, he decides it's time; time to put the past where it belongs: in the past. 'You've never talked about it—what you did in all those years between leaving Riversend and returning.'

'There's not a lot to tell.'

'Ten years?'

More silence, the city sounds again penetrating, washing over them, the restless city.

'I worked for a while, down in Melbourne. Bar work, waitressing, whatever. Some modelling. Saving up, so I could go to uni. I went to Wollongong, to study literature. Like my mum did up at Bathurst. But it didn't work out.'

'What happened?'

'The books. They no longer spoke to me.'

Outside, in the street, someone is shouting. A man's voice. He sounds angry or drunk or both. A dog is barking, the sound bright above the constant traffic. Martin can't remember Surry Hills being this noisy. 'So it didn't last?'

'No. The other students, they were like kids. Like they'd never lived, never known that life leaves tracks. I felt like a refugee. I didn't know anyone. Just the normal zit-faced losers getting drunk and hitting on me, and sleazy lecturers. I wanted friends, but I didn't understand how to make any. I'd never really had one. It all got too hard; I dropped out.'

A car alarm goes off, joining the nocturnal symphony. 'To do what?'

'Not a lot. I went back to bar work. Floated north to Sydney. Did some fashion shoots, catalogues, that sort of thing. Paid well, but I hated it. I didn't like being photographed. I didn't want to be out there, in the world, my image, just like that, people staring at me.' A pause, as she considers what she is saying. 'So I drifted. It was a drifting life. Eventually I hooked up with the bass player in a band, lived in a squat with him. We were always broke, but he was a good guy. Billy the bass player. The band broke up. We did some drugs. We did some more. He did even more than I knew. In the end, his guitar was stolen, the last thing of any value. He was in tears, inconsolable. Then I saw it in the window of a Cash Converters around the corner. I went inside, asked where they got it. He'd pawned it.' She pauses, takes a breath, letting the memory pass. 'I got him into rehab. I told myself I was helping him, but the truth is I was glad to be rid of him. He was no longer fun, no longer a good guy. A lesson learnt. I drifted more. Then he was back from rehab and we were together again—not because I wanted it, not because he wanted it, but because we didn't have the will to do anything else. Who knows how it would have ended if I hadn't met Tarquin. He was so different. So very different. Except he wasn't. Just another creep.'

Martin frowns, waits for her to continue. There is a strange quality to her voice, as if she is reciting a story she's heard somewhere.

'He got me a job. A good job with good money. A respectable job, a desk job. Working in Pyrmont, in an office block. At a merchant bank called Mollisons. You heard of it?'

'No. He was working there?'

'Sort of; he was on secondment from a law firm. I forget its name.'

'He was a lawyer?'

'So he claimed.'

'He helped you?'

'I thought so. Now I know he was only using me.'

'How do you mean he used you? To infiltrate the bank?'

'Yes. And now you're telling me he was a cop as well.'

Martin wonders how to move the conversation forward without offending her, but she speaks unprompted, her voice still far away.

'For a moment, it was all so golden. So perfect. And then I began to suspect. Not that he was a criminal, or that he was a cop, but that he was cheating on me. I heard a rumour, dismissed it. Then I . . .' She swallows. 'I found them together, he and Zelda. It broke my heart.'

'Zelda? The woman who kidnapped you?'

'Yeah. Her.'

'What happened?'

'I dropped him.'

'How'd he take that?'

'Not well. He begged me to take him back.' And now Martin can hear the emotion behind her words; not a lot, but it's there, though she appears to be trying to control it. 'He swore Zelda was

59

nothing, a stupid dalliance. Swore everlasting love. And when that didn't work, he proposed.'

'You said yes?'

'I said yes. And I was happy. For a whole month, I was exultant. And then he disappeared. I came to work one day. There were flowers on my desk and an envelope with a plane ticket to the Gold Coast. I rang him. He said he was already there, working, that he had a penthouse for the weekend. Asked me to take the next day, a Friday, off work. So I did; I called in sick, flew up. But he wasn't there. I had a text message saying he'd be there soon, but he never arrived. And I never heard from him again.'

In the half-light, Martin can see her eyes, moist and glittering. She senses his attention, rolls onto her side, back to him. And yet she continues. 'The next week, the rumours started to swirl. I was questioned. Interrogated. They arrested Zelda. And when they couldn't prove my involvement, I was sacked. And I was drifting again. More like sinking. You don't need to know. Drugs, squats, couch surfing. I didn't even have Billy to look after.' She rolls back, again gazing upwards, before turning to face Martin for the first time in their conversation. 'Do you believe in karma?'

'You've asked me that before.'

'I have. In Riversend and in Port Silver. What's your answer?'

'I guess I do,' says Martin, remembering his childhood in Port Silver. 'I've learnt that we can't outrun our past.'

'That's what I'm worried about. It's all still there. The ugliness and the betrayal coming to claim us, to claim Liam.'

'No,' says Martin, reaching out to her. This time she doesn't move away. 'Why would it? If you did nothing wrong? You've said it yourself. We are the barricades. That's our job, to protect him, to make sure our past is not his future.'

She lifts a hand to touch his face. 'Thank you, Martin.' And then, after a moment, 'I'm just not sure how we can achieve that.'

Later, when she's finally tumbled into sleep, exhausted by her ordeal and by her revelations, Martin wonders what she thinks of him, whether she has ever truly trusted him. Perhaps it would be more surprising if she did. First there was Tarquin Molloy, an undercover policeman who played her for a fool, picking her up only to send her spiralling downwards. And later there was Byron Swift, out in the scrublands, the homicidal priest who also lied and deceived. Will she ever truly open herself to him, tell him all of her past? Maybe. Maybe tonight is the start.

And in the dark, he feels a tug of guilt. For more than a year now, she has helped him come to terms with his own past, his childhood trauma, acting as his own personal counsellor. And not once has he questioned her about her own dysfunctional history. She's alluded to her miserable childhood in Riversend, but never spoken about her twenties, the lost decade between leaving her home town and returning to it. Why hasn't he asked? Is he really that self-centred?

———

She lies awake. The room is beginning to fill with light and the noise of traffic is ramping up as the city stirs. She must have slept, but she doesn't feel like it. Instead, it's as if she has tossed and turned all night. Beside her, Martin is snoring softly. At home in Port Silver, she'd find his wheezing irritating; here it's a comfort.

At least she has him. He's taken it so well: this revelation that she was betrothed to another man, had loved Tarquin Molloy. She wonders once again why he persists with her, with her faults and her falsehoods. Why he trusts her.

But Martin is not the source of her anxieties and she knows it. It's Tarquin; it's always been Tarquin, playing with her, even now, toying with her sense of self. These past five years she believed he'd deceived her, that he won her trust in order to steal his millions and vanish. Left her empty-handed and empty-hearted, without a job, out on the streets with no discernible future. But that wasn't what happened, she knows that now. Montifore told her: Tarquin hadn't escaped, he'd been killed; Martin told her: he hadn't been a thief, he'd been a cop. What does that mean?

Not a lot, when all is said and done. What difference does it make if he was an undercover investigator, probing the bank, or a fraudster, intent on stealing millions? He used her to access the bank's systems; he betrayed her trust. Same thing.

And yet, once again, her thoughts wind back down into the labyrinth. She had always trusted the untrustworthy: Tarquin Molloy and Byron Swift and lesser lights like Billy the bass player. And they all ended up hurting her, betraying her faith in them. For God's sake, she'd even been duped by that thug Livingstone, fooled into believing he was a cop. What is wrong with her? Is she as dumb as her hair colour suggests, like some bar-room joke rolled out for the amusement of half-cut bogans? Has she not progressed at all from her days on the street? Can Martin Scarsden really be any different? Is he laughing too? No, she tells herself, that is unfair and unworthy—but the thought stays with her, lingering, unable to be dismissed.

More like it's herself she shouldn't trust, her own faulty judgement.

A memory comes to her, so vivid she can smell it. The school bus between Riversend and the high school in Bellington, a forty-five minute drive there and a forty-five minute drive back across the arid plain, trapped inside with her classmates, trapped inside with the stigma: the bastard child, her mother unmarried, the progeny of scandal. *Bastard.* How the other children loved to spray the word about—carelessly repeating the slurs of their parents, supporters of her father—as if it didn't hurt, more like a nickname than a weapon. Only she knew how hurtful it was, branding her as different, an outsider. And somehow, she'd come to believe she deserved it, that it was a penance she had to pay for her mother's courage.

The smell is the same: the dust and the bus driver's body odour, the heat of summer lifting chemicals from the vinyl seats, the boys' excessive deodorant, the girls' green-apple shampoo, the hint of a clandestine cigarette. It lasted four years, an eternity. Most days weren't so bad, not objectively; when her fellow students had other things to entertain them, when they simply ignored her. But that made the trip no less laden with dread, sitting up behind the driver, reading her books, ears alert for incoming invective. Four years of hell, until somehow her mother found the money to send her to boarding school in Albury for her last two years.

The worst was Trina's birthday. She hosted a party every year. On that Friday, the bus would stop at Trina's kilometres-long driveway, out there on the plain, and practically the whole bus would alight, only some seniors remaining up the back. The balloons tied to the milk-can letterbox, laughter and excitement filling the air. The first year, it had caught her by surprise. She'd buried her face in her book, pretending not to notice. 'Not you, love?' the driver had asked, voice gentle, before putting the bus into gear and driving on. A weekend filled with tears.

Now, lying in bed, she contemplates the lesson of the school bus. She'd left it out there on the plain, once her karmic debt was paid, that's what she's believed. She's done so well, these last few years, moving beyond Riversend and Sydney, finding sanctuary in Port Silver, putting distance between her and Tarquin Molloy and Byron Swift. Reinventing herself, a new Mandalay Blonde. Motherhood, her fresh start with Martin, her inheritance and the house on the cliffs: the foundations to a new and better life, a new and better her. She's been a good mother, she knows that, and she's been rewarded with Martin. Isn't that how it works? You do good things and good things are delivered to you; you do bad things and you get the same back, often with interest? Maybe not literally, but psychologically: doing good lifts you up, doing bad weighs you down. And these past few years she has done good. She's been good for Martin, and he's been good for her. But now it feels like she's back in the bus, pretending she's fine, even as she's waiting for the next affront. Does good cancel bad on the karmic ledger, or does the bad demand some new act of atonement?

Martin. Why hasn't she told him of her past, the lost years between finishing school and returning home to Riversend, the ten years of flailing about? She's told him something of the privations of her childhood, so why has she never recounted her twenties? That decade-long winter, leavened only by the brief summer of

Tarquin Molloy, the unfulfilled spring of Byron Swift. Why didn't she confide in him when she had the chance? Was it because she thought that decade unimportant, an uneventful hiatus between her school days and her life with him? Was she still buried in her book, unwilling to raise her head?

This past year, Martin has become more and more open, telling her about his own awful childhood, the deaths of his parents, his sisters. She's seen him changing, softening, become more giving, shedding the persona of foreign correspondent, losing his shell. She'd believed herself maturing alongside him, the psychic wounds healing, the scar tissue growing over. She and him and Liam: nothing else mattered. That was what she had told herself up there on the cliff: nothing else mattered, the world couldn't reach them there. Not the bushfires, not the virus, not the past. So she didn't tell him about Tarquin Molloy, convincing herself it no longer mattered. But it wasn't true. They didn't live quarantined from the consequences of their actions; they could not travel unimpeded to new worlds; there was no vaccine against the past.

That thought traps her; she can't move on, can't escape it. And now sleep is reaching out, its tendrils stroking her. Her thoughts start to swirl, a vortex pulling her downwards, inviting her to surrender consciousness, to give in to her dreams. And yet every time she slips towards the soft bed of oblivion, they are waiting, the ghosts of Tarquin Molloy and Byron Swift, their haunting presence.

'It's your money Martin wants,' whispers Tarquin. 'You've got millions.'

'It's your looks,' insists Byron. 'It's his dick that wants you, not his heart.'

She bites her lip, emerging once again from the slippery pool. How can she sleep with these spectres waiting for her?

Then she thinks of Martin with Liam, surely the clincher. His love for the boy is so evident, so selfless. And Liam is not even his biological son.

Beside her, he emits another whistling exhalation, and again she feels her love for him. The ghosts cower. She rolls over once again, trying to drift off, but the sheets are wrinkled and the duvet twisted, too warm in the cold apartment. She yearns for sleep before the day begins in earnest, if only to escape her maddening thoughts.

But still she can't fall into the void. Her mind switches back from Martin to Tarquin. All this time, she's believed he'd used her, deceived her, abandoned her. It's what the case against Zelda Forshaw established: that the accountant had abetted him in defrauding the bank. The prosecutors asserted he'd bolted, leaving Zelda to face the music. Of course, Mandy accepted their version of events. Why wouldn't she? It was proven in a court of law.

But now she knows different. Tarquin was dead, murdered. He hadn't got away with it, he'd never left the country. He'd been killed, shot, back then, maybe while she still fretted in the Gold Coast penthouse. And he wasn't a thief, he was a cop.

And suddenly she is fully awake, the knowledge clear in her mind, the real reason she can't sleep. All this time, she's thought he was the one who had betrayed her. Now she realises the opposite may be true: that she had betrayed him, condemned him. That her jealous heart and her spiteful tongue had killed him. My God, what had she wrought?

They convicted Zelda but not her. They concluded she was innocent, of course they had. For hadn't she reported him, in a jealous fit, after she found him sleeping with Zelda? Told them he'd asked for her passwords, claiming he'd inadvertently allowed his own to expire. She'd done that; there was no denying it. It had been a petty thing, a childish retribution, a reminder that he shouldn't take her for granted.

Ever since, she's thought maybe that was why he had abandoned her, disappeared with the money and left her behind, knowing that he couldn't trust her. That was what she's been telling herself for five years; her rationalisation, the reason why she hadn't ever told the police and the bank all she had known. Why she had lied, why she had protected herself, why she always denied helping him. But he hadn't fled; he'd been murdered. Why? Because someone had discovered he was a cop? And how had they discovered him? Could it be because she had reported him, his misdemeanour, using her passwords instead of his own?

Suddenly, it's hard to breathe, the sobs coming. Fuck. She'd got him killed. The poor bastard. Maybe he hadn't sent her to the Gold Coast to get her out of the way. Maybe Zelda was right, and he had sent her north to make sure she was protected, that she had an alibi as he probed the bank's computers. He was a cop and she'd got him killed.

Beside her, Martin grunts and rolls over. She turns to look at him, his profile now clearly visible in the rising light. How dare she suspect him, after what she's done? How can she ever tell him? How could he ever want her if he knew the truth? How could he ever trust her? He wouldn't stay with her and Liam.

He'd write a story about her, put it in the paper, reduce her to clickbait and leave.

And with that she rises from the bed and heads towards the kitchenette, knowing that sleep is beyond reach. Feeling as if she may never sleep again.

TUESDAY

chapter seven

ALDO'S IS UNCHANGED. THE CAFE ON A LANEWAY OFF CROWN WAS MARTIN'S regular haunt back when he worked full-time at the *Herald,* in the years after he bought his apartment. He ignores the outside tables, like everyone else in the chill of the morning. Inside, two steps lead down, giving the place a slightly subterranean feel, but it's warm and welcoming, the polished concrete floor softened by the dark stained wood of tables and stools. Aldo himself is nowhere to be seen; his son Louie is manning the espresso machine.

'Martin. Your usual?'

'Thanks, Louie.'

'I'll bring it over.'

It's been two months since he was last here, but suddenly Martin feels like he's home, so much more than in the apartment. He sits at the bench by the concertina windows, usually open but closed today. Outside the sun is shining: an exemplary Sydney winter's day, the perfect rebuttal of the night's rain, the sky a vivid blue above the persistent shadows of Surry Hills. Soon it will warm up, but not yet. Across the street a cat is curled in a doorway, soaking up the sunlight in anticipation. When the coffee arrives, it tastes as if it's been consecrated: rich, strong, smooth. He hasn't missed Sydney, but he's missed Aldo's coffee. For all his efforts and expensive gadgetry, he's yet to master the perfect cup at home. He closes his eyes and takes another sip. The world has corrected itself: his late-night concerns seem inconsequential. Mandy is safe and nothing else matters. She'll spend the morning with Montifore; sooner or later, the police will arrest her kidnappers. With any luck, long before that, the two of them can leave Sydney, drive back over the Hawkesbury, back to Port Silver, the cogs of this great machine of a city whirring on without them. He imagines the scene: he and Mandy reunited with Liam. A big sprawling lunch with Vern and Josie and their extended family to celebrate, outside in the balmy weather of the north coast. Later, they'd head down to the beach, go back to waving at whales. And then, in private, over many months if that is what it takes, he can help Mandy come to terms with her past, just as she has helped him.

But first he needs to go and see Max, to explain in person why he can't stay in Sydney, why he can't participate in the scoop of the century. At the same time, if he's being honest, he's still intrigued. Not in the story, but in what his former editor might tell him about the mystery man, Tarquin Molloy, the man whom Mandy agreed to marry. The wall on his flat has enough trophies; he doesn't need any more, but he desperately wants to help Mandy reconcile with her past.

His phone buzzes in his jacket pocket. It's Winifred Barbicombe.

'Winifred. Hello.'

The lawyer doesn't bother with greetings, her voice matter-of-fact. 'I've just arrived in Sydney. The police want a statement from Mandy and probably a formal interview as well. I'm heading straight to the station.'

'Does Mandy know? She was asleep when I left her.'

'Yes. I just spoke to her.'

'So how can I help?'

'It's probably inconsequential now, but I looked up those names—the ones Montifore mentioned up in Port Silver. Atticus Pons and George Giopolis.'

'Never heard of them. Who are they?'

'Giopolis is a property developer. Pons is a lawyer, a senior partner in Phipps Allenby Lockhart. Commercial law. Phipps is where Molloy purportedly worked while he was undercover.'

'So, about sixteen months ago, Montifore floated Pons's name in an interview with Mandy?'

'That's right.'

'What does that mean?'

'I don't know. It's possible Pons was helping with the police investigation, that he provided Molloy with his cover. But that's just a guess.'

'What about Giopolis?'

'He's wealthy, self-made, well connected. His family develops industrial parks. I can't see any reason why Montifore raised his name.'

'Right. Well, it probably doesn't matter now Mandy is safe. I'm off to see my old editor. He may know something about Molloy. I'll see if the names mean anything to him.'

He hails a cab, deciding to leave the Subaru cosseted in the underground car park. Hopefully, by tomorrow they'll be gone. The taxi winds through the familiar streets, up Moore Park Road and along Oxford Street, Martin gazing out at the morning rush, the commuters at bus stops, the clog of traffic, the city back to normal. And then turning off, into the quieter streets of Bellevue Hill. The air is sweeter up here: less exhaust, more money. The cab drops him outside the protective wall surrounding Max's place. Martin has been here many times, at dinners hosting the city's movers and shakers, at more informal weekend lunches full of wine and conjecture. Today, the gate is open and welcoming. For a moment he stands and breathes in the street: the trees, the peace under the cloudless canopy, the post-rain clarity. Between the houses opposite, he can catch glimpses of the harbour, the blue expanse, the glittering city, all of its promises within reach.

He walks through the gate, following the path via a small garden towards the front stairs. There he finds Max's wife Eileen, sunning herself on the stairs, sitting with her eyes closed.

'Eileen. Good morning.'

'Oh. Martin. It's you.'

'Yes. Lovely morning, isn't it?'

'Just beautiful.' She smiles.

'Is Max in?'

'Yes, he's in the sitting room.'

'Can I go through?'

'Of course. And Martin?'

'Yes?'

'He's dead.'

Words fail him. He stares at her. Her face is benign, but on her hands, clasped tightly before her, is the smallest smear of blood. And her eyes, their faraway look, the thousand-yard stare. He's seen that before, more times than he would like to count, but rarely in Australia.

He doesn't want to enter the house, but he knows he must; he owes it to the traumatised woman quietly going into shock on her own front step. And he owes it to Max.

He smells it, of course, before he sees it: the blood and the shit and the other thing, that strange sweet smell that accompanies death. Max is indeed in the sitting room. He's slumped against a sideboard, naked from the waist down, wearing stockings gone awry. Around his neck, a choker leash, tied to a sideboard, cutting into his neck. His face is blue and distorted, eyes engorged, tongue bulbous and blue. *Jesus.*

Lying face down on the other side of the room is another body. A woman, not a young woman: a bra, stockings, no knickers, her flesh flaccid, the back of her head a volcanic red hole, a gun in her limp hand. *Jesus Christ.*

He takes one more look then backs out of the room, creeping, as if not to disturb them, as if to exclude himself from their reality.

Outside, he lowers himself onto the steps beside Eileen, holding his breath, trying not to shake, trying not to make a sound. He places his hand on her shoulder, looks down at her hands with the red streak. She doesn't flinch, doesn't move. The morning remains sunny and still, resolutely untarnished by what has occurred inside the house. In the distance, through the houses, the harbour still glints, white sails carving through the gaps.

'I was in Bowral last night,' she says. 'I just got back. I knew something was wrong. The door wasn't locked. The alarm wasn't on. I've called the police.'

'It's okay, Eileen, they'll be here soon enough.'

And they are. No sirens, just a quiet swoosh as the squad car pulls up to the kerb beyond the wall. Two constables walk through the open gate, a man and a woman, stiff and apprehensive. To Martin they seem too young to witness what the world is about to show them.

'Mrs Fuller?' asks the policewoman. 'Are you Eileen Fuller? The woman who phoned?'

'Yes,' says Eileen. 'They're inside. Please go through. You'll forgive me if I stay here?'

'Of course. And you, sir?'

'Martin Scarsden. A friend of the family. I just arrived.'

The police enter, spend no more than a minute inside. The policeman, looking grim, is speaking on his phone as he walks back down the path towards his car. 'Homicide, please,' he says.

chapter eight

IT ISN'T AN INTERVIEW ROOM, MORE LIKE A MEETING ROOM, WITH A SMALL conference table surrounded by a dozen chairs, and on the walls innocuous black-and-white prints of the harbour city: the bridge, the Opera House, Luna Park. It might as well be wallpaper, for all the difference it makes: she's still in police headquarters, there's a tape recorder on the table and a constable in the corner. Mandy feels as if she's about to be grilled, as if she's guilty. She feels guilty, knows herself to be guilty; she's just not sure of which crime. At least her lawyer, Winifred, is here with her, as supportive as always, showing no sign that her advancing years or the early morning flight from Melbourne have blunted her scimitar mind.

Morris Montifore enters, looking dishevelled and apologetic. Not so his assistant, Ivan Lucic, his suit a cut above his superior's; superficially neutral and businesslike, he carries with him unspoken aggressions. Mandy tells herself it's his default disposition, directed at the world in general and not at her in particular. Montifore sits, Lucic remains standing. The senior man mouths the niceties, then the necessities, and launches into it, as if time is short and this is just one more task on a long list.

'We are investigating the murder five years ago of a man known to you as Tarquin Molloy. Our investigators have confirmed that you were interstate, on the Gold Coast, at the time that Molloy disappeared. You are not a suspect in his murder. However, we are hoping you might be of assistance to our investigation. Are you willing to assist?'

'Of course.' Mandy keeps her voice measured, cautious.

'Ms Blonde, you're aware that Tarquin Molloy was a police officer, working undercover?'

'I am now. But I wasn't then.'

'When did you find out?'

'Last night. After you neglected to tell me at dinner.'

'I see.' Montifore makes a note. 'My apologies. I should have told you.' Behind him, Lucic grimaces, as if apologising to the public contravenes the code of conduct.

'What was he investigating?' asks Mandy.

'Sorry?'

'He was an undercover police officer. He was murdered. Now you want my help. So perhaps you can tell me what it was all about.'

Winifred nods her support and encouragement, but Lucic shakes his head as if in disbelief. Mandy glares at the junior officer.

Montifore notices the exchange and turns to his subordinate. 'Ivan, give us a minute, will you?'

Lucic shrugs, as if indicating he couldn't care less about the interview, and saunters from the room. The constable in the corner remains impassive.

Montifore leans back, pauses to think, but answers the question nevertheless. 'Money laundering. Tax evasion. High-level corruption. You name it, Molloy was chasing it.'

'Right.'

The policeman spreads his hands, a conciliatory gesture. 'But that's not why I'm here. I'm a homicide detective; I'm investigating his death, nothing more.'

'Okay, how can I help?' she asks, her tone measured.

'Tell me about Molloy. How did you meet?'

'At the casino—the Star—late one night. He'd had a big win in the high-rollers room. He took a shine to me, bought me a drink, then something to eat. He was handsome. Nice hair, nice smile, nice suit. Charming. Polite. He didn't try to race me off. Instead he listened to what I had to say. At the end of the night he requested my phone number, asked if he could call me.'

'He liked gambling?'

'Loved it.'

'And you were already working at Mollisons, the investment bank?'

'No.' She pauses, then wonders why she is hesitating. 'He got me the job there.'

'Really? When was this?'

'A few weeks after we met. It would be six years ago now, the year before he disappeared. We started seeing each other. I needed a job, he found me one in their graduate program.'

'You were a graduate?'

'Only from high school.'

'So you were indebted to him?'

'I was in love with him.'

Montifore blinks at her frankness. 'Where did you work? What section?'

'I was on the trading floor.'

'I see. But you weren't a trader?'

Mandy smiles. 'Hell, no. I was just there to double-check trades, to make sure all the records were in order. To fetch coffee, take phone messages, do the photocopying. All the tedious stuff the traders were too busy or too important to do.'

'But you had a desk, a computer?'

'Of course.'

'Did you have digital access to other areas—Mollisons' wider business dealings, their financial records, their trading platforms, human resources, that sort of thing?'

'No, I don't think so. Not anything commercially sensitive. I had access to the personnel files of the trading floor staff, to update holidays, rosters, that sort of thing. I could access email, the company intranet and the trading software—but only to see the records; I wasn't actually able to trade. Beyond that, I don't know.'

'You don't know?'

She shrugs. 'I never tried to access anything else. I just did what I was meant to do.'

'And where was Tarquin Molloy working?'

'For a law firm—Phipps something or other.'

'Phipps Allenby Lockhart?'

'Yes, that's it. But he spent three days a week at Mollisons. He told me they were a major client, that he was working on some sort of restructuring with them.'

'Did he ever discuss who he was dealing with at Mollisons?'

'If he did, I can't remember it. My impression was that it was senior people. He had an office up on mahogany row with the other executives.'

Montifore steeples his hands, looks her in the eye. 'I've said that you're not a suspect, that we know you were on the Gold Coast when he disappeared and that all I'm interested in is finding the killer, not investigating any other criminality, not by Molloy, not by the bank.' He pauses, either for effect or to choose his words. 'There is evidence that Molloy gained unauthorised access to Mollisons' computer systems and stole something like ten million dollars. You're aware of that?'

'Of course. Everyone was talking about it.'

'Is it possible that he used your passwords to gain access to Mollisons' systems?'

She frowns. Why is he asking her this? 'Yes. I told the company investigators at the time. He used my passwords.'

'Take me through that. How did he get your passwords?'

'I think he recruited me, played me for a fool. Got me the job at Mollisons as another conduit for him to infiltrate their networks, either as a cop or a fraudster—or both. I should have seen it, but I was blind.' She allows herself a knowing smile. 'Love's like that.'

'So you think, in retrospect, that you could have picked up on what he was doing?'

'Maybe.'

'How did he get the passwords?'

She sighs. 'This should all be on the records from the police at the time.'

'If you wouldn't mind repeating it, please.'

Winifred interjects. 'If this is some sort of attempt to find inconsistencies in my client's evidence, given five years apart, it's a clumsy one.'

'I said she's not a suspect. I meant it.' He turns from the lawyer. 'Mandalay?'

'It's pretty mundane. He was over at my apartment one weekend, after we'd been going out for a few months. He was working on his laptop. He told me the system had locked him out because he'd forgotten to do his monthly password update, some reason like that. So I gave him mine. I didn't think anything of it.'

'You had no suspicions?'

'No. I had very low-level clearance. Even now, I can't believe it would have been much use to him.'

Montifore is looking at his notes as he speaks. 'And yet you reported him, some months before his disappearance.'

'It was a formality. Routine. There was a questionnaire; I answered it truthfully.'

'Who sent the questionnaire?'

'I don't recall.'

'Clarity Sparkes, the head of physical security. Does that sound right?'

'Yes. Thanks. That was her. She interviewed me about it at the time. She didn't seem to think it was serious.'

Montifore is looking at her intently; beside her, Winifred is unmoving. 'I don't understand. He was your boyfriend, you only had low-level access, it was no big deal. Yet you dobbed him in?'

'That's right.'

'Is there anything else you want to tell me?'

And the memory comes to her: hard and clear, as if illuminated by stage lights. Discovering the two of them at it, in the most tawdry and compromising of situations, his snow-white bum pumping up and down, her groans filling the air like a porn star. Mandy frozen there, staring through her tears, anger filling her. And later, when the questionnaire had arrived in her inbox, she'd answered it honestly. Such a petty betrayal, such juvenile vengeance, a schoolyard retribution. What was she thinking? To punish him? To demonstrate he shouldn't take her for granted? What?

'Mandy?'

She swallows. 'I discovered he was having an affair.'

'He was unfaithful?'

'Yes.'

'With whom?'

'With Zelda Forshaw.'

'Zelda Forshaw? The woman you allege abducted you?'

'It's not an allegation. It's a fact.'

'So he was in a relationship with you, then you discovered he was also involved with Zelda Forshaw. When was this?'

'I'm not sure. Some months before he disappeared.'

Montifore looks at his notes. 'About eight weeks before?'

'If you say so.'

The detective leans back in his chair. 'Let me get this right. You're in love with Molloy. You trust him. You even give him your passwords. Then he betrays you; you discover he's having an affair with Zelda Forshaw. You're pissed off. Understandably so. And then a security questionnaire comes to you, just at this time, and so you report him.'

Mandy feels her face flush. She's not sure if it's guilt or shame she feels. But she nods. 'Yes.'

'Did you confront him about this fling with Zelda Forshaw?'

'I did.'

'And what did he say?'

Mandy stares down at the desk, not allowing her emotions to rise. 'He begged forgiveness. Said he'd been a fool. He was very convincing.'

'You believed him?'

'I did when he asked me to marry him. After that, my doubts disappeared.'

'He proposed; you said yes?'

'I said yes.'

'Did you know Zelda Forshaw?'

'Not really. We'd met socially. I didn't like her.'

'Why not?'

'She liked to play the slut.'

'You mean she was a flirt? Or something more?'

'With Tarquin she was definitely something more. None of the women liked her.'

'Where did she work?'

Mandy blinks. The policeman must already know that, surely. 'She was an accountant. I'm not sure which floor she was on.'

'Okay. Let's move forward to around the time he disappeared. Tell me about the night you spent on the Gold Coast.'

'It was a weekend. He rang me beforehand, on the Wednesday night. He told me he'd had to go up at short notice, he'd be there for a week. He suggested I come up, we could make a weekend of it. I went to work on Thursday; there were plane tickets and flowers on my desk. So I took the Friday off. Called in sick and flew up with the ticket he left me. He said he'd see me there.' She pauses, as the memories start to solidify, images coming to mind, building upon the foundation of her narrative. 'It was a beautiful place. A penthouse. Amazing views over the beach. Lots of marble. Its own plunge pool. He was a lawyer, well paid, liked the good life, but even for him it was flash. There was champagne waiting, and flowers. But he never showed. I never saw him again.'

'Did you hear from him?'

'Just a text that night, the Friday night. Late. I'd been trying to ring, to text. Then finally I got a message.'

'You remember it?'

'How could I forget? *Sorry. Delayed. There soon. Love you.* And some kisses. That's all.'

'And then?'

'And then nothing. Not on the Saturday, not on the Sunday. So I was there two nights. I flew back to Sydney Sunday night. I went to work on the Monday, no one had seen him.'

'You reported him missing? Notified the police?'

'Yes, I did. Along with others. There was nothing for a couple of days, then they came and interviewed me. A man and a woman. Plainclothes. I could tell from their questions something wasn't right, that it had something to do with money.' She looks away, again swept back in time to those days of grief, those days when her dreams crumbled and reality replaced them. 'Then the next week they arrested Zelda Forshaw and the rumours turned to fact. They'd been in it together. Embezzlement. He'd still been on with her after all, both of us at the same time, proposal or no proposal. The only difference was she knew what he was up to and I didn't.'

'You felt betrayed,' says Montifore, a statement not a question.

'What do you think?'

'What did you tell your superiors?'

Mandy shrugs. 'The police cleared me pretty quickly, but Mollisons were more thorough. They did their own internal investigation. The rumour was that millions were missing. They gave me the third degree.'

'You told them about giving him the passwords?'

Mandy shrugs. 'They already knew that months before.'

'You were cleared?'

'Formally. But they sacked me all the same. A bunch of us, about a month later. I guess they didn't completely trust us. The whole section went. So did parts of human resources, also some of the accountants who worked with Zelda.'

'Your whole section was sacked? How many people?'

'About five. Something like that.'

'Was it your section the money had vanished from?'

'There was no suggestion of that. We didn't oversee any money. But we were out. Escorted from the building by security. That was that.'

Montifore takes this on board. 'Why do you think Zelda Forshaw abducted you?'

'I guess she thinks I know where the money is.'

'So she doesn't?'

Mandy shrugs. 'I guess not. But she went to jail for it. They established she conspired with him.'

'But if Tarquin Molloy was already dead, maybe she never got her share.'

'Yes. So she says. But she's mad if she thinks I know where it is.'

'So what do you think happened to Tarquin Molloy?'

That gives her cause to pause, to take a deep breath, to re-centre herself. 'I don't know. If he was a cop, maybe there was no missing money, maybe it was something else, all those other things you mentioned. Money laundering, corruption. Maybe someone killed him to keep him quiet.'

'That's possible,' says Montifore, his expression non-committal.

Mandy has the impression he's about to wind up the interview. Before he does, she asks her own question. 'Tell me one thing then. Tarquin Molloy was his name while he was undercover; what was his real name?'

'I can't tell you that.'

'Why not? He's dead. Has been for five years. It's not going to hurt him now.'

Montifore looks genuinely apologetic. 'It's not possible.'

Winifred is frowning. 'My client has been most forthcoming. She has helped you when she didn't need to. You should tell her.'

Montifore looks at the table, unable to meet their twin gaze. 'He was married. There are children.'

Mandy goes to say something, but finds herself unable to speak. Married? *He was married? The whole time?*

There's a silence, an awful interregnum, before Ivan Lucic bursts into the room, eyes wide, ignoring the two women. 'Boss, we've got to go. Two dead. And Scarsden is there.'

chapter nine

IT'S LIKE A SLOW-MOTION SWARM, BEES COMING TO A NEWLY DISCOVERED SOURCE of nectar. No sirens, no urgency, just an efficient hum. Two more uniformed officers, then a woman weighed down with camera gear and a grim expression, followed by a van full of forensic investigators. Quietly, without comment, they don pale blue oversuits. Plastic, Martin thinks. Disposable.

He and Eileen leave the steps, clearing the way for the police, and move to a garden bench, from where they watch without seeing. Off in the distance, the harbour shimmers, that other Sydney, so far away now.

Ten minutes later, two men wearing suits walk through the gate.

'Good morning, Martin,' says the elder of the two, his face wearing a frown as if it has been cast that way.

'Morning, Martin,' says his younger colleague, apparently unperturbed.

'Morris. Ivan.'

'In there?' asks Lucic.

Martin nods.

The young detective grimaces and heads up the stairs to the house.

'You okay?' asks Montifore.

Martin shakes his head. Inside him, something is starting to move, to shift. Beside him on the bench, Eileen Fuller is staring out into the uncaring beauty of the day.

Forensics start moving up past them and into the house. Montifore offers Martin a last look of concern then follows the plastic-encased team. Martin looks at his watch: more than an hour has somehow disappeared. A young policewoman, voice gentle, guides Eileen away. Montifore comes back some undeterminable amount of time later, his face pallid. 'You okay?'

The question makes no more sense the second time around. Martin can only shake his head.

'Come on. Let's sit in the car.' Montifore leads him back down through the still-open gate. Martin pauses to close it after him. Montifore watches him closely.

Inside the car, the detective speaks. 'You saw. Inside.'

Martin nods. 'Yes. I saw.' The words feel foreign on his tongue, a language belonging to some other tribe.

'Accidental death, then suicide,' says Montifore flatly.

That has his attention, bringing him into the present. 'You think so?'

'Don't you?'

'No.'

'Why not?'

Martin thinks it through. 'If it was accidental, if Max choked, then surely the woman would have tried to free him, to revive him. Maybe if she failed, then she might have shot herself. But she didn't try. He was still hanging there.'

Montifore examines him. Martin can feel the weight of the detective's scrutiny, but he doesn't care.

'I agree,' says Montifore. 'Murder-suicide, then.'

'Or made to look like it.'

Montifore lets more time pass. 'What were you doing here?'

'Max Fuller is my old editor. Semi-retired. He called to say he had a big story, wanted me to help with it. I couldn't. Not with what happened with Mandy. Once I knew she was safe, I decided to drop round and tell him in person before we headed home.'

'What was the story about?'

'I don't know. He wouldn't tell me over the phone.'

'Nothing?'

Martin turns to look at him for the first time. 'I asked him if he'd ever heard of Tarquin Molloy. He told me I should come and see him.'

'When was this?'

'Yesterday. When I was driving down. Mid-afternoon.'

'And he knew about Molloy?'

'He just said it was too big to discuss on the phone.'

'Too big . . .' he muses. 'And that was the last time you spoke to him?'

'I rang him last night, but it went through to voicemail.'

Now it's Montifore's turn to stare out the windscreen. When he returns his attention to Martin his face is stern, his voice heavy. 'Mandalay Blonde encountered two men pretending to be policemen. They scared off her captors. Their names are Henry Livingstone and Joshua Spitt.'

'And?'

'These guys, they're worse than ruthless. Psychotic. Livingstone killed his high school teacher at sixteen. Got out of prison in his mid-twenties, killed again. Spitt's almost as bad. You need to get Mandy and get going. Back to Port Silver. Or New Zealand. Somewhere safe.'

'Seriously?'

'Yes.'

'You think this is connected, that they killed Max?'

Montifore shrugs. 'Maybe they did, maybe they didn't. But if whoever did kill your editor searched his phone, they would see he's been talking with you.' The policeman waits a couple of heartbeats before continuing. 'This thing, whatever it is, it's not finished. Livingstone and Spitt—these are men who operate in the shadows, using fear and intimidation. Now they're out in the open; Livingstone even told Mandy his name. And I'm scared.'

'What are you scared of?'

'That more people are going to die.'

Through the windscreen Martin can see a helicopter come in low, close enough that he can see the camera operator in his harness. 'Who was the other victim?' he asks. 'The woman with Max?'

Montifore begins to shake his head, then relents for some reason. 'Not for publication?'

'Agreed.'

'Max Fuller's sister-in-law, Elizabeth Torbett.'

'Torbett? Isn't she some sort of judge?'

'New South Wales Supreme Court.'

'Fuck me.'

Montifore leans forward, starts the car. 'I'll take you to the station. We'll need a formal statement. Then you and Mandalay should make yourselves scarce. You and that boy of hers. If they're killing Supreme Court judges, they'll kill anyone.'

Martin waits until Montifore has navigated the smaller streets and is heading down Bellevue Road before he speaks. 'How are Atticus Pons and George Giopolis connected to Molloy's murder?'

Montifore looks at him, apprehension spread across his face, before returning his eyes to the road. Then he pulls over, bringing the car to a stop so he can give Martin his full attention. 'Where did you hear those names?'

'From you, as it happens.'

'What?'

'Winifred Barbicombe says you dropped them into an interview you conducted with Mandalay in Port Silver last year.'

Montifore says nothing, averts his eyes. Martin lets him stew on it; he's not helping him out. The policeman is shaking his head as if in regret, some internal remonstration. Finally he turns back to Martin. 'If you ever publish this, I'll lose my job.'

'Then I won't publish it.'

'Don't even talk about it.'

'Whatever you say.'

'Did you ever wonder why I was sent to Port Silver last year to look into the death of a small-town real estate agent? I'm one of the state's most senior investigators.'

'We did. Winifred and I. We thought it might have something to do with Mandy.'

'Correct.' The policeman closes his eyes, squeezes them tight, an expression of discomfort, as if experiencing pain. 'When I was assigned to the case, I was told to keep it out of the media.'

'That worked well.' Martin laughs at the memory of the media storm. Even Montifore cracks a smile. 'Who assigned you?'

'My boss. As usual. But I heard the request for me came all the way from the top. Roger Macatelli. Deputy commissioner. I asked around, spoke to a few trusted colleagues. A source told me your girl Mandy might be involved in some investigation involving Pons and Giopolis.'

'What investigation?'

'I don't know.'

'So why throw the names up in an interview with Mandy?'

'To see if she knew who they were.'

'You were fishing for information?'

'Sure. I was trying to work out why I'd been assigned the case.' He's about to say something more, when his phone rings. 'Montifore,' he answers, voice dropping in pitch, assuming a more officious register. 'Right.' He pauses for a moment, glances at Martin. 'I want full police protection. No one gets in or out without my say-so. Get the authorisation. I'll be there as soon as I can.' He ends the call.

'What is it?' asks Martin.

'Claus Vandenbruk. He's regained consciousness.'

chapter ten

RIGHT NOW, SHE HATES THIS CITY. SHE FEELS IT CROWDING IN ON HER: THE
buildings, the people, the insistent past. She'd thought she'd left it
all behind, the facts undeniable: Tarquin had fled overseas with his
stolen money, leaving her bereft, unemployed and utterly gutted.
He was never coming back, he would never contact her. There was
no need to tell anyone of her heartbreak, least of all Martin. Why
would she? But now it's all come rushing back, to catch her out,
to insert itself between them. What must he think of her now?
And again her thoughts return to Port Silver, the house on the
cliffs, her haven. She can't wait to get back there, to start tending
to the future once more and to seal Tarquin Molloy in the past,
as surely as his killers had sealed him in his concrete tomb.

Right now she has more pressing concerns: clothes and toiletries.
Martin brought her phone and her wallet, but nothing more. All
she has is the ill-fitting charity wear Montifore gave her. So she

walks along George Street, intent on finding some anonymous store where she can purchase a temporary wardrobe. A tram rolls past; she considers it for a moment but decides she needs to walk. To stand still, even inside a moving tram, would be intolerable.

Yet as she walks up the hill past the cinemas towards Sydney Town Hall, she's not alone. Memories stalk her; memories of a younger, more naive Mandalay. Living the low life with Billy the bass player, living the high life with Tarquin Molloy, living the half-life after Molloy had disappeared and she'd lost her job. This city has always been her fair-weather friend: revelling in her highs, spurning her in her lows. She sees herself with Billy, living hand-to-mouth but still able to laugh, still able to dance in circles in the rain and splash in the Hyde Park fountain, busking together, her singing weak harmonies as he belted out enough standards to earn them drinking money. Sometimes they'd head to a Sydney City Mission soup kitchen for a free feed. They were desperate days but simple ones, driven by simple imperatives: get enough money to eat and drink, find somewhere to sleep, get hold of some booze or some gear to take the edge off. Simple.

She stops outside the town hall and sees herself stepping out from the back of a limousine onto a red carpet, armoured in the glamour of designer clothes, on the arm of Tarquin Molloy, her dashing and gallant beau, attending a ball. A charity ball: all proceeds going to the Sydney City Mission.

Outside the Queen Victoria Building she stops once again, staring into a shop window, studying her reflection, seeing the fractured ghosts of her former self. She was beautiful, they constantly assured her, all those Sydneysiders: 'like a model', 'like a movie star', 'like a muse'. They said it so often there were times she'd begun to believe it. Billy would say it best, most sincerely, telling her she'd inspired some of his most memorable bass lines. She smiles, wishing she could recall even one of his riffs.

God, how she had loved Sydney back when she was with Tarquin, even when she'd been with Billy, believing its pulse was her pulse, that its energy belonged to her, that it was the source of the destiny she felt coursing through her veins. And yet it had never been real: the men were liars, actors in a scripted drama, the city a movie set. This city; those men. She wonders at herself: how could she ever have been so blind, so stupid, as to allow herself to be washed this way and that on the tides of happenstance? How had she allowed those men to shape her fate, to write her script, to feed her lines, instead of writing her own?

Today, as if trying to win her back, the city is aglow, putting on its tourist livery, shining blue and white, the clear light and the seductive breeze, as if the facade might fool her one more time. As if. She knows that it's all there waiting, easy enough to access, should she wish to: the city's public face. Not the back lot but the big sets: the harbour, the bridge, the Opera House. Bondi Beach, the Manly ferry, Luna Park. On a day like this, they would be iridescent with assurance: the bright veneer, the cheery gloss, the self-deceiving face. The Sydney of the winners, the Sydney of Tarquin Molloy in his pomp. But today she doesn't feel like a winner; today she feels like she belongs in the Sydney of Billy the bass player.

Another tram passes, bringing her back to the present. Martin is safe; she knows that much. He'd called, told her he wasn't harmed, was never in any danger, but that Max Fuller, his old mentor, was dead. Murdered. He needs to help the police. Another victim amid the sunshine, another death behind the scenes. Montifore is right: they should leave this place.

She shops in David Jones. She's rarely been through its doors, dismissing it as an old lady's store. It holds no memories, houses no ghosts. She spends with practicality, not pleasure: underwear, jeans, flat shoes, nondescript tops, toiletries. Enough for a day or two, nothing more. It's not easy: the store is too opulent, it offers too many temptations. She'd be better off in Kmart, where the necessary trumps the discretionary. A coat catches her attention, leather lined with quilting, a cut blending edge with quality, something to keep the winter chill out. She can afford it, of course she can; she can indulge all sorts of whims in this post-inheritance life. But she doesn't buy the coat. It doesn't feel right, spending money, not here, not now. She wants nothing to remember this trip by; she wants clothes she can rid herself of when she gets home. She returns to the perfunctory and the utilitarian.

Shopping done, she checks her phone. Nothing more from Martin. He must still be with the police. She texts through a burst of question marks, then hails a cab, deciding to head back to his apartment. But at the last moment, she has a better idea. He's always going on about Aldo's, how much better the coffee is than anything in Port Silver, or anywhere else. She asks the driver if he knows it. He doesn't, but his GPS does. It's not far from the apartment, smaller than she's imagined, less impressive, but the moment she enters she feels its warmth, its welcome. She can see why it has survived when others haven't. The wooden tables and benches have the patina of long use, polished by years of customers. On the wall are faded travel posters from a time when ocean liners were still glamorous and aeroplanes were the preserve of the wealthy. Even before tasting its brew, she understands why Martin likes the place.

She orders a skinny latte from a cocksure young barista, his flirtatious banter a welcome distraction, then takes a seat at a table in the corner. She has only just sat down when a woman slides onto the chair opposite her. Zelda Forshaw, wearing wraparound sunglasses.

'You?' Mandy can't believe the woman's gall. She looks around, but there is no man in a ski mask, no flunky. 'What do you want?'

'To talk. That's all.'

'You're joking. After what you did to me?'

'It was a mistake. We need to move on.'

'Move on? The police are searching for you.'

'So we need to talk before they catch me.' Zelda removes her shades, and Mandy sees the accumulated evidence of the intervening years. Zelda was always pretty, there was never any doubt about that. She still is, but she's aged. Mandy had thought her more or less the same age as herself, with her powdered face, large mascara-lined eyes and schoolgirl titter. Now the voice is half an octave lower, and husky with it: more Lauren Bacall than Marilyn Monroe. She looks closer to forty than thirty. Her hair is an unconvincing mix of brunette and something redder, her eyebrows over-plucked. A vein is pulsing between her left eyebrow and her temple. Prison cannot have been kind to her and, by the looks, neither has liberty.

'You want to talk,' says Mandy. 'Why didn't you try that at Port Silver, instead of drugging and abducting me?'

Zelda shrugs. 'That's what I intended, I swear. But that man was there. He warned us off.'

'He's a cop.'

'Another one? He didn't tell us that.'

'What happened?'

'He told us to fuck off. When he turned his back on us, Derek clobbered him. You don't remember?'

'No. Thanks to you drugging me. If you were only coming to Port Silver to talk to me, how come you had chloroform or whatever it was that knocked me out?'

'Not chloroform. Some shit Derek brought along; something he cooked up using an internet recipe. He figured if you didn't want to talk, it could help persuade you. Like a home-brewed truth serum.'

'Derek sounds like a real charmer. Where did you find him?'

'It doesn't matter.' There is something defensive in her voice, something protective.

'Where is he now?'

'Getting his teeth fixed. Those goons pistol-whipped him.'

'Good for them.'

Zelda stares at her and Mandy can see anger in her expression. 'Do you know who they were? What they were doing there?'

Mandy leans forward for effect. 'Killers, Zelda. Killers. That's what the police said. Henry Livingstone and Joshua Spitt. I don't know how they found us or why, but that's not my problem. They were looking for you, not me. So now you have the police after you, plus a pair of violent criminals. Congratulations. Well done.' She can't help it; she enjoys the consternation on her old rival's face. Nevertheless, her tone is more conciliatory as she continues. 'All I know is people like you and me should not be getting involved with people like them.'

The waitress arrives, delivering Mandy her coffee. 'Anything for you, love?' she asks Zelda.

Zelda looks to Mandy, eyebrows raised.

'Sure,' says Mandy. 'Whatever you like.' *Does she not even have the price of a cup of coffee?*

'Iced mocha, please,' Zelda tells the waitress. 'With whipped cream.' Then she turns back to Mandy. 'You never liked me, did you?'

'You drugged me and abducted me, then left me for dead when those goons came along. What do you think?'

'Not now. Back then.'

'No. I didn't like you then either. You were shagging my fiancé.'

Zelda grins. 'Yes. There was that.'

Mandy feels her irritation rising. For someone asking for help, Zelda Forshaw is no Dale Carnegie. 'Listen, Zelda. I don't have to sit here. I don't have to speak with you.'

The woman extends her hand and closes it around Mandy's wrist, causing her to recoil, taken aback by the attempt at intimacy. Zelda doesn't seem to notice; instead she persists, gripping hard as Mandy tries to pull away. 'Please. I need your help.' Her voice sounds sincere. 'I believe what you told me, that you don't know about the money. I checked you out.'

'So what are you doing here?'

'Look.' Zelda fossicks in her shoulder bag a moment, withdraws her phone, a dated model with a cracked screen, opens a message. She holds it out for Mandy to read. *Sorry. Delayed. See you tomorrow. Love you xxx.*

Mandy looks at the date next to the green text bubble, knowing already what it confirms: the SMS is five years old. It leaves her unable to speak.

'It's the same, isn't it? Exactly the same words?' asks Zelda.

Mandy nods. She deleted the message long ago, but there's no forgetting the words.

'I was in Melbourne that Friday,' says Zelda, her voice lower. 'Did you know? He flew me down for the weekend. Champagne. Flowers. Sound familiar? Said he was leaving you. Then this message. Then nothing more. Ever. Until now. Until they found his body.'

Mandy says nothing.

'The same message. To both of us.'

'What are you suggesting?' Mandy asks, unable to help herself.

'He didn't send the texts. Whoever shot him did. To buy themselves an extra day or two.'

'You can't know that.'

'I can't know anything for sure. I've learnt that lesson. But what if I'm right?'

'What if you are?'

'It means the murderer, or murderers, knew all about us. You and me. They sent us messages from his phone.' Now Mandy sees the emotions playing through Zelda's eyes: grief and anger and frustration. And fear. 'And if they knew about us then, they know about us now. Now that his body has been discovered.'

'But I didn't know he was dead. Did you?'

'No. Of course not. But those men, they came looking for me.'

'Yes. But not for me. Because we weren't the same,' says Mandy. 'You knew he was planning to steal the money; I didn't.'

'So you say. Or did you take the deal they offered?'

'What deal? Who are you talking about?'

'You know.'

'I don't. Spell it out for me.'

'The cops—they offered me immunity. Tell them what I knew and they wouldn't arrest me. They made you the same offer, surely.'

'I wasn't a suspect. I didn't know about the money.'

'You've already said that.'

'If they offered you immunity, why didn't you take it?'

'Because, like an idiot, I thought he was still alive. Waiting for me. So I tried to stay quiet, to protect him. But they had too much evidence. They nailed me.'

'I heard you pleaded guilty.'

'Yeah, I did in the end. But by then it was too late: the offer of immunity was off the table.'

'Did they believe he was gone?'

'Sure. They told me he ran off overseas. That you were in on it. I believed them. You were always better looking than me, he always preferred you.'

Mandy grimaces. 'He confided in you, not in me. He never told me he was going to steal any money.'

'But in the end he treated us both the same, didn't he? Lied to us, betrayed us. Protected us.'

'Protected?'

'Made sure we were interstate, out of harm's way.'

'Or out of his way, so there were no complications. So that we didn't discover what he was doing and blow the whistle on him.'

Zelda smiles sadly. 'You maybe, not me. I knew what he was planning, remember. I wasn't about to stop him. I was cheering him on the whole way.'

Mandy considers that, admiring the woman's brutal candour. And wonders why Zelda's come looking for her, what she really wants.

The waitress returns, delivering Zelda's cream-topped drink in a heavy-duty parfait glass, with a straw and a spoon.

Mandy waits till they are alone again. 'Did you know he was a cop?'

The shock on Zelda's face gives the answer before she can vocalise it. 'Is that what they're saying?' Her voice is lower, a confidential whisper.

'Yes. Tarquin Molloy wasn't even his real name.'

Now there are signs of distress playing on Zelda's face. 'Shit. No. I didn't know. The cops told me he'd been shot, but not that.'

'He was married. There are children. They told me this morning.'

Now the distress is plain to see, a shudder running through the woman. 'A wife? While he was screwing the two of us? Did she know?'

Mandy shakes her head. 'How could I possibly know that?'

'Do you know his real name?'

'They wouldn't tell me.'

Zelda looks bewildered, uncomprehending, as she slumps back in her seat. 'So he did con us. You and me both. We meant nothing to him. A means to an end, nothing more.'

'I'd say so.'

'Fuck him,' Zelda spits, real anger in her subdued voice. 'I went to prison for that bastard. I ruined my life for him. I can't get work, not as an accountant, not with a criminal record for embezzlement and fraud.' She stares at her drink with distaste. 'He didn't give a shit, did he?'

'Probably not,' says Mandy. 'He was dead by then. But probably not when he was alive either.'

'So was there ever any money?' asks Zelda.

'I don't know,' says Mandy. 'I'm not sure about anything anymore. Maybe it was just a way of manipulating you. To get into the accounts.'

'But I went to jail for being an accessory. It must have existed, he must have taken it.' There's a note of desperation in her voice. 'It must be what those men are after, the killers. Livingstone and the other one.'

'Spitt.'

'Yeah. Spitt. The ones who bashed Derek and chased me. They have to be after the money.'

'Maybe.'

'What else would they be after?'

'Maybe what he knew. He was a cop. Maybe he got killed for the money, maybe he got killed because he uncovered something that could be worth chasing down.'

'You think?'

'Does it matter? He's dead.'

'You won't help me?'

'Help you do what?'

'Find the money. Find out what happened to him. Find out what he discovered that was worth killing him for.'

Mandy is shocked by Zelda's desperation. 'We know what happened to him. Someone put a bullet in his head. And if the money ever existed, it's long gone.'

'Easy for you to say.' And now Zelda is sneering. 'You've got your money, you've got your man, you've got your little boy. You've got your castle on the clifftop.' She looks down at her iced mocha and its layering of cream. 'I've got sweet fuck-all.'

'Zelda, it's not worth it. It's not worth dying for.'

'So you won't help?'

'No.'

'All right then, we're quits.' Zelda stands, sucks hard at her drink, slurping up the dregs, before thumping the empty glass on the table. 'Thanks for the coffee. You always were a selfish moll.'

chapter eleven

THE RAIN RETURNS FROM NOWHERE. IT SEEMS PUNITIVE TO MARTIN, SLICING AT him as he walks along Riley Street, as if it senses his vulnerability, with his light clothing and no umbrella. The sky was blue when Montifore dropped him at the police station to make his statement; it was merely overcast when he left. Yet it had come in, with all its force, the same as the night before, when he'd been halfway between the station and the apartment, too close for a cab or Uber. But he doesn't care; the storm can do as it pleases. Its wrath seems appropriate. Max is dead, murdered, and now the numbness is passing Martin is feeling guilty. He doesn't know why, he just does. Maybe if he'd called Max earlier, visited him as soon as he had arrived, he might have somehow averted his mentor's death. Or maybe he would be dead with him. But that thought only elicits more guilt, and the rain's cold needles feel all the more deserved.

The weather is still cutting in from the south as he arrives at his apartment. He swings the gate open, takes the three steps up into the portico. The tramp is back, sheltering in the alcove. He looks bad and smells worse.

'Not bothering anyone,' says the man defensively, staring Martin down, as if he doesn't remember him.

'Not bothering me,' says Martin. 'Stay here until it blows over.'

The man blinks, shakes his head, trying to rattle the world into coherence. 'Martin? Is that you?'

'Yeah. It's me.'

'Right. Thanks. Thanks so much.'

Through the street door, past Mrs Jones's uncollected mail and up the stairs. Then Martin sees it: his door is closed but the lock has been smashed. He eases the door open; the apartment has been eviscerated. The lounge is a sea of detritus: books with the covers ripped off, pages strewn, floating amid the body parts of his sofa. In the bedroom, the bed has been gutted, the mattress hacked open, his wardrobe disembowelled, the chest of drawers mutilated. Not ransacked, not someone rifling through the drawers, but dismembered. He can't believe it: stumbling through the abattoir of his life, astounded by the violence. This was no search; this was a massacre of the inanimate. Who could do such a thing? And why?

A rattling sound at the window brings him back to the present. Hail. He considers lifting the sash, letting the cleansing ice enter, but there is nothing considerate about the weather. Rather, it has returned to remind him of its contempt, as if the exterior might replicate the cyclone that has so wantonly demolished the interior. So he begins to search, not for what might be saved, for that seems entirely unlikely, but for what has been lost. He finds one of his passports, ripped in half: a valuable document, surely worth something on the black market, defaced for no better reason than the inconvenience it will cause him to renew it. In the kitchenette, food has been sprayed around the walls; the only thing left in the fridge is a shit, neatly presented on a plate. Martin removes it, places it in the now empty freezer. DNA, he thinks. Evidence. The possibility of retribution. He checks to make sure the fridge is still operating, relieved to find that it is. One small break, the best the day can offer: a turd in the freezer.

His laptop is missing. Of course it is. So too his television, a decade old and surely worthless by now. A shattered window gives him the clue: the TV, hurled through the pane, is lying broken in the brick-paved laneway. But not the laptop. His Mac is gone; the only thing that is truly missing. He offers the world a weak smile. There is nothing on the hard drive of any use to them. How could there be? He knows nothing. And yet they have it, and with it the photos of his son, of Mandy, of a life now so remote, the golden beach and the months of respite, Port Silver.

Downstairs, the vagrant is still there, mumbling to himself amid his thin and soiled belongings.

'You see anyone go upstairs in the last few hours?' Martin asks.

'Cunts,' says the old man.

'That's them,' says Martin.

'Threatened to knife me if I didn't fuck off.'

'And?'

'And I fucked off.'

'And came back once they'd gone.'

'I was only gone an hour or two. The rain came in; I came back.'

'Can you describe them?'

'Why would I do that?'

'Because they're cunts.'

'Aye, there is that.' The man nods, appreciating the logic. 'They gave me some shit. Some good shit. If I promised not to tell.'

'And?'

'Short bald arsehole, spider web tattoo on his neck. And a tall fucker. Three-piece suit. Smelt like a funeral parlour.'

'Thanks,' says Martin, voice calm but mind alive. Spitt and Livingstone: the men Mandy described. It has to be. 'Here.' He extracts a twenty-dollar note from his wallet, goes to give it to the old coot, but withholds it at the last. 'Two conditions.'

'No such thing as a free lunch,' observes the coot.

'One: don't piss in here. It's not a urinal.'

'Mate, never. What do you take me for?'

'Two: if the most glorious woman you've ever seen in your life turns up here, tell her to call Martin. And tell her: don't go upstairs.'

'They fucked you over?'

'Well and truly.'

Walking down the hill, his feet wet, cold and growing numb, he rings Mandy, but she doesn't respond. He wonders why not. He looks at the screen; he missed a call from her not fifteen minutes ago. Spitt and Livingstone: destroying his apartment. The men who had found Mandy imprisoned and left her there, while searching for Zelda Forshaw. Why trash his apartment, why steal his laptop? He remembers what Montifore told him: *If whoever did kill your editor searched his phone, they would see he's been talking with you.* Christ; maybe they think he knows what Max was working on. He rings Montifore, but the policeman doesn't answer, so he leaves a message, describing the destruction of his apartment, the missing laptop, the old tramp's description of the men responsible. After ending the call, he's still standing there, lost in speculation, when he hears it approaching like a freight train, another squall, bleeding the light from the day, darkening the city, coming from Tasmania, the Southern Ocean, Antarctica. All that way, just for him. He looks for shelter, finds he's standing outside the computer shop, Ichiban Computers and Scarvery, suddenly bright in the darkening day. He enters.

The space between the door and the counter is cluttered with bargain bins full of assorted paraphernalia: wireless mouses, external hard drives, video cards in boxes depicting bare-chested gods and lightning bolts. The counter extends across the store, before making a ninety-degree turn to the right. The 'scarvery' begins, occupying its own small corner, maybe a quarter of the floor space. Glass cabinets display cravats, gloves and handkerchiefs. Ties, scarves and shawls hang, artfully presented, from racks. Umbrellas, hats and walking sticks adorn a pair of hatstands. A row of vintage opera glasses complete the setting, their steam-punk aesthetic at odds with the glistening computer peripherals dominating the rest of the store.

Behind the barrier, a young man wearing a scruffy white lab coat is working on the innards of a computer. Roof-high racks crammed with cartons and plastic storage bins extend behind him to the back wall. He has long white hair, dead straight. He's wearing jewellers' glasses and is wielding a soldering iron.

'Can you fix it?' asks Martin.

'Nah, just mucking about, mate.' The accent is as broad as the continent itself. 'Cheaper to gut it; cheaper to chuck it.' He looks up, smiles at Martin. His eyes are pale and red-tinged, his eyebrows like they've been dusted with snow. An albino. 'It's like dissecting frogs,' he continues. 'You can't bring 'em back to life, but it's fun seeing what makes 'em tick.' He puts the soldering iron down, removes the jeweller's eyepiece. 'What can I do for you?'

'I'm looking for a new laptop. My last one got stolen.'

'What sort? It might have turned up in the back there.'

'I doubt it.'

'You never know.'

'Last couple of hours? A Mac?' Martin knows the request is futile; his computer is off being dissected.

'No. Have you tried tracking it?'

'You can do that?'

'Maybe. You have an iPhone?'

'I do.'

'Give us a look then.'

Martin unlocks his phone and hands it over, but the young man takes no more than a minute before handing it back. 'No good. You haven't got it turned on.' He shakes his head, as if pitying the technological ineptitude of older generations. 'So what are you after? Anything special? Gaming? Video production? Another Mac?'

'Yeah, but I don't need anything fancy. Internet, email, word processing. That's it.'

'Right. Let's see what I've got.' The man checks his inventory on an ancient beige monitor on the counter. 'Here we go. Second-hand MacBook Pro. Two years old. Five hundred bucks. Interested?'

'Sounds perfect.'

'Goodo. I'll clean up the hard drive, reinstall the operating system and throw in a copy of Word. You can pick it up tomorrow. Cash in hand.'

'Deal.' They shake hands. 'I'm Martin.'

'Yevgeny.'

The rain has stopped again. He's just leaving when his phone rings. It's Mandy.

———

Mandy ends the call and stands shell-shocked amid the wreckage of Martin's apartment. The derro downstairs had tried to warn her. 'No,' he'd mumbled, waving his hands like a drunken conductor. She'd ignored him, refusing to make eye contact. Instead, she'd pushed past and through the door, dismissive. She should have listened.

A deep conviction comes upon her: it's the past again. It has tracked her into the present, like a pack of hounds, baying at her guilt. What else could have visited this level of destruction upon them, if not the past? It isn't just Zelda, it isn't just the police, it isn't just the people who have trashed the apartment; they are only the physical manifestation, like the city's fickle weather. Something larger, something more intangible, more malevolent has her scent. What was it the fake policeman, Henry Livingstone, said, his cigarette voice wheezing? *Don't get mixed up in this thing. It's going to get ugly.* But she is mixed up in it. The past knows it; it knows her and it knows where to find her.

Port Silver is nothing, she realises, their sixteen months there a mirage, a faux reality, seducing her into false assumptions of wellbeing, the future spreading out to the horizon like the ocean viewed from her clifftop. Now she sees it for what it is: an illusion. For there can be no future if the past forbids it.

A memory of Tarquin comes to her. The night they met, that mad evening at the casino. Billy the bass player's desperate ploy, so simple it almost worked, inspired by a random find in a charity bin: a cocktail dress, sequined, short at the hemline and plunging at the neckline. They'd hatched the plan, drinking to give themselves the courage to carry it off. She'd dolled herself up, spent an eternity on her face and hair, before striding into the casino like a catwalk model, full of alcohol and nerves. And yet it wasn't hard, it was easy. She stood there and they came to her, the drunken gamblers, and all she had to do was smile and flirt and flash her dimples, distracting them while Billy, dressed in anonymous black, surreptitiously pocketed their chips. The scam was spectacularly lucrative while it lasted, all of fifteen minutes. Then the security men moved in, well muscled and well dressed, guffawing at their stupidity, detaining them even as they ridiculed them. And that was when Tarquin stepped in and rescued her. Tarquin, dressed in his elegant black suit, smooth and imperious, the consummate performer. The security men believed him immediately, his claim that the two of them were there together, convinced by the cut of his clothes and his utter confidence. And she responded in kind, calling him 'darling' and bringing her dimples to bear on the security men. He offered her his arm, and walked her away. Poor Billy was left to receive an instructive pummelling before being thrown into the street, while she was swept into a bar and off her feet by this knight-errant.

He bought her drinks and listened to her story, seeing through her first flimsy fabrications, pushing until he had the truth, plying her with champagne and sympathy. And then, later, he took her back onto the gaming floor, losing at roulette and losing at craps and then winning it back at blackjack, a demonstration of his prowess. And, as she realises now, all the while assessing her: deducing that she was smart enough to understand and desperate enough to participate.

In the ruins of the apartment she can still see him. Young, vibrant, handsome, thick blond hair a reflection of her own, not a strand out of place, laughing and toasting her with a brandy balloon, eyes full of her, smile full of himself. Overflowing with confidence, engorged with it. But who was he? A thief, a conman, a police officer? All three? Did he act to protect Zelda and Mandy, sending them out of harm's way, or did he make sure they weren't there to interfere with his larceny, or to share in its profits, or to disrupt his police work? What were his motives, his objectives? Does it even matter? He stole the money, ruined their lives. What is she to make of him now? He was cut down, murdered with a bullet to the brain, his killers sending a duplicate text to pacify her and Zelda. And maybe to leave a trail for the police to find. *Jesus.*

She tries to move, to wade through the destruction, but loses her footing amid the flotsam, collapsing down among it, landing awkwardly, a sharp edge catching her in the ribs. She barely feels it. The tears that start to well have nothing to do with physical pain. She lies there, unable to find the motivation to stand. Was she responsible for Tarquin's death? The question returns to her now, won't let her go. Was it all her fault? The new facts, her new knowledge, have distilled everything down to that one question: did she get him killed? Her logic cannot supply the answer but her emotions can: she feels an abiding sense of guilt.

She'd reported him over the passwords, the useless, low-level passwords. At the time, her section head, Pam Risoli, had counselled her, a formality, pretending it was serious. Something similar happened to him: a slap on the wrist, nothing more. It was a misdemeanour; the passwords were changed, life went on. They'd laughed about it, the two of them, being cautioned over something so innocuous. And for the next five years she'd been convinced informing on him was inconsequential, at least for him; he had still managed to steal the money and go, off to live the life of Riley.

Yet it was the questionnaire that saved her, her truthful answer about the passwords, elevating her above suspicion. Pam Risoli cited it in her defence: Mandy had done the right thing and dobbed on Molloy, raising a red flag, and they had ignored the warning. Instead of condemning her, Pam argued, they should be rewarding her for her honesty, for her prescience. Clarity Sparkes and the overall head of security, Harry Sweetwater, interrogated her, but their attention soon shifted to a hapless Zelda Forshaw. Mandy remained free, while Zelda went to prison, confessing to collaboration, pleading guilty. There was no trial, no need to testify: it moved straight to sentencing, been kept out of the papers.

Now, in the detritus of the apartment, Mandy revises her assessment of the questionnaire and its impact. It had helped keep her out of jail, but had it condemned him, alerted Mollisons' security? Had they started to keep a closer eye on him? Molloy was a policeman, playing a double game; he had used Zelda and herself ruthlessly, but that didn't mean he deserved to die. Yet unwillingly, unknowingly perhaps, she is implicated in his death. She finds herself unable to plead innocent any longer. Maybe manslaughter instead of murder, but guilty nevertheless.

In a shard of a broken mirror, she catches her own reflection. She picks it up, examining herself. She can see the green eyes, the sculpted cheekbones. She tries a smile, deploying her dimples, her exemplary teeth, just as she had that night at the casino. For a moment she can see what they saw, those drunken gamblers, those gullible security men, or she thinks she does. The beautiful, mysterious stranger. It's so easy—they believe what they want to believe, projecting their own inventions upon her like she's a blank screen built for the purpose. Then the glass shifts, the reflection alters. She sees what they don't: the imperfections; the bloodshot eyes, that unfortunately placed mole, the strange elevation of her ears, her eyes slightly offset. Why are they always so blind? Why do they only see what they want to see?

Another memory comes to her. Back on the school bus once more, back on the breathless plain, heading into summer, the afternoon trip full of heat and hormones. She's fifteen, turning sixteen, and the boys have found they like her very much and the girls have found they hate her all the more. At least Trina is gone, belly swelling with her own little scandal. Mandy still sits up the front, behind the driver, still buries herself in her books, unimpressed by the clumsy advances of those who had shunned her for so long. But secretly, inside, she is revelling in it, this new power, experimenting on the hapless adolescents, learning that a skirt hitched high or a blouse button undone can so easily incite more attention. Her books and her beauty: her two safeguards against the world, her dual armour.

She tilts the mirror fragment, considering herself. Always so proud of her looks, always so self-conscious, always so unsatisfied. Always wanting to look so good for all of them; yet always so distrustful of them, suspicious that all they see is the performance, never the performer. Even Martin, dear Martin, the best of them.

She thinks of Liam. It's as if fate conspired to grant her a year and a half of happiness, lifting her up so the fall would come that much harder. She wants to flee, to get back to her son, to protect him. And yet the past is coming, it's here, she can't carry it back to Port Silver; she can't risk it getting a trace of her boy, picking up his scent as well. No. Whatever happens, she needs to leave the past here. Let Sydney have it, let the city keep it.

She feels a surge of anger, anger at Tarquin. For a moment it's a relief, this new emotion replacing the guilt. Even at the end, he was lying. He hadn't dropped Zelda, after all; if anything, his affair with her had intensified. He was still fucking her, assuring the accountant that it was Mandy he was leaving, sharing with her his plan to steal millions. *Bastard.* He had lied to her, he had lied to Zelda; he had lied about being single. He was married the whole time. And did the wife know? His soft words and his hard cock, screwing both Mandy and Zelda and then returning home to his wife. And then.

And then, lying there amid the carnage of Martin's apartment, she feels a strange resolve come to her, a peculiar strength. She's right: the past is after her, there is no escaping it. So she can lie here, pathetic, waiting for it—or she can get up and fight back. For Liam, for Martin, for herself. For their future. It may smell blood, it may have its fangs out, but that doesn't mean she has to always be the victim. She's tried that: she knows it doesn't work. Her books and her beauty won't protect her now; she needs to push back. *Fuck it*, she whispers to herself, and struggles to her feet.

She can start with the truth: she'd known. She has to acknowledge it, even if she still doesn't intend incriminating herself. She'd known; she'd always known. Known that first night, seeing his mastery in the casino, known in the following nights, as he taught her how to count cards and more. Making a game of mnemonic techniques, teaching her how to construct a memory palace, recalling random strings of letters and numbers by placing them in familiar locations. And she'd known that there was more than one Tarquin Molloy, more than one man inside that handsome body: the serious corporate lawyer and the charismatic player. She'd known: not that he was a thief, planning to steal millions, nor that he was a policeman, working an investigation. But she should have suspected. For she knew he was probing the bank's networks. She knew because she had helped him. She had denied it ever since: to the police, to Clarity Sparkes and Harry Sweetwater, to anyone and everyone. But Mollisons must have suspected, just as Zelda suspected. No wonder they sacked her; no wonder Zelda had come searching. She'd thought she had got away with it, deserved to get away with it. After all, she was fundamentally innocent, he had still betrayed her. Even now, no one knows, no one needs to know. But the past knows, and it has her scent.

There's a noise downstairs: Martin arriving. Martin. Is he really different? Is he genuine, the real deal? Yes, she tells herself, he must be. He lacks the swagger of Tarquin and the self-belief of Byron Swift. But that is no bad thing. She can see where it was; sometimes, when he is engulfed by his journalism, his purpose, she can detect the same signs. It had been here on the walls around her in his self-affirming trophies, now lying broken on the floor. Are all men like this, intrinsically untrustworthy, ultimately self-obsessed? Immediately she censures herself: she of all people should not be entertaining such thoughts.

Martin appears in the doorway, concern writ large on his face. He doesn't even glance at his broken trophies. In that moment, she sees his love; she sees his concern for her.

'C'mon,' he says gently. 'Let's go.'

'Where?'

'A hotel. We can't stay here.'

'Do you need to pack?'

'There's nothing left to pack.'

She looks around. He's right. 'I think it's coming for us.' There, she's said it.

That stops him, drains the momentum from him, so that he is standing absolutely still, eyes locked on hers, forehead creased. 'What? What's coming?'

'The past.'

He speaks slowly, softly, across the gap between them. 'Do you believe that you were somehow responsible for Molloy's death?'

She matches his gaze, tells the truth. 'Yes. I think maybe I was.'

Movement returns to him. He threads his way through the debris to stand with her. He takes her hand. 'You can't know that. No one knows who killed him, no one knows why.'

She studies his eyes. She likes them so much, how expressive they are, how they reveal his vulnerabilities. He's different from Tarquin, different from Byron. Different. It occurs to her that he's suffering as well. 'Martin, I am so sorry. About Max. It's so awful.'

His gaze falls to the floor, but she can see the anguish in his face, the grief in the slump of his shoulders. She takes him, holds him. He's cold, his clothes damp from the rain. She strokes the back of his head as she might a child's.

'It was terrible,' the words come from him with difficulty, as if he's choking on them. 'I saw it. What happened to them.'

'It's not your fault, you know. There was nothing you could have done.'

'Wasn't there?'

'No. Of course not.'

He leans back from her a little, so she can see his face, see the pain in his eyes. And the love. And she is secretly pleased: they are in this together, she's no longer the isolated schoolgirl on the bus to Bellington.

WEDNESDAY

chapter twelve

FOR A MOMENT, AS HE LINGERS, DRIFTING BETWEEN SLEEP AND WAKEFULNESS, IT seems all might be well with the world: the sheets are crisp, the air refined, her body warm under the covers. But with consciousness comes awareness; this is no holiday, the hotel no indulgence. The memory of the night comes back to him first: Mandy roiling in her insomnia, unable to settle, disturbing his own attempts at sleep. Now he's waking properly and the memories of the previous day return: Max murdered, Eileen in shock, his apartment eviscerated. The recollections incite a rush of adrenaline and suddenly he's utterly awake. Yet as he rises, he feels washed out: too awake, too exhausted.

It's half past six in the morning. He looks across to her, sleeping at last, her face towards him, the innocence of unconsciousness.

He pulls back the heavy curtains a fraction, peers out. The light is flat and grey, the sky overcast. He closes the curtains, he showers, he dresses, as Mandy sleeps on.

Outside, the day is humourless, the wind hard and persistent. It comes gusting down the city canyons, swirling coffee cups and advertising flyers and takeaway wrappers. It's not so long after dawn, the morning should still be at peace, yet the blustering day suggests much is underway, as if the story is already half told, that events can wait no longer. He walks with his head down: the air is full of grit, eager to get at his eyes.

Despite the weather, Martin feels the need to walk, as if exercise might dispel his fatigue. And so he stalks the city, past the sleeping homeless who care nothing for the first commuters emerging from the subway, who in turn care nothing for them. Martin sees it all and sees nothing, falling into step with the zombie workforce. And without making a conscious decision, he finds himself walking all the way through Hyde Park back into his own neighbourhood, back to Surry Hills and Aldo's.

The wind leaves him at the cafe door: inside Aldo's cocoon, the atmosphere is warm and the smell of coffee embracing. His old friend is manning the espresso machine, twisting the knobs and pulling the levers like the engineer on a steam train. His face breaks into a broad smile at the sight of Martin.

'Marty! It's true, you're back.'

Martin reaches past the machine; they shake hands.

'Aldo. Good to see you. How's business?'

'Shit, mate. Retail drought. People still aren't spending.'

'That bad?'

'We've survived worse. We've all survived worse.' He works the machine as he talks. 'And coffee, mate; people need their coffee.' And Aldo cracks an Aldo smile and the morning doesn't seem so bleak, despite the rolling recession and the malicious squalls.

The steaming bowl of milk coffee, when it comes, is hot and strong and honest. The wind outside is starting to howl, but the cafe, with its worn wood and tired travel posters, is timeless, offering the sort of comfort only familiarity can bring. Martin carries his drink to a bench alongside the window, where he can look out onto the street, and picks up a gratis copy of the *Sydney Morning Herald*, still relatively unsullied this early in the day, and leafs through it, hoping his old paper might offer some clue to the horror of Max Fuller's death. But the journal of record is silent—until he reaches page thirteen. And there it is, making it real, a brief report by his former colleague, crime reporter Bethanie Glass, under a say-nothing headline.

TWO DEAD AT BELLEVUE HILL

Police have confirmed that two people found dead at a Bellevue Hill house on Tuesday morning were the former editor of the *Sydney Morning Herald*, Mr Maximillian Fuller, and the distinguished Supreme Court judge Justice Elizabeth Torbett AO.

Police say there were no suspicious circumstances. The two were lifelong friends.

Justice Torbett was an eminent jurist, having served for more than a decade on the bench of the NSW Supreme Court. Previously, she was a District Court judge. As a prominent barrister and Senior Counsel, she was a leading light in the NSW Law Society in the 1990s. Justice Torbett was the daughter of the former justice of the NSW Supreme Court and the High Court of Australia, Sir Talbot Torbett AO.

Max Fuller was a distinguished newspaperman working across four decades, beginning as a copyboy on the Sydney evening paper, the *Daily Mirror*. Until recently he was the editor of the *Sydney Morning Herald*. Under his stewardship, the *Herald* was twice named PANPA newspaper of the year.

Martin finds it hard to believe. Ten centimetres on page thirteen, the last news story in the paper before the sudoku, the comics and the sport. *No suspicious circumstances?* The old media shorthand for suicide. And *lifelong friends?* What is that designed to convey? He pulls out his phone, rings Bethanie.

'Martin? Jesus. Is that you?'

'Yes.'

'Do you have any idea what time it is?'

'Half past seven. Normal people are up and going to work.'

'Fuck that, I'm not a person, I'm a journalist.' She takes a deep breath, loud enough for Martin to hear it down the phone. 'What is it? What can't wait?'

'Your report on Max and Elizabeth Torbett—I thought Max might have been worth a bit more than ten centimetres.'

Bethanie doesn't answer straight away and Martin wonders if she's taken offence. Instead, when she does speak, she sounds apprehensive. 'Martin, there's something wrong. Can we meet?'

chapter thirteen

SHE WAKES ALONE, MARTIN GONE, HIS SIDE OF THE BED ALREADY COLD. SHE LIES still for a moment, gathering herself, and in these first moments of consciousness, she's aware that during the night, even as she slept, the resolve that first came to her in Martin's apartment has solidified. The fear has diminished, the determination grown. Good.

He's left a note. *Couldn't sleep. Gone walking. Call me.* She knows Martin. Max's death has badly shaken him, but he won't let it overwhelm him. He'll be out there now, working it through, reverting to his journalistic identity. He'll want to know what happened and who's responsible. And when he's learnt the truth, he'll publish it, tell the world. It's time she did something similar: find out what Tarquin Molloy was really doing at Mollisons, find out what threats the past might pose. She showers and prepares herself, applying make-up as if it were subtle war paint; she wants to look sharp, she wants the world to know she means business.

Before leaving the hotel room, she Facetimes Vern and speaks with Liam. The boy is elated to see her, burbling with excitement. But soon enough he grows distracted; she can hear his cousins yelping and laughing in the background. It brings her relief: he is happy and he is safe, glad to see her but not desperate to have her back. He's resilient, cheerful and secure; life is still an adventure. She loves him all the more, feeling the connection arcing out through her phone, north to Port Silver. She tells him again she loves him before cutting the connection and ringing Martin.

When he answers, she hears the bustle of the city coming through the ether and into the silence of the hotel room. Is that what money buys? Silence in the big city; insulation? He tells her he's on the tram, on the way to meet Bethanie Glass; that there is something he needs to find out, that he'll be back soon. He says to stay in the hotel, stay safe.

'Sure,' she says. She hangs up, gathers her bag and leaves. Bethanie. She remembers her: young and vibrant. She is surprised to feel a spear of jealousy, of suspicion. It's a long time since she's felt anything like it; it reminds her of the days of Tarquin Molloy and Zelda Forshaw, like a taste of poison, creeping back into her thoughts, the past trying to reassert its hold over her. *Fuck that*. She holds tight to her resolve: she needs to act, she needs to push back, lest the past reassert itself.

The hotel lobby is small: small and expensive, designer furniture and original art. Boutique. The concierge is obsequious, almost servile, despite being old enough to be her father, as he guides her to a small room, wood panelled and plush carpeted, with new computers and a printer. 'You won't be disturbed, ma'am,' he promises her, with a quick bow. Has he mistaken her for some sort of celebrity? Maybe she's paying too much for their room.

The computer is new, the internet lightning fast; it's surprisingly easy to find her old boss from Mollisons, Pam Risoli. Google. Is there nothing that can't be found online? It takes her a little longer to track down a phone number. She breathes, looks at the number on the screen, hesitating, unsure whether she really wants to do this, resolve wavering momentarily. She closes her eyes, her mind winding back to those first days at Mollisons, to Friday night drinks at a bar down by the water. Tarquin shining, hair bouffant and mood expansive, his eyes dancing blue. She was happy, so happy, but also careful, not drinking too much, keeping her wits about her, trying hard to fit in. She found herself in a group of four with Tarquin and Raff and another trader called Phil, Tarquin doing his best to put her at ease. She was finding it difficult to make small talk: Raff was a head trader and one of the shift supervisors overseeing the bank's round-the-clock deal-making, a serious man. The conversation shifted from markets and margins to the state of the economy here and abroad. It seemed as if Phil was attempting to impress Raff with his knowledge of the European bond market. She listened, trying to learn, to fathom the jargon and guess at the acronyms, doing her best not to embarrass herself or Tarquin. She could see Pam hovering in the background, a busybody vacuuming gossip for a Monday morning debrief. Then a woman sauntered over, inserted herself into the group: Zelda Forshaw, laughing at the men's jokes, smiling broadly and flirting effortlessly with all the sincerity of an Instagram influencer. Mandy felt grateful for the diversion; she wasn't troubled by Tarquin's gaze shifting to Zelda. Perhaps Zelda, a woman of a similar age, might even be an ally.

That lasted until the bathroom, Mandy standing before the mirror, adjusting her make-up. Zelda entered, stood next to her.

'You're very pretty,' Zelda observed.

'Thank you.' Mandy smiled at the other woman's reflection. 'So are you.'

Zelda nodded, as if acknowledging a universally accepted truth. 'Tarquin Molloy. That's some catch.'

Mandy was still smiling, still too happy to pick up on the undercurrent. 'We're going out together. Yes.'

'I heard he organised your job for you. Are you enjoying it?'

'Yes. Very much. Thank you.'

And now Zelda smiled too, though there was no amity in her eyes. 'How's your back?'

'My back?'

'Just remember, some of us got our jobs through hard work and on merit.' And she left.

It was Pam who found Mandy, not weeping but mortified, in a cubicle. Pam, who comforted her, who ushered her out, who took her home to her new apartment. Who reassured her that she was good at her job and a valued member of her team. And who, for all her gossipy persona, never mentioned a word of it to anyone.

Mandy was dreading returning to work the following week. But on Monday she found that Pam had orchestrated it so she spent a part of each day in the team office, in Pam's den, with the rest of the crew and away from the isolation of the trading floor. Mollisons had its own cafe, with subsidised meals and free coffee and cakes for employees, yet Pam had decided doughnuts were required from the shop across the road and made it Mandy's job to fetch them, so the team could enjoy them in their office: Pam,

Mandy, Wendy, Raneesh and Stan. And Mandy wasn't the first one Pam had helped, she would discover; some weeks later Raneesh confided that the previous year, when Wendy had abruptly left her violent husband, Pam had put her up in her own house for almost two months while Wendy had got back on her feet financially and emotionally.

Mandy had never known anyone like her; her own mother was loving but reticent, Pam was loving and ebullient. She was everyone's mother: equal parts unbearable and supportive, a gossip and a confidante.

Now, five years since she last saw her, Mandy bites her lip, resolve returning. She knows she needs to do this. She calls the number she's found.

Pam answers. And it's the same Pam, warm and accommodating, who always has time for others, is happy to hear from Mandy. Of course she would like to catch up. This morning? No problem. Come now.

Out in the CBD, the wind shifts and swirls, lifting the dirt and the dust and the neglect, pushing it into people's faces, so that they hunch and they squint and they hurry, as if social distancing has returned by some overnight decree. No one is happy, no one smiles, no one pauses to chat or joke. It's a grim place today, this city, a foreign country, faded and cold, concrete and glass, steel and cladding, its denizens silent, smartphones on and life-cancelling earbuds in.

Even so, she eschews a cab, feeling a need to be out in the midst of it, to challenge and resist. Instead, she takes the train to Redfern, lets Google Maps guide her to Pam Risoli's terrace. The street is tree-lined, gentrified, the traffic local; in another season, with the trees in leaf, it would be charming. Not today, not with the wind and the scowling sky.

She reaches through the bars on Pam's security door, knocking on wood.

Pamela Risoli is much as she remembers, maybe a little larger, and just as friendly, throwing open the door and swallowing Mandy in an embrace. Maybe it's the bonding that survivors feel. Cats mill around the woman like a friendly cloud, brushing against Mandy's legs. Her old boss looks relaxed, content. Her hair is grey, no longer dyed for work, but shaped into a sharp inner-city cut. Pam clucks away, inviting her in. Despite the extra kilo or two, Pam still manages to glide, that curious walk that once so intrigued Mandy, a walk so smooth and constant that Pam's head doesn't seem to rise and fall but rather floats as she leads Mandy down a narrow passage, as if levitated a constant five foot six above the floor, accompanied by an entourage of felines. No scrawny catwalk model ever moved with such grace. Pam passes the stairs, a bedroom door, making her way through a book-strewn lounge room and into a kitchen that stretches the width of the terrace. The kitchen is open and bright, a new addition, a wood stove glowing in a corner. The smell is of baking and good things. The decorative style is retro kitsch, a mix of op-shop discoveries, estate auction collectibles and found objects: there are ceramic ducks on the wall, the kitchen table is mid-century laminate ringed with aluminium, the four chairs differ from each other. At a guess, Pam spends a lot of time at garage sales, school fetes and neighbourhood markets. If Tarquin Molloy did steal millions from Mollisons, none of it made its way here.

'I was so surprised to hear from you,' says Pam, busying herself making coffee with an antiquated stove-top espresso pot. 'After all you've been through.'

'You've been following me?'

'Not intentionally. But you were in all the papers. First out west in that town, Riversend, then in Port Silver.' Pam smiles. 'And of course I read the books. Martin Scarsden. Wow.' And she bestows a luminous smile on Mandy.

'Yes. It's been . . .' Mandy searches for the right word '. . . eventful.'

Pam turns from the stove, her face serious. 'I tried calling you— you know that, don't you? After he disappeared, after we were let go.'

'I remember. I saw your messages.'

'You just vanished.'

'I'm sorry. I know you wanted to help. But I couldn't face anyone, not after what he'd done to me. To all of us.'

'You could have come here. I would have looked after you.'

'I know. I just wanted the ground to swallow me.'

'I understand,' says Pam. 'Maybe it was for the best.' And her countenance lifts and her voice returns to its normal positivity. 'Now you have Martin, you have your home, and you have a little boy. How wonderful to have a child. Such a gift.'

Mandy glances about the kitchen. There are the ducks on the wall, elephants of glass and wood and ceramics on the ledge above the sink, a framed Martin Sharp poster, but no photographs of family. 'Yes. He's gorgeous. This is the first time I've been away from him.'

'He's still in Port Silver?'

'He's not in Sydney.'

A frown brushes Pam's face, and is gone. 'What is it, Mandalay? You look troubled.'

'Tarquin. Did you hear? They found his body.'

The woman's lips tighten. 'Yes. I heard. How horrible for you.'

'He was a policeman.'

'What?'

'A policeman. Working undercover, investigating Mollisons.'

Now the woman appears distressed. 'I never knew that.'

'No. Neither did I.' Mandy tells her what she knows, choosing her words carefully, not wanting to upset the older woman.

The coffee pot announces its readiness with a throaty gurgle, and Pam busies herself with stoneware mugs and homemade fruit cake. They sit at the table.

'I like your house,' Mandy says. 'It's very you.'

'Thanks. Paid off my mortgage with my redundancy package.'

'You're not working?'

'Don't have to. I was there for more than thirty years. Good super. Good enough.'

Mandy sips at her coffee. It's not Aldo's, but her host knows what she's doing. 'Pam, when they were investigating Tarquin, you helped me.'

'Did I? How?'

'You defended me. Reminded security that I'd been upfront about lending him my passwords.'

'I was just doing my job, standing up for my team.' The woman looks puzzled, shrugs. 'I'm glad if it helped. I felt sorry about what happened to you.'

'What do you mean?'

'Him treating you like that, deserting you. That's what we thought, of course—that he'd run off with the money, been in cahoots with Zelda Forshaw. That's what management said, the official line.' She looks at her coffee, still assimilating what Mandy has told her. 'But that didn't stop them sacking us.'

'Is that what they said?'

'They didn't have to. Officially, it was a restructure, the one that they'd been planning for months, but there was a lingering sense that they suspected Zelda wasn't his only accomplice.'

'Who was it? Who had us sacked?'

'Security ran the internal investigation. So Harry Sweetwater, assisted by Clarity Sparkes. She was asking a lot of questions. At first she defended you, defended us, but I guess she smelt which way the wind was blowing.'

Mandy remembers Clarity, Montifore asking about her. 'Her job. Physical security. What does that mean?'

'Passes mainly. Swipe cards. CCTV. The guards on the front desk. Not the computers, not vetting people, none of the financials. The simple stuff.'

'Is she still there, do you know?'

Pam looks shocked. 'No. Didn't you hear?'

'What?'

'She died. Not so long after we were laid off. A month or two later.'

'I'm sorry,' says Mandy, if only because it's the polite thing to say, the sort of thing Pam would expect. 'How did she die? She seemed really fit to me, like a gym junkie.'

'No. Turns out she was a real junkie. Overdosed in a hotel room. Heroin and cocaine, of all things. A speedball they call it.'

'An overdose? Clarity?' Mandy shakes her head, finding it hard to believe. 'She always seemed so, I don't know, officious and in control.'

Pam sighs at the description. 'Seems there was a whole different side to her. The word was that she'd been hooked for years but was highly functional. Nobody knew. There was office Clarity and after-hours Clarity. After she died, it all came out; she moved with some strange types: artists and musos and druggies. And worse: bouncers, debt collectors, pushers. The funeral was a very peculiar mix of people.' A frown comes over the woman's face, as if she's considering the implications of what she is saying, or maybe she feels bad speaking ill of the dead. A ginger cat leaps onto her lap and she pats it while it settles. When she speaks again, her voice is low. 'What is it you want to know, Mandy? Why did you come here?'

'Three days ago I was abducted by Zelda Forshaw. She still thinks the money is out there somewhere.'

Pam blinks, looking distressed. She fidgets with the cat; it stands in protest and circles, clawing at her trousers before resettling. 'I always thought Tarquin disappeared overseas with it. We all did. They arrested Zelda. But now . . .'

'Now?'

'Well, now that we know he was killed, it seems that he didn't get away with it. And you say he was a policeman, so maybe the whole story about missing millions was a smokescreen.'

'Maybe. But if he was a cop, what was he investigating? Did you ever get the impression something was wrong with Mollisons, that the bank was involved with anything criminal?'

'No. Never. Not that.' She pats the cat some more. 'I knew they were astute, minimising tax for clients, using legal loopholes and offshore havens and schemes at the margins, but that's what investment banks get paid to do. Use the law, bend it maybe, but not break it. That was just my impression, though. I was in support services, nothing to do with the financials. How could I know?'

'But they sacked all of us. They must have thought we knew something.'

Another frown. 'I guess.'

'I remember Sweetwater. He interrogated me with Clarity. What was his position?'

'Her boss. Head of security.'

'He seemed very wound up.'

'Still is, so I'm told.'

'He still works there? At Mollisons?'

'Apparently.'

'Maybe I should go see him.'

'I wouldn't bother. It's his job to keep Mollisons' secrets secret. He wouldn't confirm the time of day.'

Mandy stares at the ginger cat. No doubt Pam is right. But the thought, having settled in her head, won't let go. 'Would anyone else know about the passwords, besides me, you, Clarity Sparkes and Harry Sweetwater?'

'Stacks of people. There was an internal investigation by the security team when the money was discovered missing; they would have interviewed scores of people. Senior management would have been briefed about the whole thing, it would have been discussed by the board. I'm sure people in IT would have been involved when they tried to find out if Tarquin had improperly accessed anything. And maybe the Turtle. He might have discovered something, or Clarity could have put him on the case.'

Mandy's skin crawls. 'Jesus. The Turtle. I'd forgotten all about him.'

The look on Pam's face suggests she doesn't believe her.

'Clarity was his boss; the Turtle reported directly to her,' says Pam.

'Really?'

'Of course. To Clarity and up the line to Sweetwater.'

'What was the Turtle's real name? Did anyone ever know?'

'Kenneth someone. Kenneth Steadman? I hear he survived the purge; he still works there. At Mollisons. The rest of us were sacked, but he's part of the furniture.'

chapter fourteen

BETHANIE MEETS HIM AT A FOOD COURT INSIDE A SHOPPING MALL AT DARLING Harbour. It's a good choice: out of the wind, yet no self-respecting Sydneysider would be seen dead here. Instead, tourists mill around, disappointed at the choice of food, insulted by the prices and apprehensive of the birds scavenging for scraps. Even this early in the day, there is a pervasive smell of fried food and sugar. She's already seated at a plastic table when he gets there, running a disposable spoon around the rim of her coffee cup, absent-mindedly harvesting froth.

'Bethanie.'

She stands, gives him a smile and a peck on the cheek. She's changed since he last saw her, more than a year ago. Her practical bob has evolved into a more fashionable cut, longer with high-lights. Her face has matured and grown leaner, cheekbones more defined. She looks self-possessed and confident.

Martin orders himself a coffee and mass-produced muffin, declining the offer to have it microwaved. They sit across from each other amid the clattering noise bouncing around the hard surfaces of the mall. The glassed-in food court has evolved into some sort of unintentional aviary: seagulls squabble, just for the heck of it or practising for the discarded chips that will come later in the day; a couple of pigeons warble on a ledge above a sushi booth; and an ibis, one of the much-maligned bin chickens, stalks around like an escapee from Jurassic Park. Martin and Bethanie exchange pleasantries: she inquires after the health of Mandy and Liam; Martin compliments her work and her promotion to the investigative unit; she praises his latest book, recounting the events in Port Silver early the previous year, when they had worked so closely together.

He's the first to break the superficiality. 'So, what's the story with Max?'

She avoids his gaze, looking instead out at the passing parade. One of the seagulls has lost a few feathers and is holding its wing at an unusual angle. 'I wrote a much longer piece. It was cut by the subs. Severely.'

'Not so unusual. These straitened times, these straitened resources.'

'It wasn't just cut. That crap about no suspicious circum-stances—I never wrote that.'

'And "lifelong friends"?'

'Of course not.'

'So what happened?'

'I don't know. Some sub changed it.'

'What's that even meant to convey, do you think? Lifelong friends?'

'I told you. I didn't write it.'

'I know. I'm just asking your opinion.'

'It sounds like they were having an affair.'

'So why would a sub insert that?'

Bethanie frowns. 'I heard that the bodies . . . That they were found in a compromising position. It was all over the newsroom. Maybe the sub was alluding to that.'

It doesn't sound right to Martin. Why cut so much of Bethanie's copy, only to insert that? He tries another tack. 'Sometimes women have a very different opinion of men than other men do. Particularly of men in positions of power. Did you ever get the impression that Max was a player?'

Bethanie must see the distress it causes him to ask the question: she reaches out, takes his hand. 'Never, Martin. Never. Not personally, not second-hand, not on the rumour mill. You know that: Max was the mentor to generations.'

Martin feels a moment of relief, but it's fleeting. Maybe it's true, maybe Max and Elizabeth Torbett were long-time lovers. Maybe someone at the *Herald* knows it. Maybe that explains why they wanted to curtail the story.

'I raised it with D'Arcy Defoe,' says Bethanie, as if following Martin's thought process. 'He's the head of investigations now, did you know that?'

'I heard.'

'I wish you'd come back full-time. It's just D'Arcy, me and a cadet in investigations. He's not always the most collegiate.'

Martin laughs. 'Yeah. He likes to run his own race. Nothing wrong with that.'

Bethanie returns the laugh. 'Yeah. That may be about the only thing you two have in common.'

'He's a good reporter, don't forget that. And a better writer than I'll ever be.'

'You're the one with the bestselling true crime books.'

Martin smiles that one off. 'So what did D'Arcy say?'

'He agreed it was outrageous and said he'd raise it in conference.'

'You know if he did?'

'No. You should ask him.'

'Maybe I should.' Martin pauses. A bin chicken has come to contest the turf with the seagulls. They squawk, scatter and reassemble, bubbling with resentment. 'You don't think D'Arcy was behind the changes to your copy?'

'No. Why would he be? He's working on an obituary for Max, pushing for a full page. I thought he might call you, ask for a few anecdotes.'

'Not yet.' He picks at his muffin, wondering what's taking so long with his coffee. 'Did you have much to do with Max recently?'

She shakes her head. 'Not a lot. He wasn't in the office so much. I reckon he was still gutted over losing the editorship, especially after our coverage of the murders out west was vindicated. But just lately, he seemed really happy, like the old Max.'

'He'd found a big story, a cracker,' volunteers Martin.

'You knew that?'

'Yeah, he told me. Wanted me to work on it with him. Do you have any idea what it was?'

'No. But you're right. There was a gleam in his eye and a spring in his step. He was working on something significant, for sure. Mainly from home, but he was in the office sometimes.

Remember all those filing cabinets of his? All those old clippings, decades' worth? He was dumpster diving, going back to look at the pre-digital stuff.' She sips some coffee, grimacing at the quality. 'He was keeping it close to his chest, though. One time he asked me how much I knew about Changi.'

'Changi? The airport in Singapore?'

'No. The prisoner-of-war camp. Second World War. He wasn't sure if my generation knew about it.'

'And do you?'

She looks at him sardonically. 'Martin, my generation has been force-fed the Anzac tradition until it's coming out our ears.'

'You're probably right about that.' *My generation?* How old does she think he is?

'When I heard that Max was dead, I tried to find out what he was working on, but there was nothing. His personal baskets were empty, the drive clean enough to eat your lunch off. Nothing.'

'You'd need his passwords to know that.'

'So I would. Don't ask. The important thing is that his drive has been erased.'

'What are you saying?'

'I don't know. But it smells, don't you think?'

'Who could wipe his drive? Who would have the authority?'

She shrugs. 'You'd need someone from IT, I guess, but someone high up in the *Herald* would need to authorise it. I made inquiries.'

'And?'

'I've a friend in IT. We're on the same indoor cricket team. She had a look for me. First thing she could tell me was that it was deliberate. She ran a data recovery program; you know, they use it all the time when some boomer accidentally deletes a file. There was nothing left. Not a byte.'

'Does the *Herald* have the software to do that? To scrub a disc to that extent?'

'Apparently, but it could take hours. They must have done it overnight.'

'So the night Max died, or the following night? Monday or Tuesday?'

'No. Before he died. Probably Sunday night. That's what my IT friend says.'

'What about the shared drives? Aren't the files automatically backed up in the cloud or somewhere?'

'No. She checked. Max had turned off all the backup options.'

'Sounds like he was being deliberately secretive.'

'Doesn't it.'

'And all you know is that it had something to do with Changi? How could that possibly get him killed? That was a long time ago; all the men who were there must be dead by now, or near enough.'

'You should ask D'Arcy. Maybe he knows something. But if he does, he's not telling me.'

Martin's coffee finally arrives; it's already cold.

chapter fifteen

THE DOUGHNUTS GLISTEN WITH SUGARY MENACE, ALIGNED IN RANKS WITHIN THE glass display cases, a battalion of indulgence ready to march. Mandy is surrounded by them on three sides, caught in a frozen pincer movement of calorific weaponry. She hates them: their cloying dough, their camouflaged fat, their superficial appeal. Most of all she hates their iridescent icing. She hates them not for themselves, but for the memories they come armed with. They surround her, battle-ready in their trays, primed for deployment. A doughnut army.

It was one of her duties at Mollisons, as the most junior member of her team: the doughnut run to the shop just across the road in Pyrmont. Doughnuts and coffee. Sitting here now, in the over-illuminated store, with its coconut-ice decor of pink and white, she can still remember the orders. Pam: strawberry doughnut, large skinny cappuccino; Raneesh: large flat white with caramel syrup and a gluten-free chocolate doughnut; Wendy: large long black and a low-cal watermelon doughnut; Stan: weak white tea and a chocolate doughnut with sprinkles. A skinny latte for herself, maybe a macchiato, no doughnut. At first she used to enjoy the run; it got her out of the office and, on her return, gave her a chance to mingle for a time with other members of the team before heading back to her isolation on the trading-room floor.

The doughnut shop was where she first met the Turtle, talked to him, unsuspecting, learning that he also worked at Mollisons. He seemed so nice, so avuncular, with his spare-tyre tum and his oversized spectacles. His name was Kenneth, he told her, never Ken, but to everyone at Mollisons he was simply the Turtle, with his wide body, his rounded shoulders, his incongruously long neck emerging from his shell-like cardigan, his lack of a chin completing the image. A large and amiable Turtle. A nice man, totally inoffensive. That's what she thought. At first.

Then it became clear that he was timing his doughnut runs to coincide with her own. Initially, she shrugged it off, but then it began to irk her. There was no set time within her team: some-times she did her run in the mornings, sometimes afternoons, sometimes neither, occasionally both. Pam would ring and she would go. And yet there he always was, his smile losing its charm, becoming oily in her mind. How could he know? She eventually confided in Pam, told her boss of her uneasiness, and was informed Kenneth worked for security. He was the closed-circuit television guy, the man behind the monitors. Pam wanted to intervene; Mandy begged her not to. But she began to dread the trips; behind his outdated spectacles, the Turtle's eyes had become vacuums.

Some days he would buy the lemon doughnuts, with their tangy white icing, some days caramel, some days licorice. Licorice doughnuts: a more revolting concept she couldn't imagine. Then, one day, he bought boysenberry.

'Purple?' she asked. 'Trying something new?'

'Thought I should.'

'Why's that?'

'You'll never guess.'

But she did. That evening at home, undressing for bed. Her underwear, usually white, tan or black, was purple. The dread came down upon her like a diagnosis.

She didn't know what to do, not believing she could be right. Could she possibly tell Pam? Three days later she wore red knickers. The Turtle bought a raspberry doughnut, salivating as he sank his teeth into it, leering repulsively.

That pushed her into a whole new void of anxiety: he knew that she knew, but he wasn't trying to disguise it. It was like he was deliberately escalating. She hesitated. It was a preposterous allegation to make: that he was selecting colour-coded doughnuts.

Now she sits in the store and grimaces at her younger self. How exposed she was, so unsure of herself, how slow to act. But she did act. In the toilets at work, she located one of his cameras, an optical fibre as small as a pinhead. She stuck chewing gum over the lens. That day, when she did the doughnut run, he didn't cross the street to the cafe. She had him. And she had another option: Tarquin. She told him, and together they dug the end of the fibre out of the toilet wall. And that same night, Tarquin waited for him after work, beat him senseless, bad enough to put him in an ambulance. The Turtle wasn't at work the next day, or the day after, and when he did return a week later his face was still swollen and bruised. He never followed her to the doughnut shop again. She remembers her relief. It was fixed; she shunted it into the past. For six months, all was well. Then Tarquin disappeared. And she was sacked.

Thinking back, she sees herself as pathetic. Why did she rely on Tarquin? Was she really so helpless? Moreover, why didn't she question Tarquin taking matters into his own hands? Surely they should have reported it, exposed the Turtle, got him sacked. Got him arrested. Got him jailed. That's what should have happened, so why didn't it?

She looks up; the door has opened, the wind gusting him in. The Turtle. By the size of him, pants hitched high above his belly, he hasn't given up the doughnuts.

He sees her. She smiles at him, an expression as sickly sweet as the glowing doughnuts. 'Join me,' she says, voice superficially friendly.

He does what he is told, belly vibrating jelly-like as he squirms onto a seat opposite her.

There are no pleasantries, not with the Turtle. Mandy starts in on him, not giving him time to gather his thoughts. 'You know I could have ended your career. Finished it.'

He sneers. 'So you say.'

'We found the cameras. We found the evidence.'

He leans forward, voice a whisper. 'You recording this?'

'No,' she says. 'I don't have to.'

'Well, I'm not saying anything, anyway. I'm not stupid.' But he can't help himself; his eyes flicker momentarily downwards, drawn to her breasts.

'You haven't changed, have you?' she says, seething. She counts to three, calming herself. She so badly wants to abuse him, to vent her anger, but she knows that will get her nowhere. She considers the doughnuts; they stare at her, impassive.

She looks back at him, his eyes jerking up to meet her gaze a moment too late, guilt written on his face.

'What did Tarquin say? When he confronted you over the cameras?'

The Turtle licks his lips. No doubt it's an unconscious gesture, but it makes her flesh creep all the same. For a moment she thinks he won't speak, that he will call her bluff. But something—maybe it's her withering contempt, maybe not—elicits a response. 'He beat the shit out of me. The jerk. Said if I ever spied on you, followed you, bothered you, he would destroy me. He would kill me. *Kill me.* That's what he said. He was horrid.' The Turtle's voice is low and full of self-pity, as if he's the victim, the one who has been wronged, the one deserving of sympathy. 'I never did you any harm. I only ever looked.'

The anger surges once again, almost impossible to control, but again she keeps it contained. 'That's not all, though, was it?'

Now there is panic in his eyes. She's hit a nerve. 'What do you mean?'

'He knew you had cameras everywhere. Could spy everywhere. He recruited you.'

'What are you suggesting?'

'He was a policeman.'

'So they say.'

'Did you know?'

'Back then? No.'

'Do you have any idea how relentless they are, the police, when someone has killed one of their own?' She notes, with pleasure,

that the Turtle has begun to sweat, his face glistening with perspir-
ation. She lowers her voice, fills it with menace. 'They're coming
for you, Kenneth.'

'Are you police?'

'No. But I'm helping them.'

'What do you want?'

'To know what happened to him. That's all. Tell me and I
will leave you alone.'

The Turtle looks around, furtive as a back-alley stray. 'You
swear you're not recording?'

'If you help me, I won't tell the police. If you don't, they're my
next call.'

He starts shaking his head. 'No. If they killed him, they'll kill me.'

'Who? Who killed him?'

'I don't know. How could I know?'

Mandy stares at him, trying to keep the pressure on. 'Let me
buy you a doughnut,' she says. 'Today, I think you would like one
with coffee icing.'

The Turtle's eyes grow wide, his mouth goldfishes. She leaves
him gaping while she goes to the counter and orders his delicacy.
She can feel him leering at her, but she also feels the power she
has over him.

'What do you want?' he manages as she sits down, sliding the
doughnut across to him.

'I told you: tell me what happened with Tarquin.' Now it's a
command, not a question. She keeps her eyes locked on his, not
averting her gaze for a second. She can see the indecision in his
face as he tests first one possibility, then another and another, before
abandoning them all. He glances around, looking for something

to help, as if the doughnuts might still ride to his rescue, a sugar-coated cavalry. Still she glares at him—surely he can see the hatred in her eyes—and so she sees the moment he concedes.

'He beat me up, he threatened to kill me, that's all true.' He swallows; she can see his long neck flex. 'But he demanded more.'

'What?'

'Passwords.'

'You gave them to him?'

'Not straight away. I had to adjust the cameras, record people as they logged on.'

'But then?'

The Turtle nods, apparently forgetting his fear of surveillance. 'Yes.'

'And?'

'What do you mean?'

'When he went to use them, you were spying on him. You alerted Clarity Sparkes.'

'No. No, it wasn't like that.'

'Tell me, or I tell the police.'

'You said you wouldn't.'

'I say many things.' She stares him in the eye, finding that intimidation comes easily. 'You violated my privacy, you abhorrent shit. You help me or I tell the police. I have no other reason to protect you.'

'What do you want?'

'You're the one who gave him the passwords, gave him access, enabled him to steal the money. If I tell the police, you're fucked.' She gets to her feet. 'I'll be back here tomorrow at two. I want passwords too. I want the access you gave Tarquin. Or I'll tell the police what you've done and explain that you had a motive to murder a police officer.'

She leaves him there, shaking visibly, amid the florid display cabinets, the doughnuts in retreat. Outside, the bracing wind is no longer irritating but cleansing. She's desperate to get back to the hotel and shower. Every pore of her body feels tainted.

chapter sixteen

'YOU WANT SOME GUM?' THE COMPUTER GEEK OFFERS HIM A SQUASHED PACKET of Juicy Fruit, its top ripped off to reveal cracked pieces of gum. Today he's wearing a military-style jacket and a second-hand policeman's hat. With his long blond hair, it gives him the look of a faded rock star, despite his youth.

'Not right now, thanks.'

'Suit yourself. Wait here. I'll get your laptop.'

He returns from the back of the store with a computer that looks remarkably similar to Martin's old one, except for the marijuana-shaped sticker adorning its lid, proclaiming *Legalise it!* He props it on the counter, opens the lid. It boots silently, the screen welcoming Martin and offering to take him through the set-up.

'You can do the set-up here, if you want to make sure it's working okay,' says the young man. 'I tested the battery; it's in good nick. Whoever owned it, they barely used it.'

'I'm sure it's fine,' says Martin. He hands over the five hundred dollars and asks for a receipt.

'A receipt? Really?'

'Actually, no, forget about it.' He puts his wallet away. 'Tell me—Yevgeny, isn't it?'

'That's me. Call me Yev, if you like.'

'As well as fixing computers, are you any good at using one?'

'Of course. Why?'

'I'm looking for someone who's good with the internet. Researching things, finding things out.'

Martin sees the casualness drop away, the back stiffen, the intelligence cutting in like an over-clocked processor. 'You don't know how to use Google?'

'I do, and I can handle social media, bulletin boards, that sort of stuff, but beyond that I'm useless.'

'Beyond that is the badlands. The deep web. The dark web.'

'Deep? Dark? What's the difference?'

'It doesn't matter. I'm not taking you there.'

'I'll pay cash.' The moment he says it, Martin knows he's said the wrong thing.

Yev straightens. He's tall and spindly, slightly ridiculous in his fancy dress, but his face is serious. 'Maybe you should set it up at home,' he says, indicating the laptop with a flick of his head.

'I'm a journalist. An investigative journalist.'

But the assertion only makes matters worse; the expression on the young geek's face turns from caution to hostility. 'Is that meant to impress me?'

'No, but—'

Yev doesn't let him finish. 'No. I am not hacking celebrities. I am not stealing photos, I am not accessing voicemail, I am not supplying locations. See you later, Mr Investigative Journalist.'

Martin is taken aback. 'I'm not that sort of reporter,' he retorts, but he knows he's lost the argument. He powers down the computer, waiting for it to finish before leaving.

'So what sort of journalist are you?' asks Yev.

'The right sort.'

'Prove it.'

Martin pulls out one of his business cards. 'My name's Martin Scarsden. I've spent the last twenty years working for the *Sydney Morning Herald*.'

The change is near instantaneous, the hostility fading from the young man's face. 'Martin Scarsden? You're Martin Scarsden? You're shitting me.'

'Google me if you don't believe it. You don't need the dark web for that.'

'Man, I love your stuff. The Middle East—I read all your stuff. My best friend is a Leb. Wait'll I tell him. He'll be stoked. Martin fucking Scarsden. Why didn't you say? Creeping in here all incognito, going the bargain-basement deal. Doesn't the *Herald* give you a laptop?'

'I'm kind of part-time right now.'

'I know. Writing books. True crime. Not as interesting as the Middle East, but not too shabby.'

'Thanks.'

'Shit, I could've given you something really sick, if I'd known. You want free internet?'

Martin is still feeling a little wrong-footed by the change in attitude. 'Tempting. But perhaps not right now.'

'So what do you want me to do?'

'You'll help?'

'Sure. Provided it's not illegal. Or immoral.'

'Definitely not immoral. Not sure about the legality.'

'What is it?'

Martin wonders where to start. 'Well, first off, tell me about the deep web and the dark web. What's the difference?'

Yev smiles and shakes his head, as if astounded at how such an accomplished journalist could remain so ignorant. 'Most of the internet isn't readily accessible. Only about four or five per cent is open to the general public. More than ninety percent is corporate or government material, but the sites don't show up in web searches and are protected by usernames and passwords. Everything from your webmail, to the cloud, to your bank account.'

'Right,' says Martin. 'So with the *Herald*, I can log on from anywhere and file stories, check my pay slips, that sort of thing.'

'Exactly. So not publicly accessible, but totally legal. That's the deep web. But sitting within the deep web is the dark web, sites created for illegal activity and only accessible to those in the know, often using encryption and accessed through VPNs.'

'Like drug sites, paedophile rings?'

'That's it. All sorts of bad shit.'

'That's not what I'm interested in,' says Martin.

'So what then?' Yev is smiling, eyes a-twinkle. 'Is this an investigative journalist thing? Robert Redford and that other dude?'

Martin laughs. 'Something like that. We'll see.' And he looks around, conspiratorially, as if confirming they're in private, half of him hating the manipulation, half of him loving the play-acting. 'This is a major investigation. It's absolutely vital you don't talk about this to anyone, not even your Lebanese mate. Understand?'

Yev nods, a fish on a hook.

'It's for your own protection as much as anything, including legal protection. You okay with that?'

'Oh, shit, man. Can't I tell him I met you, at least?'

Martin pretends to ponder the question in all seriousness. 'All right. But just tell him I bought a laptop. Okay?'

'Yeah. Cool. My lips are data-locked and my tongue is encrypted.'

Martin blinks, wonders momentarily if he's doing the right thing. 'Okay. First question. How difficult is it to wipe a hard drive clean, so clean none of the data can be retrieved, even by police forensics?'

'Dead easy. The software comes standard on Macs, is easy to download for Windows. You overwrite the disc, up to seven times if you're feeling paranoid, with random data. After that, recovery is practically impossible.'

'Practically?'

'Can't be done by software alone. Rumour has it the spooks and the military have specialist technology that can pick up digital ghosting. But that would be in clean rooms, using classified techno-logy, shaving discs. Massively expensive, massively time-consuming. Even then, it probably wouldn't work if the data wipe has been done thoroughly enough.'

Martin thinks on that, pondering how much he should be taking the geek into his confidence. He decides to keep the information general. 'Here's the scenario. A computer hard drive inside the *Sydney Morning Herald* has been wiped clean. Overwritten.'

'Right. On a stand-alone computer, or a corporate drive?'

'Stand-alone.'

'Anyone with passwords could have done it. As I say, dead easy.'

'Is there any way to find out who did it?'

'Maybe. There's probably a record. A log. I could check, if I had the computer and the passwords.'

Martin grimaces. 'Too late. The police have it.'

'Why? What happened?'

Martin swallows. Can the young man possibly help? He decides to trust him. 'My old editor, Max Fuller, was murdered the night before last. Before he died, he was working on a big story.'

'And his hard drive was scrubbed?' asks Yev.

'Yes.'

'And there was no backup in-house at the *Herald*?'

'Apparently not. He was keeping it close to his chest.'

'Even so, he might have been backing up to the cloud using a private account, like Dropbox, iCloud, Google Drive.'

'How could we find that? Access it?'

'We couldn't. Not without knowing the provider, the account name, the passwords.'

'Sounds like a dead end, then.'

'Hang on. This computer, the one with the erased hard drive— it was at the *Herald*, right?'

'That's right.' And the moment he says it, Martin realises what Yev is driving at. Bethanie said Max was only rarely in the office, that he worked mainly from home. 'A second computer.'

'Worth checking out.'

But Martin is shaking his head. 'He was murdered at his house. If it was because of the story, they wouldn't kill him and leave the laptop.'

Yev shrugs. 'There's not a lot I can do then, short of you finding an account in the cloud.'

'I guess,' says Martin, gathering up his second-hand computer and thanking Yev. 'I'll let you know if I find anything useful.' And he leaves, contemplating how he might broach the subject with the grieving Eileen Fuller.

chapter seventeen

MANDY SITS BY THE WINDOW, LOOKING OUT ONTO THE STREET FROM THE HOTEL lobby, waiting for him. The world flows through the dusk, dressed in greys and monochrome, heads down and unsmiling, as if the people of Sydney have been subjugated by the weather, have adopted the grimness like a fashion, a throwback to the days of pandemic. But no, look. There is a couple, their child between them, the three of them laughing, oblivious to the surrounding bleakness. Each parent has a hand, swinging their daughter off her feet and back again as they walk along. The parents are singing, the child is laughing. Mandy watches them pass, wishing she could hear the words of their song through the double-glazing, wishing she and Martin were back home swinging Liam between them.

Now she sees Martin, emerging from early evening anonymity. He's on the other side of the road, at the far end of the block, walking towards her. Despite the distance, she can sense his mood:

intense, distracted, consumed. Among the commuters he seems unremarkable: he has none of the bravado of Tarquin Molloy, none of the presence of Byron Swift. Instead, she can see the self-doubt and the vulnerability, balanced by conviction and duty. *Can* she see it, or is this simply her imagination, her view imposed on the world like a filter? She'd caught a glimpse of it the very first time she met him, back in her bookstore on the lonely plain of Riversend. She sees it again now as he walks alone among the crowd, deep in thought. He's still too distant for her to see his expression, but she knows his forehead is furrowed, that his eyes are unseeing.

Journalism is his calling, his vocation. She realises that now. And it's how he copes, burying himself in his work when the world goes awry. Maybe that's what his whole career had been, the globe-trotting correspondent, forever on the hunt for the next story, the next woman, the next escape: a way to cope. She hadn't known Martin then, wonders if she would have liked him, been attracted to him. Probably; she'd fallen for Tarquin, for Byron Swift. But she likes Martin as he is now: more exposed, more self-aware. Not perfect, but so much better. Not too good for her. Someone she should trust, someone she should believe in. Someone not always calculating the angles. The pretence is gone, but the journalist remains.

A memory of Tarquin comes, clear and well defined. A day at the races, at Royal Randwick, the Autumn Racing Carnival, the two of them dressed to the nines. He led her into the betting ring, the bookmakers in suits, like politicians or car salesmen or policemen, standing in front of their boards, odds displayed. 'Behold,' he said. 'The great game.'

'Are you betting?' she asked.

'No. Watching. Learning.'

The place was busy, teeming with people, but started to empty soon enough. The next race was approaching. 'Shall we watch it?' she asked.

'No. This is where the real race is being run.'

'Is that so?'

'It's a market. They need to frame it, constantly adapting, changing the odds. Against bets already laid, laying off with other bookies, trying to stay attractive and competitive to the punters, while backing their own judgement of form.'

'You understand it?'

'Not well enough. But I will.'

A car passes, a horn blares, loud enough to penetrate inside the hotel, jerking her back to the present, causing her to flinch. She scans the street, finding him standing opposite, unharmed, waiting to cross the road, apparently lost in thought, still unaware she's watching him. He proceeds across the street through a break in the traffic and she loses sight of him as he enters the hotel.

And now he sees her across the lobby, and his frown lifts. They meet. They touch. His hand moves to her face, his eyes find hers. She wants to fall into him, to hold him close, but she doesn't feel she can. Not here, not now. There is a barrier, enforcing a formality. He's not the relaxed man of the north coast, the death of Max rewriting his features; she is not the gentle mother of their clifftop sanctuary, the confrontation with the Turtle destabilising her. Port Silver is gone; Sydney has them.

They move deeper inside the hotel, into the bar, midnight-dim and the decor dated. At this hour, they have it almost to themselves. There's an older couple in a booth drinking in silence, not talking, not looking at each other, just staring into space. A barman is propped at his counter, bored and scrolling through his phone. On the wall there is a muted television, the liveliest thing in the room. At Port Silver, at this time of day, with the breeze easing in off the ocean, they might sit side by side watching the shading horizon, the rising moon, drinking gins and tonic, but somehow clear spirits won't suffice here; Sydney demands something tainted. Mandy orders a brandy and dry, Martin a whisky on ice, the barman glad for something to do but unable to conjure any banter. They withdraw to a table, well away from the other couple. They clink glasses, not in celebration or in welcome, but in a gesture of mutual recognition and solidarity.

'Maybe you should head back,' he says.

'To Port Silver?'

'Yeah. Look after Liam.'

'You think?'

'It's dangerous here. Max and Elizabeth Torbett murdered, my apartment destroyed. And Morris Montifore says those guys, Livingstone and Spitt, are psychotic.'

'I know,' she says, considering her drink. 'Livingstone warned me. He said it was going to turn ugly.'

'What was he talking about?'

'I'm not sure. He didn't say.' She shrugs. 'The murder of Tarquin and discovering his body. The money and Zelda Forshaw.'

They sit in silence, staring into their drinks.

'Would you come with me?' she asks. 'To Port Silver?'

He continues to examine his whisky, talking with his eyes on the drink. 'I want to find out what happened to Max. What he was working on. I don't think I can leave.'

She considers her own drink. 'I went and saw my old boss today.'

'And?'

'I think I got Tarquin killed.'

That lifts his eyes. 'You said that yesterday. I don't get it; how could you be responsible?'

So she tells him of reporting the passwords, of her reprieve, of how she had thought it inconsequential, even fortunate. Of how she had thought, then and for the next five years, that he had evaded capture, was living abroad with his millions. And how, in retrospect, reporting him had seemed a good thing, allowing her to escape retribution, unlike Zelda Forshaw. She tells him all of that and then, hanging her head, she tells him how Tarquin being a cop changes everything. That reporting his use of her passwords might have eventually cleared her, but it could have condemned him. She looks Martin in the eye, as if addressing a jury. 'I think I alerted them. I think I got him killed.'

She watches his reaction, the emotional weather moving across his face: sympathy, affection and disquiet, where there could so easily be condemnation, accusation and revulsion. And she sees curiosity and intelligence and eagerness. She sees the man, and she sees the journalist. She sees him framing his words, careful not to upset her but probing all the same.

'Your old boss—what did he say?'

'She. Her name is Pam. She's the one who counselled me about the passwords after I filled in that questionnaire.'

'What did she say?'

'The questionnaire was conducted by a woman called Clarity Sparkes, from security. She interviewed me about it at the time and again after Tarquin disappeared. Pam told me Clarity died not long after Tarquin disappeared.'

And now she really can see the interest sparking in his eyes. 'How?'

She explains Clarity's lonely death, the overdose apparently out of character. But she doesn't mention the Turtle. Something prevents her. Shame, perhaps, or fear that her attempts to manipulate him will come to nothing. Or her desire to be like Martin, to pursue her own leads. Instead, she keeps it general, says that Pam thought a man called Harry Sweetwater was ultimately in charge.

Martin shakes his head. 'I can't see how you bear responsibility for anything. Molloy was an undercover cop, but he didn't trust you. He conspired to steal money from Mollisons, but he didn't tell you. He manipulated you in the worst possible way, did something similar with Zelda Forshaw.' He picks up his glass. 'Despite being married the whole time.' He takes a slug of whisky. 'You don't owe anything to anybody. Only to Liam.'

Irritation flickers to life within her. 'You want me to go back to Port Silver, but you intend to stay here.'

He shrugs, defensive. 'I owe it to Max to stay.'

'Well, I owe it to myself.'

The barman approaches to deliver a bowl of snacks. The peanuts have softened from being too long out of the packet, but the salt tastes good on her tongue. Martin orders another round of drinks, and by the time the man has returned to the bar, an equilibrium has been restored, the kind of minor truce that emerges when neither partner considers it worth pushing an issue.

'Don't you want to know what happened?' she asks.

'Of course,' he says. 'But I'm not sure how you can help.'

She takes a breath, a sip of her drink, another breath. This is the first time she's told anyone, trusted anyone. 'I knew Tarquin was probing the bank.'

'What?' His eyes are wide, lit by intelligence.

'I knew. And I helped him.'

'But you denied it.'

'Of course I denied it. I didn't want to go to prison.'

'Shit.' He looks around, a nervous gesture, as if to make sure no one can hear her. 'You knew about the money?'

'No, not that. And I didn't know he was a cop.'

'What then?'

She closes her eyes, not wanting to witness Martin's response. 'He took me into his confidence. Or so I thought. After we got back together, after the password thing, after we became engaged. He said he had stumbled across some irregularities in the bank, potentially criminal. He told me Harry Sweetwater and the board had authorised him to investigate, as a lawyer. He was lying, of course. I know that now.'

'What did you do?'

'Collected data for him.'

'What sort of data?'

'The trading records ran on Greenwich Mean Time. Universal time. Don't ask me why. At around midnight, London time—so ten or eleven in the morning in Sydney, depending on daylight savings—there would be a data dump of that day's trades. There was a five-minute window when I could see them.'

'You copied them?'

'No, that would have left an electronic trace, and we were worried we were being watched.'

'By whom?'

'There was a lot of CCTV.'

'So what did you do?'

'Each day's dump was protected by a thirty-six-character alpha-numeric identifying number.'

'You'd write them down?'

'I'd remember them.'

'Remember them? Thirty-six characters? Alpha-numeric? How could you do that?'

'Tarquin taught me mnemonics, at the casino.'

'The casino?'

'Counting cards.'

And for a moment, Martin says nothing, mouth open, at a loss for words. And then he laughs, shaking his head. 'Well, I'll be fucked.'

She feels herself starting to smile, his unexpected reaction a lift. But it's a passing sensation. 'I'm scared, Martin.'

'Why? You didn't do anything wrong. The guy was still an arsehole. He still manipulated you, lied to you. You didn't know about the money, what he was planning to do.'

'Zelda suspects I was involved. Others must too. Claus Vandenbruk. Mollisons must have had some reason to sack me.'

'Maybe. After they reset your passwords, did you share them with Molloy again?'

'No. He thought that was unwise.' She takes a drink. 'Do you think I should come clean and tell the cops? Montifore?'

He shakes his head without hesitation. 'No. No way. Right now, you're in the clear. Neither the police nor Mollisons found against you. If word gets out you were in the know, either you'll end up in prison like Zelda Forshaw or some arsehole with a gun will think you can lead him to ten million dollars.'

'I guess,' she says. And she smiles. He's on her side. Martin is on her side! And for a moment that's enough. She sips her drink, which is already tasting better. 'Do you believe in fate?' she asks.

'This again? We've had this conversation before.'

'You still say no?'

'That's right.'

'And karma?'

'I don't see what karma has to do with anything.'

'You don't think it strange? Down in Riversend, I tried to put Byron Swift behind me, but he wouldn't stay buried. You come along and I find out that Byron Swift wasn't his real name. And now it's happening again. Tarquin Molloy was someone else. How can that happen twice? I couldn't leave Riversend until I learnt who Byron was and why he did what he did. How can I return to Port Silver, to our life, unless I find out who Tarquin was, what he was really doing?'

And now she can see there is no longer any conflict on Martin's face; there is only concern. And love. She takes another slug of her brandy. She needs to tell him about the Turtle; maybe this is a good time.

But suddenly, the affection leaves his eyes, and his eyes leave hers. 'What the hell is that?'

She turns, sees what he is looking at: the television. The news. She recognises the reporter, Doug Thunkleton, remembering him from Riversend and Port Silver. He's standing in front of a police car, addressing the camera, his face communicating gravity, even with the sound down.

'That's Max's house,' says Martin as he leaps to his feet, rushes over to the barman. 'Hey, mate. The remote. Can you turn it up, please?'

The barman looks confused. On the screen is a slow zoom in to a page in the *Sydney Morning Herald*: TWO DEAD AT BELLEVUE HILL.

'Please. It's important.'

The barman retrieves a remote from beneath the bar, points it at the set and releases the volume. On the screen, Doug is walking up to a man fetching his mail from a suburban letterbox. His voiceover is deep and weighted with significance. *'And yet the neighbours know of no such investigation.'* The edit cuts to a close-up of the man.

'Yes, I read about it in the paper. It's terrible.'

'Have the police interviewed you?'

'No. Why would they?'

'You do live next door?'

'Yes. Of course.'

Before the man can add anything else, the shot returns to Doug. A second piece to camera. *'Police may say they are investigating the possibility of foul play, and yet almost two days after Max Fuller and Elizabeth Torbett died, homicide detectives have not even asked neighbours if they witnessed anything suspicious.'* There's an ominous pause, then the sign-off, full of confected portent. *'Doug Thunkleton. Ten News.'*

Martin turns to her, eyes wide. On the television, the news has moved on to a story about the government's budget plunging even further into the red.

'Bludger pollies. You want to watch?' asks the barman.

'No,' says Martin. 'No, thanks.' The barman happily mutes the prime minister in mid-spin. 'Good old Doug,' Martin says to her, grinning.

She can see the glint in his eye, his nostrils dilated as if to catch the scent of the story. He's not going back to Port Silver, she knows that. And neither is she.

THURSDAY

chapter eighteen

HE'S AWAKE EARLY, EYES OPEN, MIND CHURNING A GOOD HALF-HOUR BEFORE HIS alarm. Beside him Mandy is asleep, limbs splayed, covers in disarray, testimony to another restless night. Yet he imagines she has slept easier. She'd told him, trusted him with her secret: that she'd helped Molloy to steal his millions after all. Not knowingly, to be sure, but the police were unlikely to be sympathetic: she'd stolen confidential information, memorising the alpha-numeric codes. Technically, she's guilty of theft, maybe of fraud, or of being an accessory to fraud. And afterwards, when the police investigated, when the company did the same, she had lied, pleading ignorance of Molloy's activities. So the police could pursue her for obstructing the course of justice as well. And now she's a wealthy woman, the bank could possibly pursue her for reparations.

But for all of that, he can't help but sympathise with her. When Molloy disappeared, when she heard of the missing millions, who could blame her for denying any involvement? Surely her heartache was punishment enough? True, she had never confided in Martin, not even told him of her engagement to Molloy, but she's trusted him now. He looks at her sleeping form and tells himself it must remain their secret, too dangerous to share. It gives him extra motivation: he wants to find out who killed Max and why, to see them brought to justice; he wants to protect Mandy and make sure her complicity isn't discovered. And the story—surely at the end of all this is one hell of a story.

He gets out of bed, careful not to disturb her, and his mind, having made its decision, moves on. His yearning for coffee is profound, a physical need. Up on the coast, he might not brew a cup until mid-morning. Some days he'd go without altogether, not even missing it. But back here, in the city, in the midst of it, chasing a story, the craving is back. He's considering heading to Aldo's even before showering, when his phone rings.

It's an unknown number, but he answers nevertheless. Things are moving in the world and he wants to know what they are: the lassitude of Port Silver is gone.

'Martin Scarsden.'

'Good morning, Martin. It's Eileen Fuller.' The voice is no-nonsense, the inflections of grief absent.

'Eileen? How are you?'

'Cheesed off. That's what I am.'

'Right.' Martin can hear the irritation in her voice. 'How can I help?'

'Come and see me. I'm at my brother's place.' She gives him the address and terminates the call.

Martin showers and gets dressed, all the time thinking, his mind alight even without caffeine. He considers Eileen, who appeared shattered just two days ago, sitting outside the house containing the bodies of Max Fuller and Elizabeth Torbett, now demanding his attendance, sounding as hard-headed and focused as her late husband. What has happened to stir her? Doug Thunkleton's report maybe.

The apartment block in Elizabeth Bay looks plain from the street: three solid storeys of brown brick softened by a few Art Deco flourishes, fronted by a small, well-tended garden comprising lawn and rosebushes. Polished brass handrails lead up the short flight of steps to the entrance alcove. Six intercom buttons are mounted on a panel beside the door, one of the top flats apparently empty, with a CCTV camera hovering above. Martin buzzes apartment five, identifies himself to the disembodied voice, hears the wooden and etched-glass door click open.

Inside the entrance hall, an expensive-looking kilim leads across a polished hardwood floor; there's an oil painting in a gilt frame on the salmon-painted walls. There's money here; this is a common area. Martin eschews the lift and climbs the steps, solid oak with matching banisters, soft carpet held firm by brass runners. Apartment five is on the top floor. There is no apartment six: the door is still there, but a sign says TRADE. The door to apartment five opens before Martin can knock. There is a middle-aged Asian woman wearing an apron over a grey cotton dress. 'Mr Scarsden? Please come through.' The maid's accent is Singaporean; more refined than most university graduates.

Inside, she has him wait for a moment, giving him an opportunity to look around. The apartment is saved from opulence by its taste. The ceilings are high, the walls are white, the rooms are flooded by light, skylights augmenting windows. Martin searches for the seam where the two apartments have been joined but looks in vain; the entire interior must have been gutted and rebuilt. The furnishings are traditional but their arrangement is uncluttered, almost minimalist, the walls adorned with paintings by artists prominent enough for Martin to recognise some of them: John Brack, Fred Williams, Grace Cossington Smith. Everything is spotlessly clean, everything perfectly positioned, nothing out of place. Martin feels admiration for the maid's work ethic.

She returns and leads him through to the back of the apartment, bathed in the glowing light of Sydney Harbour. The entire top two-thirds of the front wall has been replaced by glass concertina windows, superficially similar to those at Aldo's, double-glazed and framed in cedar. This day they are closed, yet the space is flooded with the view, the harbour stretching out before him towards the heads. The apartment sits high above the shoreline, and the panorama is full of sky and sea: the world in cinemascope. There is more sun today and the wind has slackened, but it's still strong enough to animate the vista, propelling small clouds, their shadows scuttling across the ruffled harbour surface. He wants to open the window and reach out, check that it's real and not a projection, this other Sydney of water and sky and dynamic light. Even glassed off, it reaches back into the room itself, embracing Eileen Fuller as she sits in a wicker chair alongside a man who must be her brother, the two of them looking out into the azure abyss, their backs to Martin. There's a moment of silence, a pause, with only the harbour moving.

'Mr Scarsden,' announces the maid, breaking the tableau.

'Martin, thank you so much for coming,' says Eileen, rising to greet him, as does the man. Her handshake is firm, yet her eyes are red. Her hair is pulled back in a loose bun, a few stray hairs resisting containment. 'This is my brother Benjamin,' she says.

Martin shakes the man's hand and looks into his face, seeking and finding the family resemblance. The siblings are of similar size and age; Eileen wears little make-up and her hair is grey; her brother's face is more polished, the tan of a sailor or a sunbaker, and his hair appears to be dyed haystack blond, a professional job. Martin has words of praise for the apartment forming on his tongue as Eileen continues: 'Ben is married—was married—to Elizabeth Torbett.'

'I see,' says Martin. 'I'm so sorry for your loss. How terrible for the two of you.'

'Thank you,' says Benjamin. He too is showing the strain, slightly bent in his posture, deflated by the events of the week. The two must be in their early sixties; today, they look more elderly, as if old age has arrived precipitously during the night.

'Come, let us sit,' says Eileen, leading them away from the luminous view, back into the apartment where armchairs circle a polished stone coffee table and the world is more grounded.

'Something to drink?' asks Benjamin. 'Coffee? Tea? Something wet, something strong?'

'Coffee, thanks,' replies Martin, and the hovering maid departs.

Eileen cuts to the chase, speaking softly yet firmly. 'Martin, we are concerned. We are unsettled.' Her eyes are steady, grief replaced by determination.

'Why?'

'For starters, the paper. What is the *Herald* up to?'

'How do you mean?'

'The reporting of our spouses' deaths.'

'Eileen, you know I only work for the paper intermittently nowadays, more or less on commission. From home, not the office. I know that D'Arcy Defoe is writing a lengthy obituary.'

'Well, I'm glad Max won't be here to suffer it.'

Martin takes that on board. As far as he knows, Max always liked D'Arcy.

'Have you seen the coverage?' Eileen demands.

'Just a short piece yesterday by Bethanie Glass, and a segment on Channel Ten last night.'

'Precisely. That's it. At least Ten appreciated that something is amiss. Unlike the *Herald*. "No suspicious circumstances" and "lifelong friends"—what a steaming pile of horseshit, if you'll pardon the French.'

Martin smiles. So much for the fragility of the grief-stricken widow. 'Eileen, I think the police are deliberately holding back information, trying to flush out the killers. You can't blame Bethanie for that.'

'Of course I blame Bethanie for that. Max and Elizabeth couldn't stand each other, and I told her as much. It's one thing to omit and obfuscate, it's another to write deliberate untruths.'

'It was changed in the subediting,' Martin says in Bethanie's defence. 'She wrote a longer piece.'

'She told you that?'

'Yes.'

'Who ordered it cut?'

'She doesn't know.'

Eileen harrumphs as the maid returns, pushing an antique trolley bearing a silver service and small tower of petits fours. Like high tea at the Ritz. There is silence as the servant pours coffee and tea.

'Macaron?' inquires Benjamin.

'No, thanks,' says Martin.

The brother takes up where his sister has left off, albeit in a more measured tone. 'Martin, to be honest, we don't have a lot of confidence in the police. They don't seem to be doing very much.'

'Well, it's early days. They're probably waiting for the forensic report.'

'What? Before interviewing the neighbours, asking if they saw anything?' interjects Eileen. 'Balderdash. They're only getting around to it today, and only because we insisted.'

'You talked to Doug Thunkleton?'

'Yes, I did.'

'Right,' says Martin. Eileen talking to another news outlet, not the *Herald*. He takes a macaron after all. It explodes in his mouth like a sugar bomb, overly sweet. He sips some coffee to dilute it, burning his tongue. 'Eileen, what is it that you want to tell me?'

'To pull your finger out. Max treated you like a son; you owe it to him. Stir the possum, shake the tree. We can hardly rely on Channel Ten to fight our battles for us. I've spoken to Wellington Smith; he's more than happy to take your copy if the *Herald* doesn't want it.'

Martin can feel his hackles rising; much as he likes Eileen, he resents her interference. Wellington has been an enthusiastic champion of his books, but he owes the *Herald* first option on any features. He considers another macaron, decides against it, instead pouring some milk into his coffee to cool it. 'So what do you think really happened to your spouses?'

'They were murdered.'

'I know. So do the police.'

'So why are they sitting on their hands? Why is Channel Ten the only one with the guts to question the official line?'

'Okay. I want to help. Tell me: what were Max and the judge doing together? You say they couldn't stand each other. How come?'

'That's better, Martin. Much better,' says Eileen, appearing to relax a little. 'Now. Where to start? Max and Elizabeth never got on. They were too much alike in some regards, too different in others. Elizabeth thought the ultimate guarantor of democracy is an independent judiciary; Max believed a free and unfettered press is the bedrock. Elizabeth thought freedom was delivered from the top down; Max thought it grew from the bottom up. Elizabeth was a Tory; Max was a socialist. Elizabeth was a Mason; Max was Jewish. They were different in nearly every belief, or so they thought. Ben and I knew better: they were both obstinate buggers who wouldn't concede an inch to the other. We gave up years ago trying to negotiate a détente. We'd just catch up with each other and leave them out of it.'

Martin looks at Benjamin, who nods his agreement.

'Sorry. This is awkward, but I have to ask. The bodies. They presented as if they were, well, intimate.'

'Screwing,' says Eileen, distaste evident on her face.

'You said they couldn't stand each other?'

Eileen turns to her brother. 'Tell him.'

Benjamin shrugs. 'Elizabeth wasn't interested in men. Ours was a marriage of convenience. For both of us.'

Martin blinks. 'In this day and age?'

Benjamin smiles. 'Probably unnecessary even thirty-five years ago. But we became very fond of each other. Attached. Platonic. I could always trust Lizzie and she could always trust me.'

Martin nods. 'You've told this to the police?'

'Of course. As you say, they know the murder scene was a set-up—which makes their lack of progress even more mysterious.'

'So why were Max and Elizabeth together when they died?'

'That's the thing,' says Benjamin. 'They were thick as thieves for the three weeks before their deaths. Lizzie and I got back from a mid-winter break in Noosa about a month ago. She was fine, relaxed after the holiday. Shortly after, she came home from court very upset. Something had happened. Her being peeved and disagreeable wasn't out of character, but this was different. She was troubled more than angry. Morose. But she wouldn't confide in me.'

'Why not? Was that unusual?'

'No, unfortunately not,' he says, looking a little embarrassed. 'She was quite open about her private life, about all sorts of things, but never about her work. She was quite aloof when it came to the law. I'm an accountant, not a lawyer. She never discussed what occurred in court with me. Not like Max and Eileen. Max told my sister everything about the *Herald*; Lizzie told me nothing.'

Martin turns to Eileen. 'So what was Max working on? I spoke to him on the phone the night before his death. He said he was on to some huge story, some grand conspiracy.'

'I don't know.' For a moment her grief rises as if to reclaim her: a life together of trust and mutual support, and at the last he had kept his project from her.

Benjamin fills the silence, as if in consideration for his sister: 'One night we were having dinner, Elizabeth and I, eating in silence. She was still preoccupied by whatever it was that had happened at work. It was like you could hear the cogs grinding inside her skull. Eventually she asked me what I'd been doing during the day. It wasn't a real question, she didn't care about the answer; she was only asking out of politeness, to acknowledge I was there. I said I'd had lunch with Eileen. And it was like a little light turned on in her mind. After dinner she went to her study. Nothing strange about that. Next morning, before heading to court, she asked me for Max and Eileen's number. Next thing we know, the two of them, Lizzie and Max, are locked away together, working on something.'

'But on what?'

'We don't know. But the obvious conclusion is that Max was writing something based on what Elizabeth had learnt at work.'

'Okay, that makes sense. But you really have no idea what that might be?'

Now it's Eileen who answers. 'None. Sorry. They were very secretive about it. Perhaps they were trying to protect us.' Again, some emotion creeps into her voice, however fleetingly. 'It started getting on my wick. That's why I went to Bowral to visit friends. To get away.'

'Tell me,' says Martin, 'did Max work on a laptop or a desk computer?'

'He had a laptop,' says Eileen. 'It's missing.'

Martin blinks. 'Do the police know?'

'Of course.'

'Did he have a second laptop, one he kept at the *Herald*?'

'He did, but it won't do you any good. He wiped it.'

'He wiped it? How could you know that?'

'He told me. I called him from Bowral on Sunday night, but I couldn't get him on the landline. I got him on his mobile instead, and he said he'd been in to work to pick up some files and to wipe his laptop, that he wasn't comfortable leaving it there.'

'Did he say why?'

Again, Martin sees emotion shadow Eileen's face. 'He said he wasn't sure he could publish with the *Herald*. He wanted to ask your opinion of Wellington.'

'What?' To Martin it sounds unbelievable, heretical: the *Herald* was Max's life. 'What happened? Did he say?'

'No. He said he wanted to talk to you about it.'

'To me? Why?'

'He wouldn't tell me.'

Martin blinks. 'So everything was on his personal laptop. Do you know if he had a backup? A hard drive? Did he save things to the cloud?'

'If there were a hard drive, it's gone as well.' She shakes her head, as if in dismay. 'Just another question the police have failed to ask. But I know where he kept some of his passwords. I'll check to see if there's anything there.'

'Thanks, Eileen. It's essential we learn what they were working on.' He turns to Benjamin. The brother is holding a china cup, his little finger extended. 'Tell me: your wife was a Supreme Court judge—I'm guessing she was very well connected in the legal and political establishment.'

'I should say so.'

'So what could possibly disturb her so badly yet leave her unable to address it either through formal channels or through her establishment connections? Why would she feel her only outlet was to go to the media and cooperate with Max?'

'I can't imagine what it could possibly be. She was very discreet, very cautious. As I said, she would never discuss her cases with me. To speak to a journalist was anathema. She was a conservative: she believed in the system.'

Martin looks from one to the other. 'Did either of them ever mention a man called Tarquin Molloy?'

Benjamin shakes his head. 'No,' Eileen says, but there is a gleam in her eye. She thinks Martin knows something.

'I see. Well, if there is anything you recall or discover or even guess at, tell me. Without knowing what they were working on, I doubt I can find out any more than the police. Writing a piece on what really happened to them may be a lot more difficult than it sounds.'

'Do your best, Martin,' says Eileen. She reaches across the polished tabletop to place her hand on his. 'Like I said, stir the possum, shake the tree. Don't let those usurpers at the *Herald* bury this under their clickbait and frippery.'

Martin finishes his coffee and is about to stand when he remembers what Bethanie told him.

'What about Changi? Did either of them mention Changi?'

'Changi? As in Singapore Changi?' asks Benjamin.

'Yes. There was a Japanese prisoner-of-war camp there during the Second World War.'

'Thanks for that insight, Martin; our generation is well aware of its history,' says Eileen. 'What about it?'

'It's possible what they were working on may have had something to do with Changi. Neither of them have been there, I suppose?'

'No. We've been to Singapore but not the old prison. I don't even know if it's still there.' Eileen is adamant, but a cloud has come over Benjamin's face.

'What is it?' asks Martin.

'Elizabeth's father, Sir Talbot. He was there.'

'At Changi?'

'Yes. During the war. But he never talks about it.'

'You mean he's still alive?'

'Very much so.' Benjamin shakes his head. 'He's absolutely gutted by Elizabeth's death. She was always the apple of his eye.'

'Do you have a phone number for him?'

'Of course.'

When they've finished talking, the maid shows Martin out, as if to ensure he hasn't trousered the silverware. The door closes, the glowing light from the apartment is denied him, and the stairwell seems almost dingy, less impressive on the way down than it was on the way up.

Before he leaves he makes the most of the foyer's privacy, ringing Sir Talbot on the number Benjamin has given him. But the phone rings out, clicking through to a recording, the tape hiss audible, the judge clearing his throat, then the stilted message: *This is the Torbett residence. We can't come to the phone at this time. Please leave a message after the beep.'* There's an excruciatingly long delay, shuffling noises above the hiss, before the beep finally comes.

'Sir Talbot, this is Martin Scarsden from the *Sydney Morning Herald*. I am preparing an article on your daughter. Your son-in-law Benjamin has been most helpful and suggested I call you. I wonder if we might talk?' Martin leaves his mobile number, repeating it as slowly as he dares without sounding patronising.

chapter nineteen

MANDY'S PHONE RINGS. SHE'S AWARE OF IT, ITS INSISTENCE, BUT SHE'S UNABLE to rouse herself from the hotel bed to answer it. Instead, she drifts, between sleep and consciousness, floating in and out of dreams. She's in her memory palace, back in her mother's bookstore, but she's lost her way; the shelves all look the same. A man is following her, a man in a suit, a policeman. He's desperate to tell her something, something bad, but she can't hear him; can't hear him because she's trying to listen for Liam, trying to detect the boy's breath. He's here in the bookstore, but where is he? Where is Liam? Wasn't he here a moment ago? She's starting to panic. Where is he?

And then the dream is cut: the phone rings a second time and now she's instantly awake. She answers, thinking it might be Vern, ringing to alert her to some mishap. Or worse. But the voice on the other end of the line is neither the laidback tenor of

Martin's uncle nor the joyful falsetto of her son; instead, it's the baritone of authority, identifying itself as belonging to Detective Sergeant Claus Vandenbruk, police investigator. The man in the suit. He wants to meet, to come and see her. And now she truly is awake; she doesn't want him anywhere near the hotel, lest he really does carry unwelcome news. The fewer people who know the location of their bolthole, the better. She suggests they meet at a police station.

'A police station is not appropriate.'

'Why not?'

'I don't want people to see us together; they'll think you're still a person of interest. I don't want that. I don't want you to be put in unnecessary danger.'

That shakes her: Vandenbruk doesn't trust his fellow police. 'Why would I still be a person of interest?'

'Because you were engaged to Tarquin Molloy.'

'Morris Montifore says I'm not a suspect.'

'I didn't say you were.'

She bites her lip, thinking. Is it possible the investigator suspects she helped Tarquin and is coming to interrogate her? Was that why he came to her house in Port Silver? Whatever the case, she has little choice. 'Okay. I'll help if I can. Where do you want to meet?'

'Thank you,' he says. They agree on a rendezvous: a cafe near Central Station, in an hour.

Before showering, she calls Winifred Barbicombe. The lawyer is already back in Melbourne.

'I agree, you don't have much choice. You should talk to him,' says Winifred, when Mandy tells her of Vandenbruk's request to meet. 'But why not put it off until tomorrow? I'll fly back.'

'No. I want to hear what he has to say.'

There's a pause on the other end of the line. 'Why?'

'What do you mean, why? I want to know what's happening with the investigation. What happened to Tarquin.'

'But Mandalay, why? Seriously. You need to be extricating yourself from this situation, not getting more entangled. You should be leaving Sydney, going back to your boy and your life. None of this concerns you, not anymore.'

'If only that were true.'

'What do you mean?' The solicitor sounds unsure.

'I am involved, Winifred, whether I like it or not. And if Martin's here, I want to be with him.'

Now there is firmness in her solicitor's voice. 'That is no good reason. If Martin wants to return to journalism, that's up to him. But he's putting himself in danger and you with him.'

Mandy pauses before responding, not wanting to upset her most loyal supporter. 'Okay. I'll speak to Vandenbruk, but I won't tell him anything I haven't already told Montifore. Once that's out of the way, I'll talk to Martin about leaving.'

'I'm still not comfortable with you talking to him on your own,' Winifred says. 'And Mandy?'

'Yes?'

'Remember, your own interests come first.'

'Right.'

The cafe is subterranean, opening onto a pedestrian tunnel leading from Central Station, with a glass counter displaying fries, spring rolls and hash browns; the sort of place you might buy a takeaway coffee if you were in a rush, but not the sort of place you would choose to sit and eat if you had any other option. Claus Vandenbruk is seated out of sight around a tight little corner. If he's trying to meld in with the surroundings, it's working: he looks every bit as dingy as the cafe. The remains of an egg-and-bacon roll lie on a chipped plate before him; a trickle of yolk adorns a lapel of his suit. She takes a seat. He doesn't offer coffee; she's not sure she wants any.

'I've already been through all this with Morris Montifore,' she says.

'Really? I haven't seen a transcript.'

'Will he see one of this?' she counters.

Vandenbruk smiles, a crooked thing, out of kilter, possibly from lack of practice. 'No, I think we might leave this conversation off the record. Otherwise I'd want you to have your lawyer with you, for your own protection. And, as I say, I don't want to put you in danger.' He tries the smile again; it's no more convincing the second time around. Mandy concludes charm is not Vandenbruk's favoured approach; that wading in with a couple of phone books might be more his style. There is something bottled up about the man, some sort of inner tension. 'Do you remember me?'

'Not really. I'm told we met briefly at Riversend, but I don't recall much.'

'And in Port Silver? Last Sunday?'

It's Mandy's turn to shrug. 'I remember a man in a suit, an impression. And your name. You told me your name. But that's all. What happened?'

'I was knocked out.'

'And I was drugged.'

'Do you know who hit me?'

This gives her pause. Surely he knows; he must be testing her. 'Didn't Morris Montifore tell you?'

'He did. But I don't entirely trust Detective Inspector Montifore. He has his own priorities.'

'It was Zelda Forshaw. Or her accomplice.'

'Good. He was telling it straight.' He hesitates, then decides to clarify his priorities. 'Morris Montifore is a homicide detective, focused purely on murder, on finding who killed Tarquin Molloy. I'm not. I'm also a policeman, but I have been seconded to the ACIC. Do you know what that is?'

She does, but figures he'll be happier explaining it to her; he's that sort of man. 'Not really,' she says.

'We run criminal intelligence, investigating organised crime, drug syndicates, that sort of thing. We build up models of illegality, of criminal organisations, instead of acting after the fact, like most police.'

'I see. What has that to do with me?'

'Tarquin Molloy was working for the ACIC when he was killed.'

That surprises her; Vandenbruk offering up new information. 'Did he work for you? Is this personal?'

'No. Not for me.' Vandenbruk laughs, a strange and hollow sound. 'If he did, they wouldn't let me within a country mile of this case. Just the opposite. They need someone unconnected, someone with clean hands. I met him briefly a couple of times, but I was unaware he was undercover. I thought he was some sort of pretty-boy profiler. Which just goes to show how good he was.'

'Good at what?'

'At deceiving people.'

'What was his real name?'

Vandenbruk shakes his head, sighs. 'I can't tell you. You must know that.'

'So what do you need to know?'

'Molloy was working under deep cover. His identity was kept a closely guarded secret, even after he disappeared, just in case he was alive out there somewhere. That's what the brass told me when I was assigned to this investigation. Of course, it's just as likely that, at the time, they believed the story about him absconding with millions and wanted to keep it hushed up, to avoid embarrassment, questions in parliament, lurid reporting. But now we have confirmed he was murdered, that's changed things big time. Maybe he was killed for the money. Maybe for trying to steal it. But there's another possibility, one that has the ACIC exercised. It's possible that the whole story of the stolen money was a smokescreen, invented by the bank, Mollisons, as a way to cover their tracks, to explain his disappearance. It's possible he was killed for doing his job. That he found out something truly damaging. Something worth killing a cop for.'

'But Zelda went to prison over the money.'

'Yes, but all the evidence was provided by the bank. How could she stand against that?'

'What are you saying? That the bank suckered the police? Is that possible?'

'It's unlikely, but my job is to check every angle. So let me ask you this: at any time, did Molloy ever mention to you, his fiancé, that he intended to steal money from the bank?'

'No. Never.' She draws a breath, thinking. 'I do recall him saying on one instance that the bank's cybersecurity was lax and should be looked at, but he didn't express any intention to exploit that. But Zelda—I thought she confessed.'

'And I have no doubt she's telling the truth. That's what she believed happened.'

'It's why she kidnapped me. She thought I knew where the money might be.'

'And do you?'

'Of course not. I only became aware of the rumour that he had stolen the money after Tarquin disappeared.'

'You believed the rumour?'

'Everyone did, once they convicted Zelda.'

'The police investigated you at the time. What about the bank? They ran their own investigation, didn't they?'

She finds herself frowning: Vandenbruk must know all this. 'Yes. I was cleared.'

'They sacked you.'

'They sacked a lot of people.'

Vandenbruk smiles his unnatural smile, leans back, hands behind his head. The seam of his suit under his right armpit is beginning to give way. 'So you know of no evidence that Molloy ever actually took any money?'

'No. Only Zelda's conviction. As I said, I only heard the rumour after he disappeared.'

'And did Molloy, at any stage whatsoever, ever mention any other information he had found about Mollisons? Not about stealing the money, but evidence that the bank was in any way acting against the law?'

Mandy shakes her head, looks him in the eye. 'Evidence? No. Absolutely not. And I certainly had no idea he wasn't who he said he was.'

Vandenbruk drops his hands back on the table, smiles again before growing serious. 'Listen, I don't want to upset you, but this needs to be said. Tarquin Molloy was an exceptional undercover agent. I've come to appreciate that since I've been working on this case. He maintained a false identity for almost two years. He may well have infiltrated a significant criminal operation. But exceptional agents aren't typically exceptional human beings. Just the opposite. They're like spies. Ruthless. Manipulative. Amoral. Quite prepared to break the law, to break the normal rules of society, to live outside the acceptable. To bribe, to blackmail, to coerce. They become such exceptional liars that they live their lies, inhabit them. You understand what I am saying?'

'I do. You don't think I haven't thought about that? He manipulated me. He slept with me, told me he loved me, proposed marriage to me. And all the time he was sleeping with Zelda. And with his wife.'

'You know about that? That he was married?'

'Is it true? He had children?'

Vandenbruk shakes his head, sadness in his eyes. He doesn't speak for a time, and when he does, he doesn't answer the question. 'So all that time, you never suspected he was a police officer?'

'No.'

'And even now, looking back, do you know of anything he discovered about Mollisons?'

'No. I told you. I don't.'

'It's important,' Vandenbruk persists. Then he seems to change tack, staring past her into an imagined distance, as if considering something of great import, before returning his gaze to her. 'Can I take you into my confidence? Can I trust you?'

Mandy frowns. 'How do you mean?'

'I've been combing through the evidence. In the end, Zelda Forshaw confessed, you know that. She told the police all she knew, all about the help she gave Molloy. There's one problem: it wouldn't have been enough to give Molloy the access to steal all that money.'

'What are you saying?'

'He must have had other help. Others inside the bank with greater access.'

'Well, that counts me out. I had very low-level clearance.'

Vandenbruk smiles. 'Relax. I'm not accusing you. But you were engaged to him, knew him better than anyone. Can you remember anyone else he was close to, apart from you and Zelda? Sometimes, even the smallest memory can help, something that seems inconsequential in itself can help inform the larger picture.'

Mandy shrugs. 'No. He was always interested in my work, who I met, who did what. The office gossip. I thought he was just interested in me. It was refreshing. In retrospect, maybe he was trawling for information. But I was very junior. I didn't know anything, I didn't know anyone important, I had nothing to give him.'

'But you looked after the records of the traders. Rosters, holidays, and so on.'

'Yes. That was part of my job.'

'Did he ever ask about your co-workers? Their foibles, for example? You know, colleagues who liked to gamble, or who were having trouble with their bills, or who were in the closet, or who indulged in a bit of recreational drug use, that sort of thing?'

'It's possible. And if I'd heard something, I'm sure I would have told him. But, thinking back now, I can't recall anything like that.'

'Were you aware of any illicit drug use?'

'No. Not then.'

'Now?'

'I was told someone died from a drug overdose not long after we were made redundant.'

'Who was that?'

'Clarity Sparkes. She worked in security.'

'You didn't know her?'

'She interviewed me a couple of times. About my passwords and again when Tarquin disappeared. So I met her, but I can't say I really knew her.'

'And Tarquin? Was he close to her?'

Mandy shrugs. 'Not that I know.' Then she frowns, disturbed by the question. 'But she was young and quite pretty in her own way.'

'Who told you about her death?'

She recalls Winifred's advice: 'Remember, your own interests come first.' She doesn't want to tell Vandenbruk about Pam. Not Pam. 'I think it must have been Inspector Montifore.'

Vandenbruk moves on. 'So why do you think Tarquin Molloy was killed?'

She shrugs. 'I really don't know. He was an undercover cop; he manipulated me, he cultivated Zelda. But what he was really doing, what he was investigating, I have no idea. And the same with the money. The bank said it was missing, so we all believed it. Why wouldn't we?'

Vandenbruk nods. 'It probably was the money. We're double-checking the accounts, but it looks pretty solid. It's important we rule out all other possibilities, though.' He smiles. This time it doesn't look so forced. Maybe all the practice is starting to pay dividends.

But Mandy is not smiling. 'Do you think I helped get him killed?'

'By answering that security survey? By telling your boss about giving him the passwords?'

'Yes.'

Vandenbruk shakes his head. 'I doubt it. I really do. I don't think you had much to do with what happened at all.' He reaches out, gives her hand a reassuring pat. She allows it, even though she doesn't need his comfort. 'But rest assured, between Morris Montifore's team and mine, we will get to the bottom of this: Morris will find out who killed Tarquin Molloy and I'll find out why.'

Mandy feels as if the conversation is coming to an end, as if she is being discounted, a loose end tied up. 'You never did explain: why did you come to Port Silver to see me?'

Vandenbruk smiles again. 'To have this conversation. I didn't want anyone to know I spoke to you.'

'Why? Why the secrecy?'

The smile slides off the policeman's face. 'This is just between you and me, understood?'

'Of course,' says Mandy.

Vandenbruk frowns, choosing his words. 'We're working on the theory that Molloy was killed either because of the money, or because of his undercover work, or both. But there is another issue. How was he discovered? We have to look at all the possibilities.'

'Such as?'

'That someone on Molloy's team gave him up. That there was a leak in the ACIC, the police.'

'Are you serious?'

'We have to be sure. Bloody sure. That's why I didn't want anyone to know I was talking to you. I still don't.'

Mandy stares out past the counter at the bustling commuters, the uninterrupted flow of people. 'Can they monitor you? Tarquin's old colleagues, members of his team. Can they find out what you're doing?'

'Not easily. All the members of Molloy's team have been moved on.'

'As a precaution?'

'I think I've said enough.'

'Are they dangerous?'

He sighs, shrugs. 'I don't know. But let's not risk it.' He looks at the remains of his egg-and-bacon roll, forlorn on his plate. He picks it up, sinks his teeth into it. He wipes his hands on his pants, stands up, still chewing. 'I'm glad we've had this talk, away from curious eyes. I'm most grateful to you. You are free to go, free to leave Sydney. In fact, I'd strongly recommend it.'

chapter twenty

EVERYTHING ABOUT FLANAGAN MORT IS CRUMPLED: HIS CLOTHES, HIS FACE, HIS demeanour. The court reporter is among the last of a dying breed. Martin finds him in a bar full of suits—all of them in better repair than Flanagan's—called the Flynn, a couple of blocks from the courthouses of Phillip Street. He's inside, out of the wind, sitting on a lunchtime middy and studying the form guide so intently that he doesn't notice Martin approaching.

'Anything take your fancy?'

Flanagan looks up, his face breaking into a beaming smile. 'Martin, my boy! How the fuck are you?'

Martin shakes the old reporter's hand. 'All the better for seeing you, Flanno. What are you drinking?'

Flanagan looks forlornly at his beer. 'Don't really drink much nowadays. Just like to have one to keep me company. Same with the gee-gees.' He pushes the form guide away. 'But seeing as you're buying.' And he breaks into another grin.

Martin orders a couple of schooners at the bar, brings them back to the table, pulling up a stool. Flanagan drains his beer and accepts the larger glass with a welcoming chuckle. 'Good on you, Martin.'

'How's things, Flanno?'

'Shit, mate. Pure shit. You down here for Max's funeral?'

'Has a date been set?'

'Nah. Can't be long, though. Thought you might have heard.'

'Not yet.'

'So what brings you to the harbour city, if not that? I hope you're working up another true crime book. I fucking loved the first two.'

'Something like that.'

'You couldn't put in a good word for me with Wellington Smith, could you? He's your publisher, isn't he?'

'Sure. You writing something?'

'Not really. But the bean counters at the *Herald* will pension me off soon enough. Too old, too expensive. They'd prefer me to die, of course, but fuck that.'

'Cheer up, Flanno. You must know how highly they value you.'

'Nothing is valued anymore, let alone highly. Look what they did to you. Look what they did to Max. Look at this shithole of a bar—not a decent pub left within spitting distance of the courts.'

'Listen, Flanno. I need your help. You heard what happened to Max and Elizabeth Torbett?'

'Who hasn't? Word is it wasn't suicide. Far from it.'

'You're on the money there.' Martin takes a draught of his beer; it would taste better in summer. 'Here's the thing: they couldn't stand each other. Yet when they were killed, they were working closely. On a big story.'

'I know. Max told me about it.'

'Really?' Martin wasn't expecting this. 'What did he tell you?'

'Tell me? Nothing. Ask me? Plenty.'

'Like what?'

'If I'd heard any rumours of jury fixing, of judges taking bribes.'

'And had you?'

'No. It was news to me. Still is.' Abruptly, Flanagan looks forlorn. 'Forty years here, and I didn't even have the foggiest what he was on about. Says something about me, doesn't it? How much I really know, how much I don't, all the skulduggery that goes on under the wigs and beneath the gowns.' Martin is unsure what to say, is deciding whether he should be pushing for more information or offering moral support, when Flanagan continues. 'It has to be connected to the suppression order, but he hardly needed my help with that. Not if he was working with Elizabeth Torbett.'

Martin is alert. 'What suppression order?'

Flanagan looks surprised. 'Sorry. I thought you would've known about that. Everybody else does. I thought that protégé of yours, Bethanie Glass, would have told you.'

Martin lets the reference to the police reporter pass: tensions between crime and court reporters are nothing new, nor are intergenerational stresses between old male reporters and up-and-coming women. 'Tell me about it.'

'I can't; I'd be breaking the law.' And Flanno beams with mischief, raises his glass and downs a healthy chug of beer. 'Even the suppression order is suppressed. So don't go telling anyone I told you about it. It'll put both of us in the shit.'

'Scout's honour. You ready for another beer?'

'My shout.'

Martin has barely touched his drink, Flanagan has almost finished his. 'It's okay, Flanno. I can claim it.'

'You sure?'

'Absolutely.'

After Martin returns with a fresh schooner, the court reporter is ready to talk. 'Okay. The order is very broad and very vague. It simply prohibits the publication by any means of material that might compromise the reputation and standing of a Land and Environment Court judge.'

'The Land and Environment Court? Sounds like a bit of a sideshow.'

'Don't let a millennial hear you say that. They'll string you up by the balls. Crimes against wokefulness.'

'But does it carry much weight? The court?'

'Are you shitting me? It has the same standing and status as the New South Wales Supreme Court.'

'So what's the story with the judge?'

'The scuttlebutt is that there are compromising photographs. Sexual photographs.'

'Male or female judge?'

'Probably a bloke, but I can't say for certain.'

'Oh, come on. Lawyers gossip as much as journos. Someone must know.'

'The gossip's the problem. I've heard four different names already, and there are only half-a-dozen judges. Wouldn't be surprised if someone is running a book on it.'

Martin thinks it over. 'A big part of the court's work would be ruling on whether developments go ahead or not, right? That sort of thing?'

'That's it in a nutshell.'

'So, there's big money involved.'

'Shit, yeah.'

'Sounds like local government. Ripe for corruption.'

Flanno shakes his head. 'No. You're right about local councils; crooked as a dog's hind leg. Same with some of the cops. But not judges. If they wanted money, they'd have stayed barristers or corporate counsels. Moolah is not a motivator.'

'What is?'

'Status. Reputation. Service to the community.'

'Christ. You make them sound like saints.'

'Only compared to the rest of us.'

'Flanno, these photos. Has anyone seen them?'

'Not firsthand, not that I know of. It's only rumour, but what I've been told is that the photos have the judge going at it, dressed in kinky underwear. Wearing stockings and a suspender belt. Doing the business.' Flanagan starts to look concerned. 'You all right, Martin?'

Martin isn't: the description has sucked him back to the murder scene in Bellevue Hill, the bodies dressed in lingerie. He can see the gore, smell the blood, Max Fuller's bulging blue tongue, the yawning hole in the back of Elizabeth Torbett's head. 'Sorry. It's nothing.' He drinks some beer, as if to cleanse the taste from his mouth. 'But, tell me: the suppression order—you sure it's a Land and Environment Court justice?'

'Yeah, that's about the only fact we know for sure.'

'Is there any way to find out who the judge is?'

'I can ask about. But I can't promise you anything. As I said, it's like the Melbourne fucking Cup: everyone has a favourite.' Flanagan drains his beer. 'Sorry. I've got to be getting back. There's a fascinating case involving a celebrity chef, a stolen recipe and an adulterated container of garam masala.'

chapter twenty-one

THE DOUGHNUT SHOP IS OVERHEATED AND OPPRESSIVE, THE AIR SICKLY WITH THE odour of fat, sugar and broken resolutions. Mandy checks the time. He's late. Will he come? Or will he call her bluff, stay away?

Then she sees him, waddling across the street, same clothes, same as always. He pushes the door open, sees her, sidles over, sits down. He seems smug, none of the jitters of yesterday. He doesn't bother with a greeting. 'So what colour am I eating today?'

'Tartan.'

He smiles, a leery expression, like a Halloween mask. 'That's new.'

Suddenly she wants this over. 'Passwords,' she says, making it a statement, not a question.

'Here,' he says, handing over a piece of folded paper.

She unfolds it, examines it. Three usernames, three passwords. She starts to stand.

'It won't get you far. Nowhere near the financial systems he penetrated. Nowhere near the money, if that's what you're after.'

'Right,' she says, frowning. 'More like my old clearance level.'

'Exactly. But I have something better. Something much more useful. You should sit.'

She hesitates, but does what she's told. 'What?'

'Do you have your phone with you?'

'Of course. Why?'

'I have a video for you.'

'What's on it?'

'You can look on mine.'

He stands, shimmies around the table and sits next to her. She can sense his body: its closeness, its heat, its smells. Not rank, not body odour, surprising in a creature that sweats so profusely. No, not the smell of hard work and honest labour, but something more insidious: something sweet, as if the doughnut icing is being extruded through his skin.

But her unease is forgotten the moment she sees his phone. There's a video, full-screen, instantly recognisable: a wide angle looking down from ceiling height to the trading-room floor at Mollisons. Closed-circuit TV. He points at a figure walking into view. It's Tarquin Molloy. 'There he is, your young copper. You see? Walking through the office as if there's no tomorrow. Which, of course, there wasn't.' And he emits a syrupy snicker.

Her sense of discomfort reasserts itself. What has happened to the Turtle that he can now laugh, appear relaxed? Where is the panicked jellyfish of the day before? But again, the video draws her attention, the details difficult to discern on the small screen. 'What's he doing?' she asks.

'He's stopped. Recognise where?'

'My desk.'

'Logging on to your computer.'

The hair on the back of her neck rises. Tarquin at her desk?

'Your desk, your computer. That day. Lucky for us.'

'Lucky? How?'

'Because you had your own camera.' The Turtle closes the video, opens another one. This one is directly above the desk, looking down. Mandy squirms. How often did this horrible man sit in his cave of monitors, his Turtle shell, leering at her?

'Watch,' he says.

She has no choice, the vision is compelling her to bear witness. She can see Tarquin typing, quick short bursts.

'What's he doing?'

'Entering your passwords, of course,' says the Turtle.

'The ones I gave him?'

'Yes. To get into the system.'

'And the ones you gave him?'

'He uses all sorts of passwords from all sorts of sources. If you play it frame by frame, you can make them out.' The Turtle cuts the video off, switches back to the original wide-angle view. 'He was there a good twenty minutes. Knew exactly what he wanted and how to get it.'

'Do you know what he took?'

'Ten million dollars, or close enough. Transferred it out, there and then. Middle of the day, middle of the floor. He had balls, I'll give him that.'

'So it's true? He stole the money?'

'It's true all right.'

Mandy wants to ask more, but the Turtle has restarted the video and the screen has her. Tarquin is standing, looking around him. He checks the screen, seems to shut the computer down. Then he bends towards the machine.

'He's ejecting a flash drive,' says the Turtle. 'It contained the software he used to steal the money, exploiting the information and passwords he got from you and from me and from Zelda Forshaw and from God knows who else.'

Mandy can no longer move; she's transfixed. She watches as the undercover cop stops to talk with someone, leaning over a cubicle wall. It looks like Raff, one of the chief traders. Then he saunters away. She can see the confidence in his gait, full of exuberance, the jauntiness of an Olympic track star.

She watches as he enters the lift. She's about to speak, when another figure enters the shot: a tall man with long greasy hair and an elegant suit inserts his hand, preventing the doors from closing. The man enters the lift. Mandy's breath fails her. It's Henry Livingstone. She finds it hard to speak, but speak she must, voice tremulous. 'Is there more?'

'No. No cameras in the lift. It must have gone to the basement, otherwise another camera would have picked them up. No cameras down there either.'

'The videos. Can I get copies?'

'Yes. But only if you promise that's the end of it. No more approaching me. Ever. No telling anyone where you got them from. Nothing about me at all. Or else.'

'Or else what?'

'I have other videos. Other cameras.'

'What does that mean?'

'You and Tarquin. Going at it. In the storeroom, in the boardroom.'

'Bullshit.'

'You're public property, lady. You think the tabloids or one of those trashy current affairs programs wouldn't want a piece of them? I reckon they'd pay big dollars. After what happened out west and up on the coast. What did they call you? The Suicide Blonde. You, having it off with the dead cop. They'd lap it up. You'd break the internet.'

'Bullshit. They couldn't publish them.'

'They would certainly report their existence. Use still frames and pixilation. Great publicity: I could auction the originals on the dark web.'

She feels sick to the stomach. 'What's the point of giving this to me if I can't show the police?'

'You can show them. You just can't tell them I gave it to you. That's the deal, understand? You don't tell the police, you don't tell that boyfriend of yours, you don't tell anyone. Otherwise you and Molloy go viral.'

'Right. Yes. Of course.' Now she gets it; he's using her as a conduit.

'What's your email address? I'll send it to you.'

She hesitates. Does she really want to give him her email? 'Why don't you just AirDrop it to me?'

'Sure. We can do that. And then we're done, you got me? Otherwise we both crash and burn.'

'Agreed.'

A few minutes later she's back in the fresh air, filling her lungs, but there is no relief, no cleansing, as if the Turtle has pulled her down to his level. She knows what happens to sex tapes: they spread across the internet like a Blue Mountains bushfire: flaring and spotting and destroying lives. But unlike bushfires, they never truly go out; there's no cloudburst big enough to extinguish them. They smoulder deep down, like mallee roots or peat bogs, always threatening to burst into life, wreak new havoc. They'll be everywhere, and they'll still be everywhere as Liam enters preschool, and they'll still be there when he catches the bus to high school, and they'll still be there when he's an adult. They'll still be there when she and Martin are old and grey and decrepit. She needs to give the police the video, but she needs to tell them she received it anonymously.

She finds herself on the platform at the light rail stop, deep within a sandstone cutting, where once she would catch her tram home from work. She has stumbled there by instinct, following her old route without realising it. She takes a seat, watches a tram arrive on its way from Dulwich Hill to Central, disgorge one set of passengers and ingest a new load, and leave again. She doesn't rise, doesn't attempt to board it, she just stares.

The video. The Turtle knows she's taking it to the police, must know she'll show it to Martin. He must know that he risks identification, interrogation. So why give it to her? Why insist on anonymity? He could always claim to have shown his superiors—Clarity Sparkes, possibly Harry Sweetwater—back when Tarquin first disappeared. Maybe he did, at that. Yes, she concludes, he probably did. They would have slowed it down, established the passwords Tarquin had used. Zelda's and whoever else was implicated. But not hers; Tarquin hadn't asked for her replacement passwords. He'd used her desk, but not her log in. It makes sense: that's what exonerated her. They must have seen it.

She thinks it through. If the video had gone up the line, helped management to accuse Tarquin of larceny, what then? They brought criminal charges against Zelda Forshaw. The video was critical evidence, him typing in her passwords. Surely the police must have seen it. But if she could identify the man entering the lift as Henry Livingstone then surely the police would have done the same, back then. The man was notorious; Montifore had even known his brand of hair oil. The thought makes her shiver: the police had seen Livingstone, a convicted killer, enter the lift, yet the accepted wisdom was that Tarquin had got away with millions and fled overseas. Could Vandenbruk be right? Could the police and the ACIC be complicit? *Jesus.*

Another tram eases in to the platform, heading in the opposite direction. Still she remains seated, still she stares. She can feel her imagination starting to career away from her, her own runaway tram. She tries to stop it, tries to organise her thoughts. The video. It all comes down to the video.

She pulls out her phone, finds the clip, plays it. The date stamp identifies it as the last day Molloy was seen alive, the Friday when she was already on the Gold Coast. The stamp could be fabricated, she knows that, but she doesn't doubt its authenticity: she knows she's watching Tarquin Molloy's last moments of freedom. Of life. The thought sends a shiver through her. Again she watches him saunter across the trading floor, moving to her desk, as if nothing could be more natural. She'd never known that, that he'd used her desk. Why? Why use her desk but not her log in and passwords? Was he trying to implicate her or protect her? Maybe neither. Perhaps he needed a computer on the trading floor, one accessing the same servers as the traders. Was that why he'd lured her to the Gold Coast, to make sure her computer was free? Was it that simple?

She watches the video. Tarquin reaches down by the side of the desk. That must be him inserting the flash drive. It makes her remember: the drives on her computer were disabled, a security measure. So how had Tarquin managed to use it? He must have had help. Or the computer skills to activate the drive. Training. The police would have been able to supply that. She watches the screen. His confidence is high; he doesn't even look around to see if anyone is watching him. And now he is tapping at the keyboard, although the camera is too far away to identify what he is typing.

She pauses the video, overcome by a new realisation. This is the wide-angle version, showing much of the room. The Turtle has not given her the close-up. Of course not; he doesn't want anyone to know about the spy camera he installed above her desk. And he doesn't want her to slow it down and work out what passwords Tarquin did use. She pauses the video and unfolds the slip of paper he gave her again. Passwords all right, but probably of little use.

She starts the video again. It runs for twenty minutes, with Tarquin typing for less than a minute here, less than a minute later, and again a third time. At one point he leaves the desk altogether, walking away, coming back after almost ten minutes with a coffee, standing there, chatting to a person or two, then logging off from the computer and removing the flash drive. Again she watches the ending, again he leans over Raff's cubicle, talking briefly. Again he heads to the lift, jaunty, without a care in the world.

And again, at the last moment: Henry Livingstone. Montifore described Livingstone and Spitt as hard men, as killers. How could such a notorious criminal even come to be on the trading-room floor? Not by chance. There was swipe card security in the lobby, again at the trading-room entrance. Maybe he had stolen a card, like he'd stolen police ID. No, that's unlikely. He must have been invited in. *Christ*. Invited in to confront Tarquin, to wait for the lift so there were no witnesses on the trading floor. Into the lift, to the basement, away from the CCTV. Again, she shivers.

Another tram enters the station, heading towards the city. And this time she stands, boards it. She feels the need to ride, to set events in motion. If the Turtle has worked through the implications of taking the video to the police, she needs to do the same. She needs to work out what to tell Montifore. And what not.

chapter twenty-two

MARTIN IS STILL STANDING ON THE FOOTPATH OUTSIDE THE BAR WHEN HIS PHONE rings. It displays a number, a landline, but no identification.

'Martin Scarsden,' he answers gruffly.

'It's Talbot Torbett here. You rang me, I believe.'

The father. 'I did. Thanks for returning my call. I wonder if I might talk to you about Elizabeth?'

'Hmmm. Yes. I think we might manage that. Can you come to my home? Centennial Park.'

'Of course.'

'Good. You can come straight away, if it's convenient.'

'It is.'

The judge gives him the address and finishes the call with no further discussion.

Martin hails a cab, replaying the short conversation in his mind. Is he mistaken, or did the old judge sound eager to talk?

*

The house in Centennial Park is modest in its dimensions and impressive in its status. Having spent twenty years based in Sydney, Martin is not immune to the city's obsession with real estate, even if he's less fixated than most. He's long been aware of this enclave, a couple of blocks of houses between the green expanses of Moore and Centennial parks, but he's never had a reason to visit it. There is no through traffic; it's an island of wealth, surrounded by parkland. The cab drops Martin off. There are security gates protecting a circular driveway, but a pedestrian gate is open wide. Inside, there are palm trees and a couple of massive Moreton Bay fig trees, leaves rustling in the wind. A big BMW sits in the drive, polished to a gleaming black, the sort of car that the owner doesn't drive but rides in the back. The house is made of sandstone, brick and render, a century old, a melange of Art Deco and something older and more ambitious. It's sited on a slight rise, gifting it an imposing air beyond its two storeys.

The door is opened by a man too well-dressed to be a butler. The suit is immaculate, the tie from somewhere a lot more expensive than Ichiban Computers and Scarvery. 'I'm Titus Torbett,' the man says, offering his hand. 'Elizabeth's brother.'

'Martin Scarsden,' he replies, covering his surprise. He wasn't aware there was a brother. 'I'm sorry for your loss.'

The handshake is unremarkable, neither pretentious in its firmness nor disappointing in its limpness. A Goldilocks handshake. The same can be said for the man himself: his face is neither handsome nor ugly, his hair neither thick nor thin, his physique neither impressive nor dissolute. Martin places him at about sixty, a professional in his prime.

'Thank you. Before you come in, would you mind? Father will be ninety-eight this year.' He hands Martin some alcohol-based sanitiser.

'Of course,' says Martin, cleansing his hands.

'Thank you. Father won't be a moment.'

Titus leads him into a modest lounge and leaves him there, a comfortable room lacking ostentatious displays of affluence or influence. It's furnished with aged chesterfields. A bay window overlooks a rose garden, the breeze animating a large tree. The paintings are the giveaway; one looks suspiciously like a Drysdale, another like a Nolan. On the mantelpiece are a couple of fading family photographs. There's one from way back, maybe the 1970s, Sir Talbot and his wife, plus the two children, Elizabeth and Titus, the elder brother with a protective arm around his younger sister. There's not a single indication of Sir Talbot's lofty career: not an oil painting of him in his robes, no photos of him with prime ministers, no images of him receiving honorary doctorates. Martin pulls out his phone and takes a snap of the family pictures. Then he takes a seat in a large leather armchair, before realising that he's subconsciously chosen the correct position: the chair opposite is clearly Sir Talbot's favourite, worn and lopsided from use, close to the window for light and the view over the gardens, sandwiched between occasional tables stacked high with books. One carries all four volumes of Churchill's *A History of the English-Speaking Peoples*. He remembers it from university: well-written, if self-serving.

He's sitting there when his phone pings. It's a message from Mandy. *See attached*. She's sent him a video. But before he can open it, Sir Talbot enters the room. Martin has been expecting some sort of invalid, wheeled in by Titus, not this spry old man, rake-thin and only slightly stooped, with a mop of white hair, as if a teenager has been photoshopped into an old man. He's rather small; Martin had somehow thought that High Court judges should carry significant heft. Maybe he once did. Martin stands and shakes the man's hand, feeling the bones through the thin skin, like chicken bones in a paper bag.

'Martin, forgive me for keeping you waiting. I wanted to reassure Titus I'm happy talking to you.' He eases himself into his chair. 'He hides it well, but he's devastated by Lizzie's death. We all are. He's moved home for a day or two, set himself up in the dining room. Work can be a great salve at such times.' The old man's blue eyes are unnaturally clear. He's not wearing glasses and there are none on the side tables. Martin wonders about lasers or cataract surgery. But now that he looks more closely, the indications of great age are easier to see. The judge's nose and ears have grown over-large, the earlobes appear to have run like old glass, the eyebrows have taken on a life of their own.

'You're an admirer of Churchill's, I see,' Martin says, making conversation.

'Not at all. Pompous windbag. He gave us Gallipoli. And Singapore. Thanks to him I spent three years in and around Changi.'

'I heard you were there. It's why I wanted to talk to you.'

'Long time ago now, son. Why the interest?'

'I was very close to Max Fuller. I believe he and your daughter were working on a big story when they were murdered. It may have been connected to Changi.'

The old man smiles. It strikes Martin as an odd response. 'You think they were murdered?'

'I do.'

'And you're trying to find out why?'

'That's right.'

Again the smile, teeth unnaturally well aligned. 'That's good enough for me.' The voice is reedy, but Martin can detect an underlying strength. 'Do you know why I agreed to see you at such short notice?'

'Not really.'

'Right. Do you have a notepad and dictaphone with you? No? Here, use these. There's a fresh tape and batteries.' He hands Martin an old-fashioned micro-cassette recorder, a museum piece, a fresh notebook and pen. 'Ready to start?'

'Of course,' says Martin, covering his surprise. He'd come prepared to ask questions, uncertain how to frame them to a man he'd imagined incapacitated by age and grief. Instead the old judge is taking the lead. Martin starts the cassette recording, duplicating the function with an app on his phone.

'Good. Do you know anything of the big exposé my daughter was working on? What it was about?'

'No.'

'Well, let's start at the beginning then. Have you ever in your journalistic exploits come across an organisation called the Mess?'

'No. What is it?'

'It's why Elizabeth was working with Max Fuller. So listen.' The old judge pauses for a moment, perhaps considering how to get to the core of his subject. 'It started in Changi, almost by accident. We were just trying to survive, to keep body and soul together, and to keep our spirits up. I was just nineteen when Singapore fell. I'd only been there two weeks. I was a lieutenant, brittle, callow, ostensibly responsible for older and tougher men, men who had wives and children and experience. Imprisonment was hard, but not so hard for me, being an officer, albeit a junior one. The Japanese cared about such hierarchies. I became a firm friend of a young fellow my own age, Joe Murphy. It's a long story, largely irrelevant. The important thing is that we survived, partly because Joe and I and a couple of others looked out for each other. We were mates. Good mates. It's an overused expression these days, bowdlerised by advertising and politicians, but that's what we were: mates. Bonded for life. You won't understand, but you don't have to.

'The war ended, we were repatriated. I was keen to restart my life: I had escaped the trauma of the railway and the other atrocities, unlike so many of those poor devils. I went back to Sydney University, back to law. So did Joe Murphy. Life was full of promise. It was easy for me. My family was well off. A large property up in New England, cousins in the law. Joe relied on the Repatriation Board: it paid his fees and a living allowance, and he worked nights at a knitting mill in Chippendale. Then Joe came across a young bloke called Barry Diamond, a chap we had known briefly in Changi. Barry had lied about his age to enlist, got to Singapore in time for the Japs to overrun us. He was very young, very scared, no weight on him even before the privations began. Later, he suffered terribly on the railroad; he copped dysentery and malaria. We lost track of him, until Joe found him down and out, not far from Chippendale, down the road in Redfern. We took him out, gave him a decent feed. A week or two later, a few of us held a dinner in his honour, raised a few pounds to help him out. And that's how it started. The Mess.'

'Why was it called "the Mess"?'

'Honestly, I couldn't tell you. It was connected with Changi and the war. The whole defence of the Malaya Peninsula was a mess, Changi was a mess, the officers and men messed in together. Strange, isn't it? I was one of the founders, but I don't know. It's just what we came to call ourselves.'

'Sounds pretty innocuous to me,' says Martin, unsure of where this is leading.

'It was. Absolutely. It became a regular thing. We were different, you see, us ex-servicemen. We didn't really fit into university life. There weren't that many of us, and we were a bit older, of course, and we'd experienced all sorts of things. Some were traumatised by the war, had a hard time coping with the carefree life of their fellow students. Not me and Joe: we were the opposite. We'd lost years at the war, in the camps. We were hungry for life, eager to make up for lost time and not easily daunted. We'd stared down Jap guards; a university lecturer was unlikely to intimidate us. Anyway, the dining became a monthly event. Barry became a member, and we assisted him. Fed him up and got him healthy, found him somewhere to live, helped him through the last few years of school, got him a job. Later we got him into uni. We did good, like our own private RSL, our own chapter of the Freemasons. I reckon Joe and I and a couple of the others felt something akin to what they now call survivor guilt—we'd got off so lightly—but it didn't feel like that at the time. Anyway, it felt good to support others.

'Somewhere along the line, one of the chaps had the idea of forming a secret society, of formalising it. He'd heard that American universities had these clandestine clubs, so that's what we called ourselves. But we only had one secret: that we existed. There were no rituals, no inductions and no clubhouses. None of that palaver. We simply existed to have dinner once a month and occasionally give a helping hand to poor fellows less fortunate than ourselves.'

'Very noble,' says Martin. 'So the Mess became a dining club, a secret one. But a lot of it was helping yourselves, wasn't it? Isn't that what secret societies do?'

'Oh, yes. No getting away from that.'

'So why were Max Fuller and your daughter working on an exposé? What was there to expose? And why were they killed? I don't follow.'

'I'm not sure I can shed that much light on Elizabeth and Max Fuller, but let me continue. The Mess outlived university, prospered. The dinners were held on the first Tuesday of the month. We dressed formally. The membership became restricted to just thirty members. Every now and then someone would leave, usually because they moved interstate or overseas, sometimes because they got sick of us, and we'd replace them.'

'Women?'

'No. Not initially. That didn't change until the seventies.'

'I see.'

'Our first explicit rule, that the Mess be kept secret, was joined by a second implicit rule: no member could refuse any reasonable request for assistance from another, provided it was legal and provided it didn't harm anyone.'

'An influence exchange?'

'That's one way of putting it. And as the decades passed, the membership changed. As Joe and Barry and I progressed in our careers, so did the remaining original members. Within ten years, by the late fifties, new members were always up-and-comers, movers and shakers. It seemed natural: we were all on the same trajectories, all riding the wave of the new Australian prosperity.'

'Barry Diamond? Wasn't he some sort of politician?'

'State attorney-general. Appointed me to the Supreme Court.'

Martin blinks. 'I see.'

The judge smiles grimly. 'I think you might.'

'So who else was a member? Can you reveal names?'

'All in good time, Mr Scarsden. In the mid-seventies I was appointed to the High Court, and I resigned from the Mess. I thought membership of a secret society was incompatible with such a high office.'

'But wasn't it just a dining club?'

'For many of us it was. Primarily. But it was evolving. I feared that sometime in the future my membership could come back to bite me. I want to be absolutely clear here: I had never done anything illegal, I had never done anything to be ashamed of as a member. Quite the contrary, we had done much that was good.'

'So you're saying that you haven't had anything to do with the Mess for almost fifty years? How do you know it's even still in existence?'

'Because in the eighties I called in one last favour from Joe and Barry. Membership, first for Titus and then for Elizabeth.'

Martin pauses, trying to catch up with his own cascading thoughts. Max researching Changi, Elizabeth disturbed by information from the courts, Elizabeth a member of the Mess, the two of them collaborating on a big exposé.

'Did Elizabeth talk about it much?'

'No. Titus didn't stay a member for long. It became a sore point within the family, so we never discussed it—until recently, when she confided in me. She said it had gone too far. It needed to be cleared out. "Lanced" was the word she used.'

'What did she mean? Did she elaborate?'

'No. She said she wanted to keep me out of it. But we did spend an afternoon talking about its origins. In this room. I sat here, she sat where you are. I told her a story very similar to that I've just told you. The origins of the Mess.'

'When was this?'

'Just a couple of weeks ago.'

'So you think that was what she was collaborating on with Max Fuller? Something to do with the Mess?'

'Yes. That's what I suspect.'

'Why do you think your daughter was killed?'

The old man swallows and Martin catches a glimpse of the distress her death has visited upon him. But there is little emotion as he speaks, the forensic mind in control. 'I think she upset powerful people connected to the Mess. But I have no idea who, and I have no idea how, and I have no evidence. That's why I'm talking to you. Titus and Benjamin aren't satisfied with the police investigation. Nor is Max Fuller's widow, Eileen, as you may be aware.' And the old man smiles in a self-deprecating way, looking out the window as he speaks, his voice growing more wistful. 'All those years, all that accumulated influence: it melts away, you know. There was a time I could call up ministers, prime ministers, police commissioners. But it's more than four decades since I joined the High Court and left the Mess behind, more than twenty-five years since I retired. I wouldn't even know who to call, now that Lizzie is dead. It's gone, all the connections, all the influence. Remember that, Martin: when all the sound and fury is over, when they've given you the gold watch and pensioned you off, all that is left is family.'

Martin looks at the old man, wonders why he doesn't feel more sympathetic. 'What you've told me is intriguing, but I'm not sure why you're telling me this instead of the police. I'm not sure what I can do.'

Sir Talbot's eyes narrow, a squint somehow signifying insight. 'I don't have too much faith in the police. The Mess has influence, and if it's turned rotten, then who knows how far its tentacles might reach.'

'Understood. So can you tell me the names of the members? You said there were about thirty.'

The judge shakes his head, a wan smile on his lips. 'Not really, not after nearly fifty years. The people I knew are all dead. And, as I said, it's not something we talked about within the family.'

'No one?'

'Titus might know more. He's still out there, out in the world.' The judge gazes through the bay window as if at something fondly remembered, something denied him. 'There was Lizzie and Titus, and Clarence O'Toole—another young lawyer, a classmate of Lizzie. His father was a member. We signed them up together. He might still be a member for all I know.'

'Do you know where I might find him?'

'Through the courts, I'd imagine.'

'He's still a lawyer?'

'A judge. Land and Environment Court.'

chapter twenty-three

MANDY SENDS THE VIDEO TO MARTIN, HOLDING HER BREATH AS SHE MESSAGES him. He'll want to know what it is, where she got it.

Her phone rings. Just like him: so focused, so quick on the uptake. 'Martin.'

'Hello? Is that Mandy?' The voice is female.

'Yes. Can I help you? Who is this?'

'It's Pam.'

'Pam? Is everything all right?'

'Yes. Champion. I've just been doing a bit of research on the internet. You know, seeing what I might find out about Mollisons. What Tarquin might have been looking into.'

'On the internet?' Mandy can't keep the incredulity from her voice. She likes her old boss—Pam was always supportive, practically the only one who was, and she always meant well. So Mandy doesn't want to insult her, but the idea of using Google to find

Tarquin's killer is ludicrous. She needs to finish the conversation so Martin can get through.

'Well, not just the internet,' Pam continues, seemingly unaware of Mandy's scepticism. 'Zelda Forshaw has been helping.'

'Zelda? You're joking.'

'I know you don't like her.'

'Don't like her? Are you kidding? She kidnapped me. Tied me up and gagged me.'

'But, Mandy, listen. She went to prison—but if Tarquin was a cop, if he never stole the money, she might be innocent.'

'She confessed. She was convicted.'

'Of what? Conspiracy to defraud? But there can't be a conspiracy if one of the parties isn't conspiring, if Tarquin was simply using the illusion of money to win her over.'

Mandy can't believe she's having this conversation. 'Pam, I know you see the best in everyone, but trust me, Zelda is interested in one thing and one thing only: getting her hands on the money.'

'Too right she is. But not Tarquin's money.'

'Sorry?'

'If there was no money, if there was no theft, if Tarquin never stole it or intended to steal it, then she can't be guilty. There was no conspiracy to defraud.'

Mandy thinks of the trading data, the thirty-six-character alphanumeric codes she committed to memory and conveyed to Tarquin. And she thinks of the Turtle, his confirmation that millions were missing. 'I don't follow.'

'She deserves compensation. For false imprisonment, for loss of earnings, for damage to reputation. The lists goes on. She hasn't worked as an accountant since. She could get millions.'

Mandy can't help laughing: Zelda the gold-digger has found a richer vein. 'You trust her?'

'I trust her to pursue her own self-interest. And I tell you, she's good.'

'At what?'

'At being an accountant. We've worked it out.'

'Worked out what?'

'How Mollisons works. Who owns it. Who controls it, anyway.'

'Why would I be interested in that?'

'Because it might help us to work out what Tarquin was investigating. Now, should I come to you, or do you want to come here?'

An hour later Mandy is in the State Library, waiting for Pam in the reading room in the new wing, next to a wall of glass, where it feels as if a quiet conversation won't be frowned upon. Outside, the afternoon has grown sunny, the wind easing. All around her, people are at desks, working in silence, using the library's computers.

Then she sees her, Pam, gliding down the stairs, carrying a brown leather tote bag. There's purpose in the woman's movement, but also pleasure; Pam is back at the centre of things, the den mother. Always first at the sausage sizzle and always the last to leave, always offering a shoulder to cry on, always the dispenser of hugs. A heart of gold. Mandy had forgotten how overwhelming she could be, simultaneously well-meaning and irritating.

'I got the train in,' whispers Pam, as if divulging a saucy secret, a tidbit of gossip. 'It's so nice to be back here, in the city. I didn't realise how much I missed it.' And she pats her bag, as if it's the first time she's used it in a long time.

Mandy doesn't respond. She hasn't missed it a bit, not living in splendid isolation up on the north coast with Martin and Liam. Immediately, she feels guilty. She has her family, her new life; Pam had prioritised her career. It had been her life, her colleagues her family, and she'd lost them five years ago. All that energy, all that ability, all that compassion. What a shame, what a waste. Maybe she sees this as a way of bringing them back together. A family reunion. 'What have you learnt?'

Pam casts her eyes about. 'Not here. Zelda is meeting us upstairs in the cafe.'

'She's coming too?'

'Yes. She doesn't trust you.'

Mandy surprises herself; finds herself laughing. 'Fair enough.'

A middle-aged man at a nearby table casts a disapproving scowl in their direction.

Zelda is waiting for them, sitting at a table of pressed wood next to a man with a scarf around his face.

'Who's he?' asks Mandy bluntly, not bothering with a greeting. 'What's he doing here?'

'This is my brother, Derek.'

'Ah, the man in the mask. What's with the scarf?'

Derek lowers it; his face is a mess, his jaw appears to be wired shut.

Mandy winces. 'I'm sorry,' she says, not sure what she's sorry about. 'I assume that's Henry Livingstone's handiwork?'

Another nod.

'Derek, mate,' says Zelda, her voice surprisingly soft, all the hard edges taken from it, 'would you mind giving us half an hour or so? Have a walk or something?'

The man nods compliantly, stands, and walks away. Mandy senses there's something unusual about him; recalls feeling the same way when she first encountered him.

'He's fine,' says Zelda, as if she's used to explaining. 'On the spectrum, but not too far in.'

'He seems lovely,' says Pam in a very Pam voice.

The three women sit at the table, surrounded by a quiet babble of voices, enough to offer them privacy. Mandy offers to buy coffees: Pam selects a large skinny decaf and a slice of carrot cake, Zelda chooses two iced coffees with whipped cream—one for herself and a takeaway for Derek—plus an eclair for herself and a mousse for her brother. Mandy orders at the counter, making do with a skinny latte for herself, returning to the table with a number on a pole.

Once she's seated, Pam takes charge. 'Here,' she says, 'let me show you.' She extracts a clear plastic folder from her bag, removes a piece of paper and unfolds it. It's two pieces of A4 stuck together. There's a drawn diagram, as neat as any school assignment. At the centre are three large squares arranged in a triangle, each neatly labelled: Mollisons at the top, Diamond Square and Large Sky below. Each square is linked to the other two by arrows going in each direction, forming the sides of the triangle, each arrow containing a percentage between twelve and twenty-four. To the right of the diagram is a list of about two dozen names.

'Mollisons I know,' says Mandy. 'What are the other two? They sound familiar.'

'Zelda?' prompts Pam.

'Mollisons is a bank, Diamond Square is an unlisted property trust, Large Sky is a property developer. All privately held companies, so not on the stock exchange.'

'And the arrows and percentages?'

'They represent the cross-ownership. Each company possesses a significant holding in each of the other two. Not enough for outright control, but enough to get a couple of board positions. The companies are separate legal entities, but because of the cross-ownership, and because of common board members, it's safe to assume they operate in concert.'

Mandy looks at the list of names. Most are male, most appear to be Anglo-Saxon, but that's not what draws her eye. Six names have a suffix, like some sort of qualification, except instead of PhD or AO, the names are followed by a mixture of the initials M, DS and LS. Four have all three of the initial sets, another two have two each. 'And these?' she asks.

Pam is beaming with pride. 'Board members.'

'Six of them are on more than one board,' Mandy observes.

'That's right,' says Zelda. 'And three of the four who sit on all three boards are the deputy chair of one of the companies.'

'Very symmetrical,' observes Mandy. 'Who's the odd one out, if he's not a deputy chair?'

'Here.' Pam pulls out another single piece of A4 paper. It is headed *Phipps Allenby Lockhart*.

'That's the law firm Tarquin was working for,' says Mandy.

'Correcto-mundo,' says Pam.

'It's a partnership, like a lot of law firms,' says Zelda. 'Look at the names of the partners.'

There are a dozen partners, but only two matter: the bottom ten names have no suffixes. One man, Atticus Pons, has the trifecta—M, DS and LS—and another has DS and LS.

Mandy compares the two documents. 'So these six men, they're across everything?'

'It seems that way.'

'Let me guess,' says Mandy. 'The bank sources money, some of which is invested in the property trust, Diamond Square, which in turn invests in new developments being built by Large Sky. Or Large Sky sources money directly from Mollisons. And if there are any legal hurdles, they turn to Phipps Allenby Lockhart.'

Zelda smiles. 'That seems likely. We can't say for sure how the money flows, but it seems logical enough.'

Mandy looks at the flow charts, the numbers in the arrows. 'Is there anything illegal or improper in the cross-ownership?'

'Not really,' says Pam. 'But it's interesting, isn't it?'

'Yes. And these six, the inner circle, they own the companies?' Mandy directs the question at Zelda.

'No. It's not that simple. They do seem to have some holdings, but the controlling ownership of all three companies is held offshore. The board members represent the owners, but that doesn't mean they themselves are the owners.'

'So who are the owners?'

'Don't know—and it's nigh on impossible to find out. Some shares are held through custodial accounts; some are held directly through companies domiciled in offshore tax havens: the Caymans, the Bahamas, Switzerland. Bits and pieces through Vanuatu. Here . . .' Zelda hands over a third piece of paper, a list printed off a computer. 'You can see for yourself, there are hundreds of shareholders.'

'What's a custodial account?'

'An account run through a large stockbroking firm or some such. It can be a way of disguising the true ownership.'

'Is that legal?'

'Yes.'

Mandy stares at the diagram of the companies and the list of names. It's like looking at the Rosetta Stone: as if seeing great knowledge, but lacking the key to decipher it. 'What does all this mean?'

'Maybe everything, maybe nothing,' says Zelda. 'All those small holdings might be just that: dozens of small holdings. Which would mean the Australian directors really do have effective control. But so many foreign owners, nearly all of them untraceable, raises a more likely possibility: there are a handful of foreign owners who are disguising their control.'

'Is that possible?'

'It is. There's even a name for it: bank capture.'

Mandy stares at her, blinking. 'That sounds serious.'

'The tax haven ownership sends up a red flag. It suggests that this has something to do with evading tax, or money laundering, or even ownership by organised crime syndicates.'

'Shit a brick,' says Mandy.

'I know, right?' Pam is grinning madly now, like a schoolgirl receiving an A-plus for her homework.

'Money laundering? How would that work?' asks Mandy, again directing her question to Zelda.

'Well, these diagrams don't tell us anything about that. They show cross-ownership and board directors, not how the companies make money. There's nothing here about revenue, margins, profits, cash flow.'

'Any guesses?'

'Well, no doubt all three companies and the law firm have multiple customers, including legitimate clients and investors above and beyond any money that flows in from offshore.'

'Do we know who their clients are?'

'No. Even less than we know about the owners. You won't find that in any publicly available company records. But more than likely there's a big overlap.' And Zelda smiles once more, as if in admiration. 'If it's what we suspect it is, then it's very clever. Whoever is washing their money through Mollisons is not only getting their cash laundered, they're getting it invested in legitimate businesses and property, and they're making a profit along the way.'

'And the authorities can't track this?'

'Only to an extent; once it goes offshore, it's very hard to trace. And remember, Mollisons runs its own trading floor: foreign exchange, bonds, derivatives. So there is money washing in and out all the time, large amounts of it, big trades.'

'That's where my desk was,' says Mandy. 'On the trading floor.'

'There you go,' says Pam.

Mandy ignores her, still focused on Zelda. 'Is it possible, then, that all of Mollisons' activities, here in Australia, are above board, totally legal? That it's just the source of funds and ownership that's questionable?'

'Yes. Entirely possible.'

'What about Phipps, the law firm? Same owners?'

'No, that's different. A partnership. Twelve partners. All Australians, mostly in Sydney, one in Brisbane and one in Melbourne. The interstate partners aren't on any of the company boards.'

'Which explains why Tarquin was positioned there. In Phipps.'

'Yeah. Working for Phipps, working three days a week at Mollisons, he was in the perfect place to find out what was really going on.'

Mandy stares at Zelda. 'This is amazing,' she says, her antipathy towards her erstwhile rival on hold. 'Have you found out anything else?'

'Not a lot. But all three companies are profitable. Although Mollisons in particular doesn't seem to like paying much tax.'

'But again, nothing illegal?'

'No,' says Pam. She looks as though she is starting to feel left out. 'Apparently it's just mug punters like you and me that pay full tax.'

Mandy leans back, thinking. 'So we have our suspicions. With so much money flowing in from overseas, and the companies controlled in large part by unknown foreign interests, you can see why the authorities might assign someone like Tarquin to go undercover and check them out. But we still don't have any hard evidence of what it was that he found.'

Zelda shakes her head. 'No. It's not exactly going to be filed away with the financial statements.'

Pam chimes in. 'And you can also see, with so much money moving through, that Tarquin might have been tempted to pocket some.'

'Possibly,' says Mandy. 'Or maybe he stumbled across someone else who was doing just that,' she suggests. 'They found out and it got him killed.'

The three women continue to speculate, but to Mandy it seems they're going in widening circles, suspicion orbiting with nowhere to land. Eventually, Pam excuses herself, heading off to use the bathroom. With her gone, the remaining two lapse into silence.

'You don't like me, do you?' Zelda says eventually.

'No,' says Mandy. 'I already told you that.'

'But you can trust me,' says Zelda.

Mandy can't help herself; she shakes her head, disdain evident. 'Is that right?'

'Because you know what I want.'

'Money?'

'That's right. If Tarquin never stole any, then I want compensation.'

'Are you sure it's worth it? You saw what Livingstone did to your brother.'

At the mention of Derek, the hard-faced shield cracks a little, and Mandy can see the edge of emotion. Suddenly Zelda is talking with a low intensity. 'You have no idea what it's like, no idea— being unemployed, unable to practise, to have a police record, only able to get menial work. To look after a brother like Derek. You can't even begin to understand, with your perfect partner and your perfect house and your perfect child.' She spits the words out. 'If I can't have the life that Tarquin promised me, then at least I want my old one back.'

Mandy blinks; she can't quite make Zelda out. The brassy go-getter has been replaced by a woman of compassion. 'The last time I saw you, you were still convinced the money existed. Enough to kidnap me. I can't see why you've done a one-eighty-degree turn.'

'You,' says Zelda.

'Me?'

'Don't you see? I thought Tarquin was a lawyer who stole ten million dollars and skipped the country. We all did. For five years I thought that, and the known facts supported it. But then the facts started changing. Fact one: he was dead the whole time. Fact two: he was an undercover cop, investigating Mollisons. Fact three: he was married. Fact four: he didn't tell you about the millions. So I reckon there never was any money. He sized you up and he sized me up and he pretty quickly worked us out, how he could manipulate us. I wanted the good life, you wanted a knight in shining armour; I wanted money and you wanted love. So he gave us what we wanted, or at least the facsimile of it. Promised me millions, promised you marriage. And in return, we let him fuck us, even as we gave him the keys to the kingdom: access into Mollisons. Face it, Mandy: he screwed us good and proper.'

Mandy says nothing; there is nothing to say. Zelda's words are sharp with truth and heavy with conviction, enough to excoriate, enough to penetrate, enough to wound. Tarquin had used them, nothing more. She had supplied Tarquin with the alpha-numeric keys, but she still has no idea what he used them for. Was it to collect incriminating evidence or to plunder millions? Either way, Claus Vandenbruk was right: the undercover cop Tarquin Molloy was every bit as amoral and every bit beyond the law as any ASIS spy.

They're still sitting there in silence when Pam returns, as cheery and enthusiastic as ever, bouncing around like a dog in a graveyard. 'God, it's good to be back together, working like this,' she says. 'The old team.'

Later, outside, Mandy, Zelda and Derek walk Pam up Elizabeth Street to the entrance of St James station. Derek finishes slurping his iced coffee out through a straw and embarks on the more diffi-cult task of spooning micro portions of mousse into his mouth.

'I showed you how Mollisons works,' says Zelda. 'Now, I need your help.'

'How?' asks Mandy warily.

'I have no money. If I'm going to win compensation, I'm going to need a lawyer.'

Mandy says nothing.

'In return, I'll give you everything I find, everything I know.'

'All right,' says Mandy eventually. 'I have a lawyer. A very good one. I'll instruct her to assist you.'

'I'd prefer my own.'

'You won't find one as good as Winifred. And if you're her client, you're protected. Lawyer–client privilege; she can't tell me anything.' Mandy hesitates. 'Are you sure you want to pursue this?'

'Why wouldn't I? I want what's owed me.'

'Henry Livingstone? Organised crime?'

Zelda looks at her ruefully, then laughs. 'Fuck it. What have I got to lose?'

Derek makes a guttural exclamation; the spoon is caught up in his mouth, tangled in the wiring, mousse smeared across his chin.

chapter twenty-four

TITUS TORBETT GIVES MARTIN A LIFT BACK TO THE CITY IN THE BMW. IT SEEMS the limousine belongs to him, not his father.

'This is very good of you,' offers Martin as the car glides away from the house.

'No problem. I have a hearing at the courts.'

'You're a lawyer as well?'

Titus's eyes are on the road, but Martin thinks he detects a smile as he answers. 'All Torbetts are lawyers.'

'A barrister?'

'Of course. I'm a corporate counsel.'

'What does that mean?'

'I work for a select group of corporations.'

'Sounds interesting. Which ones?'

'Sorry. That's confidential.'

'Of course.'

Martin watches the greenery of Moore Park slide by before attempting to restart the conversation. 'Were you close? To Elizabeth?'

'Of course. She was my little sister.' Titus is concentrating on the traffic; his face betrays no emotion. 'I'm told you found them.'

'Not exactly. But I witnessed the crime scene.'

There's a red light, giving Titus Torbett the opportunity to turn his eyes from the road to Martin. 'Do you think she suffered?'

Martin shakes his head. 'No. She wouldn't have felt a thing.' Which is true, he thinks. Not when the bullet entered her brain and blew out the back of her skull. But in the minutes before, she must have been terrified. But why tell her brother that? 'Your father told me you were once a member of the Mess,' Martin states.

'A long time ago. I quit after a couple of years.' The man's face is neutral, eyes back on the road.

'Why?'

'Never really interested me. Father signed me up, but I found it tedious. A bunch of self-promoters, sitting around drinking fine wines and eating roadkill. Not my scene.'

'Roadkill?'

'Their dinners. They eat rare and endangered species, if you can believe that. Makes them feel special. Elite.' The lights change and he moves off with the traffic, face still impassive. 'Perverse, if you ask me.'

'Shark fin soup made from white pointers, that sort of thing?'

'Exactly. Bloody disgusting.'

'You don't approve?'

'I don't. Father had the good sense to distance himself when he went to the High Court. Elizabeth should have done the same when she went to the bench.'

'You think that's what got her killed? Being a member of the Mess?'

Titus laughs, amused at the idea. 'I doubt it.' He seems about to add something, hesitates, then refrains from saying anything more.

'Your father said you might be able to help me. Thought you might know some of the members.'

'Me? I resigned thirty years ago. More than thirty years.'

'You never discussed it?'

'No.'

'Your father thought Clarence O'Toole might still be a member.'

Titus shrugs. 'More than likely. He'd be right at home there.'

'What do you mean?'

'Likes the sound of his own voice.'

'I see. Anyone else you can think of?'

Titus grunts. 'Just one—your pal at the *Herald*: D'Arcy Defoe.'

'D'Arcy? Are you sure?' Martin reaches up, takes hold of the Jesus handle, even as the BMW continues on its smooth trajectory along Oxford Street.

'That's what Elizabeth said.'

'When was this?'

'A couple of years ago. She was on her high horse. Thought it was outrageous having a journalist as a member. Said he was always sniffing around, trying to get the inside running on some story or another.'

'Sounds about right. She wasn't impressed?'

'You could say that.'

'Anyone else?'

'No, sorry.'

'Atticus Pons? George Giopolis?'

Titus takes his eyes from the road to cast a doubtful look at Martin. 'Never heard of them. Who are they?'

'Never mind. Just some names I heard. Probably unconnected.' They're almost at Whitlam Square now; Martin can see the trees of Hyde Park.

'Somewhere here do you?' asks Titus.

'No. The courts will be fine,' says Martin, wanting to ask a few more questions. 'Tell me, though: do you have any idea who might have killed them? Max and your sister?'

'Me? No. Not at all.'

Titus turns right onto College Street. An orange light at the corner with William Street invites acceleration; instead, Titus takes the opportunity to stop. He turns to Martin. 'My father comes across as rather modest and self-contained, I know. But men like him, men who have wielded real power, they're used to being at the centre of things. They can have a difficult time believing events no longer revolve around them, that they now inhabit the periphery. Father has settled on the belief that Elizabeth's death is connected to the Mess, and therefore to him. But there is no evidence of that. None. The Mess is most likely irrelevant. And so is he. The Mess is not a criminal organisation—it's a dining club for blowhards. I'd be very careful about leaping to conclusions. I know you've got yourself into trouble doing that previously.'

'You've researched me?'

'Of course.' The light changes and Titus returns his concentration to driving. He turns into Macquarie Street, pulling over to let Martin out. He smiles, offers his hand, gripping Martin's with the same Goldilocks handshake. 'I do wish you the best with your investigations. Please contact me if there is anything else

I might assist with.' He hands Martin a business card. It seems to be a pro forma farewell; courtesy by the numbers.

Back on the street, Martin watches the BMW glide away, a yacht afloat in the corporate liquidity of the CBD, off to dock in some subterranean marina.

He looks for somewhere off the street and out of the wind, somewhere he can make a call in private. There's the lobby of a small building, a row of lifts. Good enough. Inside, he rings Jack Goffing, ASIO agent, praying he will pick up. Goffing has been helpful in the past, down in Riversend, up in Port Silver. But that was when Martin had something to offer him. This is different. Still, no harm in asking.

'Martin Scarsden. This is a surprise.'

'Jack. Long time, no talk.'

'Busy times. How can I help?'

'I'm in Sydney. Thought you might like to catch up.'

'I'm in Canberra, so maybe stop with the small talk and tell me what you want.'

'Have you ever heard of a secret society, a dining club, calling itself the Mess?'

Goffing laughs. 'That sounds like something Enid Blyton would cook up.'

'It's serious, Jack. Could you possibly check it out?'

The laughter stops. 'Tell me.'

So Martin does. The murders of Max and Elizabeth, the Mess, an apparent go-slow on the investigation by the police.

'Jeez, Martin, it's not exactly a national security issue. Not really one for the secret police.'

'Thought you might say that. But tell me, am I still on your books as an informant? You told me last year, up in Port Silver, that you'd registered me.'

'Yeah. So what?'

'Do you ever pay informants?'

'What? You want money?' Goffing sounds confused and just a touch worried.

'Fuck no. But I want payment. Information.'

And Goffing is laughing again. 'Okay. That's the thinnest cover story I've ever heard. I'll see what I can do. On one condition.'

'What's that?'

'If you find anything useful, you make sure I'm the first to know. I don't want to read it in the *Herald*.'

'Of course.'

Call finished, Martin dials Wellington Smith, publisher of *This Month* and Martin's two true crime books.

'Martin? What news?' Martin can barely hear the man's voice over a background ruckus: music, voices, the sound of cutlery on crockery.

'Yes. Yes, it's me.'

'Fuck, I can't hear a thing. I'll ring you right back.' The phone goes dead.

Martin waits for half a minute before giving it away and walking out into the street. But he's only advanced half a city block before it rings.

'Martin?' This time he can hear Wellington clearly, the background noise reduced to the white noise of traffic. 'Sorry about that. Celebratory lunch. End of financial year. We're almost back in the black. Thanks to you and those terrific fucking books of yours.'

'Yeah, Wellington, sure.'

'When are you going to give us another one? And for that matter, when are you going to stop pissing around with those half-arsed specials for the *Herald* and come back and do some real work for *This Month*?'

'That's why I'm calling, I might have something for you.'

'Seriously? Fan-fucking-tastic. What have you got?'

'It'll take too long to explain. I don't want to keep you from your lunch.'

'Come on, give me something. Just the top, just the headline.'

'Later, Wellington. But tell me one thing first: did Max Fuller ever talk to you about doing an investigative piece for *This Month*?'

There is a moment of white noise, nothing more, and when Smith talks again, the ebullience is gone and the voice is sober and serious. 'Jesus, Martin. Max. I have to tell you, I don't believe for a minute that he suicided. Have you talked to Eileen?'

'I have. And you're right. He didn't kill himself. It was murder and the police know it.'

'Fuck me. Is that what you're working on? Who killed him?'

'Yes. It's part of a bigger story.'

'The Mess?'

Martin stares into a moving cityscape. 'So he told you about it? He was working with you?'

'Too right,' says Wellington. 'But he only came on board during the last week or so. I never got a full briefing. The Mess, a secret society, some sort of corruption. That's it.'

'His laptop was stolen when he was killed. Do you know if he had a backup on the cloud? You give it to me when I'm working on a book.'

'Yeah. He had the facility. No idea if he ever used it. I'll check. But I'm not sure I can access it, even if he did.'

'I see. Let us know. And do you have any idea why he swapped allegiances? Max was a *Herald* man, through and through. Why you?'

'I don't think he trusted them.'

'Did he mention D'Arcy Defoe?'

'No. You think D'Arcy was trying to gazump him?'

'Wouldn't be the first time.'

After the call, Martin looks about him at the unchanging city, bustling and disinterested, hectic and impersonal. He needs to find somewhere quiet to sit while he tries to hunt down Justice Clarence O'Toole.

chapter twenty-five

MANDY HAS RETURNED TO THE STATE LIBRARY BY HERSELF. NOW SHE SITS, CONTEM-
plating Pam and Zelda's diagram. It doesn't prove criminality,
but there's the intimation of malfeasance: the tightly held cross-
ownership; the high percentage of foreign ownership; the true
identity of shareholders disguised; the low level of tax. She can
imagine why the authorities would want to scrutinise the companies.

She tries to imagine how it might work. Money coming in
from overseas, directed to the bank by its foreign owners. Clean
money, dirty money, blood money. The funds being reinvested
into Diamond Square and Large Sky and who knows what other
companies, then the profits, suitably laundered, returned to the overseas investors, the Australian owners taking their share of the profits
and the transaction fees. So nothing illegal, nothing underhand,
the Australian operations totally legitimate, save for a bit of tax
minimisation. But every company in Australia minimises tax.

She uses the library's computers, googling away, trying to glean what she can about international money laundering, and quickly learning that it's serious, involving unquantifiable billions, maybe trillions, of dollars. She reads that it usually runs at a loss, almost like a fee for service—you only get a percentage of your investment back. That would explain why the bank is so profitable—it would be able to charge extravagant fees. Of course, if the owners and the investors were one and the same, then they would keep their profits, and the profits from the bank would be doubly laundered. Was that the business model? Was that what Tarquin was investigating?

She looks up, and is surprised to see Martin walking through the stacks, head down. Martin. Here. Why? She watches him for a moment, fascinated, reading his intensity, his quiet resolve. It's good to see him. How serendipitous. She stands, creeps up behind him, places her hands over his eyes where he stands. He flinches, stiffens, twirls, wrenching her hands from his face, his eyes revealing his momentary panic, before relaxing immediately into a smile when he recognises her.

'Shit. Don't do that. You scared me,' he says.

She rubs her wrists. 'You hurt me.'

Immediately he is apologetic. 'I'm sorry, I didn't realise it was you. I'm a bit on edge.'

Contrition washes over her. 'Sorry. It was stupid of me.'

'Never mind.'

'I was just glad to see you.'

'And me you.'

They find a quiet corner over by the window, sitting by a small, up-ended cylinder, covered in cloth, a cross between a table and an ottoman.

'Did you watch the video I sent you? What do you think?' Mandy asks.

'The video? Not yet. Let me see.' He pulls out his phone, opens the attachment, watches it as she leans close. 'Okay,' he says. 'What am I looking at? Is that time stamp accurate?'

'It is. Most likely that's the last time Tarquin Molloy was seen alive. It shows him on the trading floor of Mollisons, downloading data onto a flash drive. Then, as he gets into the lift, he's joined by Henry Livingstone.'

'Livingstone?'

'Killer and standover man.'

'What?' He appears shocked, scrolling through to watch it again. 'Jesus. The guy who found you, when you were abducted?'

'Same guy. Always dressed to the nines, wears antique suits, oils his hair with something called California Poppy.'

Martin's eyes are still on the screen. 'And by the sound of it, the same guy who trashed my apartment.' He looks up, mind working. 'Where did you get this?'

'An old work colleague. Security camera footage.'

'Jesus. Montifore needs to see this.'

'I know. I wanted to show you first.'

'Thanks, but I can't do anything with it before we give it to the police. It's evidence in a murder investigation. We don't want to get charged with withholding evidence or perverting the course of justice.'

Mandy smiles. 'Of course not. But I promised not to involve my old colleague. I'll have to claim I got it anonymously.'

'You're going to tell Montifore that?'

'Don't look at me that way. You're the one who's always banging on about protecting your sources.'

He gives her a puzzled look. 'If you have to. I guess it's what's in the video that's important, not who gave it to you.' He smiles. 'And I guess if Montifore is after him, then Livingstone isn't going to be bothering us.'

'Exactly. Maybe you could give it to him for me? I'm not sure I want to see him again. Not without Winifred.'

But Martin doesn't accede. She recognises the look on his face: he wants to ask a question; he's just deciding how best to frame it. When it comes, his tone is conciliatory. 'What is it, Mandy? What's the problem?'

'I told you. I don't want to get my colleague into trouble.' It's the truth, or a variation of it. She can't reveal her dealings with the Turtle, not to the police and not to Martin. The thought of him knowing about the sex tapes, the Turtle's nuclear option, fills her with dread.

'I don't think I can,' says Martin. 'I'm sorry.'

'Okay. I understand,' she says, deciding to move on. 'I've been talking to some of the other people I used to work with. My old boss, Pam Risoli, gave me this.' She unfolds the pieces of paper with the diagram of the structure of Mollisons and its sister companies, Diamond Square and Large Sky. She sees Martin's initial confusion, then his widening eyes as he realises what he's looking at.

'Holy shit,' he whispers. The video is forgotten.

She takes satisfaction in explaining it to him, pointing out the cross-ownership, the board memberships.

Martin stabs his finger at the paper. 'These two names. Atticus Pons, senior partner at Phipps, member of all three boards. And over here, George Giopolis, property developer, member of the Large Sky board.'

'What about them?'

'They mean nothing to you?'

'No. Why would they?'

'Last year, in Port Silver. Montifore threw them into an interview he was conducting with you. You remember?'

She shakes her head, frowns. 'I do remember a strange interview. He was bouncing all over the place, throwing in names I didn't recognise.'

'Winifred took notes. Pons and Giopolis. Any idea how they're connected?'

'Other than this?' she indicates the diagram. 'None. You?'

'No.'

Their focus returns to the diagram, voicing theories, exploring the possibilities of money laundering, speculating about what it was that Molloy had found. She sees it then, experiences it: the thrill of the story, like she's an explorer entering an unknown world, the first outsider to set eyes on a new civilisation, already preparing a report to the Royal Geographic Society. For the first time she's seeing Martin's world from the inside, the reporter on the scent of a big story. And she feels it too, the euphoria. She feels the intoxication and she feels the power. The power to push back, to expose the past instead of letting it hunt her down. She and Martin, fighting back. She starts to laugh with exhilaration. 'This is sensational.'

He laughs as well. 'It certainly is.'

'So where do we go from here?'

'You need to see Montifore. Give him the video. I've got a few leads to chase down. Nothing to do with Molloy—people who might know why Max and Elizabeth Torbett were killed.' He recounts his meeting with Sir Talbot, explains the existence of the Mess, how Max and Elizabeth were investigating the secret society, how he wants to track down Clarence O'Toole.

'Jesus,' she exclaims when he has finished. 'Do you think there is any way they're connected? Tarquin's murder and the killings of Max and Elizabeth Torbett?'

Martin grimaces. 'Max certainly knew about Molloy, said he was investigating a grand conspiracy, or words to that effect. Apart from that, I can't see any connection. It could be coincidental.'

Mandy stares at him, feeling as if they're almost there, that answers lie just beyond their grasp, waiting to be revealed. 'You think?'

He shrugs. 'Let's keep digging. We might only be scraping the surface, but we're making progress.'

A warmth spreads through her. He said 'we'. 'So what next?'

'Go see Montifore. Ring Winifred if you want. She'll know better than me how to handle it.'

'Can we trust him?'

Martin frowns at the suggestion. 'We don't have much choice. But don't tell him anything you're not comfortable with.'

'Okay. And what about you?'

'I'm going to find Clarence O'Toole. And, hopefully, have a chat to D'Arcy Defoe.'

'D'Arcy? Why?'

'He's a member of the Mess.'

'Do you trust him.'

'Right now, the only person I trust is you.'

chapter twenty-six

ELIZABETH STREET IS A WORLD OF SHADOWS, THE SETTING SUN UNABLE TO penetrate, only the peaks of buildings framed by its failing lumin-escence. Sydneysiders might deny the season, but the rhythms of the sun are beyond the influence of public opinion. There is an old woman outside the wine bar, a high-vis vest an outer skin on layers of overcoats that threaten to swallow her. Her face is red and her eyes are bleary; she's selling copies of the *Big Issue*. Martin fishes around in his pocket, but he has no change, no cash at all. He pushes past, apologetic.

It's a plush place, set inside colonial-era sandstone. Brass and polished wood, red velvet and warm lighting imbue an air of opulence. The bar may be old, but the clientele is young: bankers, lawyers and political staffers; good-looking achievers, orthodon-tically correct, confident of their upward trajectories, filling the space with the boasts and braying laughter of infallibility.

He feels underdressed in his jeans and open-necked shirt as he works his way through the crowd by the bar. The glorious young take micro-seconds to scan his face, register him as unknown, unimportant and undesirable, before averting their gaze towards more promising prospects. He spots D'Arcy Defoe occupying a prime spot by the window looking out on the street, sitting in a dark leather armchair, a glass of red resting on the antique marble table before him. He rises when he sees Martin, extends both hands in welcome, a politician's handshake, and smiles a well-calibrated smile, a smile that simultaneously says he's glad and grateful to see his former colleague but regrets the circumstances of their meeting. Martin can't help but admire D'Arcy's presence, his well-tailored suit and his ability to secure them two seats in the packed bar.

Pleasantries exchanged, D'Arcy signals effortlessly for a waitress and offers Martin a drink.

'Why don't I try what you're having?' says Martin, glancing at the glass of red.

'Excellent suggestion. In which case, let's get a bottle. On expenses. Agreed?'

'Of course.' Martin wonders why he feels as if he's sparring whenever he encounters D'Arcy.

The two men sit not opposite each other, but at right angles. D'Arcy's view extends across the table towards the door, where he can see all those who enter and leave. Martin sits to his left, looking across the table and out through the window at pedestrians and traffic hurrying along Elizabeth Street, his back to the aspirational young. If the two men both lean forward their faces are close; they have no trouble hearing each other over the background babble of ambition.

'How are you doing then, Martin? We don't talk often enough.'

'I'm good.'

'Have you given any more thought to coming back on full-time? I could really do with your help.' Technically, D'Arcy is head of investigations; technically he's one of those authorised to commission work from Martin. Yet for the past eighteen months, Martin has only filed intermittently, mainly updates based on his books about the crimes in Riversend and Port Silver. He knows it's an arrangement that can't last forever, not with the financial pressures bearing down on the *Herald*. It was tough enough before the virus tanked the economy.

'No, not really. But I'm working on something. Max's death.'

'Yes. Max.' D'Arcy takes a considered sip of his wine. 'I'm glad you got in touch—I'm writing his obituary. I'm pushing for an entire page; he deserves it. Here's what I'm thinking: if you give me some good anecdotes and some good character obser-vations, I'll marry them with my own and I'll write it up. Once I'm done, I'll send you the draft and then it's up to you: you can correct any errors or rework sections or rewrite the lot. Up to you. The way I see it, we'll share the by-line. What do you think?'

'That sounds fine. Thank you.' Martin has always thought of himself as a better-than-average writer, capable of rising above the formulaic when time and circumstances permit, but he also knows he's no D'Arcy Defoe. His colleague can write in any number of styles, all of them well: the analytical, the emotive, the satirical, the portentous, the elegiac. He's been pumping out a book every second year for a decade, all of them well received, all of them selling well.

So the two former colleagues drink wine and Martin recounts stories about Max. D'Arcy seems to know many of them, but prompts Martin to flesh them out. An hour later, they have reached the end of the bottle and D'Arcy has ordered another of a lighter wine, 'to toast the great man'. They raise their glasses and take a sip. To Martin it tastes very fine; Max deserves nothing less.

'D'Arcy, there are a few other things I'd like to ask you about.'

'Sure. Go for your life.'

'Why was the report of Max's death so short? Page thirteen. Half-a-dozen sentences.'

D'Arcy looks at him, sizing him up. 'That was me.'

'What? Why?'

'I was asked by the police to play it down. They wanted to keep the real situation under wraps for a few days. We debated it in conference; agreed it was a fair trade-off if it helped them find the killers.'

'What was the trade-off?'

'Full access when they decide to go public.'

'You spoke to Morris Montifore?'

'No. Who's he?'

'The detective inspector running the investigation.'

'Right.'

'So if it wasn't Montifore, who was it?'

'Roger Macatelli.'

'The deputy police commissioner? He asked you to hold off on reporting the true nature of their deaths?'

D'Arcy shrugs, but looks a little unsettled. 'Yes. I dealt with Macatelli. So what?'

Martin recalls Morris Montifore saying it was Macatelli who had sent the detective to Port Silver over a year ago, and now the deputy commissioner is again bringing his influence to bear on an active investigation. Martin changes direction, hoping a blunt approach might elicit a response. 'Tell me about the Mess.'

There is no immediate reaction from D'Arcy, no sign the question has ruffled him. Instead, he offers Martin an amused smile. 'So you've come across the Mess. What do you need to know?'

'I was told you're a member.'

'That's true, I am.'

'Is Macatelli?'

But Defoe simply shakes his head. 'I'm not at liberty to say.'

'One of the rules, right?'

'The only rule, really.'

'So how come you joined?'

'How come? Why wouldn't I, given half a chance? It's an unprecedented networking opportunity: a journalistic goldmine. I'm not going to tell you who any of the members are, but suffice to say there are some heavy hitters. Politicians, lawyers, businesspeople. And as fellow members, they talk to you as an equal, and they talk to you confidentially, they talk to you on the basis of mutual trust. *Trust*, Martin, the most valuable commodity any journalist can possess. A ready-made, off-the-record insight into how this city really works.'

'But it's a secret organisation. Doesn't that bother you? Aren't we the ones who are meant to be shining light into dark places?'

'What makes you think it's a dark place?'

'Because Elizabeth Torbett was a member, she and Max were investigating it, and they were murdered,' says Martin.

D'Arcy nods, suddenly serious, considering his options. 'So that's what Max was working on.'

'I believe so.'

'All right.' D'Arcy sighs. 'It's true, Elizabeth was a member. I believe her father—Sir Talbot, the old High Court judge—was one of the founders.' He frowns into his wine. 'Do you believe there is a link between the deaths and the Mess?'

'Do you think it's possible?'

D'Arcy doesn't answer straight away. Instead, he turns and gazes out the window. Martin is unable to see his eyes. He turns back, leans in close. 'Martin, I need to take you into my confidence. This is just between you and me, okay?' Martin signals his agreement. 'I have no idea how much you know about the Mess, but you're right: there is something amiss. What I told you is correct; I joined for the contacts and the connections. I've been a member for three years. But in recent months, I've become concerned that it's been infiltrated by some rather unsavoury elements. No, worse than unsavoury—criminal. But I must emphasise: most of the members are beyond reproach; that's why I won't identify them. However, I think one or two may have succumbed to temptation. I'm considering blowing the whistle on them.'

Martin blinks. 'What? How?'

'An investigative series. In the paper. How else?' D'Arcy smiles. 'I reckon there's a book in it, if I play my cards right. I hear true crime is all the rage.' He chuckles, two colleagues sharing a joke. And then he's serious again. 'But I need to tread carefully. I don't want to burn all my bridges.'

'Of course,' says Martin, trying to keep his voice neutral.

But D'Arcy picks up on his scepticism. 'You of all people should understand. If I'm seen to be betraying confidences, giving up the names of sources, that would destroy my reputation. It would be career-ending.'

'Right.'

'And if you are correct, and Max and Elizabeth were killed because they were investigating the Mess, then I'd prefer not to join them. No story is worth dying for.'

'Did Max ever talk to you about the Mess?'

'No. Never.'

'But Elizabeth knew you were a member?'

'Of course.'

'So why didn't he discuss it with you?'

D'Arcy shrugs. 'Maybe he was planning to do just that. Maybe he figured I didn't have much to offer; Elizabeth would know as much or more about the Mess than me. She'd been a member for decades, her father before her. Maybe he was just playing his cards close to his chest.'

'But you knew he was working on a big story?'

'I did. I am titular head of investigations, after all.'

'Don't you think it's strange he didn't tell you what it was?'

D'Arcy looks unperturbed. 'I'm sure he would have told me sooner or later. I mean, it's not as if I always told him what I was working on when he was editor. And neither did you.'

Martin has to accept that. He drinks some more wine. It really is very good; there is no faulting D'Arcy's discernment. 'What can you tell me about her then? Elizabeth Torbett, I mean.'

'What's to say? Supreme Court judge, pillar of the community. I've known her for years, even before I joined the Mess. She's also a member over at the SCG. Big cricket fan. Tests, not the pyjama games. We sat in the same group at the New Year's test match. I always found her a bit stand-offish. Always polite, but a little aloof. I don't know if that was simply the way she was, or because I was a journalist. I got the impression she wasn't a big fan of the media, that she only tolerated me because I was a fellow Mess member.' D'Arcy again considers his wine. 'That's why I was surprised when I learnt she'd been cooperating with Max. Then again, I didn't know they were related through marriage.'

'And Max didn't tell you they were working together?'

'No. He said he thought he might have something for me, that we could brand it as a *Herald* investigation. But that was it. He told me nothing else.'

Martin considers that. Max had rung him in Port Silver, had been eager to involve him in the story, and yet he hadn't confided in the *Herald*'s own head of investigations, another of his protégés. Instead, just recently, he'd started working with Wellington Smith. 'The night before he was killed, Max went into the *Herald* and scrubbed his hard drive clean. Why would he do that?'

D'Arcy smiles once more, although this time it doesn't look like there's much humour underpinning it. 'I see you have good sources. I can't imagine who.' And then he again becomes serious. 'I don't know why he would do that. Perhaps you're right: perhaps he no longer trusted me because I'm a member of the Mess. If so, that's a tragedy. He should have; we should have been working together.' He sips some wine. 'A lesson for us all.'

'Clarence O'Toole?' asks Martin.

That elicits a knowing grin. 'What about him?'

'I know he's a member of the Mess. You're betraying no confidences there.'

'What can I say? I assume you heard about the photographs and the suppression order?'

Martin suppresses his own smile; it is as he suspected: O'Toole is the Land and Environment Court judge, the one Flanagan Mort told him about, the one covered by the suppression order. 'Yes. I know about the order.'

'Of course, who doesn't?' D'Arcy continues. 'Bit of a buffoon, if you ask me, but that could just be an affectation. You know, the sort who appears to have had more to drink than they really have. And the underwear thing, not totally out of character, if you get my drift. But he does have a reputation as a solid judge.' Defoe pours more wine, topping up Martin before filling his own glass. 'There's an obvious parallel between the photos of O'Toole and the murder of Max and Elizabeth Torbett, but whether that's Mess-related, or court-related, or unrelated, I can't say.'

'You say the Mess may be harbouring some sort of criminality. Is there any suggestion O'Toole is involved?'

'No. None that I know of.' Martin is about to pose further questions, but D'Arcy cuts him off. 'Listen, Martin, I need to be somewhere. But here's a thought. We're both investigating the same thing, both prying into the Mess. Let's work together, a collaboration. It may take a long time, it could be a lengthy dig, but it has the makings of a mighty yarn. We research it together, we write it together, we collect the Walkley together. We dedicate it to Max.'

Martin is a little surprised; he and his rival have never shared anything more than a drink, a bit of banter and the occasional contact number. 'Are you sure?'

'I am. It might prove useful to have you as a co-author. If one of my contacts cracks the shits, then I can lay the blame on you.' And D'Arcy laughs, that rich baritone laugh of his. He raises his glass, compelling Martin to join him. They clink glasses. 'It would be great to have you back on board,' says D'Arcy, before taking a mouthful of wine.

But Martin holds off drinking any more. 'Okay, as we're working together, can you put me in touch with Clarence O'Toole? All I could find was a number for his chambers, and they weren't telling me anything.'

'Let's try.' Defoe pulls his phone from his inside coat pocket. Its case is maroon leather, perfectly in accord with the bar's expensive decor. Martin watches as he taps out a text. Defoe looks up at him, raising his eyebrows in a 'let's see' gesture.

Almost immediately the phone vibrates. Defoe nods. 'Well, blow me down. He says yes.'

'Do you have an address? I can go there once we're done.'

D'Arcy taps again, then holds his phone out as the reply comes in. Martin notes down the address. Paddington. Ten minutes by cab, fifteen at most.

'Thanks, D'Arcy.'

'Don't mention it. I'll be keen to hear what his honour has to say.' He glances at his watch, an elegant affair sliding from under his cuff as he lifts his arm. 'I'm sorry, Martin. I do need to leave. Let me know how you go with his justice.'

The waitress appears, as if by magic, and D'Arcy signs the chit. 'I run an account,' he explains. Of course he does. He stands, leaving his glass unfinished, with more wine left in the bottle. He departs and the young aspirants of the bar turn to watch him go.

Martin sits alone, restored to anonymity. He's tempted. D'Arcy is a man on the inside. Connected. He will ensure they claim the front page, extract maximum coverage for the story. But another part of him feels wary, uncomfortable. D'Arcy is still a member of the Mess, and Max is still dead. It comes down to trust. Does he trust him? Martin twists his neck, looking back towards the bar. The waitress steadfastly ignores him. He stays a moment more, wondering if the wine really is as good as it seems. He thinks of Max, defecting to Wellington Smith. That's good enough for him. Wellington Smith and *This Month* it is. He gets up and leaves, unnoticed by the throng. Outside, the woman selling the *Big Issue* has disappeared and the sun has set. At least the wind has died.

chapter twenty-seven

SYDNEY IS WINTER DARK, THE COLOURS OF SUMMER NOWHERE APPARENT, STORED as if with mothballs to be aired occasionally but not worn seriously until spring. Not now that night is here. Office workers walk quickly, eager to be home. Dixon Street seems tired, the trees without leaves, no one dawdling, tourists absent, the neon signs of the restaurants more garish than joyful. The pandemic has gone but Chinatown is yet to regain its buzz. A busker stands around the corner from the Covent Garden pub, trying valiantly to attract interest, or at least a coin or two, but is thwarted by lack of talent, a broken guitar string and the general impatience of passers-by.

Mandy finds Morris Montifore upstairs in the same Chinese restaurant, the one on Sussex Street he brought her to after her release from Zelda Forshaw's captivity. He's seated in the same corner, apparently eating the same food, this time with Ivan Lucic at his side. Martin has told her Montifore has a wife and children, and it's true the man wears a wedding band, but that's the only evidence. He seems married to his job, living it twenty-four seven, surgically attached to his suit, addicted to MSG and catching killers. She approaches the table. Montifore at least has the good grace to study only her face; Lucic gives her the once-over.

'Please, take a seat,' says Montifore. His words are shaped by formality, but tinged with sympathy. Yet nothing feels comfortable or relaxed as she joins them. 'Have you eaten?' asks the policeman, gesturing at the dishes on the table.

'No thanks,' she says. 'I'll eat with Martin later.'

'Understood,' says Montifore. 'So what is it that you have for me? You mentioned a video.'

'Yes.' She opens her phone, pulling up the video, making it full screen. 'Here,' she says, handing it over, believing it to be self-explanatory. She watches Montifore's eyes as he views it, bracing herself for the stream of questions she knows must be coming.

Montifore watches only long enough to get the gist of it before handing the phone to Lucic. 'The date stamp,' says Montifore to her, 'you believe it's accurate?'

'Yes. It's Tarquin Molloy on the last day he was seen alive,' she says. 'On the trading floor, inside Mollisons.'

'Yeah, we've already got it,' says Lucic matter-of-factly.

'What? How?' asks Mandy, addressing Lucic, aware that Montifore's eyes are on her, studying her reaction.

Lucic shrugs, speaking to his superior more than to her. 'The original investigation into Molloy's alleged theft had it. It shows him walking to Mandalay's desk on the trading floor, inserting a flash drive into a port that was meant to have been disabled, feeding in the software enabling him to transfer several millions of dollars. And leaving.'

Mandy can't believe it. 'So you knew about him, all the way back then? Henry Livingstone?'

Montifore looks at Lucic, then back to her. 'What?' His voice is muffled, his mouth full of noodles, but his frown is communicating his displeasure. Lucic looks blank.

Mandy fills the space. 'Right at the end, when Tarquin gets into the lift. Just before the video cuts out, a man joins him. It's Henry Livingstone.'

Montifore looks back to Lucic, who is watching the video again. 'Shit. She's right, boss,' the younger man states, handing the phone back to Montifore.

There's a moment of silence as the senior detective reviews the clip before delivering his verdict. 'The dickheads. They missed it.'

'I guess they weren't looking for it,' says Lucic. 'Their eyes were on Molloy, their thoughts full of stolen money. Livingstone was just a man in a suit in an office full of suits. If they weren't looking, they weren't seeing.'

Montifore addresses his subordinate. 'Okay. Can we get the techs to look at it, to see if they can enhance the vision? It's been five years—the technology must be better now. And get in touch with Mollisons, see if they still have any other video footage from that day. I'm guessing they handed over everything with Molloy in it, but maybe there's other footage with Livingstone. I want to know who he met, who he talked to—and how he managed to get into a secure area of a bank in the first place.'

'I'll do it in person. Ring tonight, go in first thing,' replies Lucic.

Montifore nods, turning his attention back to Mandy. 'Where did you get this?'

'An old workmate from my time at Mollisons.'

'Not from a police source?'

'No,' she says. 'I don't know any police.'

She's expecting him to demand she identify her source, but the inspector's thoughts have moved on. 'Is Martin investigating this? Another of his true crime potboilers?'

'I think he's more interested in the murders of Max Fuller and Elizabeth Torbett,' she deflects. 'Max was like a father to him. He feels a debt.'

Montifore looks at her for a moment, unseeing, before resting his head in his hands, chopsticks abandoned and food forgotten. He remains like that for long seconds before addressing her. 'Listen, Mandalay. Mandy. You've done us a favour here, a big favour. We were unaware Livingstone was in the video. But listen, I'm serious: this is dangerous. Livingstone and Spitt are psychopaths. They've killed before. Brutally. Martin would never forgive himself if anything happened to you.'

'Is that a threat?'

Montifore laughs, a real laugh, a belly laugh. Lucic is shaking his head in disbelief. 'No,' says the senior man. 'No. I'm not threatening you. Just the opposite. I'm trying to save your life.'

chapter twenty-eight

THE CAB DROPS MARTIN OUTSIDE A LARGISH TERRACE IN PADDINGTON, DOWN BY Trumper Park: a modern house, doing enough to sympathise with the suburb's nineteenth-century row housing to win council approval and not much more. The street is tree-lined and quiet against the background hum of New South Head Road up on the ridge above the park. Bats move soundlessly across the luminous greyness of the night sky. He opens the gate, climbs up a couple of stairs to a narrow concrete verandah and the front door, inaccessible behind a locked security screen. A floodlight trips on; a camera peers down at him. There's an intercom with its own lens; Martin rings the bell, identifies himself. A maid unlocks the door, then the security grille, and ushers him in. No, not a maid. The uniform is different, the watch attached above her breast the giveaway: a nurse. As well as the uniform, she's wearing a bored look, as if answering the door is beneath her.

'He's in here. In the lounge.' She indicates the way but doesn't enter herself, retreating deeper into the house.

Justice Clarence O'Toole of the New South Wales Land and Environment Court is slumped in an armchair, looking nothing like his photographs. In Google searches, he looks hearty and red-faced, Santa Claus with an executioner's glower. In reality he is pallid, his skin parchment yellow. There's a cannula in the back of his hand and, Martin can just make out through an opening of the man's robe, another in his chest.

'I'm dying,' O'Toole says by way of greeting, not attempting to rise, perhaps aware of the dawning awareness on Martin's face. 'The big C. Pancreatic.'

'I'm sorry.'

'So am I. Please, take a seat.' The voice is deep and resonant, a voice used to being obeyed, a voice whose opinions matter. A voice that is yet to catch up with the dire reality of its owner.

Martin finds a seat, looks quickly about. It's an old room, growing musty, as if it too is growing ill. On one wall there is an oil painting of two boys hugging a labrador, the style dated. This was once a family home, but now Martin is guessing it's the sole preserve of O'Toole. Like a museum. Or a mausoleum. 'When?'

'When did I find out? About a month ago. When will I die? I won't make the summer. No chance of parole, none of a pardon. All appeals to a superior court exhausted.' O'Toole offers a weak smile at a joke Martin suspects is becoming threadbare. 'And yet death is, in a sense, liberating.'

'How so?'

'I no longer give a shit.'

'Right.' Martin wonders what medication the judge is on.

The judge smiles wickedly. 'I don't have to worry about the consequences.'

'Of what?'

'Talking to journalists, for a start.' And O'Toole laughs, as if at the absurdity of his predicament.

'I see,' says Martin, deciding not to waste the judge's time. 'Can I ask you about the Mess?'

'Ah, the Mess. So that's what's brought you here at this time of night. I was wondering why such a fine young journalist as yourself would want to seek me out. The Mess, is it?'

'Yes. What can you tell me about it?'

'Some of the worst food, some of the most mediocre company and some of the best wine I've ever encountered. I'd do it all again, if only for the wine.' And now, as if suddenly bored by his own banter, the judge grows earnest. 'What is it you want to know, Mr Scarsden?'

'I believe a great friend of mine, Max Fuller, was investigating the Mess, together with Elizabeth Torbett.'

'Ah, Lizzie,' he responds, and there is fondness in his voice. 'Lizzie, Lizzie, Lizzie. You should have known her when she was young. She was glorious. A great beauty.' And he pauses, as if remembering. 'And feisty as all hell. There were no boundaries for Lizzie, no telling her what she should or shouldn't do.' Another pause. 'We were at law school together. She never wanted much to do with the likes of me, of course; there were far more glittering stars in her firmament. And yet, for all of that, we were pals.' There is a wistful air to him now and a misting in his eyes. Martin wonders again as to the strength of the drugs. 'There was a night, skinny-dipping up in the Blue Mountains, when I almost thought I stood a chance. Before she started batting for the other side.' But now those eyes return to focus and Martin can see the intelligence, the calculation behind them. 'None of what I'm about to tell you comes out until after I die?'

'You have my word.'

The judge smiles. 'Ask away.'

'Did you help Max and Elizabeth with their investigations?'

'I did.'

'You were a source?'

'I was *the* source. Don't give me second billing, for God's sake. Max spent a lot of time here during the past couple of weeks, sitting where you are now. He even had a set of keys, could let himself in after the nurse had left for the day. He was here as recently as Saturday.'

'The source for what? What drove Elizabeth Torbett to join forces with Max Fuller?'

'Well, my little imbroglio, for a start.'

'The suppression order?'

'Ha. You know about that? Is there anyone who doesn't?'

Martin shrugs.

'So you know the situation. I was photographed in compromising circumstances. Wearing fishnets and ladies' underwear.' The judge smiles, the humour back. 'There was a time when I was a young chap, I might have carried it off.' And then the seriousness once more; Martin is getting used to the alternating moods. 'I was here one night, feeling sorry for myself, when there's a knock at the door. Two big men, full of muscles, and a smaller one, supervising them, gone to fat. All wearing balaclavas, like a bad movie. They knock me to the ground, haul me back up, punch me in the guts. They hold my arms behind my back. The little guy has a knife, holds it to my neck, uses his other hand to give my balls a gratuitous squeeze. They force me to drink some whisky; it tastes sweet. I'm not sure what was in it—some sort of drug. In no time, I've come over gah-gah. The little guy's holding the knife up in front of me, I can see how sharp it is, how easy it would be to hurt me. I see the gleam in his eye through the holes in his mask, glistening like the blade. He wants to hurt me. I can see it. Then he gives me a choice: he can slice off a testicle, or we can play dress-ups. I'm not thinking at all straight, but the idea of dress-ups seems such an easy out. So I do it, think I'm being clever, doing something so innocuous in order to save a ball. You'll understand: I've had two of them for a very long time and I've grown fond of them. So they strip me and I put on this women's underwear they've brought with them. You know, lingerie. Make me pose for photos. They're laughing, like it's the biggest joke on earth. I'm laughing too, the drugs doing their work. Then they leave. And as they leave, the little guy says, "We'll be in touch."'

'Do you have any idea why they did that to you?'

'Oh, indeed I do. The next week, I was at court, in chambers, when I received an email with the photos attached and a simple statement: *You know what to do.* Well, I did know what to do, and that was refuse to cave in to a blatant blackmail threat. I showed the photos to my fellow judges.' Justice O'Toole issues forth another low chuckle. 'There were some interesting reactions. The photos, you understand, have me dressed in fishnets and a suspender belt, but I don't look to be under duress. Rather, I'm laughing at the camera, looking as if I'm enjoying myself. Some of my colleagues were mortified, a few were intrigued. I think a couple were impressed. At least one fancies a bit of cross-dressing himself and thought he'd found a fellow traveller. But they were absolutely united in one thing: their determination to preserve the integrity and independence of the court and resist this blackmail attempt. The chief justice herself issued a suppression order.'

'So when was this?'

'About a month ago, maybe six weeks.'

'About the time of your diagnosis, then?'

'Just before.'

'What was it all about?' asks Martin. 'What did they want you to do?'

'It was an attempt to affect the outcome of a case I've been presiding over. A development application. A large one. But I wasn't having it. Not this time. The chief justice issued the suppression order and I hoped that might be the end of it. But I installed state-of-the-art security here in the house, just in case the thugs returned.'

'Surely you knew the suppression wouldn't hold, that gossip would spread?'

'Of course. That was the whole point.' And he smiles a teasing smile, his eyes alive with mischief. It occurs to Martin the judge is enjoying their exchange. 'People would know what happened. Not the public—forget them—but the people who count. They would know that I had told my fellow judges and that they supported me. The blackmail threat would lose its potency if it was known I had the full backing of my colleagues.'

'So it worked?'

The judge grimaces, and responds in a voice carrying the weight and inflections of the bench, of a finely crafted legal opinion. 'More or less. But there was collateral damage. It alerted Elizabeth to the real nature of the Mess. She was fiercely intelligent, of course, but somewhat naive. She believed everybody else shared her high-minded view of the world. I guess that's why she maintained her membership of the Mess even after her father and her brother resigned.'

'So what was it Elizabeth discovered?'

'Not so much discovered, but came to realise. Here's what happened.' And the judge pauses, as if to gather his thoughts. Or for dramatic effect. He really does appear to enjoy performing. Maybe it's the company; much better entertaining a journalist than sitting all alone, waiting in the night.

'The Mess, as you no doubt know, is secret. It has around thirty members. We meet once a month for dinner. Ostensibly, that's all there is to it. When Lizzie and I joined we were very junior; the founding generation still held sway. We only got in because of our fathers. We sat at the end of the tables, on the periphery, listening and learning. But years pass, and generations change. We became barristers, we took silk, we ascended to the bench. And we inherited the Mess as well. And we learnt how the world really operates: patronage, nepotism, networks of influence. It's true: it's entirely possible for a member to attend the dinners, endure the exotic dining and the well-informed discourse and leave it at that. Participate in some of our philanthropic endeavours. But that's not why people join the Mess and they know it. That's not its purpose.'

Martin says nothing. The judge is on a roll and he decides to let him speak.

'Among other things, the Mess is an information exchange, and not just at the monthly dinners. It's constant. We reveal information to each other that we really should not. If I want to know what is happening inside the Labor caucus or the Liberal party room, the politicians among us will tell me, openly and frankly. I'm sure they feed information to each other on a daily basis, across party lines. You can imagine how useful that would be. Members who are stockbrokers and businessmen give insider information on business deals, allowing other members to get in on the ground floor, to profit from it. I'm sure you know that's illegal.'

'And judges?' asks Martin.

That elicits another self-amused grin. 'We too provide information, sometimes circumventing the spirit of the law, sometimes the letter. But that's not all. As well as information, we exchange favours. At the lowest level, it is petty patronage. A member has a friend who has a son who wants to do a semester interning in the courts. No problem, nothing illegal about that, happens all the time. A member has a daughter who wants a job in a big city law firm, despite having a lacklustre academic record. It can be done. A member wants some confidential information on a case before the courts. Yes, it can be arranged. There's a spectrum: some members bend the rules, others disregard them, some rejoice in the power of breaking them. Are you following?'

'I believe I am, yes,' says Martin. 'Tell me, though: I've heard that Mess members have an obligation to assist each other wherever possible, but only within the law.'

The judge laughs, a real guffaw. 'Don't you believe it, son. We break the law, no doubt about it. With impunity. I've done it myself.' The judge pauses, then decides to qualify his assertions. 'Now, to be clear, there are likely members who have not done anything illegal, although I'd rather think they are in the minority.

Elizabeth Torbett always appeared to be like that, a Galahad at the Round Table, seeing only the shining armour and the Orders of Australia, the latter-day knights of the realm, unaware that some of them are thieves and scoundrels.' He pauses again, as if to pass judgement. 'It's my opinion that over the thirty-plus years I've been a member, there has been a growing acceptance of criminality, a normalisation. The Mess today is not what it once was: there's less philanthropy and more self-interest. Although you can be sure, if and when you publish, the philanthropy will get a big run in the papers. A bit of smooth media management and we'll come out looking like the victims.' Another humourless harrumph. Martin tries to interject, but the judge holds up one hand for quiet, like issuing a decree from the bench, and Martin remains silent.

'What I am saying is that we were always on a slippery slope, always destined to become more and more a law unto ourselves. But that process accelerated dramatically about six years ago. I believe we were infiltrated by a genuine criminal, a man named Harry Sweetwater.' Martin comes fully alert; Sweetwater—Mandy has mentioned him. The judge appears to notice his reaction. 'You've heard of him?'

'Yes, I have,' says Martin.

'Well, you're one of the few who has. Have you tried to find out who he is? What he does? What his past is?'

'I know he heads up security at an investment bank, Mollisons, but I don't know anything more than that.'

'I bet you don't.' The judge closes his eyes for a moment, appears to wince. Martin wonders if there is pain. The eyes open and he continues, the facade of bonhomie gone. 'I haven't been able to find out myself. Anyway, this Harry Sweetwater becomes a member about six years ago. And he's different. Most members, perhaps all members, sign up to the Mess hoping it will advance their careers and perhaps their wealth. Lawyers wanting to become senior counsels, politicians hoping to become ministers, businessmen aspiring to become moguls. Sweetwater is a banker. He's senior management but not on the company board, so he must have had good support to gain membership. First year or so he seemed pretty quiet, learning the ropes. Then, for the next few years, he was everybody's best friend, presenting himself as a Mr Fix-it, no problem too big or too small. He dispensed favours like a fairy godmother, and if people didn't have any problems, he would offer them favours regardless. He was very good, very affable. I was foolish; I took him up on it.' And now there is regret in the judge's eyes.

'What happened?'

'Nothing outrageous, nothing illegal. He organised a job for my niece. Bright girl but wild, in danger of going off the rails. Out all night, asleep all day, experimenting with drugs. Had a rough childhood, parents went through a shitty divorce, fell in with a very ordinary crew of ne'er-do-wells. She was facing some minor charges; a respectable job would help her to stay out of prison, avoid a record, perhaps straighten her out. He learnt of it somehow, offered to help; I accepted and he came through. He got her a good position at his bank, Mollisons, working for him. And a well-paid and respectable job it was at that.'

'What's her name, your niece?'

'Her name was Clarity Sparkes. My sister's kid.' The judge looks down, as if observing a moment's silence. 'She died about a year later—accidental drug overdose.'

Martin remembers now; Mandy had told him of the death of the security officer. He can see the pain in the dying man's eyes. Not just grief, but anguish. 'You don't believe it was an accident, do you?'

'No. I don't.'

'Why? What happened?'

'Ah. Now we get to it. She came to see me here, a week before she died.' The judge pauses to make the calculation. 'It was close to five years ago. My wife was still alive then; we had lunch here, out on the back patio. Then afterwards, Clarity and I spoke. She was worried, I could see that. She'd fiddled all through lunch, had hardly eaten a thing. She told me that she was disturbed by goings-on at Mollisons.' O'Toole gathers his thoughts before continuing. 'This came as a surprise to me. She'd been there for a year, loved the work, had made something of herself. They'd given her a grand title: head of physical security. It seemed pretty menial to me, but she loved it. The sense of responsibility, of being trusted. Of being part of a team. I'd been congratulating myself on getting her in the door, but suddenly she was really upset.' The judge looks around furtively, then leans over, fishes under his cushions and withdraws a hip flask. 'Just a dram,' he says, unscrewing the cap, taking a quick swig. 'Can't hurt me now.' He replaces the cap, stows the flask. 'Right. Where was I? Oh yes. This young lawyer had been discovered plotting to embezzle money from the bank, and she'd been tasked with sorting him out. She thought this was very strange, couldn't work out at first why they didn't simply call the police. Anyway, her boss, Harry Sweetwater, said they couldn't have the police anywhere near the place because the bank had an obligation to protect the privacy of its clients. Some twaddle like that. Anyway, she believes him, organises for this bloke she knew, a low-life who'd taken a shine to her, to beat up this lawyer and warn him off. Which happens and she thinks it's all sorted. She's disturbed, but she's also happy because Sweetwater is delighted and is heaping praise on her, telling her that she's one of them now.

'Then the next thing she knows, the lawyer has disappeared and so has ten million dollars. Sweetwater is livid, threatening to sack her, wondering how she could possibly have allowed the lawyer to get away with the loot. She's in danger of losing her job, so she starts investigating, interviewing staff members at the bank. After a while, Sweetwater calms down, tells her she's still part of the team, not to worry. They end up sacking a truckload of people. She keeps her job, but her suspicions have been raised. She starts digging.'

'And found what?'

'Irregularities. The way the bank sourced money, the way it operated. And she starts to suspect her own boss, Harry Sweetwater. She told me all this and a week later she was dead.'

'So what did you do?'

'What did I do? Not enough, coward that I am. Oh, I had a word to Roger Macatelli, the deputy police commissioner. A good fellow, mind like a steel trap. I impressed upon him my suspicion that Clarity had been a victim of foul play, told him of *her* suspicions, and he assured me the case would be thoroughly examined. But it came to nothing. The police determined it was a self-administered overdose and so did the coroner. I knew then that Macatelli was either compromised himself or had been overruled by those who were. The fix was in; there was little I could do about it.' The judge smiles, a bitter expression, and adds, almost wistfully, like an aside to himself, 'You can't fight city hall.'

Macatelli. That name again. 'I'm assuming Roger Macatelli is a member of the Mess?'

'Of course.'

Martin pauses, making sure he has assimilated all the judge has told him before responding. 'That was almost five years ago. What's changed, other than your condition?'

'My condition, as you so coyly describe it, has quite a bit to do with it. It means I now give zero fucks.' Martin can't help but be amused, the youthful phrase expressed in the sonorous voice of authority. O'Toole continues, again alternating from flippancy to gravitas: 'A month or two ago, Harry Sweetwater came to me, wanting a favour. After all, he reminded me, he'd hired Clarity as a favour to me.' The judge breathes deep. 'He said that to me. Really, he did.' Another pause, emotions bubbling. 'So I smiled and I went along with it. He wanted me to find in favour of a Mess member in a court case.'

'What case?' asks Martin.

'A development application. I mentioned it earlier. A huge one. On the north shore, towering over Luna Park. Massive. As big as Barangaroo. Retail, a hotel, cinemas, thousands of apartments. A casino. Just what this city needs: more apartments, another casino. But it was never going to win approval. As the law and the regulations stand, the application didn't have a chance.'

'Was this the same development application? The one with the photographs, the blackmail attempt and the suppression order?'

'One and the same.'

'When did Sweetwater approach you? Before or after all that?'

'About a week before.'

'Let me guess,' says Martin. 'Large Sky.'

That gets the judge's attention. 'Very good. How did you know that?'

'I didn't. I was just guessing. Who was the Mess member?'

'A new man, George Giopolis. Never really had much to do with him.'

So Giopolis is a Mess member too. 'What did you do?'

'I said no. I joined the Mess to advance my career, not destroy it. To obtain a degree of power, not to become someone's pawn. Of course, that's not what I said to Sweetwater's face. I told him it was pointless; that if I were to hand down such an unsound verdict it would be overturned on appeal to the Supreme Court. Sweetwater said that wasn't a problem, he'd spoken to Elizabeth and she was onside.'

Martin blinks. He wasn't expecting this. 'What does that mean, she was onside?'

'That she would arrange to hear the appeal and find in favour of Giopolis and Large Sky.'

'You're saying Elizabeth Torbett was corrupt? I thought you just said she was Sir Galahad?'

'She was. He just didn't know it yet.'

'Sorry, I don't follow. What happened?'

'I had dinner with Elizabeth. All very civilised, at our club, a polite conversation, a few snifters. I told her what had happened. All of it. I was very candid, listed some of my past misdemeanours. It had something of the atmosphere of a confessional.' He pauses, seeks out his hip flask and takes another fortifying swig. 'She was appalled. Devastated. Especially when I told her that Sweetwater claimed she was onside. Like Galahad realising the round table was full of termites.' He clears his throat, puts the flask away. 'Sorry. Bad analogy.'

'What happened?'

'That week, the case came before court. It became apparent I wasn't going to indulge Large Sky. After I reserved judgement, I was photographed in women's underwear.' The judge shakes his head. 'And then, not long after that, the diagnosis was in. I was dying. I didn't care. My wife was dead, Clarity was dead, my sons are living overseas, and I'm dying. So why would I help that cunt?'

'And you told all of this to Elizabeth?'

'I did.'

'So she teams up with Max to do an exposé.'

'Something like that.'

Martin thinks it through. He can understand O'Toole's actions and motivations, but those of Elizabeth Torbett seem less clear. 'But it doesn't make sense. She was a Supreme Court judge, daughter of a High Court judge; no one could be more embedded in the Sydney establishment than she was. Why would she need to go to Max? I heard she held journalists in contempt.'

Now O'Toole looks serious, nodding slowly. 'That's very perceptive of you. It's true. Sydney might be rotten, but it's not that rotten. There are plenty of honourable and decent and unblemished people in this city: judges, politicians, police.'

'So why not go to them?'

'Isn't it obvious? Sweetwater had something on her.'

'Do you know what it was?'

'No.'

'Would you tell me if you did?'

'Depends.'

Martin finds himself frowning. 'I still don't get it.'

'Oh, I think you probably do. You just don't want to admit it.'

'Tell me.'

'She went to her brother-in-law, Max Fuller, the former newspaper editor. Elizabeth disliked him, to be honest; thought he was a muckraker and a socialist. But she saw a use for him. She presented Fuller with evidence that his removal from the editorship of the *Herald* had been orchestrated through the Mess. Your friend took the bait, and why wouldn't he? She was offering a huge story, a fitting epilogue to his brilliant career, a vindication, an up-yours to the people who had cut short his editorship.'

Martin shifts in his seat, trepidation growing, understanding emerging.

O'Toole smiles grimly and continues. 'Max Fuller and Elizabeth started working up a sensational piece exposing the Mess, but concentrating very much on the activities of Harry Sweetwater. As I understand it, her idea was to present the Mess as largely benign, an innocent dining club infiltrated by a career criminal. By this time, you understand, some other members were also having second thoughts about our Mr Fix-it, as they got wind of the suppression order and worked out what had happened. As you can imagine, I was enjoying the moment. My diagnosis was in, so I started filling them in, sticking it to the little shit.' The judge takes a deep breath. 'So when the time was right, Elizabeth sent Sweetwater an anonymous email with a lengthy excerpt of the piece attached. The email was untraceable, the excerpt redacted to protect informants, but Sweetwater would know that Elizabeth was the author and that Max Fuller had the influence to have it published. Sweetwater's position was already being undermined by my suppression order and the story behind it. Elizabeth's message was clear: back off or this goes to press. And she wanted Sweetwater to resign from the Mess, or we would sit as his jury. We were confident he'd overreached his position and we were going to put him back in his box.'

'She was threatening Sweetwater with exposure?'

'Yes. The nuclear option. Mutually assured destruction.'

'So he was under real pressure?'

'I would say so. Then, a few days later, she and Max Fuller were murdered. Dressed in lingerie, a clear message to me and anyone else in the Mess: keep our mouths shut or end up like them.'

Martin can't believe it. 'But that's not the nuclear option, that's the doomsday option. Surely the other members aren't going to cave to that sort of pressure. Who knows where it might end?'

The judge harrumphs. 'One would hope they won't, and eventually they might push back. But let me ask you this: how is the investigation into the murders of Lizzie and Max Fuller proceeding? Are the police getting stuck in, or are they still pretending it was suicide, the same way they pretended Clarity accidentally killed herself?'

Martin accepts the point; the judge knows what he's talking about. In the ensuing silence, he wonders how much D'Arcy knows. But for now, he stays with O'Toole's narrative. 'Let me take you back a step: you're saying that Elizabeth Torbett had no intention of publishing the piece, that it was meant purely as a threat to get Sweetwater off her back?'

'That's right. As I say, going through with the threat and publishing was the nuclear option: it would destroy Sweetwater but most likely it would also destroy Elizabeth and take the Mess and a fair few of its members down with it. No, it was a threat that was never meant to be used. I'm sorry about that, Mr Scarsden, but this was a high-stakes game and Elizabeth needed Fuller's name on the article to demonstrate it wasn't an empty threat.'

'But that's her motive. Why would Max agree to hold the story?'

'A Supreme Court injunction. A suppression order. Pre-emptive defamation writs. Board members worried about financial impli-cations. Mess members applying pressure and friendly advice. It could have been done.'

'I think she might have underestimated Max.' And Martin thinks of his mentor, spending so much time with O'Toole. Why do that when he had access to Elizabeth and her knowledge? Double-checking his facts? *Never rely on one source when you can use two.* Did he not entirely trust Elizabeth, did he suspect she didn't really want to publish?

'That's very loyal of you,' says the judge, bringing Martin back to the present. 'And yet he's dead and the story remains unpublished.' Again, O'Toole changes the tone of his voice, growing sympathetic. 'Whatever Elizabeth thought of him, I liked him. He had a commitment to the truth. Lawyers don't, as a rule: we just seek and reward the better argument.'

'You said he was here on Saturday. What did you talk about?'

'He came to tell me that they'd found Molloy's body. He was quite excited. Said the police couldn't ignore the murder. He said it might even shed some light on Clarity's death.'

'He was interested in Clarity?'

'No, but I was. It was part of our deal: I'd tell him all about the Mess if he could try to find out what happened to her.'

'What did he say?'

'He said he'd heard a rumour that Molloy's accomplice, a woman called Zelda Forshaw, was with Clarity when she died.'

'He wanted to find Zelda?'

'No. But I did. Max was more interested in Harry Sweetwater.'

Martin thinks this through. 'You suspect Sweetwater of murdering Max and Elizabeth Torbett?'

'He certainly had a motive. But possibly so did others.'

'Shouldn't you be telling this to the police rather than me?'

'The police? You disappoint me, Mr Scarsden. The police know a good deal about it. Indeed, too much for their own liking. I've made sure they do. The link between my photograph and the murder scene is obvious, but they don't dare interview me. The police are going nowhere with this. I understand the only reason any progress at all is being made is because Fuller's widow, Elizabeth's widower and old Sir Talbot have been applying pressure. But against the influence of the Mess, I can't say I like their chances. Harry Sweetwater may yet escape justice.'

'Is that why you're telling me all this?'

'Yes. I want you to get Sweetwater. Not appease, not threaten, not coerce. Not some private accommodation, not allowing him to crawl back under whatever rock he came from. Elizabeth tried that.' Now, at last, the measured tones of justice have been replaced by something more visceral. 'I want you to destroy him—to hang, draw and quarter him and stick his head on a pike on the city walls. I want you to fuck him six ways to Sunday. And if it means taking down the Mess with him, that's the price we'll have to pay.'

Martin is momentarily silenced by the judge's vehemence, then asks, 'You're sure? What about your reputation?'

'That's in your hands. My reputation. Elizabeth's. Max Fuller's. But don't delay. Once you've published, you should be safe. Sweetwater will never sue, no matter how damning the allegations. He will do anything to avoid appearing in open court, where his past, his character and his actions would be open to interrogation.' The judge takes another small swig from his hip flask, as if he's rationing life itself. 'You have a story here, Mr Scarsden, a scoop, perhaps the biggest that ever there was. It's your opportunity to avenge the death of your friend, Max Fuller. Do with it what you will.' The judge lets that sink in before slowly trying to stand, wincing at the effort and failing at the first attempt. He tries again, succeeds. He looks around the room as if it has become unfamiliar. 'I must go now. Just because I'm dying, it doesn't mean I don't have to shit. Please don't try to contact me unless it's absolutely necessary.'

'Of course.'

'There is one more thing. A most important thing. Take this.' The judge reaches into a pocket of his robe, withdraws a business card, hands it to Martin. 'Keep it somewhere safe.'

'What is it?' Martin asks, examining the card.

'A website, with the username and password.'

'It's a security company.'

'Yes. This house is now packed full with closed-circuit television cameras.' O'Toole cocks his head towards a corner of the room. Martin turns but sees nothing, even as the judge continues. 'Fibre optics. They all feed into the site. You can review at least the past forty-eight hours.'

'Why would I want to do that?'

'Not now. In case something happens to me. Something unto-ward.' The judge smiles. 'The police tell me they haven't found the keys I gave to Max Fuller.'

Martin stares at him. 'Change the locks.'

'Might be too late for that. Too late for a lot of things.' O'Toole looks him in the eye, gaze unwavering. 'I handed down my last judgement earlier today—blocking the Large Sky development.' Another swig from his flask. 'So there's no longer any reason for them to keep me alive.'

chapter twenty-nine

SHE SHOULD BE CELEBRATING; SOME PART OF HER IS TELLING HERSELF THAT. She's alerted the police to a crucial piece of information, perhaps the decisive piece of evidence: Henry Livingstone entering the lift with Tarquin Molloy on the very day the undercover policeman was shot dead. She should be in town telling Martin the news, handing him his scoop: the police had the evidence all along, they just didn't realise it. So why isn't she? Instead, she's on a train, destination unknown: a suburban train, heading west. Soon enough, somewhere in the suburbs or out at Penrith or up in the Blue Mountains, she will need to alight and get another train back into the city. But not yet; she feels too flat, too emotionally spent.

She has to tell Martin what happened with the police, knows she must. He's a journalist; she can't let him publish the wrong story. He can't trumpet the video as dramatic new evidence when in reality it isn't, when the police have had it all these years. He's done that before—publish stories that were wrong or only half true—and paid the price for his inaccuracies. But she doesn't want to face him, not yet, so she texts him, the easy way out: *Police already had video from back then. But MM didn't realise it was HL at the lift!!* There. Duty done.

The Turtle had played her, set her up to look a fool in front of the homicide detectives, Montifore and Lucic. He must have known the police already had the video; he would have been the one who supplied it five years ago. It was pure luck he'd actually provided something useful. He'd manipulated her, like a child, and she'd fallen for it; he'd given her nothing while extracting her promise to protect him in return. And even now, his threat of exposure is real. Just thinking of it makes her feel sordid.

And so she rides the night train, the commuter rush over, the office workers already home and only the after-work drunks, the homeless and the shiftworkers remaining. Up in a corner she spies the telltale black hemisphere of a CCTV camera, like an inverted snowdome. She looks away out the window instead, holding her hands up to shield her face, to cut the glare from the carriage lights. The train rushes onwards, past the high-rises, their windows chequerboards of life; past building sites, work continuing under floodlights; past intersections arthritic with traffic. The endless sprawl, the city reaching on across its basin between the sea and the mountains, millions of lives, millions of struggles.

What had she been thinking, running off by herself like that, playing such a dangerous game? Martin's been a journalist for twenty years, reporting from all round the world, from count-less hellholes, dealing with all sorts of despots. He knows how this game works: the rules, the risks, the ethics. And yet she'd sat at the Turtle's table, played with his pack of cards, and lost. The Turtle had got what he wanted: her guarantee of silence. This she understands: he wants to remain in the shadows, to escape police interrogation. But why give her the video in the first place, if he knew the police already had it? To demonstrate his prowess, his array of cameras? Or because he wanted her to identify Henry Livingstone to the police? Was that possible? To put the police on the right track, to divert any attention from himself and Mollisons? She racks her memory: she can't remember either of them mentioning Livingstone by name, but he'd been aware of her interest in the man joining Molloy in the lift. Was that it?

She desperately wants to confide in Martin. It was so liberating when she'd told him about helping Tarquin, memorising the alpha-numeric codes, the information he'd used to embezzle a small fortune. But that information only ever had the potential to harm herself, no one else. The sex tapes are different. They're nothing to be ashamed of, she knows that. She hadn't been doing anything wrong; Martin would understand. But she can't bear the thought of Liam one day seeing them, hearing the stories of his mother being screwed and discarded by a corrupt cop, a disposable tool as he planned to steal his millions. She can imagine her son, sitting on his own school bus, subject to his own ridicule, carrying the scandal of his own mother. She needs to protect him; she needs to keep the secret.

And it comes to her, a sullen revelation. It's not just the Turtle she's done a deal with, it's the past. The past, that she was so determined to confront. It's hunted her down, cornered her, and she's compromised, agreeing to keep it secret, compartmentalised away. But what choice does she have? She lowers her hands; she sees her reflection in the window, her face distorted by some flaw in the glass, a twisted version, lit by the flickering green light of the carriage. She stares at herself, her own empty eyes. She needs to keep the past in the past.

The train slows, pulls in at Strathfield, wheels screeching, not fully aligned to the tracks, tracks not fully aligned with each other. People pile off, a few get on, no one speaks, seemingly possessed by their smartphones. The platform is lined with billboards, placards of allure, promising, always promising: the casino, off-the-plan apartments, payday lenders. And models. Glorious in their beauty, young and carefree, with airbrushed skin and photoshopped teeth, eyes luminous with confidence. Her gaze drifts downwards to the old men asleep on the benches beneath the hoardings, huddled against the cold. The real Sydney. The train eases out; the old men don't look up.

Fifteen minutes later the train squeals into Parramatta, wheels wailing like an animal in extremis. The train breathes; more passengers flow in and out into the humming night. A woman gets on, smart in her business suit, phone clamped to her ear. A successful woman, a career woman. It makes Mandy think of Pam. Pam with her career. And her self-respect, her empathy, her principles. Mandy had pitied her once, back in the day, when the world was golden, illuminated by Tarquin's promises, when she shone out from her own imagined billboard and Pam was just a member of her audience, another commuter on the platform beneath. How is it possible that she felt sorry for Pam? Pam, who'd been to university, earned a degree, had won her position at Mollisons on merit, her promotions through ability and hard work. Who had been so kind and so caring. And yet Mandy had felt superior, courtesy of Tarquin, her high-flying fiancé. But none of it had been earned; it was airbrushing and photoshopping, her existence a vacuity. Before Tarquin, she'd been down and out, a borderline junkie, hopeless and helpless, floating on the Sydney pond with Billy the bass player. And then Tarquin had pulled her up, a latter-day Pygmalion, arranging her job, arranging her life. But it was a play: Tarquin was an actor, a professional imposter. God, how could she have sneered at Pam?

'Are you all right?' It's the corporate woman, standing above her.

'What?' asks Mandy, even as she touches her face, feeling the wetness.

'Is there someone I can call?'

'No. It's fine.'

'Are you sure? You have somewhere to stay?'

Mandy smiles. 'It's okay. I have money. I have a hotel. I'm just upset, that's all.'

The woman smiles back. 'All right then.' She looks up, the train is slowing. 'This is my stop. Take care.'

Mandy watches the woman disembark. Then, at the last moment, she scrambles off herself. Time to cross the tracks, to return, to re-engage. She thinks of the woman, the woman who cared. She thinks of Pam. It's time to push back, to respect herself.

———

Walking. He walks through the emptying streets, the air still and taut, the streetlights losing their struggle against the encroaching night. He passes through Hyde Park, the fairy lights sparkling in the trees, bequeathing a wonderland glow to the ice addicts yabbering incoherently beneath them. He's making progress, real progress. Clarence O'Toole has gifted him a mighty story, of murder and corruption and conspiracy. He can't sit on it, he can't avoid it, he has to write it. The judge has provided so much information it's difficult to assimilate it all. But at its heart, he has connected the two murders: the murders of Max and Elizabeth are linked to their investigation of the Mess, and the Mess is connected to Mollisons and the execution of Tarquin Molloy. And to Large Sky, to George Giopolis and, most of all, to Harry Sweetwater. The story: he can feel it, almost smell it. But there is no sense of excitement, no thrill. Not this time.

Max. Not dead for some great journalistic scoop. Not Watergate, not the Panama Papers, not the Moonlight State. No. Played. Played by Elizabeth Torbett, used as a pawn in her attempts to outmanoeuvre Harry Sweetwater. The internecine squabbles of an entitled elite, corrupt and careless.

Part of him doesn't want to return to the hotel, doesn't want to face Mandy, doesn't want to explain how the man he had so idolised, the man who had made him, who had been like a second father, had been so humiliated. And part of him does. Part of him wants to run to her, to cry in her arms, to let her comfort him. What is wrong with that, after all? Aren't they in this together, the two of them? Not just this investigation, this story, but this life? Not just the easy times, cocooned in Port Silver, but the difficult times, when the world comes calling with unwelcome news?

He should tell her; he knows he should. But poor Max, lying dead and desecrated on the floor of his own home. How can Martin really write the truth, shatter his mentor's reputation, tell the world that he died for nothing? Can he front Eileen Fuller, reveal that her husband was a dupe? Or explain to Benjamin that his wife was no Sir Galahad, to Sir Talbot that his daughter was just another conniving operator? What will the old man think as he reads Martin's story, sitting in his armchair by the bay window? What then of his lifetime of service?

Martin knows he doesn't have to write the story that way. He could present Max as a victim and nothing more; he could gloss over Elizabeth's treachery. It would be easy enough. He's done it before in his books, the authoritative accounts of murder and more in Riversend and Port Silver. Wasn't that the great lesson learnt? That he should have compassion, that he should spare the innocent? But this time it feels different. This time he will be writing about the Mess, of patronage and nepotism, of favours given and favours owed. And who is he, to condemn the likes of Clarence O'Toole for using back channels to secure a job for his niece, or D'Arcy Defoe for turning a blind eye to misdemeanours in the pursuit of a bigger story, while he himself is sparing some and condemning others, playing the gatekeeper just like D'Arcy? Is that it? Is that what has him walking the impersonal streets— this sense of hypocrisy? Or is it more than that? In the past he spared some people from the full glare of publicity, but this time it's not just them but himself he would be sparing. Is he motivated by compassion for them or for himself?

Yet he knows there is no holding the story. If he doesn't write it, someone else will. Doug Thunkleton, with his limited compre-hension, tabloid sensibilities and overreliance on Eileen Fuller; or D'Arcy, playing the angles, selecting what to and what not to report. Better himself, then, than the others. The Mess needs to be revealed in all its decadence. Sir Talbot is right; it's a boil that needs to be lanced. He realises there is little room for finesse:

he must write the story, the full story. He owes it to society, he owes it to himself, he owes it to the victims. And a memory comes to him, a memory of Max, as Martin struggled with telling the story at Riversend, the awful events out in the scrublands. 'Protect your sources; everything else goes in. If it's newsworthy, the public has a right to know,' Max pronounced. 'We're not here to play God.'

Martin understands now why Max had forsaken the *Herald*. It would be too easy for them to spike his mighty exposé, or to cull it, the way they did to Bethanie's initial report of Max and Elizabeth Torbett's deaths—Roger Macatelli calling in a favour from D'Arcy Defoe. And it would be hard to argue against: the members of the Mess must include some of Sydney's most prominent and influential citizens. Even if backroom pressure wasn't brought to bear, even if the editors stood up to boardroom pressure, the lawyers would be all over it, demanding every last allegation be ironclad, lest the defamation cases ruin the company, in these days when there was so little hard cash propping up the famous masthead. And that's even before the legal impediments that O'Toole had spoken of: injunctions and suppression orders, gagging writs and sub judice, threats of contempt of court. It wouldn't be the first time a media company folded on a story because the legal risks were too great. He thinks of Wellington Smith, based in Melbourne; perhaps the influence of the Mess is weaker in the Victorian capital.

He leaves the park, crosses Oxford Street up by Whitlam Square. A memory comes to him of being out late at night, Friday nights, back when he was a cadet, back in the glory days of the *Herald*, before the classified ads migrated to the internet and the display ads followed them, back when the paper had clout and more money than it knew what to do with, and the world belonged to them, him and his fellow cadets. Of how, after an evening of drinking and carousing, they'd stagger up to Taylor Square at midnight to buy the papers fresh off the truck; the big fat Saturday papers, still warm from the presses, still smelling of printer's ink, like fresh-baked bread to the young tribe of reporters, leavened by classified ads and supplements. And waking the next day to find the paper there to greet him, among the cigarette butts and empty bottles and the hangovers, left open at the page where he had found his own newly minted by-line.

He comes to a convenience store, enters the garish light. He looks around, searching for a newspaper, finds nothing. Just a few magazines: *Home Beautiful*, *Gourmet Traveller*; a slurry of gossip mags shouting the latest inventions about Harry and Meghan; a couple of tired skin mags, their plastic covers a flimsy prophylactic in this digital age.

'Newspapers? No, mate. Try station,' says the clerk, shielded behind security glass.

So Martin does just that, walks towards Central, suddenly motivated. It can't be true; surely the *Herald* cannot have vacated the field so completely.

Another convenience store. When did all these carbon copy eyesores proliferate, these pustules on the inner-city streetscape? Was it the backpackers, the tourists, the foreign students? The family milk bar, the corner store, unable to compete with corporate efficiencies and wage theft. But this one, at least, has some newspapers. Friday's are yet to arrive, printed who knows where. One copy of Thursday's *Herald* languishes. Martin picks it up. Thinner than it used to be, emaciated, but still here. He feels proud; proud of his former colleagues, of their rearguard defence. But he knows it's not where his story will be published; he's come to the same conclusion as Max. And he feels the same sense of grief his mentor must have experienced that night he went into the *Herald* and scrubbed his drives.

Was it really so long ago, Martin wonders, when the trucks dropped the papers at Taylor Square, when he and his workmates would greedily buy them, working their way through them, learning the fate of their stories: where they were run and at what length? He misses the camaraderie. They've all gone now, off to public relations and private enterprise, joining the government or climbing the greasy pole into management, chasing the corporate dollar and family-friendly work hours. Of his intake, there's only D'Arcy and himself left. And now it will only be D'Arcy, the winner of a two-decades-long reality TV show: *Survivor: Sydney Morning Herald*. For Martin realises he's leaving the *Herald* for good; not just for this story, but forever. When Wellington Smith publishes the story in *This Month*, that will be the end. There will be no going back, not this time. D'Arcy has trusted him, helped him gain access to Clarence O'Toole on the understanding the two of them are now working together. He knows he's about to betray that trust, maybe for a good reason, but he understands that D'Arcy will never forgive him.

He pulls out the business card Clarence gave him. He should tell Yev about it, make sure they monitor the security website. He has to admire the judge, trying to finesse his own death. Talking to Martin, establishing his side of the story. And almost inviting retribution, hoping to die, to be martyred, while the CCTV makes a permanent record. Martin can't help but think it noble: to go out with a bang, to make your death mean something, rather than just sliding into oblivion, sedated and unaware.

Martin's phone rings, pulling him from the depths of his contemplation. An unlisted number.

'Hello?'

'It's Jack Goffing. We need to meet.'

FRIDAY

chapter thirty

DURING THE STILL OF THE NIGHT, A HAZE HAS SPREAD ACROSS SYDNEY, TURNING the dawn grey and the rising sun a lurid orange. This acrid shroud, choking and ominous, carries the smell of a thousand campfires and the sense of the earth turned awry. Mandy peers into it through eyes growing scratchy, buildings disappearing in the distance. Sydney is on edge: workers wear face masks, leftovers from the summer's fires and the winter's pandemic.

'Bushfires? In winter?' she says. 'Surely not.'

She watches as Martin checks the *Herald* site on his phone. 'Hazard reduction,' he says. 'The Blue Mountains. They burn whenever it's safe. Winter and no wind.'

That's it, she realises: it's the lack of wind that's creating the sense of eeriness, as much as the smoke itself. The day sits upon her like a weight, a portent.

Martin turns to her. 'You up for this?'

'Of course—let's do it,' she says, remembering to smile.

At Ichiban Computers and Scarvery, there's a young man with dead-straight, pure white hair, sitting behind a counter in front of an old-fashioned computer monitor, helping a customer. Mandy thinks the young client would be better off buying acne cream than splurging on the latest video card, but the gleam in his eyes and the excitement in his voice suggests he thinks different. While they wait, Mandy wanders to the scarvery, where a young woman is opening some new stock: pashmina scarves. She looks like the guy behind the computer counter, except with normal colouring, her straight hair brown and her eyes grey. She introduces herself as Lena, recommending a green scarf to match Mandy's eyes. Mandy accepts the advice, buying the scarf and a set of three cotton bandanas for Martin. You never know when you might need a bandana in these days of smoke and viruses. Mandy pays. Lena smiles.

By the time she's finished the purchase the young gamer has left and Martin introduces her to Yevgeny. Then he gets straight to business. 'Yev, we need your help. Our investigation; we've made some progress.'

Yev's eyes widen. 'No shit?'

'No shit.' Martin smiles.

'How can I help?'

It's Mandy who takes the initiative. 'There's a couple of things we want to check out online. But before we do, can you enhance video? Zoom in, sharpen focus, that sort of technology?'

Yev shrugs. 'Probably.'

'We'll pay, of course.'

'Good. I'm not a charity.' A dry grin. 'What have you got?'

Mandy shows him her phone, the video of Tarquin Molloy, the CCTV from Mollisons.

Yev nods, a slight grimace, already intrigued by the challenge. 'Yeah. I can clean it up a bit. Most video software has some capability. The cops and the intelligence services have the really good stuff.'

'Can you zoom in?'

Another grimace. 'Don't expect miracles. The software can extrapolate to a very limited extent, but you can't see what isn't there. Not even the spooks can do that.'

'It runs for about twenty minutes, but we don't need all of it processed, just a few important moments,' says Martin. 'Does the man in the suit insert a flash drive into the computer? Is there any way to determine what he types on the keyboard? And right at the end, a second man gets into the lift with him. Can we enhance that, see if the new man is holding anything?'

Yev shrugs. 'That sounds like a pretty tall order to me.' Then the same dry grin. 'But we won't know if we don't give it a go.'

It's a good grin, Mandy decides, nothing duplicitous about it. She wonders how old Yev is. He seems young, like he's fresh out of uni. Too young to be overwhelmed by the guile and calculations of the world.

'Can you email me the clip?' he asks her. He pulls out his phone, selects an email address from a long list and gives it to her. She sends the file as an attachment. 'Come on. I have another work station behind the counter. Less charm, more grunt.'

It's quite a contrast to the retro box on the counter; this set-up is ultra-modern. There are two huge screens, a keyboard, a mouse, a drawing tablet and stylus, an impressive set of speakers and a bespoke tower under the desk, a case of brushed aluminium and glowing blue plastic.

'Impressive,' says Martin.

'Built it myself,' says Yev, and there is a touch of pride in his voice. He sits, inviting Martin and Mandy to pull up a chair. There is only one and she takes it, Martin standing. He can't stay long, he says. Yev logs on, opens up a web browser, goes to the email site, selecting the address he has given Mandy.

'How many accounts do you have?' she asks.

'Plenty.' He finishes logging on. There is only one email in the inbox: Mandy's. He clicks on it, retrieves the attachment, attempts to open it. But the computer baulks, bringing up a warning dialogue box. His hand hovers over the mouse, the cursor hovers over the ignore button. 'Where did you get this?'

'From a source,' says Mandy.

'A trusted source?'

'No,' she says, thinking of the Turtle. 'I wouldn't say that.'

'Right. Can I have your phone?'

'Why?'

'I just need to check.'

'For what?'

'Viruses. Malware. It shouldn't take too long.'

Mandy shrugs, hands over her phone. Yev forages around for a lead, attaches the phone, gets Mandy to unlock it.

'Right. Let's have a squiz.' He opens a program. Mandy can see a blue line running across the screen, indicating progress. It finishes its pass, declares the phone virus-free. 'That's strange,' says Yev. He checks the phone then goes online, searching a bulletin board. Mandy looks at Martin, who shrugs and raises his eyebrows.

'Okay,' says Yev. 'Let's give this a thrash.' He goes to another site, selects some software, paying with a credit card number he selects at random from a long list.

'I can pay,' says Mandy.

'No. You don't want your credit card anywhere near this.'

'Right,' she says, exchanging another look with Martin.

Yev goes offline, plugs the phone back in. The interface of the new software is less sleek, more homespun, monochrome instead of colour. The text looks Cyrillic. When Yev sets it to work, instead of a coloured bar there is simply a percentage completed ticker. It's up to seventy-four per cent when it stops. A pirate flag drops down from the top of the screen. A line of script appears, again with the foreign alphabet.

'What does it say?' asks Mandy.

'Jesus,' says Yev to himself. 'Jesus.' He hurriedly unplugs the phone from the computer, before addressing them. 'It's Russian. Cutting edge. It says: *You are fucked. Code 63457. Have a nice day.*'

'What is it?' Martin asks. 'What has it found?'

'Nothing good.' Yev takes a photo of the screen with his own phone, then shuts down the computer, turning to them. 'Your phone has a virus. Malware. Probably associated with that video. I'm just going to run a check on my computer. It shouldn't be infected, but I want to make sure. Then I'll disinfect your phone.'

'She shared it with me,' says Martin. 'The video.'

'On your phone? Did you open it, play it?'

'Yes,' says Martin, the concern evident in his face.

'Not good,' says Yev. 'Power it off. You too, Mandy.' They do as he says. He takes their devices and places them in a steel box.

It takes ten minutes for Yev to ensure his computer is clean. Then he's back online, searching for code 63457. He ends up in a chat room on the deep web, writing and reading in Russian. He closes his browser, then turns to them, face serious, delivering the bad news.

'It's new and it's sophisticated. As soon as you played the video, it essentially handed control of your phone over to a third party. They could access all your data, monitor your calls, track your location. They could turn the camera and microphone on without your knowledge. The lot.'

'Shit,' says Martin.

'Shit,' says Mandy. 'What do we do now?'

'I wipe your phones clean, reinstall the operating system. You'll lose all your data. Photos, contacts, everything. I hope you've backed up, that there's nothing too precious.'

'The video?' asks Mandy.

Yev shakes his head. 'No. It's irretrievable.'

'Jesus,' says Martin. 'My phone backup is on my laptop. The one that got stolen.'

'The cloud?' asks Yev.

'Nup,' says Martin. Then he turns to Mandy. 'The video. You showed it to Montifore. Did you share a copy with him?'

'No. I told you last night, they already had it.'

'So it's just you and me; we're the only ones infected?'

'Yes. I think so.'

'Thank God. Imagine if we'd infected the police force.' And he laughs, expressing his nerves.

'Okay,' says Yev. 'You guys want to get a coffee or something? It'll take me a while to restore your phones.'

*

The moment they walk into his cafe, Aldo is effusive, smile spread almost as wide as his arms, rushing out from behind the counter, stunning Mandy with a massive embrace before releasing her just as quickly. 'Martin! You bring her. At last, you bring her!' And then to her: *'Bellissima!* Gorgeous!' To Martin: 'You are a lucky man, mate!' Back to her: 'What do you want? Coffee? Cake? Panini? On the house.' She can't help herself; despite the phone virus, despite the smoke-laden city, she finds herself smiling.

But when they sit at a table, Martin's smile soon fades.

'What is it?'

'Nothing. Don't worry about it.'

'Martin?'

'It's just my phone. My contacts. I'll never get some of them back.'

She laughs. 'Is that all? People are dead and you're worried about your phone?' But as soon as she says it, she knows she's overstepped the mark.

She can see the anger in his eyes as he retorts, 'Your source, the video. They set you up. The cops already had it. All the source gave you was a virus. So yes. I'm upset. Twenty years of contacts wiped because you didn't have the wit to recognise what was happening.'

She spits back at him, 'Twenty years of contacts wiped because you couldn't be arsed backing them up properly.'

Martin stands, not waiting for his coffee or his panini. 'I'm going for a walk. I'll see you later.' His voice is even, reasonable. Benign. It sends a shiver through her.

'Where are you going?'

'To check on the apartment. See if I can organise a clean-up. I can't leave it sitting there with the door off its hinges.' He looks at her for a long moment. She can feel his eyes upon her, as if judging her, before he speaks again. 'And I need to talk to Wellington Smith. Like I told you last night.'

And then she's alone with her self-recriminations. Over behind the espresso machine, Aldo is averting his eyes, no longer smiling. God, is it that obvious?

She drinks her coffee, waits for Martin, but he doesn't return. She waits five minutes more, then pays and leaves. When she gets back to Ichiban he's already there, discussing some sort of website, Yev staring at a business card. The computer whizz doesn't seem to notice anything wrong between them, handing over her phone. 'Good to go. Can you set it up, please? Passwords, fingerprint recognition, facial recognition, all that stuff.' She looks across at Martin, but he's concentrating on his own phone. So she does what she's told, setting up her handset. Unlike Martin, she can't remember her PIN or passwords and she's forced to create new ones. Yev isn't bothered—another customer has arrived and he's busy at the counter—but she can feel the irritation radiating from Martin, forced to waste his precious time waiting for her to set up her phone.

Finally, she's done and Yev is back with them. 'Right. Now, can you go to the App Store and download WhatsApp? We need to be able to communicate safely.'

'Why WhatsApp?' asks Mandy.

'End-to-end encryption,' says Martin. 'Good idea.'

But nothing is simple. Now Mandy has to replace her old password for the App Store. It's another ten minutes before she's good to go.

'One more,' says Yev. 'Give me your phones.'

'What is it?' asks Martin.

'I'm installing a tracking app, also encrypted. It will let each of us see where the others are at any given time.'

'Why would we need that?' asks Martin.

'Insurance,' says Mandy, attracting an annoyed glare from him.

It's only after the phones are set up again that Yev smiles and says, 'Okay, now we've finished with the boring stuff, what else did you want help with?'

Martin is about to answer when his phone rings.

'Martin Scarsden.' He listens for a moment before speaking again. 'Yes, sorry, my phone was out of action. I'll see you shortly.' And then to Mandy and Yev: 'A contact. I'll have to leave soon.'

'Who is it?' Mandy asks.

'I'll tell you later.' There's an edge to his voice.

'So what are Yev and I doing?' she asks him, trying to keep the hurt from her voice.

Martin addresses Yev, practically ignoring her. 'Last time I was here, I told you that a former editor of the *Sydney Morning Herald*, Max Fuller, was murdered. We're trying to find out who did it and why.'

Yev looks at Martin steadily. 'I get it.'

'Like I said on Wednesday, his laptop went missing when he was killed. He had another computer at the *Herald*, but he wiped that himself. He was writing the story for a news magazine called *This Month*. You've heard of it?'

'I've heard of it; haven't read it.'

'Okay. You suggested Max might have backed up some of his material onto the cloud. I've got his details here.' Martin hands Yev a piece of paper. 'This is the site, his username and passwords.'

'Where did you get them?' Mandy asks, frustrated at being left out.

Martin responds, voice even. 'The site address from Wellington Smith—it's the same one I use for the books—and the passwords from Eileen Fuller. She emailed them through this morning.'

Yev is looking at the paper, frowning. 'Why do you need my help? This should be straightforward.'

'It's not. I tried. The files seem to be protected by more than passwords.'

Yev raises his eyebrows, then smiles. 'Okay. I like a challenge.'

'Sorry. I really need to go,' says Martin.

'Leave it with me,' says Yev.

'I'll let you know if we find anything,' Mandy adds.

'Right. Well, see you soon.'

She reaches out, brushes his hand. 'Take care.'

'You too.'

She bites her lip, watching him go, aware a gap has opened between them, unsure what to do about it.

chapter thirty-one

THE SMOKE IS GETTING WORSE, THE UNMOVING AIR A GENTLE APOCALYPSE. HE walks through a city grown hazy, the light muted and tangerine, the buildings fading away into vague outlines, their substance questionable, people moving along the footpaths like wraiths. He's making his way down Albion Street, towards the agreed rendezvous, when a white SUV pulls in, horn voicing a brief toot. The windows are tinted; the one on the passenger side slides down. 'Martin. Jump in.' It's Jack Goffing, the ASIO officer, behind the wheel.

Martin climbs in, is surprised to see a woman in the back seat. 'Jack?'

Goffing pulls away from the kerb. 'Let me find a park, then we can talk.'

The ASIO agent picks an underground parking garage, seemingly at random. He descends a floor before pulling into a vacant space. It's extremely narrow: it takes two or three goes to get a perfect fit. He cuts the engine.

'Martin, this is Griff. Not her real name.'

'Good to meet you, Griff. Martin Scarsden. My real name.'

'So I believe,' says the woman quietly. She has a stocky build, in her fifties, grey hair cut short. Her nose is flattened and crooked, as if she's been a boxer.

'What's going on, Jack? This is very cloak-and-dagger.'

'It is. But I don't want to take any risks. This is dangerous shit.'

'What can you tell me?' asks Martin.

'First, everything we tell you here is strictly off-the-record. It cannot be published unless we give you the all clear. You got that? Under no circumstances.'

Martin sighs; the same old story. 'If that's what it takes.'

'The Director General has authorised me to poke my nose in—discreetly, of course.'

'ASIO? He thinks there are national security implications?'

'He does.'

'Such as?'

'The Mess.'

'So you checked it out?'

'I did. Your suspicions were on the money. It's a lot more than a dining club. It's an influence exchange, an information hub, a conduit for power, all operating in secrecy, protected by respectability.'

'Sure. But a threat to national security?'

'Possibly. It's almost certainly been infiltrated. Probably by organised crime, potentially by foreign states.'

Martin experiences a familiar surge, the adrenaline that comes with a new or better story. This could be way bigger than he's imagined.

Goffing continues. 'Have you heard of a Harry Sweetwater?'

Martin gives a sardonic chuckle. 'Yes. I'm told he's a crook. And a member of the Mess.'

'He's more than that. Harry Sweetwater is an alias. His real name is Danilo Calabrese.'

'Italian?'

'American. Organised crime. The Chicago mob. Senior, connected. Wanted but never convicted. Deadly.'

Martin doesn't know what to say, so he says nothing, but his body reacts anyway: a shudder runs through him. The story might be bigger, but it's suddenly sounding a lot more dangerous as well.

The woman in the back seat speaks, voice soft and rasping, as if she's been gargling drain cleaner. 'Arrived in Australia twelve years ago, walked straight into a position at Mollisons. He's been there ever since.'

Martin shakes his head in despair. 'Max Fuller and Elizabeth Torbett. They didn't know what they were going up against.'

'We don't know that for sure,' says the back-seat woman. 'Maybe they did.'

'Sorry,' says Martin, 'but who are you, Griff?'

It's Goffing who answers. 'Griff is retired. Lives on the Central Coast. Breeds budgerigars. It was very considerate of her to come down and meet us.'

'It's my bridge day,' says Griff.

Martin can feel his hackles rising. He's played this game before, getting fed selective information while a source denies him the rest. Max was murdered, Martin's apartment was trashed, Mandy was kidnapped; he doesn't feel like playing now.

'I'm an old cop. Former Crime Commission,' volunteers Griff, as if reading Martin's thoughts. 'I was running the investigation of Mollisons at the ACIC. Tarquin Molloy worked for me.'

That settles Martin. That's not selective. 'You were investigating Sweetwater?'

'No. We were investigating Mollisons. We didn't know about Sweetwater. Still didn't until Jack told me this morning.'

Goffing adds his own observation. 'It's only just come to light. An FBI informant came forward in the past year or so; a totally unconnected inquiry in the States. This source mentioned Calabrese, that he was in Australia. The Americans shared it with the AFP after they realised Calabrese had been in Sydney all this time.'

Martin twists in his seat so he can look Griff in the eye. 'You think that's what Molloy discovered? That's what got him killed? Sweetwater's identity? The mob infiltrating Mollisons?'

The woman doesn't flinch, meeting Martin's examination directly. 'That's a definite possibility.'

'Why were you investigating Mollisons, if you didn't know about Sweetwater and the mob?'

'You probably don't need to know the details.'

So Martin rattles off what Mandy has told him, what she and Pam and Zelda had established: 'A large part of the ownership is held offshore by untraceable entities, there's money flowing in and out via tax havens, Mollisons is a profitable company paying little tax, there's the suspicion of money laundering and organised crime.'

Griff nods ever so slowly, as if in recognition. 'Very good. You've been doing your homework.' She pauses, then continues. 'Mollisons made some bad calls in the lead-up to the global financial crisis. Very bad calls. They were exposed, almost went under in early 2009, our own Lehman Brothers. They needed a lot of money in a hurry.'

Martin turns his attention back to Jack Goffing. 'Why are you telling me this?'

Goffing adopts a grim smile. 'First and foremost, you needed to know for your own safety. I'd hate to see you and your girlfriend wind up like Max Fuller and Elizabeth Torbett.'

'Right,' says Martin. 'First and foremost. What else?'

There is silence then, for a good minute, or so it seems to Martin.

When someone does eventually speak, it's Griff. 'What else do you know about the Mess?'

Martin is about to launch into an explanatory exposition of favour-trading and corruption, poachers' banquets and prisoner-of-war camps, but he says something else entirely. 'The membership. Roger Macatelli. The deputy police commissioner.'

'Impressive,' says Griff. 'You might be right about this joker, Jack.'

'Exactly,' says Goffing. 'Sweetwater has been extending his tentacles for years, inside and outside the Mess. We don't know how far they've reached. That's why the boss wants me on it. If the mafia are operating, he's concerned foreign powers may be exploiting the same channels.'

'Do you have a membership list?' asks Martin. 'I'm told there are thirty members.'

'So I believe,' says Goffing. 'But we've only really started moving on this today. I'm hoping to have the full list by tonight, tomorrow at the latest. It's likely to include some heavy hitters.'

'Can I get a copy?'

'Of course. That's part of the reason we're talking to you,' replies Goffing.

'We might need the media,' says Griff. 'It could be the only way.' Martin can hear the reluctance in her voice.

'I see,' says Martin, swallowing the implications. 'So tell me: what do you know about Molloy's murder? What did you know back then? What did you suspect?'

The look on Griff's face reflects the bitterness of her words. 'My opinion? We were fucked over.'

'How's that?'

'The man you know as Tarquin Molloy was good at his job—brilliant, even. But he had an ego the size of a planet. Suffered from double-oh-seven syndrome. Thought he was bulletproof. Not easily managed, not responsive to guidance. A lone wolf. But a great agent, one of the best. The last thing he told me was that he'd found the smoking gun. He just needed to get his hands on it.'

'What did he mean by that?'

'I don't know. The next thing we knew he'd disappeared, and Mollisons was jumping up and down, accusing him of stealing millions and shooting through. Overseas. They even had a witness telling the fraud squad all about it.'

'Zelda Forshaw.'

'Exactly.'

'You believed her?'

'I didn't know what to believe. It certainly wasn't impossible, given Tarquin's personality. And then we were disbanded. I was suspended.'

'What? Why?'

'Seriously? Because a member of my team had gone rogue and stolen millions of dollars. Shit was raining down on us from all quarters. I couldn't exactly argue; I would have done the same thing if I was running the ACIC. Either I was incompetent and I fucked up or, worse, I was complicit. And the bank needed to be mollified, reassured that the authorities were acting. So I was the sacrificial lamb. Me and my team. I was moved to a non-operational position. My career was over. I took early retirement.' There is no emotion beneath Griff's raspy voice; this is old territory for her.

'So in all that, do you know if the bank knew Molloy was undercover, or did they just think he was a lawyer on the make?'

'My guess? Those who killed him knew he was a cop. Others in the place probably believed the theft-and-flee cover story. But that's only a guess.'

Again there's a pause in the conversation, this time filled by Jack Goffing. 'The body was well preserved. Concrete can do that. There are signs Molloy was comprehensively tortured before he was shot.'

'Jesus,' says Martin. 'So they would have extracted everything he knew.'

'Most likely.'

Another silence as thoughts recalibrate.

Martin's phone pings, a regular SMS, not WhatsApp. *Need to meet. Come to Surry Hills ASAP.* Martin shows the screen to Jack Goffing. 'This number. Can you confirm it's Morris Montifore?'

Goffing compares it to his own phone's contact list. 'Yeah, it's him. What happened to your phone?'

'I needed to scrub it. Long story.' He puts the phone away. 'What about Montifore? Can I trust him?'

'What do you mean?' Goffing's voice is cautious.

'He's New South Wales police. Ultimately answerable to Macatelli. And he wants to see me.'

It's Griff who answers. 'I've never heard anything bad about Morris. He has a high clearance rate, no hint of unethical behaviour.' She hesitates, choosing her words carefully. 'But he's also known to be politically astute.'

'What does that mean?'

'He doesn't ruffle feathers. Has an aversion to challenging the status quo.'

'So I shouldn't deal with him?'

'Quite the contrary,' interjects Goffing. 'Griff is retired. She can't be seen anywhere near this. I'm ASIO, I don't want to break cover. Which leaves you. You're the one we need to deal with Montifore.'

'I see,' says Martin, 'I thought you were concerned about my safety.'

'Yours, and that of the realm,' says Goffing, a half-amused smile playing on his lips. 'So are you in? You want to be part of the team?'

Martin shrugs. 'I guess I am.'

'There is one more thing,' says Goffing.

'What's that?'

'Harry Sweetwater is listed as an AFP informant. He's protected.'

'What? By whom? Who's he informing to?'

'I don't know yet. The AFP doesn't hand out information about their informants.'

Martin thinks it over: even knowing Sweetwater is an Australian Federal Police source is testament to just how well connected Goffing is.

'The FBI doesn't even know the AFP is using him,' adds Goffing grimly. 'So no telling anyone. And don't even think of publishing it.'

'Surely you're going to detain him? A senior mafia figure, operating under an alias.'

'Well, that's kind of academic. He's vanished. We can't find him.'

'He's been tipped off?'

'It's possible.'

Only later, after Goffing has dropped him a block from the police station, does Martin reflect on the absurdity of the car park conversation: talking to a former cop whose name is not really Griff, about an undercover operative whose name was not really Tarquin Molloy, investigating a mafia captain whose name is not really Harry Sweetwater.

chapter thirty-two

'HELL,' SAYS YEV.

'What is it?' asks Mandy.

'Look.' Yev points at one of his screens, at an icon. 'This folder. A few minutes ago, it was chock-a-block with files. Now it's empty.'

'Whose folder? Max's?'

'Yes. Password-protected files. Encrypted. I've been trying to get into them. And now . . .' Yev hits some more keys, and lets out a long, deflating sigh. 'And now nothing. Now the folder itself has disappeared.'

'Disappeared?'

'Deleted. Gone.'

'Someone is in there, cleaning it all out?'

'Yes.'

'But how would they know where to look?'

'Your phones. Did you and Martin discuss this?'

Mandy thinks back to their conversations, last night and this morning. And he must have talked to Eileen Fuller and Wellington Smith. 'Yes,' she says, voice small.

'Too late, then. Look.' Yev refreshes the screen again and the remainder of the files are gone. 'Finished.'

'Who could do that? Clear out the files like that?' asks Mandy.

Yev shrugs. 'The owner of the files. An administrator at the company. Someone who has the passwords. Any half-decent hacker.'

'We're screwed, then,' says Mandy.

'I wouldn't say that.' Yev gives up his crooked-toothed smile. 'The first thing I did was download the folders, so I can work on them later. Offline.'

'Brilliant,' she says, face bursting into a huge smile. 'That is so clever. Thank you.'

'Yes. Brilliant. But it will take me some time to open them. It depends on how well protected they are.' He frowns, looking at the screen. 'It may take days. Or weeks. Maybe you want to come back? I can WhatsApp you.'

'Sure. But there is one other thing first. A different company. A bank.'

'Ha, as if,' says Yev, his tone disparaging. 'I can't hack a bank. It's not possible. Organised crime, terrorists, governments, they're all trying, big sophisticated teams. I can't compete with that.'

'Not bank accounts. Not the financial systems, not where the money is. Just admin systems, emails, personnel, that sort of thing.'

Yev shrugs. 'Maybe that's possible. But unlikely. Banks are very sensitive: any successful hack would inflict reputational damage.'

'Can we try? I have passwords.'

'Passwords? Okay, then. Let's give it a whirl.'

Mandy guides him to the login page, the web address unchanged since her days working at Mollisons. The site itself is updated with new graphics, but if anything the new layout is simpler and easier to navigate than the one she remembers. She gives Yev her old user-name and password, just in case they might still grant them access.

'No,' says Yev. 'We can't risk that.'

'What? Why? You can't be sure they won't work.'

'Yes I can be. Ninety-nine-point-nine per cent. What's worse, it will leave a trace. You try to log in, the system locks you out, then moments later someone is trying to hack their way in. You don't need to be a computer expert to work that one out.'

'Okay,' says Mandy. 'I get it. Try these.' She hands Yev the details supplied by the Turtle.

'These can't be associated with you?'

'No,' she replies, her voice more confident than she feels.

'Okay. Let's have a crack.'

'Before we do, can the attempt be traced back here?'

'No. We're cloaked. This is all being routed through VPNs.'

'So it's risk-free?' she asks.

'More or less.'

Yev enters the details. There's a circle, whirling spokes, and then the access screen dissolves into another, a welcoming page with links to various departments and files. It's been updated, but Mandy recognises it nevertheless.

'That was easy,' says Yev. 'Where do you want to look first?'

Mandy points to a link. 'Let's check the email. Find out whose account this is.'

Yev hits the link, moving through to email. 'Nothing here. You recognise this user?'

Mandy doesn't see it at first, but when she does it jolts her. The account owner's name is at the top right of the screen. Clarity Sparkes. 'Shit,' she says.

'What is it?' asks Yev, but before he can say anything else, the computer starts emitting a soft beeping. 'That's strange.' He moves the cursor to the other screen, opens software, starts typing, more and more quickly. 'Hell.'

'What is it?'

'Someone is trying to track me.'

'I thought that wasn't possible.'

'It's not.'

'Oh no. Look,' says Mandy. On the right-hand monitor, superimposed over Clarity Sparkes's email home page is a smiley face, taunting them. Then, as she watches in horror, it flickers away, only to be replaced by a dick pic. Mandy's mouth falls open; she's frozen to the spot.

Not Yev, he's moving fast. He's off the chair and onto his knees, under the desk, yanking power cords, crashing his computer, the screens flickering off, the speakers popping. He gives himself a moment, breathing heavily, before crawling back out.

'What just happened?' Mandy whispers.

'You saw. They knew we were there.'

'They were waiting for us?'

'Yes.'

'But they can't trace us?'

'No. I think it was trying. That or more malware. That's why I pulled the plugs.'

'Quick thinking.'

'I have not done that for ten years.' Yev sounds like he's talking to himself. 'I had no choice.' He's staring at the dead screens, as if he's inflicted pain on a favoured pet.

'The phones,' Mandy says. 'They could track the phones.'

'Not anymore.'

'No. Not now. But before you cleansed them. They would know Martin and I came here, both of us, that we were here for some time. And then the tracking stopped, the malware was deleted. At a computer store.'

'What are you saying?' asks Yev, although the look on his face tells her he knows the answer.

'We need to leave,' says Mandy. 'Immediately.'

'Yes,' says Yev, but instead of heading to the door, he's back on his knees under the desk.

'What are you doing?'

'Getting the hard drives.'

'Leave them. It doesn't matter.' She can hear the panic in her voice, the rising tide, the rational part of her mind being inundated. 'Where's Lena?' She rushes back to the counter, looks around. She can't see Lena, just a middle-aged woman examining her wares.

'Here.' Yev is emerging from under the desk, two slim drives in his hand. 'My files. Max Fuller's files.' And he smiles. Mandy smiles back.

And then their smiles fall away. Two men have entered Ichiban Computers and Scarvery.

'This way, madam. Police. Please leave,' Henry Livingstone says politely to the middle-aged woman, displaying his counterfeit badge. 'We're closed.'

Joshua Spitt escorts her out and locks the door behind her.

'Good morning,' says Henry Livingstone, walking over to the scarvery. 'Nice cravats.'

chapter thirty-three

MARTIN IS APPROACHING THE POLICE STATION WHEN HIS PHONE CHIRPS WITH A
WhatsApp alert. A message to their group from Mandy:

Finished here. You won't believe what we've got. Where can we meet? Where are you?

Give me an hour, he replies.

Where are you?

He doesn't have time to respond: he sees Morris Montifore out the front, hands in pockets, squinting against the smoke, waiting for him. If anything, the haze is getting thicker. Martin puts the phone back in his pocket. Yev has installed the tracking app; they can use that.

'Morris?'

'It's almost lunchtime, thought we might grab a bite to eat.'

'Off the premises. Off the record?'

The policeman smiles. 'Something like that.'

They walk two blocks, come to a street cafe, a hole-in-the-wall place with a few tables scattered outside. 'We can grab a coffee here,' says Montifore.

'Thought you were hungry?'

'I am,' he replies, checking his watch. 'But we may not have time. Grab a table. What do you want?'

'Flat white, thanks.' Martin does as he's been asked, occupying a free table. It's not hard to get one; the smoke is forcing anyone with half a brain inside to rest their lungs. At least it offers them privacy. Goffing returns with the drinks and a face lined with unease and insomnia; even the filtering smoke can't soften it. He hands Martin his coffee, places his own on the table, sits and stares at him. He's still squinting, but it's hard to know if it's from the smoke or from concentration.

'What?'

'I know you've been conducting your own investigation into Max Fuller's death.'

'His widow isn't satisfied with the official inquiry.'

'Yeah. Tell me about it.'

'Is that what this is all about? You've come to tell me to back off, pull my head in?'

'No. I already tried that, remember? Warned you and your girlfriend to get out of Sydney.'

'And?'

'And it didn't work.'

Martin takes a sip of his coffee. The barista has burnt the milk. When did Sydney forget how to make the universal beverage?

'So what is it, Morris? What do you want to ask me?' He tries another sip; maybe it's the smoke he's tasting.

'Have you ever heard of a man called Harry Sweetwater?'

Martin almost chokes on the coffee. 'That's funny,' he says, lowering his cup to the table, trying to keep his voice light, 'someone just mentioned that name this morning.'

'Right. What do you know?'

'He's a big wig at Mollisons—the bank Tarquin Molloy was investigating when he died.'

'Who told you that?'

'Is it wrong?'

Montifore leans back. 'No. Molloy was investigating Mollisons and a couple of associated entities.'

'Diamond Square and Large Sky,' says Martin, his voice even.

Montifore's voice sounds cautious. 'Yes.'

'So Harry Sweetwater is implicated?'

'Harry Sweetwater wants to meet with you. With us.'

Martin doesn't know how to respond. He catches himself gold-fishing and closes his mouth, in case something ill-considered escapes. Or he swallows too much smoke. He tries the coffee for a third time, if only to give himself some thinking room. It still tastes like an incinerator.

But the policeman has picked up on his disquiet. 'What, Martin? What is it?'

'Why does he want to meet with us? Why me?'

'I don't know. My guess is that he has information about Molloy and he wants you there as some sort of guarantor. He's checked you out, knows your reputation for covering big true crime stories.'

'He doesn't trust you?'

Montifore shrugs. 'That would be my guess. He tells us both what he knows. If I don't investigate, or it gets whitewashed, you will know. You can publish.'

'And you're okay with that?'

'As it so happens, I'm delighted with that.'

'So me as guarantor. That's one possibility.'

'What are the others?'

'He might want to kill both of us. He might want to kill you, use me as a witness. Who knows?'

Montifore laughs. 'For fuck's sake. Relax, will you? The guy's a banker.'

Martin stares at Montifore. Does he tell him? Surely he needs to trust the detective, needs to warn him that Sweetwater is mafia, potentially deadly. He's still considering how to phrase his response when his phone pings, distracting him. It's WhatsApp again; Mandy persisting: *Where are you? Urgent.*

Martin can't help himself. *FFS*, he types. *Use the app.* By the time he looks up again, Montifore is looking at a message of his own.

'Come on. Sweetwater wants to meet in ten minutes. Central Station.'

chapter thirty-four

THEY SIT IN THE MIDDLE OF THE FLOOR, HANDS ON THEIR HEADS: MANDY, YEV AND Lena. Joshua Spitt has turned the sign on the door to CLOSED and pulled down the blind. He stands there, full of menace, a gun in his hand. Henry Livingstone is over by the scarvery counter, admiring the stock. He too has his gun in his hand, a huge thing, a retro accessory, charcoal steel and glistening pearl-shell grip. He uses it to spread out neckties for his consideration. He nods a final appreciation of the quality of Lena's merchandise before turning back to them, everything about his body language relaxed, a pleasant smile playing on his lips. Mandy can smell him, a mix of hair oil and cigarette smoke, combined with her own odour of sweat and fear. He moves over, takes a seat in front of the three of them.

He casts his eyes slowly over each of his captives in turn, but it's Mandy he's looking at when he speaks, voice gentle. 'Do you know how many people we've killed? Between the two of us?'

She shakes her head, unable to speak. She can hear Lena whimpering softly.

'No. Neither do we, love.' And he smiles, gold tooth glinting. 'Where can I find Martin Scarsden?'

'Why?'

'No matter why. Tell me.' His voice has hardened.

'I really don't know.'

'Give me your phone.'

'I don't have his number.'

'Then you won't mind me looking.'

She hands over the phone.

He hands it back. 'Open it.'

She does, using fingerprint recognition.

He starts going through it, looking confused. 'Where are all your contacts?'

'Gone. We just finished wiping the phone.'

'Why?'

'Someone was spying on us, using our phones.'

'The police?'

'No. We don't know who it was.'

Livingstone looks at her phone once more, as if it might provide an answer. 'What's this?' he asks. 'WhatsApp.' He's looking intently at the phone, using his finger to swipe and select. Mandy steals a glance at Yev. 'Beauty,' says Livingstone, and starts typing away with his thumbs. He must be messaging Martin. Then he's all smiles, addressing them again. 'I like WhatsApp. All the crims use it.'

'What did you say to him?' asks Mandy.

'Nothing much, just asked where he was.' Livingstone takes another look at the phone, then resumes his seat, balancing the handset on his knee. 'Mr Spitt and me, we had a chat with Zelda Forshaw last night.'

'Jesus. Is she okay?'

'No. She's shitting herself.'

'Why?'

'She's in the frame for murder.'

'What?' She can see Livingstone smirking at her reaction, but she doesn't care what he thinks. 'Who did she kill?'

'My guess? No one.'

'Sorry. I don't follow.'

'Neither do I, love, neither do I.' And he smiles amiably and fondles his gun. Mandy wonders if he's even rational.

He stands, starts to pace. She takes the opportunity to glance across at her fellow captives. Lena has her head bowed, avoiding eye contact, snot running from her nose; Yev also has his head lowered, but looks more composed, peering out from under his eyebrows, flashing the facsimile of a smile, trying to gift encouragement.

Livingstone stops walking and sits. 'Have you ever run into a fat little cunt called Kenneth Steadman?'

'The Turtle?'

'That's him. Friend of yours?'

'No. Absolutely not.' Mandy doesn't know why she's telling Livingstone the truth, but she can't help it; her loathing for the Turtle is too strong.

'Glad to hear it.' He smiles again, his teeth stained with nicotine, except for the one gold incisor, unblemished amid the incipient decay. 'I spent this morning with the police, an officious arsehole called Montifore. You know him?'

Mandy nods, unsure where this is going.

'He had a video. Me and Tarquin Molloy. You give it to them?'

'No. They already had it.'

'You were going to give it to them?'

Again she nods. There's not much point in lying. Not to a man with a gun. Who knows what Montifore said to him? 'Yes. I was.'

'So he says.' And now there is something wicked in Livingstone's smile, a hint of remembered pleasures. But like a cloud moving across the landscape, his face turns serious once more. 'Where can I find Scarsden?'

'I told you, I don't know. He was here fifteen minutes ago, but he had to leave. He was meeting someone. I don't know who. I don't know where.'

'Tell me about Harry Sweetwater.'

She shrugs, unsettled by the change of subject, but glad they've moved on from Martin. 'I only met him once or twice back when I worked at Mollisons. He interrogated me—him and Clarity Sparkes—after Tarquin went missing with the money.'

'With Clarity?'

'Yes.'

'What did you make of him?'

'I didn't like him.'

'What did others say?'

'No one else liked him either.'

'Right. And do you know where I could find him?'

'He stills works at Mollisons.'

'Not anymore.'

'Are you sure?'

'Not as of last night. He's in the wind. Some very bad people are looking for him. Very bad people indeed. Including Joshua and me. We're bad. Do you know why bad people are looking for him?'

'No. I don't know anything about him.'

'Lucky for you, love.' And he smirks; for the life of her, Mandy can't quite make him out, can't quite follow the logic that's driving him. And it seems that he too can't quite order his thoughts. 'Let's try again, shall we?' says Livingstone, holding out her phone.

She unlocks it once more and Livingstone sends another WhatsApp message.

His face is deadly serious as he resumes the conversation. 'Zelda Forshaw—was she ever a friend of Clarity?'

'Clarity Sparkes? From security?'

'Yeah, Clarity from security. You said she questioned you. Did you know her?'

'No, not really. She seemed quiet, kind of private.'

'Yeah, that was her.' God, what is it that she can hear in his voice? A gentleness? A wistfulness? 'She was pretty, though. Like you,' he says. Yes, she's right, it's there: fondness.

'And Zelda. Was she already a junkie back then?'

'What?' Of course. The moment he says it, it's obvious. Zelda's lack of money, her skin, her desperation. 'How would I know?'

Livingstone looks sad. 'She says she got into it inside. Or it got into her. She did six months in prison. You know that?'

'Everyone who worked at Mollisons knows that.'

'She denies it. We spoke to her last night. She denies it.' Now there is a distant quality to his voice, as if he's speaking more to himself than to Mandy.

She's still having trouble following him. She tries to keep her own voice gentle as she responds. 'Denies what? The money?'

'No. I heard Zelda was with Clarity the night she died. She was out on bail, awaiting her trial.'

Mandy stares. Clarity Sparkes, dead from a heroin-cocaine speedball. She realises she's biting her lip, stops it. 'That's why you were looking for Zelda?'

But before he can answer, her phone pings in his hand. A WhatsApp message. He regards it for a couple of seconds and the smile returns, his tooth glinting like that of a fairy-tale wolf. 'A tracking app? You have a tracking app?'

Mandy says nothing.

'Show me.' He hands her the phone, gun pointed at her, denying her leeway.

She opens the app, shows him. It reveals Martin is down near Central Station.

'Beauty,' says Livingstone. 'Not far away.' He stands. 'I'll need the passcode for the phone.'

'It's already open.'

'For later. We're taking it with us. Either you give me the code or I take your finger. Your choice.'

Mandy gives him the code, watches as he trials it.

'Very good. Now listen closely. Mr Spitt and I are professionals, so we're not going to kill you, on account of the fact no one is paying us. Once we speak to Martin, we'll tell him where to find you.'

They bind and gag Mandy, Yev and Lena with Italian silk ties, Egyptian cotton bandanas and Indian leather thongs, spraying Lena and Mandy with some perfume from an atomiser for good measure, with a touch of aftershave under the chin for Yev.

But before he leaves, Livingstone crouches, placing his hand on Mandy's shoulder. 'I didn't kill no undercover cop. I didn't kill no newspaper editor, I didn't kill no judge. The coppers won't listen, so tell Martin Scarsden. Tell him—if I don't tell him first.'

chapter thirty-five

HE'S WAITING FOR THEM AT A TABLE ON THE OLD GOODS LINE NEAR HARRIS STREET, sitting at a yellow metal table, street furniture designed to thwart vandals and survive the weather, not for comfort. The old rail line, elevated above the city streets, has been turned into a pedestrian thoroughfare, a broad pathway leading from the ABC studios and the University of Technology down towards the harbour, a stunted echo of New York's High Line. The smoke from the fires in the Blue Mountains has thickened amid the absolute stillness of the day. Somewhere a siren is wailing, there are church bells up on Broadway, and closer by a raven calls. Sweetwater is staring at his phone, doesn't even look up until they sit opposite him. He stares at them now, his eyes unreadable behind aviator sunglasses.

'Montifore and Scarsden, right?'

'Right,' says Montifore.

'You know who I am?'

The policeman responds. 'Harry Sweetwater. Head of security at Mollisons Investment Bank.'

Sweetwater nods, turns to Martin. 'And you. Do you know who I am?'

Martin tips his head. 'Danilo Calabrese. The Chicago mob.' Montifore says nothing, but Martin can feel him stiffen.

Sweetwater cocks the corner of his mouth, more of a sneer than a smile. 'The cops are always the last to know.' The sneer vanishes, gone in the smoke. 'Keep your hands on the table. We don't want any misunderstandings.' And as he speaks, he reaches into his own coat pocket, retrieves a small brushed-steel pistol, and places it on the table in plain view, his hand resting on the grip. If a gun can be elegant, this gun is elegant.

'What is it you want?' asks Montifore, his voice carrying a mixture of apprehension, annoyance and uncertainty.

'Well, I'd like to live. Not that you can help so much with that.' He spreads his arms wide. 'I'd also like to clarify a couple of points before I disappear forever.'

'I don't follow.'

'Scarsden here seems to know a bit about me. I am indeed a native of Chicago. I still have a lot of friends there. There and elsewhere. One of them rang me last night. Told me an interesting tale. Told me the organisation has put a contract out on me. A hit. Me. After all I have done for them. You understand what I mean?'

'We can offer protection. You can trust me,' says Montifore, but that only elicits a snort of contempt.

'Why?' asks Martin. 'Why do they want you dead?'

'They've been told, on the best authority, that I'm a grass. Some snivelling shit in the FBI told them I'm feeding information to your Crime Commission.'

'Are you?' asks Martin.

'Fuck you, pal,' says Sweetwater, voice low and menacing, hand tightening on the gun.

'Why tell us this, if you don't want protection?' Montifore persists.

Sweetwater looks up at the sky, purses his lips. Then he looks first at Montifore, then at Martin. 'I want you to clear my name.'

'What? How?' asks Montifore.

'I'm being set up. Framed. I didn't kill Molloy, I didn't order his killing, I didn't know he was dead. And I didn't know he was a fucking cop. If I'd known that, I *would* have killed him.' He takes a breath, as if containing anger. Or regret. 'And I didn't kill the fucking judge or that arsehole reporter. I had nothing to do with any of it. And yet my connections here are washing their hands of me. I'm being made a scapegoat.'

'Who by?' asks Martin.

'Isn't that obvious?' Sweetwater smiles again, opens his mouth as if to speak, then closes it. For a moment, he's dead still, as if the mechanism running the day is changing gear, moving to a larger cog, slowing the world down. Martin watches on, unable to move, as events begin to unfold, frame by frame. He sees Sweetwater's fingers tighten on the gun handle, the knuckles whitening, the barrel lifting. 'You cunts,' spits the mafia man, as if speaking underwater, even as he begins to stand, the weapon coming to bear as he rises to his feet. It's pointed at Montifore, Sweetwater's finger on the trigger, the policeman starting to raise his hands in futile defence. But there is no shot, no flaring of gun smoke. Sweetwater's head is turning away, looking beyond Montifore and Martin. Still he doesn't shoot, moving instead, starting to run. Martin watches him, his mind still trying to catch up, even as Montifore lowers his arms to look. Sweetwater is a step away, two steps, three, accelerating through treacle.

Martin swivels, sees a man in an antique suit approaching, walking calmly, seemingly unnoticed among his fellow pedestrians, striding like a gunslinger, his long hair oiled back. That must be Henry Livingstone, some outlier in Martin's brain reports in, some distant colony informing its capital. Livingstone is wielding a gun, holding it before him at arm's length, a large and brutal thing, matt-black steel—an instrument of death, and elegance be fucked. Henry Livingstone: in the flesh, here, brandishing a revolver.

'Down,' yells Martin, reaching for Montifore, pulling the policeman from his seat, pulling him downwards towards the concrete as a shot powers above them, a booming explosion coming from the suited man. Martin witnesses the muzzle flash, believes he smells the cordite, even as he hits the ground, a shrill pain firing through his elbow as it strikes the pavement. The shot echoes in the smoke-filled day, the sound fragmenting like shrapnel, bouncing every which way from the uneven surfaces of the adjacent building. Another shot follows, booming like a cannon, like an artillery piece, echoes chasing the first.

Livingstone has reached them now, riding boots polished to a high sheen. He glances down to where they cower. For a moment, for a single frame, his eye catches Martin's. The killer smiles, gold tooth glinting, and he winks. Winks at Martin, and moves on. Close by, ravens launch into the air, cawing madly.

The mechanism behind the world changes down a gear, and life begins to speed up again, a moment after it could have seized up altogether, the moment when their eyes met, the killer and the journalist, when death stood just a metre away, wearing riding boots and a well-tailored suit, winking at him like an old friend.

Martin rises to his knees, adrenaline quieting the pain in his elbow, preparing to stand, when he hears the triple volley coming in response from Sweetwater, some distance away now and out of sight, firecracker retorts, a treble staccato, a contrapuntal response to Henry Livingstone's basso profundo revolver. A chamber orchestra of death. A bullet goes screaming, ricocheting from the metal street furniture, the chair beside Martin ringing like a bell with the impact. Martin looks to Montifore, sees his own mind reflected in the face of the detective: not fear, not panic, just the struggle for comprehension.

Pap. Pap. More shots from Sweetwater, further away now, but no less emphatic, the brushed-steel accessory singing death. A *boom*, Livingstone responding in kind, Martin and Montifore struggling to their feet, the combatants leaving them, vanishing into the smoke. And now silence, there is silence, like the city is holding its breath, no sound as pedestrians stare out of hollow eyes, unbelieving.

And then the silence is broken by an animal shriek, a howl of pain. Someone has been shot. Martin starts to move, the detective next to him, pushing forward, into the smoke, into the veil. Another gear shift, and the world spins them forward, running in the direction of Livingstone and Sweetwater, even as bystanders are starting to move the other way, desperate to get away from the men with guns, desperate to get away from the blood and the terror.

Somehow Martin knows it's too late, all too late, but they run anyway.

They come first to the woman, writhing on the ground, blood soaking her. A man is with her, an office worker, kneeling, his coat off, his shirt off, trying to stem the bleeding, trying in vain. A child stands nearby, Munch's *The Scream* vivified, unable to look, unable to look away, unable to vocalise, the terror pouring from her eyes. The gears of the world grind to a momentary halt, the teeth on the cogs slipping, making sure, even in mid-stride, the image is burnt into Martin's retinas: the dying mother, the helpless daughter.

Next they come to Livingstone, crouched down in the middle of the Goods Line, gun still in hand, oblivious to the world. He's cradling Joshua Spitt, blood running out of his accomplice onto his once immaculate suit and onto the ground. Martin and Montifore slow to a walk. It had been a pincer movement, Martin realises: Livingstone coming from one direction, Spitt from the other, trapping Sweetwater. Or so they had thought. Now Spitt is bleeding out, his life leaking from him. 'No-o-o!' howls Livingstone, a visceral protest, a cry from the soul. A bystander, a student by the look of him, is filming with a phone, moving stealthily closer.

Montifore steps towards Livingstone, arms spread wide, phone in one hand, attracting the gunman's attention. 'Henry, don't shoot. I'm ringing an ambulance.'

Livingstone whirls around as if seeing them for the first time, snapping back to reality, raising his gun, anger and despair in his eyes, looking like he badly wants to shoot someone. But instead of firing bullets, he fires words. 'Call 'em. Call 'em now!' he commands.

And then gently he lowers Spitt's head to the concrete, kneels over him, gun still pointed at Montifore. The spider web tattoo flutters with the man's failing pulse, his eyes flicker as the life leaches out of them. 'Joshua,' whispers Livingstone, the spectre of a voice amid the smoke. He leans down, kisses his dying friend's forehead. 'Farewell, brother.' And then he is on his feet and running, long lanky strides, running as if the furies are with him, running after Harry Sweetwater.

chapter thirty-six

THEY SIT IN THE POLICE STATION, THE SILENCE INSIDE AS THICK AS THE SMOKE outside. Mandy glances at Martin, but he doesn't return her look; he's staring at his hands. Yev is looking around furtively like an addict in need of a fix, desperate for a computer or a device. They've been here for hours now, the initial excitement of being freed long gone. She sees herself reflected in clouded grey glass. Still shaken by the speed of events, but otherwise unharmed, unthreatened. She can feel the weight of what's happened, though, the enormity of it all. She rubs her wrists, still sore from being bound.

The three of them sit in a glassed-in office off a room full of detectives. She sees them swarm, gather in small groups, full of urgency and purpose, full of resolve. And now they pause, all of them, looking towards a bank of television monitors mounted along one wall. It's the top of the hour and from their glass sanctuary she has a clear view as the network news channels burst into life, like time-lapse flowers, each and every one of them leading with a public shooting in the heart of Sydney. She can't hear which channel the police have chosen to listen to, but she can read the headlines. GUNFIGHT: TWO DEAD, says Channel Seven, CBD SHOOTOUT, says Channel Nine, MANHUNT, says Channel Ten. She watches, fascinated, her mind beginning to fill in the gaps that Martin has been unable to repeat. She turns to him: at least he's looking at the screens, not buried in his own thoughts and recriminations. Her heart goes out to him—he's a good man, he doesn't deserve this.

Ivan Lucic cracks the door open and enters. 'Here,' he says, handing Mandy her phone. 'We found it not far from the scene. He ditched it as soon as he could. Fortunately for you, someone handed it in.'

'Thanks,' she says quietly, taking it.

'Can I get mine?' asks Yev.

Lucic shrugs. 'Do we have it?'

'You know you do,' Yev snaps, extracting nothing from Lucic other than a smile.

Morris Montifore walks into the room, takes a seat. Lucic remains standing, a vaguely menacing presence. 'What a shit show.' Montifore sighs. 'I'll be filling out paperwork from now until the crack of doom.'

'No sign of Livingstone?' asks Martin. Mandy is relieved to see he's still engaged.

'Why should I tell you anything?' There is something in Montifore's eyes, an unspoken allegation. Then he relents. 'Nothing useful. Some CCTV caught him up at Central. But even if we can follow his trail, it will be too late. He's vanished.'

345

'His colleague, he's dead?' asks Yev. He flicks his head towards the television screens.

Montifore nods. 'Joshua Spitt. Shot dead by Harry Sweetwater as he made his escape.' The pain on his face is evident as he adds, 'And a young mum. An innocent. Wrong place, wrong time. Caught in the crossfire. From the size of the wound, I'd say hit by a round from that cannon Livingstone carries.'

'So, he's wanted for murder then?' asks Mandy.

'They both are.'

Lucic clears his throat, attracting Mandy's attention. The younger officer shakes his head, as if to quieten her. She meets his gaze, doesn't look away. She's not in the mood to take any shit.

Montifore shifts on his seat. 'Okay. Let's go through this quickly, establish the chain of events. We'll stick purely to the facts. I'm keen to hear your theories, your speculation, but not this evening. Our priority now is the crime scene and catching Sweetwater and Livingstone.'

'Do I need my lawyer?' Mandy asks. 'She's in Melbourne.'

'I can't see why. I'll need a formal statement at some stage. Right now, I just want a quick overview.' He glances at his watch. 'I'm needed upstairs in fifteen, once the brass have watched the news.'

'Okay.'

'Right. Chain of events. Mandalay, you start. Yevgeny, Martin, add anything you think is relevant but remember, just facts.' Montifore again looks at his watch, then up at Lucic. 'Have a seat, Ivan—take notes.'

Lucic grabs a pad and paper from a nearby table, sets his phone down, activating a recording app.

Mandy looks at the phone and squirms in her seat. Why has Montifore chosen her to recount events? Because he doesn't trust Martin to be transparent? Or because she's more likely to blurt out something she shouldn't? 'Where do you want me to start?' she asks.

'How did you come to be at the computer store?'

Mandy glances at Yev and Martin, realising she can't afford to appear to be hiding anything. 'We were there, Martin and I, seeking Yev's help.'

'To do what?'

'Fifteen minutes isn't long enough,' says Martin, interjecting. 'I've been investigating the murders of Max Fuller and Elizabeth Torbett, as well as Tarquin Molloy. Mandy and Yev were helping me.'

Lucic gives a derisive grunt, even as he concentrates on his notes.

Montifore turns to Yev. 'You're a computer expert?'

Yev shrugs. 'If you say so.'

Montifore returns his attention to Martin. 'You weren't there when Spitt and Livingstone arrived?'

'No, I'd already left—to meet with you.'

'Right. So what time did you leave?'

Martin tells him. Mandy thinks it sounds correct.

Montifore frowns. He returns his attention to Mandy. 'So Martin leaves, and you and Yevgeny continue to pursue whatever research you're undertaking on the computers. Correct?'

'Yes.'

'Then what happens?'

'Then Spitt and Livingstone arrived. They came in, locked the doors, held us at gunpoint. Yev and me, and Yev's sister Lena.'

'She wasn't part of your research?'

'No. She works in the scarvery.'

'The what?'

'She sells fashion accessories in a separate part of the shop.'

Montifore blinks, exasperated, as if he can feel his precious fifteen minutes leaking away. 'What did Spitt and Livingstone want?'

'Spitt didn't say much, just grunted every now and then. It was Livingstone asking the questions.'

'What did he want?' repeats Montifore, undeterred.

'Martin. He wanted to find Martin.'

'Is that all?'

'And he wanted to know what I knew about Harry Sweetwater and where to find him.'

'Sweetwater? What did you say?'

'I said he worked at Mollisons, he could find him there. But he said Sweetwater was on the run, that bad men were after him.'

'He said that?' Montifore is addressing Yev, inviting him to confirm it.

'That's right,' says Yev.

'Were they interested in what you were doing?' Montifore asks Yev. 'The computers?'

'No, not at all,' replies the geek. 'He just wanted to find Martin. He said the police had interviewed him this morning.'

'You let him go?' Martin asks the detective.

'Shut up, Scarsden. I'm not talking to you.'

There is unfamiliar anger in the detective's voice. Mandy wonders what has transpired between them. Does he blame Martin for the shootout?

'What else did Livingstone want?' Montifore's question is directed at Yev.

'Nothing,' says Yev, sounding a little cowed.

'And you told them where Martin was?' asks Montifore.

'They had guns,' says Mandy.

Martin interjects again. 'Our phones are connected. A tracking app. They used it to find me.'

Montifore looks between them. 'Martin, do you know why Spitt and Livingstone wanted to find you?'

'To beat me up? To kill me? To tell me their side of the story? No, I don't know.'

Montifore turns his attention back to Mandy. 'Did they know Martin was meeting with Sweetwater?'

'I don't know. If they did, they didn't tell us,' she says.

'I didn't know we were meeting him until you told me, remember?' adds Martin, but it does little to improve Montifore's mood. 'Who else knew he'd been in contact with you?'

The anger is just below the surface now. 'No, Martin. We are not going there. Not now. Not ever.' The detective again addresses Mandy. 'Back before that. How did they find you? At the computer store?'

Mandy doesn't know how to respond and is glad when Yev answers. 'They might have tracked the phones.'

Montifore looks intently at Mandy and then at Martin. 'Is that right?'

'I thought you didn't want speculation?' Martin says.

Montifore gives him a hostile stare, as if he can sense they aren't revealing all they know, but before he can speak, his own phone vibrates. He checks the screen. 'I'm needed upstairs. You can go, but I want you back here tomorrow morning. Eight-thirty. We'll get a formal statement. Bring your lawyers if you think you need them.'

'Are we safe?' asks Mandy.

'What?' Montifore pauses, even as he's getting to his feet, as if considering any continuing threat to them for the first time. 'I would say so. Livingstone is on the run; he won't be bothering anyone.'

'Sweetwater?' asks Martin. 'He wanted to speak to me, remember?'

Montifore stares at him, mind working. 'I doubt it. Not now, not if he thinks we led Livingstone to him. But if he does try to get in touch, you must tell me, okay? No going off on one of your crusades. This is too serious, too dangerous.'

'You mean he might come looking for us?' says Mandy, trepidation in her voice.

Montifore is already heading to the door as he addresses Lucic. 'Please arrange for a uniform to escort them back to their hotel.' Then he turns to Mandy, his voice almost kind. 'Get your stuff, find another hotel. Send the officer back once you feel safe.'

'Thanks,' says Martin.

'Can I get my phone back?' asks Yev.

Montifore shakes his head in mock despair. 'For God's sake, give the geek his phone.'

SATURDAY

chapter thirty-seven

MARTIN CAN'T BELIEVE IT. HE JUST CAN'T FUCKING BELIEVE IT. HE'S SITTING IN the waiting room of Surry Hills police station reading the *Sydney Morning Herald* on his phone. Mandy is with him, reading a book; Winifred too, tapping away at her laptop. Outside, life swirls through the smoke, the morning given an additional edge by the shootout, as if Sydney's cosmopolitan credentials have been elevated to the level of Los Angeles and New York. A television on the wall recounts the events of the Goods Line for the umpteenth time. Witnesses recount their own close calls, bullets missing by inches, unprompted heroism, a friend of a friend who knows the deceased. But Martin hears little of it; his attention is captured by the *Herald*. First, there's the headline story—BLOOD ON THE TRACKS—the dramatic gunfight, complete with photos retrieved from social media, including one of Montifore and himself cowering under a table, and a link to the video of Montifore approaching Livingstone as he held a dying Joshua Spitt. There's a bird's-eye-view graphic, with Martin and the police inspector labelled *Policeman* and *Journalist*, an X marking the spot where they met with Sweetwater, as if they somehow bear responsibility for the deaths of Spitt and the young mother. Yet that's not what irks him. What irks him, when he calms down enough to admit it, is Bethanie Glass getting all the glory; looking the reader in the eye with calm authority from her picture by-line. And down at the bottom of the story, the slimmest of acknowledgements: *additional reporting by Martin Scarsden*. Additional reporting? Christ, he was there in the middle of it, living it, as Livingstone opened up with his Wild West revolver and Sweetwater returned fire with his mafia-issue Glock, bullets ricocheting off the concrete and the steel street furniture, as an innocent fell, as Spitt bled out. There, amid it all, the terror and the noise and the panic and the death, the daughter frozen with horror, and all he gets for it is a footnote to Bethanie Glass's front-page screamer, as if he himself has become a footnote. At least the graphic suggests some kind of importance, some relevance.

'Fuck it,' he says quietly to himself, looking up to see Mandy's concern and Winifred's disapproval. An elderly man a few seats away looks at him with anxiety.

He knows he has only himself to blame. He'd gone with Montifore to the station, cooperated with the investigation, compared notes with Mandy and Yev. It was only after they'd been left waiting for hours that it had occurred to him to ring Bethanie, well after her first iteration had been published. It's as if his instincts had gone missing, as if the primacy of the story no longer mattered. What had he been thinking? Cooperating with police; since when was that a priority? Was it some sort of subconscious compensation for withholding Sweetwater's identity from the detective? Had he become somehow captive to the authorities, instead of the eternal sceptic, holding the powerful to account? For if it wasn't for the story, why was he even involved, why stay in this smoke-filled shithole of a city? He and Mandy could be back home with Liam. But he'd made the decision to remain: to honour Max, to write the first draft of history. So why hadn't he? And so it rankles: *additional reporting by Martin Scarsden*. What would Max think of that?

Yet his displeasure at Bethanie's story, and his failure to insert himself into the moment, is as nothing once he scrolls further into the *Herald*'s coverage. For waiting on the inside pages, as it were, is D'Arcy Defoe's exclusive. It drills him right between the eyes, claws at his stomach.

EXCLUSIVE. The Mess: Inside Sydney's Blood-Drenched Secret Society
A Herald Investigation. By D'Arcy Defoe

D'Arcy's by-line photo is twice the size of Bethanie's; he stares out at Martin: wise, knowledgeable, superior. 'Shit,' breathes Martin as he begins to read. 'Shit, shit, shit.'

'You okay?' asks Mandy.

'Fine,' he fumes.

Winifred grimaces and resumes typing. The elderly man moves a few seats further away. Martin reads on, unaware.

Few know of its existence, fewer still know of its power. Yet the Mess is not just Sydney's most secret cabal, it's the state's most influential. And possibly its most corrupt.

Now, for the first time, the *Sydney Morning Herald* can lift the veil of secrecy on this most secret of societies, revealing a clandestine club implicated in a series of bloody murders and suspicious deaths, leaving a blood-soaked trail that leads directly to the shootout yesterday afternoon on the Goods Line in Ultimo.

The *Herald* can reveal that one of Friday's gunmen is a notorious US mafia captain, Danilo Calabrese, long wanted by law enforcement in his home country. This man is known in Australia as Harry Sweetwater, an influential member of the Mess.

And yet for years, the Mess has been able to operate in the shadows, growing its malevolent influence, spreading corruption and operating with impunity, providing the perfect entrée into Sydney power circles for Sweetwater and his ilk.

For the best part of a decade, I have been researching this most covert of organisations, slowly, year on year, developing an overview of its sway.

Full disclosure: to investigate, to get inside, I willingly became a member of this secret society, passing myself off as an adherent to its rules, its etiquette, to its oath of absolute secrecy.

In short: I risked my life for this story.

'Holy shit,' Martin exclaims. He doesn't know whether to laugh, or cry, or vomit. 'You fucking fraud,' he hisses at his phone. The elderly man gives up trying to move further away and leaves altogether. Martin doesn't notice; the article commands his full attention:

But now a young mother, an innocent, lies dead on the Goods Line at Ultimo. And I must break the most fundamental rule of the Mess   the rule that subordinates all others: its existence is never to be revealed.

I am breaking that rule now for two reasons: first, the public has a right to know what has been occurring behind closed doors; and second, it is becoming increasingly clear that some members of the organisation have subverted its once high-minded ideals and have engaged in criminality.

For years, I'd heard rumours of a secret society operating at the pinnacle of our community. I began digging, and step by step I was able to work myself closer. Eventually, after identifying a number of members, I received a surprising invitation: to join as a full member.

What I found, as I attended my first dinner, upstairs in a private room at one of Australia's premier restaurants, was a gathering of this city's great and good: judges, politicians, sportsmen, lawyers, business leaders, trade unionists. As an investigative journalist, I had hit pay dirt; it was like being invited to sit in on Cabinet.

The food was the best imaginable, the wine superb. But I didn't drink much; I wanted to remember every word, every detail, writing it all down as soon as I could. And so it continued, almost every month for three years: almost always in Sydney, but on occasions in Canberra and Brisbane and once in the Barossa.

And what did I uncover?

The Mess is defined by secrecy, it's defined by power, and it's defined by influence. In that sense, it is profoundly undemocratic. It operates in the shadows, away from media scrutiny and public knowledge. There is something intrinsically unAustralian about it.

And yet, at first, I could find no sign of corruption or abuse of power. A stockbroker sharing a market tip, a unionist spruiking the benefits of a favourite racehorse, a real estate agent agreeing to look out for a suitable property. In short, nothing criminal.

Or so I thought.

For now, the Mess finds itself inextricably linked to murder. In particular, one member of the Mess, mafia captain Danilo Calabrese, known by the alias Harry Sweetwater, has been playing a sinister double game. Just as I had an ulterior motive for joining the Mess, so did Sweetwater. He used the Mess to grant organised crime access into Australia's leading political and business circles, the city's power elite.

It must be stressed that of the thirty members of the Mess, the great majority are innocent of any wrongdoing, any criminality, guilty of nothing more than granting an occasional favour to a friend.

For that reason, I will not yet name the full membership, although I possess the list in its entirety. It would be unfair to traduce the reputations of fine Australians in some sort of media-fuelled witch hunt. It is up to individual members to make that difficult decision: to stay in the shadows or make public their membership and risk being judged guilty by association.

There are some I can name.

Justice Elizabeth Torbett of the New South Wales Supreme Court was a member.

I can reveal she was murdered, shot dead, as she worked to expose the Mess with revered former *Herald* editor Max Fuller.

There are others I can name, with their permission. Federal Labor Senator Janine Trelore and State Liberal MP Samson Fielding are still living. They have shown considerable courage in giving me permission to name them and should be commended for it. They have denied all knowledge of Sweetwater's true agenda and have categorically denied assisting him in any way. They are to be believed: I have found no evidence of systemic corruption within the Mess. Rather, it's likely individual members may have fallen under the corrupting spell of Harry Sweetwater.

I will be writing more on this in the coming days and weeks, exposing what I have found about the Mess and its members. The Mess may be secret, its secrecy may be undemocratic, but at the end of the day, it is merely a private dining club. The great majority of its members, almost all of them, will have never known of Harry Sweetwater's mafia ties. They do not deserve to be pilloried for going to dinner.

For a moment Martin is swept with . . . what? Irritation? Anger? Amusement? This is his story, and D'Arcy has gazumped him, got it out there into the public while he cools his heels in a police station. That's not good. But something else rankles him.

He re-reads the story, this time with more objective eyes. Now he sees what he didn't the first time around: this has none of the gravitas, the logically laid out, thoroughly legalled work tradition-ally associated with a major *Herald* investigation. It starts with a bang and ends with a whimper. D'Arcy at his best is a fine reporter and a great writer, convincing and articulate. This isn't one of his best. Far from it. The only Mess members named are Harry Sweetwater, a fugitive wanted for killing Joshua Spitt; Elizabeth Torbett, who is already dead; and the two politicians, Fielding and Trelore, who have agreed to out themselves. It has all the signs of a quickly cobbled together yarn, produced under pressure. But pressure to get ahead of the media pack on a breaking story? Or the pressure to put a spin on his own membership of the Mess before the media lights the whole thing up like a Christmas tree? Martin puts his phone down, walks over to a seat where someone has discarded a hard copy of the *Herald*. The Goods Line shootout dominates the front page, together with an inside spread, Bethanie pushing hard to compile what they could learn before deadline. But there is no mention of D'Arcy's major investigation; not only is the story itself absent, there is no tease.

Martin smiles. He knows how much work goes into one of these stories; they don't get rushed out without good reason. He can picture the newsroom, live the logic. Once D'Arcy learnt Sweetwater was wanted for murder, he would have realised he needed to get the story out there, in part to get in first for fear Martin or someone else would break the story of the Mess, but also to inoculate himself, to make sure everyone knew his own intentions in joining the Mess were honourable. D'Arcy was no fool; he could see the approaching media storm and had decided to pre-empt it. And by voicing support for some Mess members, even as he condemned Sweetwater, he was already setting himself up as the arbiter of which members were above reproach and which should be condemned. Clever D'Arcy; no doubt those he exonerated would be most grateful.

———

Mandy wonders about Martin, sitting next to her, giving a running commentary on the contents of his phone: laughing, swearing, guffawing with derision. Last night, he was shaking, overwhelmed with the violence of the shootout, withdrawn and reflective, falling into long silences, eyes unfocused and staring. It took her hours of consoling, of pampering, before he spoke, opened up to the horror of it: a man bleeding to death before his eyes, the keening as an innocent woman lay dying in front of her child. Even this morning, when they arrived at the station, he'd seemed withdrawn. And now here he is, as if nothing has happened, as if he's witnessed nothing. It's like some switch has been turned inside his head, some compensating mechanism, and he's sprung back to life. She feels nothing of it. If anything she feels deflated, waiting for Montifore, trapped here with Martin and with Winifred, who has again flown all the way from Melbourne. Mandy has the distinct impression she is a very small cog in a very large investigative machine.

'Look,' says Winifred, drawing her attention to the television. The ABC is crossing to a live event, a press conference out the back of the NSW Parliament. Someone turns up the volume. Graphics identify the pair fronting the cameras as a federal senator from New South Wales, Janine Trelore of the Labor Party, and the state's deputy treasurer, Liberal Samson Fielding.

'Ladies and gentlemen, thank you for attending at short notice.' The man takes the lead as if by right, voice sonorous and weighted with import, the pauses long and in all the right places. *'In the*

past twelve hours, Senator Trelore and I have become aware of a most serious matter. We both believe it is important that we come forward as quickly as possible and be as open as we can in regard to this matter. However, we are constrained by active investigations by the police and other law enforcement bodies. We will tell you as much as we can, but we will be unable to take questions. Janine?'

'*Thank you, Samson. Last night and this morning, we have become aware of an investigation into what may or may not be a major criminal organisation. We have also learnt that we may have inadvertently—and, I must stress, entirely innocently—come into contact, at the periphery, with some of those being investigated. This association comes through our membership of a long-established and reputable dining club known as the Mess.*' She pauses before continuing; it's not only Fielding who has been to Toastmasters. '*It is essential to emphasise this point: neither Mr Fielding nor myself have been involved in any criminal activity. We are not accused of anything; we are not suspected of anything. We have not engaged in any unethical behaviour or behaviour that is in any way incompatible with our roles and duties as parliamentarians.*'

Fielding takes up immediately where Trelore leaves off. The tag-teaming is remarkable for politicians on different sides of the aisle operating in different parliaments. '*Our first instinct was to remain quiet, so as not to jeopardise police investigations, but we also came to understand that the* Sydney Morning Herald's *D'Arcy Defoe, himself a club member, was preparing to go public with this story. We felt compelled, in the public interest, to reveal our own membership—asserting our innocence—and to defend the reputation of other highly respected members of our association who have also been caught up in this investigation inadvertently.*' He pauses for a

Churchillian moment, then continues speaking with the weight of sadness in his voice. *'You may see some very prominent names bandied around in the media over coming days and weeks. I implore all of you to act responsibly, and to remember that most of the people named, like Senator Trelore and myself, are completely innocent of, and completely ignorant of, any wrongdoing. They are simply the members of a dining club.'*

There is a murmuring among the media, an attempt to insert a question, but Janine Trelore is not about to be diverted from the script, her voice strong and clear. *'We believe inquiries centre on one rogue member, a man known to us as Harry Sweetwater. There is no evidence, as we understand it, of any other member being implicated at this stage. Should the police establish otherwise, let those cards fall as they may. If any Mess members are guilty of any crimes, of any impropriety, then they should face the full force of the law.'*

Again, Samson Fielding takes over, perfectly. It seems so practised that Mandy wonders if they might be lovers. *'Every month or so, a group of about thirty prominent Australians meet for dinner and conversation. Typically we hire out a small restaurant, or a private room at a larger restaurant. We meet to enjoy good food and wine, and to discuss the issues of the day. And that is all. The dining club is not politically aligned, it has no unifying objectives or agenda, it is simply a dining club, nothing more and nothing less. We attempt to keep the dinners confidential to protect the privacy of some of the members, who include politicians, union leaders, captains of industry, members of the judiciary and the wider legal profession and senior media figures.'*

Janine Trelore's turn. *'Samson and myself have come forward in the interests of full disclosure. The big difference is we are public figures, while most other members are private citizens. It is entirely up to them to decide whether to identify themselves. Remember that: they are private citizens. So, thank you for coming. Mr Fielding and I wish we could tell you more, although to be honest, there is not a lot more to tell. Nevertheless, we don't want to jeopardise ongoing investigations and we don't want to assail the privacy of innocent people. Please be responsible in your coverage; please check your facts. Thank you for your time.'*

There is the sound of camera shutters and yelled questions, then the vision cuts back to the Ultimo studio.

'Covering their arses,' says Winifred. 'This thing is about to bust wide open.'

———

The television coverage has returned to the studio, where a tame academic is expounding on the history of secret societies. Martin's phone rings: it's Wellington Smith, his gradually recovering contact list identifying the number.

Martin speaks before the editor can start up. 'Wellington, don't worry. There's plenty left for us.'

The mini mogul is so excited Martin can hear his enthusiasm fizzing down the phone. 'Fantastic. Did you see Sky?'

'The ABC. Trelore and Fielding.'

'What do you think?'

'They're inoculating themselves.'

'What have you got?'

Martin hesitates, looking around the empty foyer of the police station, but only for a fraction of a moment. 'It's connected. The story Max and Elizabeth were chasing, this whole thing with the

Mess, Sweetwater and the US mafia and the murder of an under-cover cop named Tarquin Molloy.'

'Mate, that's brilliant. Outstanding. Is that why they were killed?'

Even to Martin's ears, Smith's unbridled enthusiasm for death and destruction lacks empathy. Max and Elizabeth were working for him, after all.

'Here's what I'm thinking,' the editor continues, fervour undiminished. 'Something for *This Month*. There's still another fortnight before deadline, so plenty of time. I'd need it confirmed well before then, of course. And there has to be another book in this. The ones on Riversend and Port Silver are still selling well. You are *the* king of the true crime blockbuster. We really have to put you on the writers' festival circuit and . . .' Wellington stops in mid-sentence, refocuses. 'But that's for the future. We need to publish whatever you've got up online as soon as possible. We need to get ahead of the pack on this one. Put D'Arcy Defoe back in his box.'

'Online?'

'Welcome to the future, pal. Give me something as soon as you can. It doesn't have to be lengthy, it doesn't have to be compre-hensive. Just enough to stake a claim, let our readers know we're on to it, something for our newsletter, a pointer to the mag. In fact, all the better if you segment it, run it out over several days. Keep the punters interested. I'll make it worth your while. Keep something central back for the magazine, if you like. Then, once we've staked it out as our own, that will prepare the ground for the book. You good with that?'

'I'll see. I can't make any promises. It does depend on what I can dig up.'

'Are you kidding? You were there. In the middle of that goddamn gunfight. Like the O.K. Corral. Just write a first-hand account, what it was like to be there. Do that now. Nothing the *Herald* or anyone else has got can compete with that. And make sure you insert yourself right into the heart of it; make it clear that you weren't there by accident.'

After the call is over, Martin sits and wonders. Wellington is right, so very obviously right. So why has he been so slow to realise it? He's written such stories before, knows the power of them. Maybe he really is losing his chops.

Ivan Lucic emerges through a security door beside the counter, interrupting his reverie, speaking to them as a group. 'The boss wants a word. All of you.'

Inside the station, in the same glassed-in office as the previous evening, Morris Montifore is waiting, deep in conversation with Claus Vandenbruk. The inspector looks up as they enter and signals them to sit. 'Morning. I've got another meeting upstairs shortly. We've got Mess members outing themselves and the brass are shitting themselves. So we need to be fast. Claus and I have a few simple questions.'

That's enough for Vandenbruk; he launches straight in on Martin with his customary sledgehammer approach. 'Detective Inspector Montifore tells me it came as no surprise to you when Harry Sweetwater revealed himself as a member of a United States organised crime syndicate.'

'The Chicago mob.'

'Precisely. How did you know?'

Martin frowns, folds his arms. 'I'm not revealing sources.'

'Fuck that. Was it, or was it not, a member of the ACIC or the AFP?'

Martin shrugs. 'Sorry. I can't afford to play rule in, rule out.'

Vandenbruk seethes, Martin can see it in his eyes, but the investigator's voice remains even. 'I appreciate your journalistic undertakings. But this is life and death. Understand this: Tarquin Molloy was an undercover operative, a police officer, a good man with a family. He was murdered. Brutally murdered. Probably because his cover was blown. We have other undercover agents whose lives are potentially threatened. We can't afford to risk any more killings. If one of the federal agencies is leaking, we need to know.'

'There's an ongoing investigation into Mollisons?'

Vandenbruk slams his open hand down onto the table in frustration. 'Lives are at risk, that's all you need to know.'

Martin thinks it over. 'All right. I didn't learn anything from the ACIC or the AFP.'

'Good. Thank God,' says Vandenbruk, some of the intensity leaving him. He takes a deep breath, rolling his shoulders as if to relax them. 'What else did you learn about Sweetwater?'

Martin's first instinct is to keep his mouth shut, but then he sees an opportunity: maybe he can glean some information in return. Vandenbruk was conducive to such arrangements the last time they dealt with each other, down in Riversend. 'Sweetwater is registered as an AFP informant.'

A chill descends on the room. Both Vandenbruk and Montifore appear stunned, rendered motionless, as if someone has removed their batteries for a second. A journalist has somehow learnt the identity of a highly protected source.

Martin sees an opportunity to press home his advantage. 'Was he Molloy's informant?'

Now it's Vandenbruk's turn to assess his position. The longer he hesitates, the more Martin starts to believe there must have been a connection. 'Maybe,' says Vandenbruk finally. 'We're unsure of their precise relationship.'

'So why didn't you investigate Sweetwater back when Molloy was killed?'

'Because we didn't know Molloy was dead. We thought the same as everyone else: that he'd taken the money and scarpered, either with or without Sweetwater's help.'

'And has Sweetwater continued to cooperate, after Molloy vanished?'

But Vandenbruk is shaking his head. 'I can't tell you anything about his current status, other than that he is wanted for shooting dead Joshua Spitt and for questioning involving Tarquin Molloy's murder. Being an informant gives him no protection against that. None.'

'You think he did it?'

'Don't you? He had the perfect motivation and the perfect opportunity.'

'He told Morris and me that the mob had a contract out on him. That he's a fugitive: from the police and the mob.'

'Yeah. News spreads fast. That's why Henry Livingstone and Joshua Spitt went gunning for him; the contract is worth half a million dollars US. Big money.'

'So what's that got to do with me?'

'We desperately want to get to Sweetwater before they do. You can imagine what a motherlode of information he could give us.

So should he try to contact you, it's imperative you let me know. Understand?'

'Why would he contact me? After what happened on the Goods Line, Morris and I are the last people he's going to trust. He'll think we set him up for Livingstone.'

All this time Mandy has been listening; now she speaks. 'If he's desperate, maybe he'll try to get his hands on the money? Lead us to it.'

Vandenbruk frowns. 'I doubt it. He'll have plenty of money squirrelled away already.'

'Why would you think that?' asks Martin.

Vandenbruk shrugs. 'The mob must have a reason to put out a contract on him. Maybe he killed Molloy and kept the money for himself. Told his bosses that Molloy had escaped overseas.'

Martin looks to Montifore, who raises his eyebrows as if the theory is worth consideration.

Mandy is looking concerned. 'Will you give him immunity if he talks to you?'

'No,' says Morris Montifore. 'Murder is murder. More so if the victim is a cop.'

Vandenbruk purses his lips, calibrates his response. 'Personally, I agree with Morris. But decisions like that, they're well above our pay grade.'

Now it's Montifore who looks annoyed.

'Boss?' It's Lucic, still standing in a corner.

Montifore looks at his watch. 'Shit. I need to get upstairs. I'll get my arse kicked. Thanks for being so candid, but needless to say, do not tell anyone what we spoke about here. And for God's sake, don't put it in the paper. Leave the speculation to D'Arcy Defoe.'

'Can we leave?' asks Mandy.

'Yes,' says Montifore.

'Yes,' says Vandenbruk.

Martin nods as if in agreement, but it's not what he's thinking. When Livingstone appeared on the Goods Line, he'd come from Yev and Mandy, had used the tracking app to find Martin, not Sweetwater. Either he knew the two men were about to meet, or it was just a coincidence.

He's following Mandy and Winifred back out onto the street when his phone rings. Another unidentified number. His deleted contact book is really starting to give him the shits.

'Scarsden.'

'Martin, it's Talbot Torbett. Do you have a number for D'Arcy Defoe? I desperately want to speak to a journalist.'

'Where are you? At home?'

'Yes.'

'I'm on my way.'

chapter thirty-eight

MANDY IS STILL HAVING TROUBLE COMPREHENDING THE CHANGE IN MARTIN. HE'S buzzing with energy, talking on the phone as they leave the police station with Winifred, bouncing around like a frog in a sock. He puts his phone away, places his hands on her shoulders and gives her a cursory kiss. 'I've got to go.'

'You want me to come?' Mandy asks.

'No. It's a source. They'll want confidentiality.'

And now Mandy understands: the story has him. It's part of him, this journalistic fervour, she knows that, but she's not so sure she likes it. As recently as two days ago, she experienced the same adrenaline rush, the same addictive pull, at the State Library when she revealed the company diagram Pam and Zelda had prepared, and he was linking it to the Mess. But now she sees that there's something reckless about it, something self-righteous, something of the same cowboy spirit that had infected Tarquin Molloy. The sense of being different, of having a licence to flout the rules, of the ends justifying the means. She's heard Martin spouting Max Fuller's dictums often enough: 'speaking truth to power', 'holding the powerful to account', 'shining light into dark corners'. The fourth estate. But she knows that's only part of it: that the noble ideals of public service are matched by self-serving ambition. Nevertheless, right here, right now, she doesn't have time to voice her concerns. 'Okay, take care.'

'Sure, you too,' says Martin, sounding distracted. The urgency is in his eyes; the story has him in its grip.

No sooner has he hailed a cab and headed off than her own phone rings. It's Yev.

'You've finished with the police, I see,' he says.

'How do you know that?' she asks.

'The tracking app. You're back on the street.'

'The app? It's still working?'

'Of course. Where's Martin going? His phone is engaged.'

'Off to meet a contact.'

'Will he be long?' And now Mandy can hear a seriousness in Yev's voice. And something more: trepidation.

'Why, Yev? What's happened?'

'You should come here straight away. There's something you should see. Come straight away. I'll try ringing Martin again.'

Fifteen minutes later, after promising to keep Winifred abreast of any developments, she enters Ichiban Computers and Scarvery, Lena scowling at her entrance. A faint smell of the perfume lingers from Henry Livingstone's parting gesture the previous day. Yev isn't at the retro monitor on the counter; instead he's back behind the shelves, working at his homemade super computer.

'Fuck,' he says. 'Fuck. I found more. After we spoke on the phone. You won't fucking believe this.'

'What? What is it?'

'We need to go straight to the police.'

'Jesus, Yev—tell me what you've found.'

'You remember Martin went and saw an old man, a judge called O'Toole? He told you about that?'

'Of course. We tell each other everything,' she says, trying to keep the irony from her voice.

'This judge, he has his entire house wired with closed-circuit television. It all goes to an external site, triggered by any intrusion, like additional people in the house. Each time that happens, it sets off a little alarm. Early this morning, the alarm went off. I got a message, so I checked it out.'

'You got a message? Why you?'

'Martin should have got it as well. He told me about the website, gave me the username and login.'

'Go on,' says Mandy. 'What did it show?'

'Here, see for yourself.' He opens up a program on his computer, his two big screens revealing almost two dozen camera angles in and around a house.

'This is the website?' asks Mandy.

'From the website. I've been downloading. On the site, it's all grainy and low-res, black and white, easy for shuttling through. But the downloads are full colour and high resolution. Like reality TV. And I don't want to leave it sitting on the site. Too easy for someone to erase it, like the files of Max Fuller.'

Mandy counts the cameras. Twenty-two in all. 'Quite the set-up.'

'Extremely expensive,' says Yev. 'They all play back in sync, and you can switch between the cameras, bring it up here.' He indicates a larger image. 'Just like a television studio.'

'Show me,' says Mandy.

'Okay. This first bit—this was what I was watching when I called you.' Yev hits play and all the screens start moving in sync. He's right about the quality: it's like watching television. The camera by the front door reveals it to be night-time. Each screen carries a date and time stamp in the top right corner. The early hours of this morning, just after two. Suddenly, lights flare, and the night is repelled.

'Here we go,' says Yev.

A man is at the front door, the camera looking down from above. He's wearing an overcoat with the collar turned up, a scarf covering the lower half of his face, his eyes hidden by a felt hat, his hands in leather gloves; give him a cigarette and it could be Humphrey Bogart.

'Who is he?' asks Mandy.

'Someone who knows about the cameras,' says Yev. 'But watch this.' He cuts to a wider shot, looking along the narrow verandah, just in time to see the man go through the process of unlocking the door. Three keys, three locks. He enters, pausing at a keypad by the door, punching in a code. 'He's disarming the internal alarms.' Before moving on, the man relocks the front door.

'Where's the judge?'

'Inside.'

'He sets alarms when he's inside the house?'

'The nurse does, when she leaves for the night.'

Mandy and Yev watch as the man moves deeper into the house, lighting his way with a torch. The video struggles with the lack of illumination, but the shape of the man is clear enough, trailing the pool of light made by the flashlight. He enters a room, disappears.

'Toilet. No camera,' says Yev.

Seconds later the man reappears. He walks back the way he came, entering the lounge, flicking on the lights. Two of the screens flare to clarity, bright with colour, high resolution. The man is now wearing a ski mask. The leather gloves have been replaced with latex.

'Audio?' Mandy asks.

'No.'

The man is moving quickly, with confidence.

'He knows the layout of the house,' observes Yev.

'So where's the judge?' asks Mandy again. 'You said he was inside.'

'Here.' Yev switches to another camera. It's a bedroom, a grainy black-and-white picture. Mandy can just make out the shape of a man in a single bed. 'This is as far as I'd watched when I called you. But there is more.' He draws a breath. 'It's fucking terrible.'

'Show me.'

But Yev doesn't. Instead he pauses the playback. 'The intruder searches for almost an hour. Takes his time. He's methodical, searching the judge's study and the library. Here . . .' He shuttles the video forward. 'This is interesting.' The camera captures the man examining a small notebook at a desk, testing passwords on a computer. He pauses, putting on a pair of reading glasses over his mask.

'Green frames,' says Mandy.

'He's aware of the cameras, but might assume they're black and white, like on the website. And here . . .' Yev shuttles forward again. 'The library.' The man is reaching into a cavity. He pulls out some sort of electronic device, like an amplifier or home media computer. They watch as he sets it on a table, calmly opens it with screwdrivers, pulls out a component and places it in his briefcase. 'It's the hard drive. He has the recording of the camera feed.'

'He doesn't know about the live feed to the website.'

'Apparently not.'

'What aren't you showing me, Yev?'

He turns to her, eyes disturbed. 'You sure?'

'Yes.'

'This.' He moves the vision forward again, the two dozen recordings spooling forward in sync, different screens flaring as the man proceeds through the house, turning lights on and off. The final two brighten to reveal the judge's bedroom. Yev brings up one of the screens. The intruder is standing over the bed. He has a gun. He prods the judge in the face with it, waking him.

'They talk for almost fifteen minutes,' says Yev. 'At first it seems almost convivial, but by the end the man starts hitting the judge with the gun, putting the barrel into his mouth. Look here.'

The video moves rapidly forward again. When it stops, Mandy can see the judge's face covered in blood, his hands up, defence-less. She feels sick in the stomach, an unbearable dread of what is coming next. She doesn't need to see it, but she needs to know.

'And then?'

'And then he shoots him. Three times. And leaves.'

chapter thirty-nine

AS THE CAB DROPS MARTIN AT SIR TALBOT'S CENTENNIAL PARK HOME, HIS PHONE chirps in his pocket. A WhatsApp message from Yev: *Come to shop. Urgent.* Martin ignores it, pays the driver, climbs from the cab. He's not going to allow himself to be distracted from the story again; he doesn't want Torbett talking to D'Arcy Defoe instead of him.

He walks through the open pedestrian gate and sees the BMW parked outside the front door; Titus must be here. He knocks twice before the door opens. It's the former judge himself, Sir Talbot, looking less spritely and more bent over than on Martin's previous visit, as if his grief has devoured him.

'You came,' says the old man, an air of vague puzzlement in his voice.

'Yes, I came,' says Martin, not knowing how else to respond.

'Well, I guess you must enter then.'

Martin follows the old man inside the understated home, so different from his own inner-city apartment, as if the quality of Sir Talbot's furnishings insist on a higher level of neatness and cleanliness. They enter the sitting room, with its bay window and comfortable armchairs. But some of the armchairs are missing. Instead, Titus Torbett is sitting silently on the other side of the room in a dining-room carver. He offers a weak smile but doesn't get up. He can't. All too late, Martin sees his wrists: attached to the arms of the chair by cable ties, blood seeping from where he has tried to work them free. Something cold and hard presses into the back of Martin's neck before he can move or speak.

'Hello, Martin,' says a calm voice with a familiar American twang. 'And yes. It's a gun.'

Fear fetches up from somewhere deep inside and flows through him, like ice water injected into his bloodstream. 'Hello,' he says, trying to sound in control, knowing he controls nothing. He looks at Titus. A deep vertical crease has carved itself into the other man's forehead, making him appear more concerned than scared as he watches the man with the gun.

'I'm not going to shoot you, Martin. Not unless I have to.' The gun barrel leaves his neck, moves to his back. Judging by the shifting of Titus's gaze, the assailant has stepped back and to one side. 'Now, Martin, very slowly and very deliberately, please take out your phone and place it on the floor.'

Martin does as he is told.

'Stamp on it. Smash it.'

'Why?'

An explosion sounds in Martin's ear—the gun firing. Plaster falls from Sir Talbot's no longer pristine ceiling. 'Now.'

Martin does what he's told, moving slowly and deliberately off the rug, placing the phone on the oiled floorboards and stomping it into oblivion. He wonders if Yev's tracking app is restricted to real time or if it records past movements, so that at some point the computer technician will be able to work out his location.

'Good. Now, please take a seat. There, next to Torbett junior.'

There is a chair next to Titus, another carver, waiting for him. Titus nods to him, urging compliance. Martin keeps his hands aloft, a sign of acquiescence, and walks to the chair, turns around and sits down. He looks up at the man with the gun: Harry Sweetwater. The aviation glasses are gone; there are laugh lines around the soft brown eyes, setting off a face shaped by conviviality. Now the eyes speak of intelligence, purpose and violence.

'Hello, Harry,' says Martin, unsure if this pleasant face could really belong to a mobster and killer.

The armed man turns to the judge, who is steadying himself against the doorjamb. 'Now, Sir Talbot, do the honours once more, will you, please? Tie his arms to the chair. Nice and tight. I'll be checking.'

The judge shuffles forward, straps Martin's wrists to the wooden chair arms with thin plastic cable ties.

'And his ankles. To the chair legs.'

It takes time. The judge is old. He lowers himself to his hands and knees, is forced to crawl to Martin, to wind the cable ties around his ankles and the chair legs.

'Sorry,' says Martin.

'Not as sorry as I am, son,' says the former judge. By the time he's finished and levered himself back upright, he's wheezing.

'Thank you, Sir Talbot. You can sit down now. There. In your chair,' says Sweetwater, waving his gun. 'I'm not going to restrain you, but if you try to stand, I will hit you with my gun. Very hard. If you persist, I will shoot you. Understood?'

The old man nods, his eyes flaring with indignation and contempt, but the ramrod mind is not about to slip. He'll do nothing to provoke the gunman.

Sweetwater has moved across in front of the fireplace opposite the bay window, through which he can see the front drive and anyone approaching the house. The gunman has Titus and Martin to his left: Titus closer to him, Martin closer to the window. To Sweetwater's right is Sir Talbot, glaring defiantly from his armchair. The mobster makes sure everything is to his liking before he addresses Martin. 'Now you are here, we can start. We play this right and we all leave alive. I have no wish to hurt anyone, let alone kill them. But that depends on you. Or, more precisely, it relies on Mr Torbett here.' He gestures towards Titus.

'What is that supposed to mean?' asks Titus, an attempt at assertiveness that fails to disguise the underlying fear and trepidation in his voice.

'I am going to disappear,' says Sweetwater. 'You will never see me again, never hear from me. Nor will anyone else. But before I go, I'm going to set the record straight. That's your job, Martin. For some reason, you have become the note taker of this clusterfuck, the journalist of record. You and that suckhole Defoe. This is for your benefit and that of your readers. So you hear it, you remember it, later you write it.'

'If you untie one of my hands, I can take shorthand,' says Martin.

'And if I untie Titus's legs, he can dance the light fandango.' Sweetwater shakes his head, as if he's being forced to work with amateurs. 'Here's how it works. I'm going to ask questions. Titus is going to answer them. Once I am done, perhaps you can ask him some yourself. Then, when we're finished, I'm going to leave. By the time the judge unties you and phones the police, I'll be gone. Agreed?'

Martin frowns. 'I guess so,' he says, uncertainty in his voice.

'There is one catch, however,' says Sweetwater. He's smiling, and for a moment Martin catches something in the gunman's eyes, something malicious; he's enjoying their distress. Too late he remembers his hostile environment training, the instruction not to make eye contact during a hostage situation. Easy for them to say. Sweetwater continues. 'Each time Titus here answers a question untruthfully, I am going to slice his father.' He reaches into his coat pocket with his free hand and withdraws a flick knife. He activates its trigger and with a threatening snap a ten-centimetre blade flashes forth from the handle, catching the light. The judge makes some expulsion of breath, tries to rise, but Sweetwater moves quickly to him, pushes him back down into the chair. 'Easy, old man. You have nothing to fear from me. Just from your son.' From behind the judge's chair, Sweetwater looks to Titus. 'You understand the rules? One lie and your father loses an ear. The more you lie, the more he loses.'

Martin is looking at the old judge. There is no sign of fear in his eyes, just tenacity and resistance. Tough as teak. The same can't be said for the son. He's trembling, dread and fear and horror chasing each other across the profile of his face.

'Good,' says Sweetwater affably. 'The sooner we get started the sooner we get finished. First question. What is your precise position at Mollisons?'

'Corporate counsel.'

'Thank you. Easy, isn't it?' Sweetwater turns to Martin. 'Did you know that?'

'No. I didn't.'

Sweetwater grins, gleeful at the amazement on Martin's face, before returning his attention to Titus. 'How was it that I came to Australia to start working alongside you at Mollisons?'

Titus looks at his father, looks at Martin. His eyes are pleading, but there is nothing Martin can do. 'You want me to tell a journalist that?'

'I do.'

Titus glances quickly back at Martin, before facing Sweetwater again. In that moment, Martin can see the man's mind working, trying to calculate the angles; the lawyer's intellect. 'I understand you came to Australia as part of a wider deal. Your employers would funnel more money through Mollisons and take a large equity position in the company. You would be placed in the company to ensure their interests were looked after.'

'Very good, Titus. This is encouraging. But there is no need to be coy. Mr Scarsden already knows the identity of my employers. Maybe you should let your father in on the secret too.'

Martin can see the old man's eyes, wide with intelligence, the eyes of an inquisitor. Martin clears his throat, begins to respond.

'Not you,' interjects Sweetwater. 'He should hear it from his heir.'

Titus's voice is softer, lower. 'Mr Sweetwater works for, is part of, an American organised crime organisation. The mafia. Based in Chicago.'

'And as corporate counsel, did you play a pivotal role in these arrangements? The shareholdings, the investments, my visa, my employment? Disguising it, making it respectable?'

'Yes,' Titus whispers, his head hanging, unable to meet the laser glare of his father. The distaste on the judge's face is all too apparent.

But Sweetwater isn't done. Far from it. 'Now, who suggested I join this so-called dining club that Martin has been poking his nose into, the Mess?'

Titus's head remains slumped, his voice barely above a whisper. 'It was me.'

'You championed my membership?'

'Yes.'

'Why?'

Titus lifts his head, looks at Sweetwater with the eyes of a supplicant. 'I thought it would help extend your influence.'

Sweetwater is nodding. 'So I was aided and abetted by you?'

Again the head bows, again the whispered response. 'Yes.'

'But you're no longer a member yourself?'

'No. Not for many years.'

'Why did you leave?'

To Martin it sounds an innocuous question, easily answered, but for some reason Torbett is hesitating.

'The truth now,' says Sweetwater. His voice is almost placid, but of a sudden he grabs the old judge by his mop of white hair, holding his head tight, flourishing the knife before his eyes. 'The truth now. Or the old man loses his nose.'

That's enough for Titus. 'Elizabeth asked me to resign. She had someone else she wanted to join.'

'Numbers are limited.'

'Yes.'

'That must have hurt. Your own sister. Your little sister. Not thinking you important enough.' And Sweetwater smiles, releasing the father. 'You're doing very well. Hope you're getting all this, Martin. A simple question next: do you know what I'm capable of?'

That gets the son, Martin can sense it. Another tremor runs down the length of the lawyer's body and a broken affirmation escapes his lips. 'Yes.'

Martin can see the son is engulfed by fear. He looks at Sweetwater, who remains calm and deliberate and smiling. Like a snake charmer.

'Have I ever deployed violence?'

'You want me to incriminate you?'

There's something in this answer that Sweetwater doesn't like. He moves back towards the judge, knife extended, but then thinks better of it. 'Tell Martin about Tarquin Molloy. What happened to him.'

But the lawyer's mind has leapt ahead, has reached a conclusion as to where this might be heading. 'You don't need to kill us. I'll do whatever you want.' To Martin's ears, there is something pathetic, something craven in the man's voice. Across from him, a new emotion has entered the eyes of Sir Talbot: contempt.

'I won't be killing anybody. I won't even be harming anybody,' says Sweetwater. 'Just tell the truth.'

Titus's eyes are firmly on the floor as he speaks. 'Your physical security person, Clarity Sparkes, came to us. She said she was suspicious of Molloy, that he was attempting to cultivate her, attempting to cultivate other women. He was trying to access files he had no authority to read.'

'Did we know Molloy was a policeman?'

'No. We thought he was some sort of fraudster. Whoever he was, we needed to fix him, without drawing attention to ourselves or what the bank was doing.'

'We didn't want to involve the police?'

'No.'

'So what did we do?'

'The three of us discussed what might be done. The Turtle set up surveillance. I forget his real name. Clarity tried to lead Molloy on, find out what he was up to. She was authorised to use money, to bribe him. But he wasn't tempted.'

'And after that?'

Titus Torbett is looking increasingly confused. 'Why are we discussing this?'

But Sweetwater simply raises his eyebrows. 'So Martin and your father know exactly what we did. Exactly what sort of men we are, you and I.' And he smiles, a rictus of saccharine menace. 'What happened?'

'You and I discussed killing him. But you thought it too extreme.'

'And Clarity? What did she suggest?'

'She was the one who came up with the idea of beating him up, warning him off. She knew some people.'

'Who were they, these men?'

'One man. A crim. A standover man. Henry Livingstone.'

Sweetwater looks at Martin. 'The self-same man who tried to shoot me dead yesterday.'

'I haven't forgotten,' says Martin.

'Did you know they were stalking me?' asks Sweetwater.

'No,' says Martin. 'No, I didn't.'

'Lucky for you,' says Sweetwater. 'Titus, continue.'

Martin interrupts. 'Can I ask a question?'

Sweetwater frowns. This is his show; he doesn't want to lose control of its narrative. 'All right. Just one.'

'Did she know? Did Clarity Sparkes know what Mollisons was really all about?'

Sweetwater defers to Mollisons' corporate counsel. 'Titus?'

'No. I think she suspected towards the end, but no. She wasn't a member of the inner sanctum.'

Sweetwater nods to Martin as if in agreement, then says to Titus Torbett, 'Please continue.'

Torbett junior looks part perplexed, part panicked. 'Continue where?'

'What happened to Molloy?'

'He disappeared. At first we thought the beating had served its purpose. But then we found that money was missing. A lot of money. Molloy had disappeared at exactly the same time. A check of the systems revealed he'd stolen it.' He pauses. 'That's what we thought. Honestly.'

'Correct,' says Sweetwater. 'Get that, Martin? We thought he'd escaped with the money. Titus and I and our employers. We concluded he was a grifter, a very lucky grifter, a very ballsy grifter, probably unaware of whose money he was stealing. Is that how you remember it?'

'Yes,' says Torbett, but again Martin can hear the hesitancy in his voice. The lawyer is still unsure where this is leading, why Sweetwater is so eager to incriminate the two of them. Martin is wondering much the same thing: what is the purpose of all this? Sweetwater's already admitted to being a ranking member of the Chicago mob, confessed to infiltrating Mollisons. Does he want to be cleared of murder? Or does he want to point the finger at those he sees as his persecutors?

'So who killed Molloy?' asks Sweetwater, voice soft.

The tension steps up a notch, Martin feels as if his ears are about to pop, as if they've abruptly dived deeper. Is Sweetwater about to gift him the scoop of his life?

'Livingstone,' suggests Titus. 'He was told to beat him up, but he fucked up, went too far. He accidentally killed him.'

And Harry Sweetwater laughs, a high-pitched cackle. 'Accidentally? You shitting me? Someone put three slugs in his head. That ain't no accident, pal.'

Titus looks at his father, as if begging the old man to believe him. 'Okay. Someone authorised it. But it wasn't me. I didn't know about it. I thought Molloy had escaped with the money.'

'Really?' And Sweetwater steps across to Sir Talbot and rests his knife against the judge's neck. 'You sure about that?' he says, the menace in his actions not his voice.

Titus looks terrified, but he sticks to his account. 'Yes. I knew nothing.'

'So who authorised it?'

'I don't know.'

'Who do you think?'

There is no response until Sweetwater again starts to admire the edge of his knife. There is panic in Titus's voice now, the suggestion that he might lose control altogether. 'Why ask me? You clearly know more than I do.'

'Because you're a coward; whatever I say, you will agree with me. Scarsden needs to hear it from you. So does your father. So talk, please. Remember, there is no penalty for honesty.'

'I don't know. It must have been Clarity. She had him killed, then took the money.' There is a pause, Martin can almost hear Titus swallowing bile. 'Or you.' The last is but a whisper.

And again Sweetwater laughs, the same high-pitched cackle, a little unhinged. He flicks the knife up before his face, twirls the blade, examines its edges. 'So you really don't know? Not for sure?'

'No.'

'Good answer, Titus. You are doing very well. Tell the truth and nothing will go wrong. Okay? Don't worry about offending me or incriminating me. Just tell the truth.' He turns to Martin. 'For the record, it wasn't me. And I really doubt Clarity Sparkes would have the bottle to order an execution.' He turns back to Titus. 'Who killed your sister and Max Fuller?' There is silence, long and portentous. The pleasant smile still adorns Sweetwater's pleasant face, but the amiability in his voice has been replaced with steel. 'It was nothing to do with me, was it?'

'No.'

'Who killed them?'

'I don't know. Livingstone and Spitt.'

'You may be right. But if so, who paid them to do it?'

'I don't know. Honestly. Maybe it was you.'

'Wrong answer,' says Sweetwater sadly. And with a quick, assured movement, he grabs the judge's head and slices off the top of one of his ears. There's a spurt of blood, and Sir Talbot grabs at the slippery mess.

'You cunt,' he exclaims.

Sweetwater laughs and tosses the tip of the ear to Titus. It lands in his lap where it squirms slowly, like a dying bug. He looks at it in horror, mouth open, eyes wide, arms straining at the cable ties.

'Talk,' says Sweetwater.

'For God's sake, get it off me.'

'Talk.'

'I don't know. How could I know?'

This time Sweetwater moves slowly, telegraphing his intentions. 'Hold still, arsehole,' he says, taking off all of the judge's other ear, tossing it towards Titus. It bounces from his lap onto the floor.

'Jesus Christ,' weeps the judge, blood seeping out between his fingers as he holds the side of his head.

'You know, don't you?' says Titus, eyes wide.

'I do. But Martin and your father need to hear it from you. Especially your father.'

'Fuck you. Kill me then.' The defiance comes suddenly, with desperation.

Sweetwater sneers. 'You're not getting off that lightly, you fucker.' And he twirls the knife before the cowering judge. 'What appendage should we take next, Titus? Your choice.'

'For fuck's sake, tell him,' says the judge. 'You want me to bleed to death?'

'Wise words,' says Sweetwater.

There's a moment there, Martin can see it in the son's eyes, where all the possibilities narrow down to just one. There is no escape.

'It was me,' whispers Titus, his head down, eyes shut.

'Louder.'

'Me. I killed them.'

'You ordered the murder of your own sister?'

'Yes.'

'You miserable little cunt,' says the judge. 'Give me the knife. I'll take more than his fucking ears.'

Sweetwater is shifting weight from leg to leg, almost bouncing with glee, delighted at the emotional carnage. 'Settle down, children. Settle down.' He cackles once more, overjoyed that his script is unfolding so well. 'So, Titus, just to be clear, I wasn't responsible for any of these deaths, was I? Not Molloy, not Fuller, not your sister. Say it.'

'Molloy wasn't me.'

'Oh, for fuck's sake, you're dumber than I thought.' He grabs the judge by the hair, but this time the old man has both hands up, protecting what remains of his ears. Sweetwater draws the knife quickly through the fingers of the left hand, severing nothing, but leaving a deep and bloody gash, blood seeping.

'Jesus wept,' says the judge, anger in his voice. 'You'll pay for this, you arsehole.'

'No doubt I will,' says Sweetwater, before again addressing the son. 'So, tell your father, tell Martin. Why was it necessary to kill your sister and Fuller?'

'I was protecting us. You. Me. All of us. They knew all about the Mess. They were closing in on Mollisons.'

'So you took it upon yourself to eliminate them?'

'Yes. For the greater good.'

'And did you seek my advice? My permission?'

'No,' says Titus, the passion draining out of his voice.

Sweetwater shifts his gaze to Martin. 'You following this? This white-bread lawyer here, this lily-livered motherfucker, is working alongside a fully paid up member of the Chicago mob, and yet he decides to kill a couple of innocents without even thinking to mention his plan to me.' And again his attention shifts back to the son. 'Why was that, Titus? How could you have been so fucking stupid?'

But Titus seems to have sunken below speaking. He's sobbing, alternating between looking at his father and the floor, as if lifting his gaze to meet Sweetwater's is a physical impossibility. His face is racked by guilt and self-pity. The judge is also in pain, real pain. It's not the loss of his ears or the pulsing gash in his hand, Martin understands; it runs much deeper than that. His daughter, murdered by his son. How could losing ears even compete with that level of agony?

Sweetwater continues. 'So what you two gentlemen need to consider—especially you, Martin, as you write your account—is this: why did the brother kill the sister? To protect Mollisons, to protect me, to protect his own precious arse? Or was it more than that? Was it simply that he couldn't bear the thought that it was his sister who would expose him, diminish him, send him to prison, belittle him for all time in their father's eyes? Expose him as the corporate counsel to a mafia-controlled company? The High Court justice, a knight of the realm, and his high-flying daughter, a Supreme Court judge, the golden girl, always the favoured child, always the high achiever, whereas this pathetic little shit's only way to gain anything like status and money was to become a corporate criminal for Mollisons. Before that, he couldn't even keep his membership of the Mess.'

Martin hears the contempt in Sweetwater's voice, can only wonder at it. How could one criminal, a member of the mafia no less, be so scathing about another transgressor?

As if to answer Martin's question, Sweetwater, his voice imbued with true emotion at last, spits at Titus Torbett, 'You miserable little bastard. You have no idea of poverty, of deprivation, of abuse. Growing up in this house, with all your privileges. I never had a choice, not like you. Yet I made more of myself than you will ever be. And now they're coming for me. Why? Because a spoilt child got outshone in his father's eyes by a girl.'

Now there is near silence: Martin can hear Sweetwater breathing heavily with emotional exertion, Titus Torbett sobbing with self-pity and the judge wheezing with pain. *Is that it?* Martin wonders. Has Sweetwater extracted all the information he requires? Has he inflicted all the pain he desires, exacted his retribution? What now? Is he just going to walk out, leave them like this?

Martin decides it's time to talk. He looks Sweetwater in the eye. 'I've got it all. I understand it. I will publish it. There is no need to go any further. It's enough.'

But it's not Sweetwater who responds. A deeper voice speaks, backed up by a gun with a deeper register. 'No. We're not finished just yet,' says Henry Livingstone, stepping out of the shadows. He places the barrel of his gun square in Harry Sweetwater's back. 'Drop the knife, cunt.'

chapter forty

SHE TRIES AGAIN, AND AGAIN MARTIN DOESN'T ANSWER. INDEED, HE SEEMS TO have turned his phone off altogether; it's redirecting straight to voicemail. She hangs up, not bothering to leave another message. She tries to locate him on the tracking app, but it doesn't seem to be working.

'Hey, Yev, is the tracker on the fritz? I thought it was still working.'

'Should be. Give us a look.' He takes Mandy's phone, frowns. 'That's weird. I'm showing up clear as day.' He checks his own phone. 'And I can see you.' He shrugs. 'Either he has his phone powered off completely, or he's underground or something.'

'Train?'

'No. There's reception in the tunnels.'

'Right. How's the video?'

'Almost done downloading. I just want to make sure I back it all up before we give a copy to the cops.' Yev returns to his work station, spools through, double-checking. 'Okay. All good.' Then silence.

'C'mon, let's go,' says Mandy, anxious to get this done.

'Shit,' says Yev. 'There's more.'

'What?'

'Come see.'

'What is it?'

'There's a new recording. Someone else visiting.'

She joins him, silent as he works at the controls. 'This is straight off the site, so not high quality.' He starts moving through. Again it is night-time, lit up by the floodlights, the cameras and recorders triggered. But this time it's different. There is nothing furtive about the man walking up to the front door, no attempt to disguise his identity: the suit, the oiled hair, the length of his face.

'Henry Livingstone,' whispers Mandy.

'Wanted for murder,' says Yev.

'Not even trying to hide. Bold as brass.'

'Visiting a judge.'

They watch as he unlocks the door, not bothering to knock or ring the bell. He has keys, enters with confidence, with impunity. As if he doesn't know that anything is wrong, that Justice Clarence O'Toole is already two hours dead, shot by a man wearing a ski mask. Mandy finds the video chilling to watch, knowing what she knows, knowing what Livingstone must discover for himself. They watch as he disarms the alarm, saunters down the hallway as if he's done this many times before, apparently calling out as he comes. They watch him enter the bedroom, switch on the light, stand there frozen as he takes in the scene.

'He didn't know,' says Yev.

'Doesn't look like it.'

'Seen enough?'

'No. Let's see what he does next.'

What he does next is this: he takes the handkerchief from the top pocket of his suit, the dapper turned functional, and wipes the light switch, turning it back off. He closes the door and wipes the handle. He walks straight to the library, switches on the light with his kerchief-covered hand. He walks towards the cupboard with the recording gear, sees the disembowelled recording machine. He nods to himself. He takes out his phone, checks something on it.

'Shit,' says Yev. 'He's got access to the website.'

'Are you sure?'

'No, but why else would he be checking his phone at four o'clock in the morning?'

But Livingstone doesn't look at his phone for long. Instead, he turns and removes a painting from the wall.

'Jesus,' says Yev. 'A wall safe.'

'The killer missed it.'

They watch as Livingstone calmly works at the combination, checking his phone constantly, hand still cloaked in the kerchief to avoid leaving prints. It takes a few minutes, but he gets the safe open, reaches in, withdraws something, puts it in his pocket. 'Go back,' says Mandy. 'Can you see what it is?'

Yev tries, but spooling the video is clunky, and the resolution is no better the next time around. 'I'll need to download it. High-res. We may be able to see more then.'

'How long?'

'Not sure. An hour maybe.'

'Right. We need to do it anyway. The killer gutted the recorder in the house. If the only copy is on the site, then it's vulnerable.'

'Absolutely.'

'Okay. You stay here and get downloading. Can I take the first video to the police?'

'Sounds like a plan.'

'And can you contact Martin?'

'I'll see what I can do.'

By the time Mandy arrives at the police station with the video of Clarence O'Toole's murder, Winifred Barbicombe is already there. Mandy sighs with relief. Life is always a little easier with the support of her fierce solicitor. As they enter the foyer, Winifred rings Morris Montifore on his personal number.

'He's on his way,' she says.

As it happens, it's not Montifore who collects them, it's his minion, Ivan Lucic, silent and surly. 'This better be good,' is all he has to say. He leads them to the same glassed-in office where Mandy has found herself twice in the previous two days.

Montifore bustles in. 'Talk. You have two minutes.'

'Justice Clarence O'Toole has been murdered. Shot to death in his bed.'

'We know,' says Montifore. 'Nurse called it in when she arrived at work. We were just leaving. But how do *you* know?'

'We saw it happen. And we know who killed him.'

Montifore stares, blinks. 'Sit,' he says. 'Explain.' Lucic pulls out a pad and a pen.

So Mandy explains how Yev downloaded the CCTV footage from the security website.

Montifore hears her out, before he starts his questions. 'Your pal, the computer genius—how did he get access to the site? Did he hack it?'

'No. O'Toole gave the login and password to Martin. In case something happened to him.'

'That's convenient,' says Lucic.

'Watch your tongue, officer,' snaps Winifred. 'My client didn't have to come here. She could have given the video directly to Martin Scarsden without consulting you. The first you would have known about this evidence would be when you read about it in the *Herald*.'

Lucic looks like he could bite the lawyer's head off, but Montifore is all conciliation. 'Calm down, everyone, calm down. I wasn't casting aspersions.' He talks directly to Mandy. 'Your lawyer will understand. We need to ensure any evidence, including this video, has been legally obtained. If it's stolen, we need to ensure it won't be ruled inadmissible.'

'It was legally obtained,' asserts Winifred. 'O'Toole gave Martin access to the security site precisely because he feared something like this might happen.'

'Very good,' says Montifore. 'Let's see it then.'

Mandy hands over a small hard drive. 'There are multiple camera angles. Yev has cut the most relevant ones together. But we can give you the lot.'

'Of course you can,' says Montifore. 'Speaking of which, where is Yevgeny? And why are you the one bringing this to me? Where the hell is Martin Scarsden?'

chapter forty-one

ALL EYES TURN. HENRY LIVINGSTONE HAS MOVED OUT OF THE SHADOWY HALLWAY and into the room proper, his enormous handgun like a magnet, pulling in their attention. Sweetwater drops the knife, and Livingstone gives him a mighty shove in the back, sending him sprawling onto his knees in front of the bay window, between where Titus Torbett and Martin sit tied to their chairs and where Sir Talbot Torbett sits bleeding into his. And from his position, cable-tied to a chair, Martin watches the play unfold around him, not as a member of the audience, but as an actor on the stage, one who has neglected to read the script, one rooted to the spot, one who doesn't know exactly what is coming next but dreads it all the same. First, he sees the pistol—even as Sweetwater is falling, slipping his designer Glock from its holster. Now he sees the mafia man rise on his knees and begin to turn, bringing the barrel to bear on Livingstone, but before he can align it, Livingstone's own weapon explodes with a roaring violence. Martin can see the muzzle flash, see the smoke, see the recoil jerking Livingstone's hand backwards. The sound is deafening, a full-throated explosion, a sonic boom. And directly in front of him, a metre away, he sees Sweetwater lurch backwards from the impact, blood and flesh and cloth blowing out of the exit wound, smashing a hole in the window and spattering Martin and Titus Torbett. Before Sweetwater can do anything, before he can fire, before he can even fall, there is a second explosion, another torso-shredding impact. His knees go, he falls, landing sideways, still attempting somehow to bring his weapon around to return fire.

Livingstone watches him dispassionately. 'Die slowly, you cunt,' he sneers, but there is no chance of that. The life is pouring out of Harry Sweetwater, spreading in a pool of blood around him. He knows it too; it's in the mobster's eyes as he stares up at Martin. 'The truth,' he gasps to Martin. And then, with a last effort, he raises his own gun, no longer trying to twist back towards Livingstone. Titus sees him, sees his intent. Before he can speak, before he can beg, Sweetwater's own gun barks. The noise is a sharp retort, but no less emphatic than Livingstone's cannon, another punctuation mark, another story ending. Martin hears the splattering collision of the bullet hitting Titus Talbot in the chest. Horror is written on the lawyer's face, surprise. At his feet, Harry Sweetwater smiles one last beatific smile and dies, the expression easing slowly from his face as life leaves him.

There is nothing angelic about Titus Torbett's death: he is beginning to convulse, to cough blood, eyes round with fear, reading glasses and pens falling from his pockets as he slumps forward. His father, his bloody ears forgotten, has not so much stood up as fallen forward out of his chair and is crawling across the carpet towards his son, past the corpse of Harry Sweetwater, through the pool of blood. 'Titus.' He is weeping, tears streaming, face contorted. 'My boy.'

At the last, the son hears him, looks up to meet his pleading eye. 'Forgive me, Pa,' he manages. 'Forgive me.' And he collapses under the weight of impending death and acknowledged guilt. His eyes glaze, there is a final expulsion—air and blood and sputum—and he dies, his father still crawling towards him.

Martin looks up to Livingstone, who stands surveying the impact of his handiwork, devoid of emotion. He's dressed immaculately: a navy three-piece suit, polished leather shoes, a new white shirt and red silk tie. He has a red carnation in his lapel. He looks like a bridegroom. He regards Martin, acknowledges him. 'They killed her. The two of them. They killed her.'

'Who?' asks Martin.

But Henry Livingstone is already moving away, Martin can see it, not moving physically but in his mind, moving beyond questions and answers, beyond the here and now. 'Clarity,' he says. And he puts the gun in his mouth and fires. A large red hole is blown through the ceiling and Livingstone collapses like a rag doll. A red mist fills the air and Martin gags, attempting to hold his breath, not to breathe it in. But, of course, he must. And when he does, he vomits, leaning forward to add to the bestial swamp of the floor. His ears chime with the violence of the gunfire, his mind with the gore.

Slowly, ever so slowly, the ringing in his ears subsides and the room grows silent, save for the quiet sobbing of Sir Talbot Torbett.

'The knife,' Martin says to him. 'Sweetwater's knife. Cut me free.'

But the old man is not listening. He is beyond hearing, trapped within his own mind, caged by his personal grief and private horror. And so Martin too is trapped, tied to a chair inside an abattoir, eyes closed and struggling to retain some sense of himself among the carnage.

chapter forty-two

CLAUS VANDENBRUK ENTERS THE ROOM WITH HIS NORMAL BUSTLING ENERGY, anger suppressed, irritated at being summoned. 'What?' he says.

'Clarence O'Toole has been murdered,' says Montifore.

'The judge?'

'The judge.'

'Where? When?'

'Early hours. At his home. Nurse called it in.'

Vandenbruk gestures towards Mandy and Winifred. 'What are they doing here?'

'Telling us who killed him. Look at this.'

Montifore plays the video Yev has prepared, but Mandy doesn't watch the screen. Instead she watches the faces of the two police officers. Montifore is grim, knowing what's coming; Vandenbruk looks on with fascination, eyes wide, alerted to what it will show, but not knowing how or when or by whose hand.

'Who is it?' he whispers, watching the masked man enter the house and flick on the lights.

'Don't know,' says Montifore.

But then Montifore shuttles to the section in the study, when the killer puts on his glasses to examine the notebook, and Mandy thinks she sees the spark of something in Vandcnbruk's eyes. Recognition? Consternation?

'His glasses—green frames,' she says, hoping for a reaction.

And gets one. 'Yes,' says Montifore, still looking at the screen, trying to vacuum up clues, but Claus Vandenbruk turns to look at her.

'Green frames,' he says. Nothing more.

Mandy tells them of the delay before the killer gets to the judge's room, the long period when he searches the house. They spool forward.

'They talk for quite some time,' says Mandy. 'After a while, the killer starts beating the judge. Eventually, he shoots him.'

'Is there any audio?' asks Vandenbruk.

'None,' says Mandy. 'We checked.'

Montifore advances the recording, watches the beating, watches the execution. When he eventually stops the vision, he turns to Vandenbruk. 'He was expecting this. Looked like he almost welcomed it.'

'You don't know that,' says Vandenbruk.

'Pity about the audio,' says Montifore.

'Too right. Can I get a copy of this, please? Is this all of it?'

'It's all we've got,' says Montifore. 'I'll get you a copy as soon as possible.'

Mandy looks at Winifred, who shakes her head. Mandy interprets it as an injunction to silence.

'Is now possible?' asks Vandenbruk.

'If you supply a drive.'

'I'll get one,' says Vandenbruk and leaves the office.

'You don't trust him,' says Mandy.

Montifore looks annoyed; Lucic's eyes are wide, as if he's just snorted a line of speed. 'I trust him fine,' says the senior detective. 'But this is murder. I don't want him and his team of anti-corruption crusaders getting in the way.'

Vandenbruk returns with a drive, and Montifore starts the copy.

'You know about the suppression order?' offers Vandenbruk.

'I do,' says Montifore. 'You think it's connected?'

Vandenbruk shrugs. 'Could be.'

The copy finishes. Vandenbruk takes the drive and leaves again.

'There's more,' says Mandy. 'More video.'

'Tell me,' says Montifore.

So Mandy tells him of Henry Livingstone entering the house, finding the judge dead, taking something from the safe.

'You're sure it was him? Livingstone?'

'Absolutely.'

'Why didn't you bring it with you?'

'Yev is still downloading it.' She explains how the vision on the website is low-res, but once it's downloaded, it's crystal clear.

'So this video here. Is this the highest resolution?'

'I guess. It looked clearer at Yev's, but his monitors are better.'

'He might have squashed it down to fit on that drive,' suggests Lucic.

Montifore turns to his subordinate. 'Ivan, I want you to go with Mandalay straight away. I want all the video he's got, all the camera angles. Everything. I want the address of the website, I want the login and the passwords. But most of all, I want the highest possible quality video of when the killer is in the bedroom—not just the execution, but the whole thing, when the killer is talking to the judge. Both angles.'

'Lip readers,' whispers Mandy.

Montifore turns to her, a flash of anger quickly suppressed. 'Do not tell anyone. No one. You got that?'

'Of course not, Inspector,' says Winifred calmly.

'I mean it,' says Montifore.

'Mandalay has just handed you your killer on a platter,' says Winifred, her voice measured. 'What's more, I will not be advising Yevgeny to insist on a warrant.'

Montifore takes a deep breath. 'Okay. I'm grateful. We're grateful. But tell Martin Scarsden, if he ever puts in an appearance, that he publishes none of this until I give him the go-ahead.' He turns to Lucic again. 'Get going, Ivan. And send someone in here. We need to identify those glasses frames.'

chapter forty-three

MARTIN IS SITTING OUTSIDE AS THE FIRST POLICE ARRIVE, THE OLD JUDGE HAVING momentarily regained enough of his faculties to cut him free before sinking once again into shock, grief and misery, unwilling or unable to move from the room. So now Martin sits, propped on a large rock next to a birdbath, blood-spattered and wide-eyed, his body intermittently electrified by involuntary tremors. He's in a bad place, he knows it, in a very bad place. And he must look it. He's dimly aware of the two uniformed officers moving cautiously through the pedestrian gate, spread apart, wearing flak jackets, with their guns trained upon him. Martin lifts his hands above his head, demonstrating his lack of weapons.

'Inside?' asks one of the officers, fear obvious on his young face.

Martin nods, feeling the difficulty of speech. 'Gunfight,' is all he can manage.

'They're armed?'

'They're dead,' he says.

'How many?' asks the other officer.

Martin holds up three fingers, then forces himself to speak. 'There's one old man. Still alive. Unarmed. Harmless. Cut up and bleeding. Needs an ambulance.'

'Fuck. Are you all right?' asks the first officer, gun still trained on Martin as if his appearance is in itself threatening.

'No. I'm not.'

'Are you wounded? Injured?'

Martin blinks, looks down at himself, somehow bewildered by the question. 'No. I don't think so. Maybe not.'

More emergency vehicles are arriving; the air is filled with sirens. A police sergeant, also wearing body armour, jogs up.

The young police officer takes the initiative, speaking without prompting. 'He's unarmed, not injured. Says there are three dead inside. A gunfight. One old man, a survivor, needs medical care.'

The sergeant addresses Martin. 'Is it safe to enter?'

'Yes,' says Martin, but even as he's saying it, he's stopped by the sharp retort of a gun: Sweetwater's, a single, sharp retort.

'Jesus,' barks the senior man. 'Get him out of here. Set up a perimeter. No one is going in there before the tactical response boys get here.'

Martin tries to explain, but they're no longer listening, bustling him away, off outside the gate, back into the streets of Sydney where madness has not yet claimed sovereignty.

Later, how much later he can't say, he's still on the kerbside, an ambulance officer in latex gloves and a mask wiping his hands and face clean, when Morris Montifore and Claus Vandenbruk approach. All around, more and more vehicles are arriving:

negotiators, forensic science trucks, the dog squad; police dressed in everything from jeans to body armour. Mounted police from Moore Park. Mounted police? Why mounted police?

'Are you all right?' asks Montifore, voice unsure.

Martin stares up at him, eyes hollow, before remembering to answer. 'No.'

'Shock,' says the ambulance officer.

'No shit,' says Vandenbruk. 'What the fuck happened?'

Another tremor rocks Martin's body, incited by the mere suggestion of recalling the mayhem. Montifore and Vandenbruk exchange a glance.

'Can we take him away from here?' Montifore asks the ambulance man.

'Sooner the better. But he needs a doctor. Care.'

'We'll make sure he gets the best,' says Montifore before addressing Martin. 'C'mon, mate, let's get you somewhere safe. Get you cleaned up.'

Martin smiles. He can feel himself smiling, nodding. He thinks he may cry.

Montifore crouches down, modulating his voice, making it as soothing as possible. 'Before we leave, can you tell me who's in there?'

And surprising himself, he can. 'Henry Livingstone shot Harry Sweetwater. Sweetwater shot Titus Torbett. Livingstone killed himself. I think the judge just did the same.'

'Fuck me,' whispers Montifore, horror written on his face, struggling to comprehend. 'You poor bastard.'

Claus Vandenbruk says nothing for a moment, his eyes wide. 'Wait here. Don't go yet.' He strides away.

Montifore sits down on the kerb next to Martin, places an arm around him in a gesture of reassurance and support, careless of his own clothing. He speaks to the ambulance officer. 'Any chance of getting him something to drink? Tea?'

'Hot chocolate?' suggests the ambo.

'Martin?'

But Martin is staring off into the sky. The smoke seems to be dissipating. The sky looks bluer. Maybe they've finished with their burning off. Or maybe it's a sea breeze, come to cleanse the day, to push the smoke and the ash and embers inland. Back into the interior where they belong, away from Sydney, away from the postcard. A helicopter is making a run overhead, as if to celebrate.

Vandenbruk returns, his face grim, his hands covered in latex gloves and his shoes with slip-on plastic covers, like repurposed shower caps. He shakes his head, eyes filled with the horror of it. He has his phone with him; he hands it over to Montifore. Montifore examines it for a moment, then shows it to Martin. It's a photograph, the colours overly bright, like a Christmas decoration, green against red: a set of green-rimmed spectacles, lying on the blood-soaked rug.

'Who was wearing the green glasses, Martin?'

A deep breath washes through him, as if he has been resuscitated, brought back from the deep water and revived on the warming sands of a beach. Another deep sigh and he can speak, the fog beginning to rise. 'No one. They belong to Titus Torbett. Fell from his pocket when he was shot.'

Montifore and Vandenbruk exchange a knowing look. 'So Torbett murdered Clarence O'Toole,' says Montifore.

'He . . .' says Martin. He tries again. 'He confessed. In there. To killing Elizabeth and Max. Ordering their deaths.'

There's a short silence, spreading to accommodate the weight of the allegation. 'His own sister? He admitted to that?' asks Montifore.

Martin nods, feeling as if he's moving his head too emphatically, or too slowly. 'He said it.'

'Christ,' says Vandenbruk. 'I guess it makes sense. Killed O'Toole. Killed his sister and Fuller. Probably killed Molloy as well.'

'Why?' asks Montifore, semi-rhetorically. 'What was he trying to achieve?'

But Martin doesn't respond. Through the fog, his mind is slowly coming back to life. It's true Torbett confessed to killing his own sister, confessed to it in front of their father. And he killed O'Toole, by the sounds of it. So why did he deny killing Molloy? Why? But now Martin's moment of perspicacity dissolves again, and he again finds it difficult to muster his thoughts; they're drifting this way and that. 'What's the Turtle?' he asks the policemen.

chapter forty-four

SHE DOESN'T HAVE MANY OPTIONS. THE POLICE WON'T TAKE HER WITH THEM.
Martin's phone is not responding and she doesn't want to go back
to Yev's, not if Lucic is still there trawling through video. There's
the hotel, but what is she meant to do there? Take up knitting?
Remove herself from the events she has helped set in train, events
that may determine her future? Bugger that.

And so she waits in the foyer of the police station, trying to
decide her next move, trying not to panic, trying to glean what
is happening from the news sites on her phone and the wall-
mounted television. And ringing in her ears, Claus Vandenbruk's
throwaway line as he rushed out of the building with Montifore:
'Scarsden. He's like the angel of fucking death.' Martin: where is
he? What has happened?

She's sitting there as the ABC News anchor, eyebrows arched
into an overly emphatic expression of concern, announces above

a red banner declaring BREAKING NEWS that police are warning of an 'active shooter' on the loose in Sydney's eastern suburbs, with unconfirmed reports of casualties. Mandy's eyes lock on the screen, her ears straining to hear the presenter, while her mind runs free, speculating wildly, and her guts swirl in gusts of dread. Soon, the ABC has a chopper in the air. The presenter is talking about Centennial Park, an exclusive enclave surrounded by parkland. Shit. It can't be, she tells herself. Not him. Not now. Not taken from her, not taken from Liam. An image comes to her of the house at Port Silver, no longer a sanctuary, but a purgatory, she a widow, her son fatherless. 'It can't be,' she repeats under her breath. 'It can't be.'

The news anchor updates the situation. Police say there is no longer an active shooter, that the situation is under control. They are establishing a crime scene. Motorists are being requested to avoid Moore Park Road and surrounding areas. A map of alternative routes appears full screen.

'Fuck the motorists,' she says aloud. 'Who's dead? Who's alive? And where is Martin?'

By the time the television is catching up, reporting that it's believed either three or four people have been shot dead inside a house in Centennial Park, her mind is starting to contemplate the worst: that he really is dead.

And then he arrives back at the station.

The wave of relief, of gratitude, of unspoken prayers answered, is closely followed by a wave of concern and, momentarily, revulsion. There is gore all over him, spattered on his clothes, in his hair; she can see where it has been wiped from his face. But there is no checking her emotions; they propel her to him, throw her on him, thread her arms around his neck, stains or no stains, blood or no blood.

'You're alive,' she manages, standing back, considering his face.

'Yes,' he replies, sounding somewhat surprised.

'Are you all right?' she asks, unsettled by the strangeness of his tone.

'Mild shock,' says Montifore, who is holding Martin by the arm.

'Mild?' asks Mandy, then looks down at the policeman's hand. 'Are you supporting him, or arresting him?'

'He's not under arrest. Far from it. But we need to get a statement from him. We might be a while.'

'A statement? He needs medical care.'

'He'll get it. I promise.'

Martin turns to her. 'It's okay. They need to hear.'

'Can I sit in with him?' Mandy asks the detective.

Montifore grimaces. 'No. Better that you don't hear all the details.'

That angers her, as if only men can face the grisly. 'I'll be fine.'

But Montifore is firm. 'I'm sorry. No.'

'I want my lawyer there, then.'

'Your lawyer?'

'His lawyer.'

Montifore sighs. 'Yes. Send her in.' Then his voice softens. 'Seriously, he's not in any sort of legal trouble. But he is going to need looking after when we're finished here.'

Again, her anger flares at being cast in the supporting role, but one look at Martin's hapless face tells her that Montifore is trying to be sympathetic.

'How long?'

'Give us an hour.'

She kisses Martin, gives his hand a squeeze and leaves. She waits until she's outside before wiping her mouth, trying to rid herself of the taste of blood. The sensible option would be to wait in the foyer for him, but she's had enough of waiting, waiting on the pleasures of policemen, and hanging on the approximations of the ABC. She texts Winifred, asks her to attend to Martin.

She's well on the way to Surry Hills when Winifred texts back: *Sorry. 45 minutes away.*

She stalks her way to Ichiban Computers and Scarvery. Yev offers a smile as she enters, Lena scowls, Lucic looks amused. Jesus, she's assumed the policeman would have been sent out to Centennial Park along with everyone else. But he is still there, collecting his treasure trove of videos, the task apparently too important for Montifore to redeploy him.

'You hear about Centennial Park?' she says, trying to keep her voice casual.

'No,' says Lucic. 'Should I have?'

'Probably not.' She turns to the others. 'Hey, Yev. I'm getting coffee. You want one?'

'Long black,' says the computer whizz without looking up.

'Large cappuccino, love,' says Lucic, smiling. 'Lots of chocolate on top.'

'Marshmallow?'

'Huh? No thanks.'

Lena shakes her head; she wants nothing from Mandy.

*

Aldo's is getting busy when she enters, the start of the lunchtime rush.

'You,' says Aldo. 'I was wondering when you might show up. Where's Martin?'

'With the police,' she says, not following the thrust of the cafe owner's comment.

'I've got his keys,' says Aldo.

'What keys?'

'To the flat.' Aldo sees the confusion on her face and drops down a gear, explaining. 'Martin's apartment. He paid a bloke to clear the place out, get the locks replaced. I think he still owes some money.'

'I don't know anything about it.'

'Here, you take them. Give them to Martin for me, will you?'

'Sure.'

'Done,' says Aldo, looking pleased as he hands the keys over, an obligation fulfilled. 'You want a coffee, then?'

'Yeah, skinny latte, thanks. Takeaway.' She thinks of Yev and Lucic. They can wait.

She takes her coffee and walks to Martin's apartment, curious to see what has been achieved, hoping there might be some good news to give him. There's a skip outside, filled to the brim with detritus. The portico is clear and clean. There's a new lock on the outside door. She opens it with the set of keys Aldo has given her and enters, climbs the stairs, opens the newly repaired door to the apartment proper.

Inside, the place is bare bones clean, almost devoid of furnishings. There is one unfamiliar bookcase, housing a few salvaged novels and some of Martin's journalism awards, mostly in pieces. There's a framed photo she's seen before, glass now cracked, a duplicate of a photo at Port Silver showing Martin as a boy grinning at the camera, together with his mother, father and twin sisters. Martin will be happy that has been saved. There's the smell of ammonia and chlorine and paint. She can see where a couple of window panes have been replaced, the putty still fresh. She hears a noise. A face emerges from around the corner, from the kitchenette.

'Oh. It's you.' It's the doorstep tramp, Martin's pet vagrant. Except now his beard is gone and his long hair is wound back into a ponytail.

'What are you doing here?' Mandy asks.

'Cleaning.'

'Yes. I get that. Why are you cleaning?'

The man shrugs, eyes averted. 'Martin asked me to. I got a bit carried away.'

'So I see.' She looks about. The place is spotless. 'You did all of this?'

'Uh-huh.'

'Martin agreed?'

The man shrugs. 'Yeah. Gave me two hundred bucks. Told me he trusted me.'

'The skip? New glass in the windows? A locksmith? That's a lot more than two hundred bucks.'

'Yeah. I'll need to get it back from him.' And his voice is apologetic.

Mandy finds herself smiling, almost laughing. 'Fuck me. In a day that's done nothing but rain shit, you have come through big time.' And she steps forward and hugs the man tight, surprising him, and herself as well.

When they separate, he's smiling from ear to ear, before growing serious once again.

'Hey,' he says. 'A couple of things, before I forget. I forget a lot lately.' He fumbles in his pocket, hands over a crumpled piece of paper. 'From the police.'

'What is it?'

'A receipt.'

She unfolds it. It is indeed a type of receipt, a formal acknowledgment that evidence has been removed. The handwriting on the form is clear enough. *One turd—frozen.* And the signature has to belong to Ivan Lucic. She has no idea what it means, but it brings another smile to her face. 'Thanks,' she says. 'What was the other thing?'

'Oh yeah—did your uncle catch up with you?'

'My uncle?'

'He was here this morning, asking after you and Martin.'

'I don't have an uncle.'

'Funny-looking dude. Oiled hair. Three-piece suit. Smelt of air freshener.'

Mandy is suddenly alert. 'Not the same man who broke up the apartment?'

The man frowns, as if trying to remember through a haze. 'Jesus. You think?'

'Can't you remember?'

'I don't know. I wasn't all here,' he says, voice confessional, distressed. 'But it can't have been him. He was asking what had happened.' He looks like he might cry. All this good work he's done, and now he's worried he's fucked up.

'It's okay,' says Mandy. 'You've done good.'

'You sure?'

'Positive. What did my uncle want? Can you remember?'

'I said you hadn't been here for days, not since the place got smashed up. He seemed troubled by that. Asked about it. Said he couldn't wait. Something about running out of time. Gave me something for you. For you and Martin.'

'Really?'

'Here,' he says. And he reaches into his pocket and pulls out an envelope.

Mandy opens it. Inside is a bright blue thumb drive.

chapter forty-five

MARTIN'S MIND IS GROWING CLEARER, HIS FACULTIES SHARPER, LIKE AN OLD motor started after months of neglect, still blowing blue smoke, still burning out the grime, but starting to run more smoothly. He's taken Montifore and Claus Vandenbruk through the macabre dance of death that unfolded before him at Centennial Park and he's typed out a formal statement, Winifred arriving in time to run her eye over the document. It's helped him process the events, to arrive at some sort of comprehension. Now he's perceptive enough to sense the elation in Morris Montifore: his murder cases are being delivered gift-wrapped: Titus Torbett killed Clarence O'Toole, and he killed Elizabeth Torbett and Max Fuller. And, Martin notes ruefully, with Torbett and Harry Sweetwater both dead, there is little to stop the police holding the pair responsible for the deaths of Clarity Sparkes and Tarquin Molloy five years ago. Certainly,

Henry Livingstone believed Sweetwater had ordered the murder of Clarity Sparkes.

Claus Vandenbruk seems more reflective than his colleague. 'What drove Torbett to do it? Jealousy? What?'

Martin shrugs, then frowns, his mental motor skipping a beat as a memory reasserts itself. 'What's the Turtle?' he asks again.

'Who cares?' says Montifore. 'Come on. Let's get you out of here. Mandy will be waiting for you.'

At her name, Martin feels a sense of longing, emotions surfacing. Yes, Mandy. But when he enters the foyer, she's not there.

Winifred tries phoning her but gets no response.

'Let's get a cab, get you to your hotel,' says the lawyer, her voice patient, as if addressing a child.

'Now?'

'Yes.' She regards him with concern. 'You need to wash, get new clothes.'

'I guess so.' He looks down at himself. Of course. New clothes.

They walk to a taxi rank. He's vaguely aware of Winifred threatening a reluctant driver with legal action. The cabbie seems to think Martin might be trouble.

Then Winifred is gone and he is alone in the hotel room. He blinks. What just happened?

The phone rings. Not his mobile, the hotel phone. He's lost his mobile somewhere. No, that's right: Harry Sweetwater made him smash it.

The phone stops ringing. He starts removing his clothes.

The phone rings again.

'Yes?' he answers tentatively.

'Martin. Are you okay?'

'D'Arcy? Is that you?'

'Yes. Are you all right?'

'Never better. How did you get this number?'

'Does it matter?' A short pause. 'Bethanie says you were there. Inside the house.'

'I was.'

'Great. Talk about johnny-on-the-spot. We need your story. The first-hand account. No one else can touch that. No one. And a big analysis piece. THE MESS: PART TWO. Joint by-line. Graphics are already on to it.'

Martin can hear the enthusiasm in his rival's voice, the rush of the next big thing. 'You sound happy.'

'Don't you realise what this means?' says D'Arcy. 'This is your ticket back. This will blow them away, any lingering resistance. You can write your own job description. We are going to be a brilliant team.'

'And the Mess?'

'Yes. Of course. It all comes out, we hold nothing back. I tell you, Australia has never seen a story like this. Never. And you, old friend, are right at the centre of it.'

'Thanks, D'Arcy. I'll get back to you.' And he ends the call. Just like that.

He stands, regards himself, blood-spattered and haggard, in the full-length mirror mounted on the wall. Why do hotel rooms always have so many mirrors? To make the space seem bigger? To appeal to the vanity of the clientele? His reflection stares back at him, a familiar stranger, his face gaunt, his hair matted. His eyes hold him, haunted. He touches his face, wipes it. It's still him all right, inside of it all. *Jesus.*

He stands there for a long time, staring at himself. Everyone is happy. Montifore is happy: he's got his killer, Titus Torbett, who is himself conveniently dead. There will be no trial, no chance of pointed fingers, of embarrassing revelations. The powers that be can rest easy. All neat and tidy and tied up in a blood-red bow. Claus Vandenbruk is happy: the ACIC is off the hook; Tarquin Molloy can be declared a hero, no longer a thief on the run, a time bomb awaiting detonation. His real name can be revealed, he can be buried with full honours, the premier and the police commissioner and the attorney-general and the head of the ACIC can drape his casket with the flag and salute it on its way. And D'Arcy Defoe is happy: he has his hooks into an enormous story, delivered to his door by Martin and the information flows of the Mess, its members eager to placate and appease the investigations editor, the gatekeeper to exoneration. Everyone is happy; everyone else. But Martin Scarsden is not happy. All this death and he still doesn't really know what happened.

'Fuck it,' he says to the mirror.

He really does need a shower. But first he rings Wellington Smith.

chapter forty-six

is her frostiness. Mandy ignores her and walks across to Yev, back at the counter in front of his old-school monitor.

'All done?' she asks.

'Yeah. They've got the lot. Enough footage for a blockbuster.' He tries to smile, but can't quite carry it off.

'Are you all right?'

'It's different, isn't it? In the movies, it's all acting and special effects. It doesn't matter how real they make it look, you know it isn't. But this. I never imagined . . .' His voice trails off.

Mandy realises he's been sorting through videos for hours. 'I know, Yev. But it's helping the police no end. You've just helped solve a whole truckload of crimes. You've been exceptional.'

'Doesn't really feel like it.' His voice is as flat as his expression.

'I heard what happened. Martin at that house. All the shooting, the deaths. Is he all right?'

'He's going to be.' She places a reassuring hand on Yev's shoulder. 'Listen. I've got something else. It might be important.' She holds up the thumb drive.

'Not more video?'

'No. I don't think so.'

Suddenly, awareness flashes in his eyes. 'Is that what I think it is? From the judge's safe?'

'One way to find out.'

'Come around. We'll need the mothership.'

Yev fires up his new-school workstation, examining the drive while he waits, some of his enthusiasm back. 'Thirty-two gigs. Not so big.'

'Big enough,' she says.

He frowns, not knowing how to take that, but now the computer is up and running. 'Okay, first things first.' He plugs the drive into a USB socket, doesn't attempt to open it, instead running a battery of tests. 'Okay. All good. No corruption, no viruses. And it's pretty much chock-a-block. Let's see what we've got.' But when he tries to open it, two folders appear and are almost immediately covered over by a dialogue box. 'Shit.'

'What is it?'

'Password protected.'

'Can you get around it?'

'Let's see.' Yev opens some new program, starts punching in code, but not for long. He sighs. 'No good. The whole thing is encrypted.'

'You can't crack it?'

'No one can crack this. The spooks maybe, if they have months.'

'Can you copy it? Mirror it?'

Yev types more code, shakes his head. 'Nup. Not sure why not, but nup.' He smiles, admiration in his voice. 'Shit, that's clever.'

'So no one can open it, no one can copy it?' she asks.

'That's about it,' he says. He stares at the screen, brow furrowed, but eventually he shrugs, reluctantly ejecting the drive and handing it to her. 'What are you going to do with it?'

'Give it to the cops, of course. It's still evidence, even if they can't decrypt it.'

'Evidence of what?'

'Who knows?' She drops the drive into her pocket. 'I'll see you soon, Yev. We'll be in touch. And take care of yourself. Remember, you have done something remarkable—you have helped to catch killers.'

'You're leaving Sydney?'

'Not right away. But Martin needs to get somewhere more healthy. He needs to get back home.' She leans in, kisses him on the cheek, gives him a heartfelt hug. 'And thanks for everything. It's been a pleasure. Working with someone trustworthy.'

'You too. Take care,' he says.

She turns to go; Lena is looking daggers at her. She turns back to Yev. 'We owe you a lot of money for all your time and effort. Add it up and double it.'

'Seriously?'

'Absolutely. And while you're at it, do you have a laptop you can sell me?'

Yev smiles, a big smile. 'I sure do. A kick-arse Mac. Just came in. Almost brand-new. Better than Martin's.'

'I'll take it.'

*

Later, she sits at Aldo's, treating herself to a latte made with full-cream milk and a cake, as she finishes setting up her new laptop. When it's done, she inserts the thumb drive, using the adaptor Yev has sold her to access the computer's new-generation ports. She opens the drive. The dialogue box comes up. There are no words, no description of what is needed, just the space for a password. She closes her eyes, and in her mind she re-enters the memory palace. She's back in her mother's bookstore in Riversend, the way it was when she was a teenager. She threads her way through the familiar shelves, stopping at each category, extracting favourite books, each with a different letter or digit incorporated into its cover, just the way Tarquin Molloy had taught her to do. She jots the alpha-numeric code: thirty-six characters. When she's done, she again closes her eyes, repeats the route, double-checking. Then, when she's sure, she enters the decryption key, using the first mnemonic given to her more than five years ago by Tarquin, the one he'd trained her with, the one he knew she would always remember.

And for the next hour she reads, as the thumb drive spews out the secrets of the past and of the present. Only when she's read enough, when her curiosity is sated and her questions answered, does she close the computer down. It's time to go to the hotel; it's time to truly trust Martin Scarsden.

SUNDAY

chapter forty-seven

MARTIN WRITES. HE WRITES AND DOESN'T STOP, NOT FOR LONG HOURS. NOT UNTIL he has filed nine separate stories to Wellington Smith and the *This Month* website. The first are going up online, spreading out through the ether, even as he works on the next, with Mandy supplying coffee, moral support and vital information, sitting by his side, her own computer open, trawling through Molloy's cache of information, directing him to the most significant sections, double-checking facts for him, suggesting storylines.

At one point they pause, while waiting for a story to go through, and check the *Herald*'s site. Fairfax has a blog running, reporting new information as it comes to hand. Bethanie is writing it, D'Arcy filing a constant barrage of analysis into it, photographs pouring in of police cars outside Mollisons, a raid in progress, a politician with his hand over a camera lens. The *Herald* team is doing its best, but Martin knows they can't compete. They can't compete with his inside story of the Centennial Park shootout, they can't compete with the trove of incriminating evidence flooding out of the blue thumb drive. With grim satisfaction, he can see where Bethanie has given up and has started lifting material directly from the *This Month* site, giving full attribution, crediting '*Sydney Morning Herald* Contributor Martin Scarsden' for the unprecedented flow of exposés.

Wellington Smith calls on the hotel phone. 'The server has gone again. We can't keep up with demand. I'm buying more grunt. The big boys are offering more data centre capacity. We'll be back up in five. Keep 'em coming.' He hangs up.

An hour and a half and two more stories down the line, he's back again. 'We're starting to cop large-scale denial-of-service attacks. Someone very big and very ugly is trying to close us down. Get it all up. Everything you have.'

'We can't,' says Martin. 'They'll sue your arse off, bankrupt you.'

'Bullshit. Let 'em try. It'll be the greatest publicity exercise in publishing history.' There is a touch of manic glee in the proprietor's voice.

'You're kidding.'

'No, I'm not. Get it all out there, and get it out now, before they crash us for good. Before we get injuncted. We're already in court in New South Wales and the ACT.'

'At four in the morning?'

'Get it up. This is our only chance. It's spreading on every social media outlet in the world. They'll never put this genie back in the bottle. We'll get a royal commission.'

'Publish and be damned?'

'Publish and fuck the lot of them.'

And so they continue, into the night, through the night, powered by coffee and adrenaline and a sense of purpose, pumping it out, getting it onto social media, spreading it so far and so fast and so thoroughly that no court, no state, no team of cyber vandals could ever hope to bottle it up again. The Americans go feral as they realise the size of the story and the implications. Harry Sweetwater, a made mafia member, has been shot dead in Australia. What's more, he's been overseeing a massive money-laundering scheme, undetected for more than a decade, washing illicit cash for everyone from the Chicago mob through the Russian mafia to Central American cartels. It's a long night for Martin and Mandy, and it's over in a flash.

———

Martin waits inside the foyer of the police station. Outside it's cold, it's shitful and cold, the sky a hard blue, a blast of Antarctic air clearing the last of the smoke. The photographers and camera crews huddle together, waiting. He got papped on his way in by Baxter James, his old colleague, hard-nosed and unapologetic, another image for the *Herald*'s blog.

He's got a copy of the *Sun Herald*. It's already out of date, one for the archives. The cover is dominated by the carnage at Centennial Park, with the inside pages crammed with photographs and diagrams and the names of the dead. But there is no explanation as to what caused the gunfight; Martin hadn't revealed that to the world until long after the paper was put to bed. And so the *Herald* has the names—Titus Torbett and his father Sir Talbot, Harry Sweetwater and Henry Livingstone—but not how they died or what they had revealed. Martin notices, with wry amusement, that part two of D'Arcy's investigative series on the Mess has been held over.

He puts the paper down. After three hours of sleep, he's dog-tired, but he's happy with his work. Vindication can do that for you. But he's not happy with life. Mandy is still inside, still being grilled, still being excoriated over the contents of the drive and how she'd cracked the encryption.

Winifred exits from the depths of the station. She looks even more exhausted than Martin feels, moving with a stiffness befitting her age. She sits with a sigh, shakes her head.

'What?' says Martin.

'She's confessed.'

'To what?'

'Everything. The lot. I couldn't stop her, she wouldn't listen.' She sighs again. 'She was in on it with Molloy. She knew he was infiltrating Mollisons. By the end, she even suspected he was a policeman. I couldn't shut her up. The only thing she's denying is pre-knowledge of his plan to steal the money. Even then, she says as soon as the theft was reported she knew it was true, that some of the information she supplied would have helped him.'

'So he did steal it?'

'He stole it, all right. Ten million, give or take a few thousand. It wasn't just some cover story. Ten million dollars. But he was dead before he got out of the building, before he could tell her where it went.'

'How could she not know, if she knew everything else?'

Winifred looks beyond weary. 'She loved him. She trusted him. He didn't have to seduce her with money. What's the old saying?

Love is blind?' She takes a deep breath, as if unable to believe her own conclusions, before continuing. 'Then, when he disappeared, she realised the stories were true, that he had indeed stolen the money. She thought he'd fled overseas, betrayed her. So she looked out for her own interests: she lied, said she had nothing to do with it. Understandable if you consider the circumstances.'

Martin shakes his head. 'So why confess now? Did she have to?'

'Probably not. She could have sat on the thumb drive, destroyed it. Not told you about it. Or she could have spun a cover story about playing memory games with her fiancé without ever knowing what it meant.'

'Montifore would never believe that. He's no idiot.'

'No, but there's a big difference between knowing something and proving it in a court of law.'

'You could have defended her?'

'It's academic, Martin. She's confessed.'

He sits on that for a moment, stews on it. She's handed herself in, confessed to so much. He still doesn't really understand why. Sure, she had the thumb drive and knew how to open it, decrypt it, but that doesn't fully explain her determination to own up to the police. 'Surely they're not going to prosecute,' he says to Winifred. 'She's handed over all the evidence, all of Molloy's intelligence. She's done their job for them. Vandenbruk must be ecstatic.'

Winifred laughs thinly. 'You have no idea how many powerful people you two and Wellington Smith have outed. It's not the police you have to worry about, or the Director of Public Prosecutions— it's the political and legal establishment. They'll want their pound of flesh.'

'But surely, for every one who hates us, there will be two who support us, who want the sewer flushed? And even the guilty, they'll be falling over themselves to implicate each other.'

Winifred smiles at the image. 'Yes. You're probably right. But they can't be seen to be doing her any favours. Not at such a politically charged time. They'll want everything to be above board, arm's length.'

'Christ. How can I help?'

'Mandy has instructed me to draw up some papers for you to sign. If you're willing.'

'What papers?'

'Giving you full guardianship of Liam. Joint responsibility with Mandy.'

Martin blinks, shocked by the request. 'Why? What's the urgency?'

'Don't you understand? She may be going to prison.'

After Martin has signed the papers, after Winifred has witnessed them and returned inside the police station, Martin is again left alone. Outside, the paparazzi are prowling the perimeter, ready to level their telephoto lenses like game hunters. He can't leave; all he can do is wait. He lies down on the floor and falls asleep.

He's shaken awake by Ivan Lucic.

'What?'

'You look like shit,' says Lucic by way of a greeting.

'Thanks.'

'C'mon, I'll take you to the boss.' Lucic leads him through the station and into the underground car park; drives him out, Martin bent over to escape detection by the photographers. Lucic drops him back at the same cafe where he and Montifore met during the smoke haze. 'He won't be long,' says Lucic.

'He doesn't want to be seen with me?'

'Who would?' says Lucic, apparently for his own amusement.

This time Martin waits inside, out of the cold. The place is more of a bar than a cafe, almost empty on a Sunday morning, but it retains its essential smell, the aftermath of Saturday night. Of alcohol and body odour and even—is he imagining it?—the smell of cigarettes. He orders a long black, triple shot. It can't hurt. The barista brings it over just as Morris Montifore arrives, looking dishevelled and badly in need of a shave.

'Morris.'

'Martin.' They don't bother shaking hands.

'Winifred told me. Mandy's confessed.'

Montifore shakes his head, as if in regret. 'I don't want to prosecute her, the fraud squad doesn't want to prosecute her, but the commissioner is insisting we play it straight down the line. Gutless bastard.' Montifore goes to the counter, orders a coffee, returns to Martin. 'She'll be charged this afternoon. She'll get bail for sure. Make sure you're back at the station to collect her. About four o'clock.'

'Okay. Thanks,' says Martin.

The fatigue on the policeman's face reflects Martin's own state of mind, his own state of body. And yet he smiles. 'You won't believe the shitstorm you've released.'

'Sounds like you approve.'

'Too right I do. Shovel it out there, as much as you can. Everything you can.'

'Seriously?'

There is a sadness in the policeman's eye as he replies, 'All that you can. You can't rely on us.'

'We're trying our best. Wellington Smith is holding nothing back.'

'So I see.' Montifore looks fondly at Martin's coffee, then looks around, either to see what's happening with his order or to make sure no one is watching, that no photographer is lurking.

'Morris? What is it?'

'You didn't hear this from me.'

'Of course not.'

'We never made this public. It was very tightly held, just Ivan and me and forensics, the people I could trust.'

'Small circle,' says Martin.

'Very small.'

The barista arrives with the policeman's coffee. Montifore slurps gratefully before continuing. 'Molloy was killed by three bullets to the head. One of them was still inside the skull when we retrieved the body. That's what we kept secret. We've run ballistics. Identified the gun.'

'Titus Torbett?'

'Claus Vandenbruk.'

Martin stares at the policeman for long seconds while his mind catches up. 'Five years ago? He was involved all this time?'

'Yes,' says Montifore. 'Go back to the documents on the thumb drive, the ones Molloy copied, the ones Mandy decrypted. Vandenbruk's alias was SC13. As in Santa Claus thirteen. Have another look; it will all become clear.'

'Why didn't Sweetwater mention him? Or Titus Torbett?'

'My guess? They never knew about him. His job wasn't protecting criminals and money launderers.'

'What then?'

'He was riding shotgun for the political establishment. The attorney-general, the deputy police commissioner, among others.' Montifore drinks more coffee. 'We believe he was in cahoots with a man named Kenneth Steadman, nickname the Turtle.'

'The Turtle?'

'I know you've heard of him.'

'Titus Torbett referred to him, but I didn't understand who he was. Still don't.'

'He's on the run, but I'm expecting to arrest him soon.' Montifore checks his watch. 'About two hours from now.'

'You sound very sure.'

'I am. And the first thing we'll do is double-check his DNA.'

'DNA?'

Montifore smiles. 'The shit in your freezer. It was him.'

Martin smiles back. 'So not a smoking gun, a steaming turd.'

'Sounds like a headline to me.'

'Doesn't it, just?'

Montifore takes another sip of his coffee, looks at it dubiously. His phone rumbles on the table. He checks the text, stands. 'I've got to get back. One of these days we've got to have a real drink, a real celebration. You, me, Ivan and Mandy. And Winifred. The good guys.'

'Thanks, I'd like that,' says Martin. 'Can I run the story about Vandenbruk?'

'That's why I'm here. Run the lot as soon as you can, before we charge him. Before some gutless wonder upstairs tries to finesse it.'

'One question. What was he doing up at Port Silver? When he came to see Mandy?'

'To make sure she didn't know too much. He knew she was rich, suspected she knew more than she was saying. And maybe to kill her if she did. Maybe you as well.'

Martin blinks. 'How can you know that? Is he talking?'

'No. Not about that. Not yet.' Montifore gestures for Martin to stand too. 'Come on. There's someone waiting for you.'

Outside, on the street, a white SUV with tinted windows is parked by the kerb.

'Here,' says Montifore, 'a parting gift.' He hands Martin a sheet of folded paper.

'What's this?'

'The Mess. A full membership list.'

'Seriously? Thanks, Morris. Thanks so much.'

'No, mate. Thank *you*.'

Martin opens the car door, climbs in. 'Hi, Jack.'

'You got the membership list?' asks Jack Goffing.

'Yeah.'

'Good. Have a look while I drive.'

'Where are we going?'

'You'll see.'

Martin unfolds the paper, scans the membership list. It's a photocopy. The names are typed and someone has annotated the handwritten descriptions.

Jeffery Jamison—*retired brigadier and diplomat*
Samson Fielding—*NSW deputy treasurer, Liberal*
Clarissa Hawthorne—*owner Nextown executive recruitment, member NSW Liberal executive*
Janine Trelore—*federal Labor senator for New South Wales*

Harry Sweetwater—*head of security Mollisons Bank*

Elizabeth Torbett—*NSW Supreme Court judge*

Clarence O'Toole—*Land and Environment Court judge*

Chester Blythe-Janes—*company director, former commodore Sydney Cruising Yacht Squadron*

Mathilda Hope—*art gallery director and film impresario*

D'Arcy Defoe—*SMH journalist*

Gino Trombino—*businessman, former CFMEU state secretary*

Palmer Fletcher—*consultant to Nine board*

Mary Dunbar—*historian at Sydney University*

Ralph Ladders—*AWU and ACTU*

Norman Bones—*Sydney shock jock*

Gerald Jones—*celebrity stockbroker*

George Giopolis—*property developer, board member Large Sky*

Lucy Wong-Clark—*retail clothing, import export*

Delaney 'Big Deal' Bullwinkel—*mining magnate, billionaire*

Bill Townsend—*lobbyist and member of ALP state council*

Clarrie Perret—*former test cricketer, transport tycoon*

Torvald Spry—*media magnate, billionaire*

Fenella Tomlinson—*Melbourne Liberal and charity queen*

Michael Ogden—*Clarion T&S arms manufacturer*

Patrick Dougall—*Bishop of Albury*

Jeremy Plankten—*state attorney-general*

Atticus Pons—*partner Phipps Allenby Lockhart, board member Mollisons, Diamond Square and Large Sky*

Roger Macatelli—*NSW deputy police commissioner*

Joe 'Viagra Joe' Vigaro—*NSW lobbyist and public relations*

Ronald 'Banjo' Patterson—*CEO Diamond Square Property Trust, board member Mollisons, Diamond Square and Large Sky*

'Holy shit,' says Martin. Then scans it for the second time. 'The attorney-general, a bishop, a couple of billionaires. What a network.'

'Your next story,' says Goffing. 'Get it out before that publisher of yours is buried beneath litigation.'

'He's started publishing offshore.'

'So I see,' says Goffing, pulling into a suburban driveway.

Martin looks around him: his attention has been on the membership list, his eyes on the paper, his imagination linking events with people. 'Where are we?'

'It's what's known in the business as a safe house. So not for publication.'

'Right.'

Inside, the curtains are drawn and the lights are on. Sitting on a couch, watching rugby league on television, eating peanuts and drinking Coke, is Griff, as if it's any ordinary Sunday afternoon. She stands as Martin and Goffing enter, switching off the TV. She nods at Martin, as if in acknowledgement, as if in appreciation. 'Top show, son. Top show.' She turns to Goffing. 'We're good?'

'Yep.'

'Through here, mate.'

She leads the way into the kitchen, into the harsh light of an old-fashioned strip fluorescent. A man is sitting there, slumped forward onto the kitchen table, one arm extended to where it's handcuffed to a pipe on the wall.

'Wake up, sunshine,' orders Griff, before turning to Martin. 'Meet Kenneth Steadman, better known as the Turtle.'

The man raises his head. Martin takes a sharp breath. The captive's face is a mess, beaten to a pulp, his right eye swollen closed. Martin turns to Goffing. 'You did this?'

'Not us. Take a closer look.'

Martin does as he's told, seeing what he missed at first: there are stitches, scabbing wounds, bruises turning yellow and blue as they age, a brutal rainbow.

'Henry Livingstone,' states Goffing. 'Three days ago. Lucky we found this bloke before his face turned septic.'

'Is this legal? Holding him like this?'

'Close enough,' says Goffing. 'I'm ASIO, remember.'

'Who are you?' demands the Turtle, before answering his own question. 'More fucking filth.' His one good eye is baleful, contemptuous, staring at Martin.

'This is Martin Scarsden,' says Jack Goffing. 'The de facto husband of Mandalay Blonde.' The Turtle flinches, cowers, as if expecting another beating. Martin frowns at the reaction, not understanding it. Goffing continues. 'Kenneth, I need you to tell Martin what you told us, then we'll take you to the police.'

The Turtle's voice is plaintive, insistent. 'I'll get protection.'

'You sure will, Kenneth. You'll be the most protected man in Australia.'

'Immunity?'

'That's for the police to decide. But you tell us what you know, and I'll put in a good word for you.'

The Turtle smiles at that, turning his swollen face and manic eye to Martin. 'I'll get it. Immunity. You watch.' To Martin he sounds unbalanced.

'You want a cup of tea, Kenneth? Cigarette?' asks Griff, her voice almost gentle. 'A doughnut?'

'No,' says the Turtle, cowering as if trying to draw back into his shell. 'I'm good.'

Griff smiles. She pulls up a chair, indicates for Martin to do the same. Jack Goffing remains standing. Griff speaks to the Turtle. 'Tell Martin how Tarquin Molloy died.'

The Turtle smiles, a glint in his eye. 'It was Vandenbruk. He shot him.'

'I know,' says Martin. 'Tell me how it happened. And why.'

The Turtle glances up at Jack Goffing.

'Protection, Kenneth. Immunity,' says Goffing. 'Talk.'

The Turtle turns to Martin. 'Molloy. He was good. Fuck, he was good.'

Griff shakes her head. 'That wasn't the question, Kenneth.'

The prisoner nods, understanding. 'Clarity Sparkes. She started it. She suspected Molloy, got IT to track him, the ISP on his laptop. A red flag went up when he used Mandalay Blonde's passwords. Clarity thought she had him. Alerted her boss, Harry Sweetwater.' He stops, as if remembering something, looks up at Goffing. 'It's true, isn't it? Sweetwater's dead, isn't he?'

It's Martin who answers. 'He's dead. I was there. I saw it. He's dead, Titus Torbett is dead, Henry Livingstone is dead. Claus Vandenbruk is in custody. None of them can hurt you now. It's safe to talk.'

But the Turtle laughs, even though the pain is evident on his face. 'I was always safe from them, don't you understand that?'

'No, Kenneth, I don't,' replies Martin, unsure where this is heading.

The Turtle puffs up, as if with pride, head jolting forward again at the end of his long neck. 'They all underestimated me. They thought I was just the Turtle, sitting in my shell, watching the world on my monitors, as if I wasn't part of the world. Just there to do their bidding. Well, fuck that. By the end I had them all where I wanted them. I knew everything.'

'Like what?' says Martin, his voice falling to a whisper, enthralled by this spectacle of a man.

'I knew Vandenbruk killed Molloy. I knew Sweetwater killed Clarity Sparkes. I knew Titus Torbett killed his sister and the newspaper man. I knew it all. I was untouchable.' And he turns again to Goffing. 'And that's why they'll give me immunity. I guarantee it. I know everything.'

'So you say,' says Goffing, his voice noncommittal.

'You know who I am, don't you, Kenneth?' asks Martin.

'I know everything,' says the Turtle again, not boastful now but matter-of-fact.

'If I put all that information in my articles, then no one would have any reason to hurt you. Understand?'

The Turtle thinks that through, taking his time, staring into space. When he looks back at Martin, there is cunning in his manner. 'Will you mention me in your stories?'

'Would you like me to?'

'Yes. Yes, I would.'

'I'll tell them you knew everything. You understood everything. That you outsmarted all of them, Harry Sweetwater and Titus Torbett and the rest of them. That you survived them all. The world will know.'

The Turtle's one good eye glows with satisfaction. 'What do you want to know?'

'Molloy. You said Clarity Sparkes caught him out using Mandy's passwords.'

'Clarity wanted to bust him, and Mandalay, and Zelda Forshaw. So she sent out an online questionnaire; it was a trap. She wanted to catch out Mandalay and Zelda lying, demonstrate to Harry Sweetwater there was a conspiracy. Instead, your girlfriend owned up, reported Molloy's use of her passwords. Sweetwater ridiculed Clarity, belittled her. She got the shits, dug her heels in and kept up her pursuit. She asked me to monitor Molloy as well as Mandalay and Zelda.'

'So you were reporting to Clarity Sparkes, not Sweetwater?'

'Technically. But I wasn't an idiot. Sweetwater held all the power, Clarity was an outsider. She had no idea what the bank really did.'

'And you did?'

'Yeah. I worked it out.'

'That's very clever of you,' says Martin. 'So you also told Sweetwater what was going on?'

'Yeah. I wanted to stay on the right side of him.'

Griff interrupts. 'Who else did you tell?'

The Turtle stares at her, hesitating for a moment. 'Claus Vandenbruk. I was his ears and eyes.'

'On what basis?' asks Martin.

'He said he was a policeman, running an investigation. That if I cooperated, he'd see I was looked after.'

'You believed him?'

'Yes. He took me into police headquarters late at night. He had all the security passes, everything. Of course I believed him.'

Martin glances at Griff; she glances back, despairing. 'Go on,' says Martin.

'Clarity guessed something was going on that Friday when she learnt that Mandalay and Zelda were both away. I'd seen Molloy leave envelopes on their desks on Thursday morning. She alerted Sweetwater and Titus Torbett. They figured he was a thief, that he was planning to steal money. They didn't want the police anywhere near the bank. They even considered killing him. Clarity wasn't privy to any of that, but she came up with a solution. She had a tame goon who could beat him up, warn him off. Sweetwater and Torbett agreed.'

'Henry Livingstone.'

'Yeah. That arsehole.'

'How did you know all of this?'

'I was part of it. I was going to monitor what was going on through CCTV. Record what he did.'

'So what did you do?'

'I told Vandenbruk.'

'Without the knowledge of Sweetwater and Torbett?'

'That's right.'

'And what did Vandenbruk say?'

'Nothing. Not to me. Just asked me to tell him what was happening and when.'

'So what did happen?'

'Livingstone beat the crap out of Molloy, as planned. Threw him out on the street. Where Vandenbruk picked him up.'

'And no one saw this?'

'I saw it. My cameras saw it. I recorded it.'

'What happened to the recordings?'

'I wiped them. I'm not mad.'

'And Vandenbruk was in your debt.'

'Something like that.'

Martin shakes his head. 'That's awfully high risk. He could have killed you as well.'

'Not if he thought some recordings existed.'

'So do they?'

'No.'

Martin looks at Griff.

She shrugs. 'Doesn't matter. Vandenbruk has confessed.'

Martin returns his attention to the Turtle. 'Molloy had a thumb drive. You saw it. It was on the video. What happened to it?'

'Livingstone took it. But no one really cared about it.'

'What? Why not?'

'Because Molloy was smart. No one knew he was a cop. Everyone thought the drive simply held the code he used to steal the money.'

'So where was it?'

'Livingstone found it when he was beating the shit out of Molloy and he gave it to Clarity. She couldn't open it, so she put it in a safe deposit box. It's probably still there.'

Martin looks to Griff then Goffing. Neither says anything. He returns his attention to the Turtle, but instead of telling him that the police now have the thumb drive, he leaves the captive in the dark.

'How could you know that?'

'I told you, I know everything.'

'So I see,' says Martin, eliciting a smirk from Griff. 'But back to Molloy's murder. That was Friday, what happened next?'

'Monday, after the Greenwich Mean Time reconciliation, the alarms went off. Millions were missing. The transaction was traced back to Mandalay's computer on the trading-room floor, but she'd been away on the Friday. I had the video. It was clear Molloy had taken the money.'

'So what happened then?'

'Sweetwater went ballistic at Clarity. But he calmed down pretty quickly. So did Titus. So did Vandenbruk, for that matter.'

'Why? I don't understand?'

'The computer logs. They revealed Molloy had stolen the money, but nothing else. All of them were shitting themselves that he had compromised the bank's operations, uncovered its secrets. So when they learnt it was theft, pure and simple, they were relieved. Sweetwater and Titus didn't know that Molloy was dead. They didn't even want to call in the police, but they had to, to satisfy Clarity. Zelda Forshaw was the sacrificial lamb and everyone was happy enough. Sweetwater was more worried about his reputation back in the States than the money. Ten million was chicken feed.'

'So Molloy took nothing else? Just money?'

'No. That's only what they thought. That's what the computer logs said. I told you he was clever.'

Martin exchanges a look with Goffing and another with Griff. And now he understands. The undercover policeman had stolen a trove of damning information, piled it onto the thumb drive and then covered his trail in such a way as to make it look like theft. Brilliant in its way. And he'd almost got away with it.

'And Vandenbruk?'

'Same.'

'So everyone was happy?'

'Except for Clarity. Dumb bitch was like a dog at a bone. She kept probing. Eventually she probed too far.'

'You said that Sweetwater killed her. The overdose: it wasn't accidental.'

'No. That was him.'

'How do you know?'

He smiles. 'I told you. I know everything.'

'Is that what you told Henry Livingstone when he beat you up? That Sweetwater killed Clarity Sparkes?'

'Yes.'

Martin nods. So that's why Livingstone was gunning for Sweetwater: the mobster had killed his girlfriend. The mafia contract had nothing to do with it. 'I thought you were working for Claus Vandenbruk?'

The Turtle just smiles and shakes his head. 'I never worked for any of them. That's what they never understood. They never trusted each other—why should I trust any of them?'

'Thanks, Kenneth, we might leave it there.' It's Goffing interjecting. He taps his watch, signalling to Martin that time is short. 'But you've been very helpful. We'll remember it.'

'I have more questions,' Martin protests.

'I'm sure you do,' says Goffing. 'And you'll get your answers. But right now, we need to get going.'

Back in the car, leaving Griff and the handcuffed Turtle in the house, Goffing speaks. 'He was starting to bullshit you. It was time to get you out of there.'

'How do you mean?'

'What he told you about Vandenbruk and the chain of events with Clarity Sparkes is true, as far as we can determine. But not what was coming next.'

'Can you explain that?'

'Sweetwater did order the killing of Clarity Sparkes, but we're pretty sure it was Kenneth who injected her, while she was held down by his two thugs. And it was him and the same two thugs who took the compromising photographs of Clarence O'Toole, working for Sweetwater, maybe for Titus Torbett as well, we're not sure. He was with Titus Torbett when he killed Max Fuller and Elizabeth Torbett. It was him who trashed your apartment after Henry Livingstone broke in and stole your laptop. It was him who infected your phones with malware. He was at the heart of it.'

'So, rotten through.'

'You don't know half of it. A sick fuck, with a fetish for women's underwear. But between what he knows and Molloy's data dump, the fraud boys and girls, together with the AFP and the ACIC, are going to have a field day. They've got everything they need. The FBI are sending a team over, and they won't be alone. The pollies in Canberra are trying to distance themselves, claiming it's all state-based, Sydney politics. But they'll call a royal commission, you can bet on it. Half of Sydney are shitting themselves. Thanks to Wellington Smith and Mandy and yourself, there's nowhere left to hide.'

Goffing drops him off outside his hotel. Martin desperately wants to sleep. Needs to sleep. But not yet. First he must file the story exposing Claus Vandenbruk as Tarquin Molloy's killer and make sure Wellington Smith publishes the membership of the Mess, spreading it to the four corners, out where no injunction can stop it. Then maybe he can get a few hours' kip before getting back to the police station by four o'clock to pick up Mandy.

WEDNESDAY

chapter forty-eight

THE WIND HAS COME IN FROM THE SOUTH-EAST OVERNIGHT, SWEEPING THE CITY with showers, leaving the sky clear between cloud bands. The rain comes and goes, squalls chasing each other north, rinsing the city for another day, but this far west the gloss is never quite as shiny. There are stains the heavens alone can't lift. At least it's still Sydney; she's not breaching her bail conditions to be here. She sits in the Subaru, gathering her courage, outside the nondescript house in the nondescript cul-de sac. The neighbouring homes display the pride of ownership: not number thirty-one. Abandoned bikes litter an uncut lawn, the letterbox tilts at an angle, its interior blackened by some neighbourhood prank. She knows the signs: an untidy exterior disguising an even less tidy interior. She's still summoning her better self, suppressing her trepidation, when a car passes her and creaks into the drive.

She watches in fascination. It's an old car, a sedan among the SUVs, one door a mismatched colour, a hubcap missing, a puff of blue smoke from the exhaust as the driver cuts the engine. Two boys bound out of the back seat, running and arguing, another squall like the skittling clouds. They run to the house, not waiting for the driver. She emerges: a woman wearing grey trackie daks, a Harvard sweatshirt, hair in a ponytail beneath a baseball cap. A pretty woman; a harried woman. She lugs grocery bags from the boot, the boys doing nothing to help. Mandy waits for the woman to enter her home, gives her ten minutes to put away the shopping, but eventually there is no avoiding it. She can see another band of rain approaching. She takes the sports bag and leaves the sanctuary of the Subaru.

There is no long wait at the door; the woman opens it almost immediately. 'You,' she says through the screen door.

'You know who I am?' asks Mandy.

'Who doesn't?'

'Can I come in?'

'Why?'

'I have something for you.'

'The truth?'

'If you really want to hear it.'

The woman looks back over her shoulder, as if to reassure herself her children are safe, that Mandy is no threat. 'Okay. Come in. If you must.'

They sit in a kitchen just big enough to accommodate a small table of peeling veneer. There's a copy of a women's magazine, three months out of date, a bowl of fruit. Up close, Mandy can see how beautiful the woman must have been before life had its way with her. Even now, with no make-up and carrying a few extra kilos, she'd be attractive if it weren't for the anger in her eyes and the grim set of her mouth.

'I've seen you on the news,' says the woman. 'You're Mandalay Blonde.'

'Yes. And you're Evelyn Bright. Richard's widow. Tarquin's widow.'

'I am. For all the good it does me.' A tooth is missing. There is no wedding ring.

'No pension? No superannuation?'

There is hostility as Evelyn Bright answers. 'He was sacked. Dishonourable discharge, accused of stealing millions. I was told to keep my mouth shut. They told me that when he disappeared, they told me that when he was found, they're telling me that now.'

'You can say whatever you like now, to whomever you like.'

'Is that why you're here? Touting for that journalist boyfriend of yours?' Her voice curls with distaste, with bitterness. 'Soliciting?' She imbues the word with contempt.

Mandy blinks away the taunt, barely registering it. 'Tarquin— Richard—was a hero. His reputation will be restored and your entitlements honoured. The money he stole was just a cover. The information he retrieved will do more to fight corruption in this state than anything in the past two hundred years. He died a hero, in the line of duty.'

'The line of duty, hey? Did he sleep with you in the line of duty?'

Mandy grimaces, looks at the table. This isn't how she had imagined this encounter, what she had hoped for. But she's beyond lying. 'Yes. He slept with me.'

'And told you he loved you?'

'Yes.'

There's a silence, then. Mandy can hear the kids playing, shouting, out the back.

'I loved him, you know that?' says Evelyn Bright, voice challenging. 'Maybe I still do.' She casts her eyes around, searching for something to look at, finding nothing. 'I can forgive him for sleeping with you, I can forgive him all the rest. I got used to that. But I can't forgive him for dying. For leaving us marooned out here.' Mandy feels creeping emotion, but there is nothing teary about Evelyn Bright. Her face remains hard and her voice judgemental. 'He was so reckless, always so reckless. Living his little-boy fantasies, like a cut-price Jason Bourne. And then he dies. And leaves us, me and the three boys.'

'Three?'

'All under ten.' She stays silent for a moment, her voice a little less abrasive as she continues. 'They look like him, you know. Bits and pieces, always there, always reminding me, like his ghost. The youngest is shy and sensible, thank God, but the older two are wild, just like him. Fearless. Reckless. Charming.'

'I remember.'

'I imagine you do.' Another pause. 'Why have you come here? To see what you wrought, you and him?'

'Reparations.'

'What does that mean?'

Mandy lifts the sports bag, puts it on the table, on top of the magazine. 'It's yours.'

'What is it?'

'Money.'

Evelyn doesn't speak; she just regards the bag for some time, then returns her gaze to her visitor's face.

'A lot of money,' says Mandy. 'Cash. Half a million dollars.'

The woman blinks, pulls the bag towards her, opens the zip, sees the bundled notes, rezips the bag. 'Whose is it?'

'Yours now.'

'The money he stole?'

'Yes.'

'I can't take it,' she says, but she's staring at the bag. The next time she speaks, it's more to herself than to Mandy. 'It's too risky. They'll come looking for it.'

'No. It's been gone five years. If they were going to find it, they would have by now. It doesn't belong to any one person or entity. It's just cream, skimmed off the top.'

'Why don't you keep it?'

'I don't need it. I don't deserve it. He wanted you to have it.'

'You can't know that.'

'Yes, I can. That's what he told me. That's how I knew where to find it. That's why I'm here. He wasn't interested in the money, just the glory, the accolades he would have won for breaking open such a massive criminal syndicate. That was his motivation. At the very end, when he began to realise how great the risks were, what he had discovered, he realised that he might not survive. So he put a contingency plan in place. It's true, stealing the money was partly a ruse; he did it to cover his tracks, to buy himself time. You'll see that in the media. But it was also for you. For your children. In case something went wrong.' Mandy holds the woman's gaze, determined not to expose her own lie.

'Are you sure?'

'Absolutely. I wouldn't put you in danger. Never. Just spend it carefully. Gradually. And once it's gone, there is more. Millions more. Your boys' futures are assured.'

At that, the woman does grow emotional; Mandy can see it in her eyes. 'He did that? He was thinking of us?'

'I believe he always was.'

'Thank you,' she says, still maintaining her formality. 'Not for the money, but for telling me that.' She pauses, opens the bag again, extracts a bundle of fifty-dollar notes, lifting it to her face, smelling the richness of it before continuing. 'I believed it, you know—that he'd stolen the money, fled overseas, was living the high life, drinking martinis with a bevy of floozies.' She gulps down a swallow. 'I never trusted him. Not really. Only to put himself first, to look after his own self-interest. But now . . .' She closes her eyes. 'Maybe he wasn't like that after all. Maybe I should have trusted him more.'

'He loved you,' Mandy repeats. 'Otherwise, why would he have risked his cover, told me about you, stolen the money for you?'

There are no more words. The woman takes the bag, holds it to herself, hugging it as if she might be hugging her five-years-dead husband.

It's only later, back in the protective shell of the car, that Mandy allows herself to relax, to breathe properly, to shed her own tears. Evelyn had believed her fabrications, all of them; had trusted her lies. It was a necessary deceit: Evelyn needs the money, she and her boys. Tarquin's boys.

epilogue

Two months later

LIAM IS EXCITED, CHATTING AWAY IN HIS BOOSTER SEAT, POINTING OUT FEATURES in the passing scenery. And now the boy is singing, his own little ditty. 'Carn Marn. Carn carn Marn,' he trills. 'Marn Marn carn carn.' And then, inevitably: 'We there yet, Marn?'

'Yes, Liam. Here we are.'

Martin pulls into the car park: shaded by gum trees, lined by bottlebrushes, the well-maintained order of government money. The minimum-security prison itself looks more like a works depot or a distribution hub than a jail. Even the razor wire appears benign, as if guarding against break-ins rather than breakouts. The place shimmers in the clear air, spring in full bloom on the far north coast.

Inside, the entrance is almost empty, an air-conditioned void, the advantage of visiting on a weekday. Martin knows the drill: he empties his pockets, placing his wallet, watch and phone in a locker, keeping some coins for the vending machines, before he and Liam pass through security. The biometrics are on the blink once again, but his driver's licence is enough for the guards, and he and Liam step through the metal detector without incident.

Mandy is waiting for them in the open-plan reception room. Liam runs to her; she swoops him up, covers him with her kisses. Only when the boy is finally satisfied does she turn to Martin, take his hand, kiss him long and deeply.

'Thanks for coming.'

'Wouldn't miss it for quids.'

After more play with the boy, they're finally able to talk, sitting across a low table from each other.

'How's it going?' he asks.

'Not so bad. Once word got about I was somehow connected to Henry Livingstone, the ladies left me in peace. I've been getting a lot of reading done. I'm going to kill uni this semester.'

'What's Winifred say about parole?'

'No different. Out in about three months. Provided I keep my nose clean.' She smiles now, her eyes warm and her dimples easy and unforced. For someone incarcerated, she looks more relaxed than she ever did outside. Maybe even more beautiful.

'It still shits me that they locked you up.'

She shrugs. 'I guess they needed to make an example, demonstrate they weren't playing favourites.'

'I know. But even so.'

She changes the subject. 'I got a postcard. It's inside. Wish I could show you,' she says.

'Who from?'

'Zelda Forshaw.'

'Seriously? Where is she?'

'In rehab. A private centre down in Sydney.'

'Let me guess—you're paying.'

'Seemed the least I could do. I couldn't exactly give her money.'

'What does she say?'

'Thank you. And that she's doing well. Training via correspondence. Forensic accounting. I think working out what was really happening at Mollisons gave her a taste for it.'

'Really? That's good. Will she be able to practise?'

'I'm not sure.'

They don't speak for a period now, happy in each other's company, happy to hold hands like teenagers while they watch Liam. He's spotted another toddler, a little girl, and has gone to investigate.

'You look happy,' he says.

'You know, I think I am.'

'In here?'

'It's given me time to think. To work through it all. It's been bottled up inside me for a very long time now.'

'That sounds good.'

She grows serious; the dimples withdraw back into the cheeks. 'I was in love with him, you know. Or so I thought.'

'Richard Bright?'

'No. Not him. Not the real man. With Tarquin Molloy, the fake. I bought into it. I believed in him, all the bulldust, all the stardust.'

Martin says nothing, knowing his role is to listen.

'I owe him a lot, Martin, in a strange way. I wasn't coping. Drifting with Billy. Lost. Sinking. Tarquin lifted me up, showed me a different world, a different me. Made me believe I could be beautiful, gave me a glimpse of something better.'

Martin is reluctant to point out the obvious but can't help himself. 'It was all bullshit, though. None of it was real.'

'I know that. Of course.' She hesitates, smiles at Liam, who's now chatting away happily with his new friend. 'It really hurt when it all turned to shit. I really believed he had played me, taken the millions, gone overseas. Left me behind after I reported him for the passwords. The promised life, it was shut off from me again.' She looks at Martin, calm and assured, as if she is talking about someone else. 'I drifted down, drifted about. Ended up back in Riversend, looking after Mum. You know the story after that.'

'Do you believe in karma?' he asks.

She smiles again, the lovely dimpled glow that first hooked him back in Riversend, and she laughs, her own words turned back on herself. 'I do, you know. I really do.'

'You once said that we were barricades, preventing the past from infecting Liam,' says Martin.

'True. I did. But that was when the past still had the power to hurt us, before we brought out our secrets and dealt with them. Now, there are no more secrets, nothing in our pasts. Your family history, my lies about Tarquin and the money, the Turtle, everything. They're all out in the open now. Karma has come full circle. It's satisfied; we've paid our debts.'

'You believe that?'

'I do.'

Liam is back with them now, eyes wide with the thrill of a new friend, jogging up and down on the spot. Then he's up on his mother's lap, hugging her close. Maybe he senses it's almost time to go.

'I thought I loved them all, you know,' she says, looking him in the eye. 'Tarquin. Byron Swift. Even Billy the bass player. But I don't think I ever did. Not really. Not like you.'

Martin blinks. 'I'm not sure I'm so very different.'

'Oh, you are. You are.'

'What makes you so sure?'

'Because I know you. Because I can trust you.'

And to Martin, no words have ever sounded so good.

acknowledgements

FIRST AND FOREMOST, A THANK YOU TO ALL THE BOOKSELLERS, FAR AND WIDE, who have done so much to connect my books with readers. May you all emerge from the shadow of Covid-19 to recover, grow and prosper!

My thanks to everyone at Allen & Unwin: such a brilliant and dedicated group of people.

Heartfelt gratitude to the same amazing editorial team that finessed *Scrublands* and *Silver*: Jane Palfreyman, Christa Munns, Ali Lavau and Kate Goldsworthy. You are the best!

My thanks, as always, to agent Grace Heifetz for her friendship and support, as well as Felicity Blunt in the UK and Faye Bender in the US.

Thanks to Christine Farmer in Australia and Caitlin Raynor in the UK for doing so much to publicise the books.

And a big shout-out to Kate Stephenson and the whole Wildfire team for bringing Martin Scarsden and Mandalay Blonde to readers in the UK.

Kudos to Alex Potočnik for his wonderful maps, to Luke Causby who has created the eye-catching covers for all Australian editions, and to Mike Bowers for his friendship and his photographs.

And, of course, love to my amazing and supportive family: Tomoko, Cameron and Elena.

Alex Ellinghausen

Chris Hammer was a journalist for more than thirty years, dividing his career between covering Australian federal politics and international affairs. For many years he was a roving foreign correspondent for SBS TV's flagship current affairs program *Dateline*. He has reported from more than thirty countries on six continents. In Canberra, roles included chief political correspondent for The *Bulletin*, current affairs correspondent for SBS TV and a senior political journalist for *The Age*. His first book, The *River*, published in 2010 to critical acclaim, was the recipient of the ACT Book of the Year Award and was shortlisted for the Walkley Book Award. *Scrublands*, his second book, was published in 2018 and was shortlisted for Best Debut Fiction at the Indie Book Awards, shortlisted for Best General Fiction at the ABIA Awards, shortlisted for the UTS Glenda Adams Award for New Writing at the NSW Premier's Literary Awards and longlisted for the UK Crime Writers'

Association John Creasey Debut Dagger Award. His third book, *Silver*, was published in 2019. Chris has a bachelor's degree in journalism from Charles Sturt University and a master's degree in international relations from the Australian National University. He lives in Canberra with his wife, Dr Tomoko Akami. The couple have two children.